David left Sam in the living room and went to his bed-room to change his clothes. He crossed the room in the dark, moving to the lamp beside his bed. As he reached down to turn on the light, he stopped.

Lilacs.

The scent filled the air. And with it came a memory of Leah. The scent of her hair, her skin.

A shiver raced up his spine. Suddenly he no longer felt alone.

Straightening, leaving the light off, he stood in the dark-ness and listened. Something brushed past him, soft and breezy, rubbing against his arm. He flinched back, his breath coming in short, harsh gasps . . .

WASTED SPACE

ELIZABETH MANZ

St. Martin's Paperbacks

WASTED SPACE

Copyright © 1996 by Elizabeth Manz.

ISBN: 0-312-95981-8

Printed in the United States of America

St. Martin's Paperbacks edition/October 1996

St. Martin's Paperbacks are published by St. Martin's Press, 175 Fifth Avenue, New York, NY 10010.

10 9 8 7 6 5 4 3 2 1

To Margaret, a good friend and an even better sister.

PROLOGUE

She was lost. Mary Glover leaned forward in her seat, squinting through the windshield, trying to see past the fog that swirled around her car.

When she moved to Michigan, her friends had warned her about the unpredictable weather. It could be hot and humid one minute, they'd said, and almost freezing the next. She hadn't believed them. But now, staring at the thick white clouds outside her windows, she realized they had been right. Earlier, when she'd gone shopping, it had been a warm summer evening. Now . . .

She bit her lip as she inched forward. Her sense of direction was poor to begin with, but add darkness and thick fog and she was in trouble. At any moment, she would come across a main road and then she would know exactly where she was. At least that's what she'd been telling herself for the last fifteen minutes.

She slowed down as a street sign came up on her right.

"Shakespeare Drive," she read aloud.

Boy, am I lost, she thought wryly as the street dropped off behind her. She smiled to herself, some of her tension lifting, as she thought about the other streets that must accompany Shakespeare Drive.

"Yes, I live on Romeo Court. You can't miss it. It's just up the road from Juliet Street," she said quietly, shaking her head at her own bad joke.

She glanced out her side window, hoping to see some houses through the thick fog, lights blazing warmly in the windows. She saw none. Dark trees, their limbs reaching toward her car, lined the side of the road, concealing whatever civilization might be just beyond them. She sighed. Another example of modern day architecture utilizing the environment instead of destroying it.

''Where's a 7-Eleven when you need it,'' she mumbled.

Up ahead, in the middle of the road, a vague black shape cut through the fog. She slowed down. Had a branch fallen across the road? Was it now blocking her path? She leaned forward in her seat, straining to see.

''What is that?'' she muttered. But as her headlights swept over the figure in the road, she jammed on the brakes, stunned.

A woman stood in the middle of the road, her arms crossed over her chest in a defiant gesture.

Mary stared at the woman wide-eyed, her heart beating rapidly in her chest. Her hands shook. She tightened her grip on the wheel to still them.

Was this woman crazy? She could have gotten herself killed standing in the road like that.

Mary reached for the button that would lower her window. But as her finger brushed against it, she hesitated. The woman was just standing there, in the middle of the road, only a few feet from the front of her car, staring ahead. She had not spoken, had not moved at all. And as Mary watched, a gust of wind blew up. It caught the woman's blond hair, swirling it around her head, temporarily concealing her face with its thickness.

Fog crawled over the woman's body, caressing her bare feet and ankles, wrapping itself into the folds of her long skirt, stroking the exposed skin on her arms and throat.

Still she did not move.

Mary looked around, the strangeness of the situation beginning to unnerve her. She saw no car pulled off to the side of the road, a flat tire stranding this woman here in the middle of the night in all this fog. Nothing. There was absolutely nothing in sight.

No help, Mary thought. And as those two words swirled through her mind, tumbling over and over, she suddenly felt very vulnerable.

With increasing dread, she dragged her gaze back to the woman.

Hesitantly, she reached out and opened her window a crack.

"Are you hurt?" she shouted, sure she could be heard.

No reply. No change at all.

"Did you break down?"

Still no reply, just the even stare and the crossed arms.

Mary shifted uneasily in her seat, fear beginning to creep up her back. She studied the woman. Her eyes, a deep, striking green-blue, were blank, distant, as if she had no idea what was going on, where she was. Her blouse hung crooked on her shoulders, one side higher than the other, buttoned wrong. The skirt and blouse did not match.

Mary glanced around once more before making her decision. Whatever was wrong was not her problem. She would send back the police to deal with the woman but that was all. Her stint as good Samaritan was over.

Easing her foot off the brake, Mary turned the wheel to the left. But as the car inched slowly forward, the woman moved for the first time. Taking three steps to the right, she placed herself once more in front of the car.

Mary's grip increased on the wheel. Her heart picked up its beat.

Cranking the wheel to the right, she tried again. But just like before, three simple steps prevented her escape.

Mary's heart jackhammered in her chest.

What did this woman want?

And as Mary stared at the woman who blocked her way, she suddenly had the eerie feeling that the rest of the world no longer existed. Just this woman, the night and the fog.

"Let's not get carried away." She spoke quietly, the sound of her own voice helping to calm her. Above all else, she should not panic.

Taking a deep breath, she decided that the strange woman blocking her car would get out of her way or else . . .

Or else what? Could she hit her? Would it go that far?

Slowly, Mary inched the car forward. But as the hood drew nearer and nearer to the woman, she simply continued to stare ahead, arms crossed, her gaze never changing.

"What do you want?" Mary screamed as she was forced to stop again, the woman very close now, her knees almost touching the front bumper of the car.

"Why don't you say something!" she yelled. Despite her best efforts, panic began to overtake her. She did not want to hurt this woman but she would not be trapped here.

Glancing in her rearview mirror, she prayed for another car, a truck, anything. As before, the road behind her was clear, the fog her only companion.

But as she continued to look in the mirror, her eyes grew wide with realization. Reverse. Reaching down, her hand shaking slightly, she gripped the gear shift and jerked the lever from Drive to Reverse.

Taking one last look at the woman in the road, Mary turned in her seat and began to back away.

CHAPTER ONE

1

Hartwick, Michigan

"Leah!" The name burst from David Ebersol as he jolted awake, sitting upright in bed. His gaze swept the room, his heart hammering in his chest. "Leah!" he called again. Throwing back the blankets, he swung his legs over the side of the bed ready to run to her . . . help her. He stumbled forward in the darkness several steps before tripping over his own feet and falling to his knees.

As pain shot up his leg, the haze that hung in his mind since waking began to dissipate. He rubbed his sore knees, blinking into the darkness around him and wondered briefly what had awakened him.

Leah. The name floated through his mind. He had been dreaming about Leah. He struggled to remember but the images were vague—a flood of light, a dark, threatening shape. Only the deep feeling of panic and loss remained intact.

He stood, then limping slightly, he made his way back to the bed. Sitting on the edge, he ran a hand through his hair trying to release the disturbing feelings that still coursed through him.

Since their breakup three weeks earlier, he'd thought about her often, hoping she'd call to tell him she'd made a mistake and wanted him back.

This was the first nightmare.

Or was it something else?

The thought intruded unwanted in his mind, whispering uncertainties in his ear, making him wonder if she were really okay.

"She's fine," he whispered, needing to hear the words.

A cool breeze drifted in through the open bedroom window, caressing his bare chest. He shook as a chill passed through his body. But it was not the cold that made him shake.

Something's wrong.

He could not dismiss the feeling.

Something's wrong with Leah.

He glanced at the phone. He would call. When she answered, her voice sleep-filled, he would hang up. It might be rude but once he knew she was at home, safely in bed, he could go back to sleep himself.

He reached for the phone. Just as his hand touched the receiver, it rang.

He yanked his hand back, jumping slightly. His gaze locked on the digital clock beside the bed. 1:08 A.M. Alarm rippled through him.

The phone rang again.

He snatched the receiver from its cradle before the shrill cry could sound again.

Maybe it's a wrong number.

"Hello?"

"Is this David Ebersol?" The curt, unfamiliar voice grated against David's mind. This was not a wrong number.

"Yes." His body tensed with a combination of anxiety and dread. "Who is this?"

"This is Officer Timmons of the Hartwick Police," the caller said in the same brisk fashion.

David's grip immediately tightened on the receiver as the

ramification of the man's position sank in.

"I'm sorry to be calling so late," Timmons continued, not waiting for David to find his voice, "but there's been an accident."

"Accident?" David's mouth had gone dry. He swallowed several times.

"Actually, it looks more like a suicide. Earlier tonight, a woman stepped in front of a car and was killed." Timmons paused briefly. "The only piece of identification we found with her was one of your business cards. We're hoping you can identify her for us."

"Identify," he repeated.

"We would appreciate it if you could come down and try to I.D. her for us."

The officer continued speaking. Something about the inconvenience of it all but David was no longer listening. In his mind—his heart—he knew it was Leah.

2

Boulder, Colorado

Harvey Staller whistled happily as he steered his pickup into the driveway of his home. He had good reason to whistle. Today was the day he and his wife, Tammy, would finally leave for Maui. For the last week, he'd had visions of Hawaiian girls in grass skirts and exotic, tropical drinks with tiny umbrellas dancing through his mind. They'd planned the trip six months earlier; the wait for this day had felt like a lifetime.

Pushing open the door of his truck, he split in two the words, STALLER AUTOMATED SYSTEMS, painted in bright red on the side. He had been called to the office that morning for a last minute emergency but as he had promised Tammy, he had returned long before their eleven A.M. flight.

"Aloha," he called as he opened the front door. It was their private joke. The last two weeks, whenever one yelled aloha, the other followed suit, mimicking it back. "Aloha," he said again when he did not receive an answer. The word drifted through the house without response. Harvey frowned.

Glancing down, he noticed the bags they had packed the night before now stacked and ready to go at the front door. He moved to the bottom of the stairs.

"Tammy?" he yelled.

"I thought you'd never get back."

Harvey spun toward the voice, startled. A man stood in front of the door, blocking the way out.

"Who are you?" Harvey demanded.

He could see the man clearly. He was tall and lean, his dark hair cropped short against his head. A scar ran the length of his left cheek—beginning at the corner of his eye, it ran in almost a straight line to the edge of his mouth. As Harvey looked him over, the man smiled, revealing straight, white teeth.

Harvey relaxed slightly. The driver. Of course.

Tammy hated driving to the airport, hated parking there even more. Every time they took a trip, even overnight, she insisted they take one of those door-to-door limousine services.

"You must be the driver." He offered his hand.

The stranger laughed, a deep, hearty sound that rattled Harvey. "Nope. Two more guesses." He leaned casually against the doorjamb.

Harvey's initial anger returned but this time it was tinged with fear. "Who the hell are you?"

"You know, that's always the first question I'm asked."

"What do you want?"

"And that's always the second."

Harvey glanced at the phone, a quick sideways look. He dodged toward it. But the intruder was faster. Snatching the beige phone from its perch on the small table, he ripped its cord brutally from the wall.

Harvey took two steps back, frightened by the sudden violence. He swallowed hard, fighting a battle within himself, working hard to keep his fear under control.

"I'm sorry." The man held the phone toward him. "Did you want to make a call?" Before Harvey could react, the intruder threw the phone against the wall behind him, smashing it into pieces.

Harvey flinched away, throwing his arms up over his face as stray pieces of plastic struck him. His mind raced through escape routes. Could he make it to the kitchen and out the back door? Try for the stairs and the gun in the bedroom above?

Tammy.

His wife's name slammed into him with an almost physical force.

"Where's my wife?" He could hear the quiver in his own voice. He cleared his throat.

"You know," the man began, his voice cool, even. "You're a hard man to catch alone. Always with someone. Always."

Harvey's belly clenched with fear. This was not random. This man had been watching him. "You can have anything you want. I don't care. The house is yours. I won't stop you."

"Well that is generous of you. I really don't need anything though. I'm paid very well."

Harvey wanted to run, wanted to just take his chances and get the hell out of there. But what about Tammy? If she were still somewhere inside . . .

"My wife," he said. "Please, where is she?"

The man's hand came up sharply, making Harvey flinch backward. He laughed again. Holding the paper in his hand, he read aloud, "I forgot the sunblock. Ran to the store. Be back soon. Aloha." He turned the paper to Harvey so he could see the note.

Tammy was safe. Relief flooded through him. And as the realization hit him, Harvey decided to make his move.

Turning, he rushed toward the door. Behind him, he heard movement—a soft, rustling sound followed by a sharp pop. In the same instant, Harvey felt staggering pain rip through his body. As he crumpled to the floor, he heard the man utter two words, the last two words he would ever hear.

"Nothing personal."

3

Hartwick, Michigan

David stared blankly at the mahogany wood of the casket, his eyes locked on the intricate design that outlined the lid. The mortician had suggested a closed casket. No one had argued.

Why did she do it? The question whirled through his mind, invading every other thought he'd had since he'd identified Leah's body.

"How are you doing, David?" Sam Wyatt stood beside him.

"Pretty shitty." He looked up.

Although they came from completely different backgrounds, Sam was his closest friend. They had met five years earlier when David returned home to work for his father's company. Sam was a computer jockey brought in a year prior to David's arrival to update the computer system. David had liked him immediately. He was a no-nonsense type of guy not afraid to say what he felt.

Today, his normally wild red hair was pulled back into a neat ponytail. He wore the blue suit David had planned to give to the Salvation Army until Sam protested, claiming it still had a few good years in it. A purple and gold colored tie with tiny drawings of buffalo on it topped off his suit.

Sam didn't try to be a character. He truly was one.

David stared straight ahead as his friend took the seat beside him.

"How could this happen, Sam?"

"I'm good at a lot of things, pal. But this? I don't understand it any more than you do."

David leaned forward, his elbows on his knees, his hands on either side of his head. "It feels like this isn't real, you know. Like a bad dream I could still wake up from." His mind drifted back to that night. The night he'd received the call. He'd known. Before it had happened, he'd known. "Maybe I could have stopped it," he said more to himself than to Sam.

"How?"

He glanced at his friend, brought out of his reverie. "What?"

Sam turned to him, staring him squarely in the eyes. "How would you have stopped her?"

David fumbled for an answer. "I don't know. Maybe if I had been with her, I could have stopped her."

"And what if you had? You could have stopped her that night but what about the next night? Or the night after that?" He leaned back, his arms crossed over his chest. "You couldn't have been with her every minute of her life."

"I should have known," David said, talking more to himself again. "I practically lived with her for the last six months. I should have seen something . . ."

Images of his life with Leah flashed through his mind. A summer picnic. Late night walks through the woods behind her house. Leah always a little sad no matter what they did.

But even with her mood swings, her sadness, he had never once entertained the idea she might commit suicide. Not Leah. It made no sense.

"Listen, Dave," Sam continued in the same even tone.

"It wasn't your fault. You have to just put this whole thing behind you. Move on."

"Just move on." David repeated the words. They sounded good. Easy. He could just go home, get drunk, forget he'd ever known Leah Brayden. Pretend he didn't care that she was dead. Ignore the fact that he hadn't believed she'd ever kill herself. He ran a hand over his face. "I can't." He spoke quietly, the words barely audible.

Sam leaned forward so they were now side by side. "What?"

Slowly, David turned to face him. "I can't do that."

"Except for work," Sam began, keeping his voice low, "you haven't even seen her in the last month. She was *not* your responsibility."

"So I shouldn't care that she's dead?" David's tone was sharp. He knew Sam was trying to help but he didn't want help right now. He wanted answers to the questions buzzing through his mind, haunting his dreams. He shook his head, his body aching with tension. He ran a hand through his hair, glancing sideways. "Hey, man—"

"Forget it." Sam smiled that "no big deal" grin of his.

But it *was* a big deal. David shifted in his seat. He couldn't explain it to Sam because he couldn't explain it to himself but he needed answers, needed to know why.

Sam nodded toward Leah's mother on the other side of the room. "Have you spoken to the barracuda yet?"

David turned toward Rose Brayden, glad for the change of subject. He watched her circulate among the mourners, her knee-length dress twirling as she spun from person to person. Hugs, kisses, sympathy. She was the center of attention and she loved it.

As expected, she wore black from head to toe—shoes, hose, dress. Even her head was adorned with the appropriate attire: a fashionable hat and veil combo. As always, she looked stunning.

"I don't have the stomach for it," he mumbled. He had dated Leah for almost a year and in that time, he had learned a great deal about Rose. She manipulated her daughter every chance she got, heaping on guilt as if it were topping for an ice cream sundae.

But all of that stopped—or at least lessened a great deal—when Leah began to see him. He did not allow Rose's negativity to get in their way and often went head-to-head with the woman. The closer David got to Leah, the more he helped her to see how much her mother affected her. And with each passing week his relationship with Rose deteriorated until he was sure the woman despised him.

How could he bring himself to say anything to her now?

"I think she blames me for all this." And as if she had heard him, Rose glanced his way. Then putting on her most pathetic smile, she began moving toward him.

"Damn," he muttered, turning away. "Now she's coming over."

"I'll head her off." Sam rose from his seat.

As David watched his friend stop Rose and lead her to the other side of the room, his thoughts turned once more to Leah.

For a moment, her face seemed to float before his eyes. She had never been a great beauty. He'd once overheard Rose telling her daughter just how plain she was, and Leah, without thought, simply fell into the mold her mother set for her. Her mousy blond hair hung straight to her shoulders without style and her skirts, always a little too long, gave her an older appearance than her twenty-eight years. But to him, she had an inner beauty that shone through.

It was her eyes. They were a striking green-blue that belied the outward package. Some nights he'd just sit and gaze into those eyes.

David looked again at the casket before him. And the image of Leah, her dazzling eyes locked with his, vanished—replaced by the bloody image of the corpse he had identified three days earlier. Her body had been severely damaged, both arms broken, the left side of her head caved in, her nose and left cheek shattered on impact.

When he first saw her body lying on the cold metal table in the morgue, he did not recognize her. It simply did not look like Leah. But as he stared into her clear blue-green eyes, so distinct, there was no question. The torn, broken corpse before him was the woman he had once made love to.

"Jesus." David dropped his face into his hands, squeezing his eyes shut, trying to erase the bloody image but knowing it would be with him forever.

A firm hand gripped his shoulder, squeezing. "David?"

He relaxed slightly at the sound of his uncle's voice. A moment later, Edward Ross sat beside him.

The two men looked more like father and son than uncle and nephew. David took after his mother's side of the family. Both had the high Ross cheekbones, strong chin and dark eyes.

David looked at his uncle. "I appreciate you coming today."

"Was there any question that I would?"

He shrugged. "To be honest, I really didn't know what to expect . . . from anyone." He glanced behind him, taking in the faces around him. It looked as if most of the main office staff had come. But along with those, he saw several other people he didn't recognize, people he suspected were from work. "Ghouls," he muttered.

"What's that?" Edward asked.

"These people." David watched the crowd around him. "They're ghouls. I'll bet half of them didn't even know Leah."

"They came to pay their respects."

David locked his gaze on his uncle. "They came to see the boss's son fall apart at his ex-girlfriend's funeral."

"Come on, David. You don't believe that."

He held his uncle's gaze for another moment before dropping his away. "I guess not. I don't know."

"Don't get cynical on me. We have your father for that."

David stiffened slightly at the mention of his father. "I really thought he'd be here today." The edge returned to his voice. The cynicism his uncle hated. "I don't know why I'm surprised that he's not."

He knew where he father was. Working. Like every other time in his life, the company came first.

Envirospace.

Thirty years ago, when Hal Ebersol had come up with the idea of transporting America's waste to the moon, he'd been laughed at. Too costly, too impractical, too ridiculous. But he'd ignored the critics. Instead, he founded Envirospace, Inc. and proved it could be done. Now he owned one of the fastest growing environmental companies in the country.

"I'm going to my father's house after the funeral."

"Do you really think it's appropriate to confront your father about all this now?"

"I'm just going to ask him why he didn't come."

"David—"

"And I'd like the company to do something for Leah," he added quickly, hoping his uncle would drop the subject. "We have a launch coming up soon and I thought maybe we could have a ceremony and dedicate it in Leah's name."

Only ten short years earlier, Envirospace launched its first ship to the moon. Garbage was brought in from all over Michigan, Ohio and Indiana, compacted down into manageable units and then packed into Envirolift One. From that point on, everything was automated. Launch time, control and direction, landing, unloading. All was simply and efficiently maintained from the control room in the pre-launch building.

At first, the launches had earned national coverage, a worldwide media event broadcast live. Now, each was simply another day at the office.

Edward nodded at David's suggestion. "I think a dedication is a wonderful idea. Maybe even a plaque of some sort to remember her."

David smiled at his uncle, glad for the closeness they shared. A closeness he did not have with his father. "Thanks again for coming. It means a lot to me."

"I hope you know that I'm here for you if you need to talk."

David leaned forward in his seat again, uncomfortable with the turn in the conversation. "I'm okay," he said automatically.

"You say that but . . ." Edward hesitated as if he were unsure if he should continue. "I just don't want you taking this all on yourself—you need to look past it."

"You sound like Sam. He just told me almost the exact same thing."

Edward nodded. "Good advice."

"It may be good advice but it doesn't help me much." David stared down at his hands debating whether he really wanted to get into this conversation now, here. "I need to know why she did it," he said after a time.

Reaching out, Edward placed a hand on his back. "I think you're going to have to resign yourself to the fact that you will probably never know."

"I can't accept that." He glanced at his uncle. "I could put it out of my mind for a while. But it'll always be there. The wondering. I want to end it." Sitting back in his seat, his shoulder only inches from his uncle's, he added in a low voice, "I'm going to Leah's house."

Edward turned to face him full on. "You're what?"

"Leah kept a diary." David glanced around, making sure no one else was in earshot. "I'm going to get it and read it." He had thought of it last night. A fleeting idea really. But now, when he spoke the words, they seemed right. It was what he needed to do.

"You can't break into her house and steal her diary," Edward whispered, concern lacing each word.

"I won't be breaking in. I still have a key."

"What if you're inside her house and her mother comes

over? Or worse yet, the police? What are you going to say?''

"I'll think of something.''

"David, this is crazy.'' Edward's gaze was intense.

"I need to know what was going through her head. Why did she leave me? Why did she do this?''

"And you think this diary will tell you?''

David could hear the compassion in his uncle's voice but there was no missing the message behind the words: Don't do this. It's a mistake.

"She used to write in that thing *every day*. Maybe the answers to my questions are between the pages of that book.''

"Leave it alone.''

"I can't.'' And once more, David's gaze locked on the casket before him. "She had my name and number in her pocket. Why didn't she call me?''

"David, this isn't helping. You have to put it out of your mind.''

"You didn't see her.'' Several heads turned as his voice rose higher than he intended. He paused, telling himself to calm down. "You didn't see her. How she looked . . .'' He trailed off as images of her shattered body flashed through his head with crystal clarity. "I did. And it's burned into my mind. If I have to remember her that way for the rest of my life, then I damn well want to know why.''

Edward stared at him, his gaze sympathetic. "You do what you feel you need to do to get through this. Just don't get caught.''

But David did not hear his advice. Over Edward's shoulder, he could see a small group of people from work, all eyes on him. They shook their heads, nodding toward him, murmuring to each other, staring.

The sudden feeling of suffocation was overwhelming.

"I can't sit here anymore.'' He stood, needing to get out of that room away from all the eyes. "I'm going to get some air.''

He walked away and was almost out of the room when someone caught his arm, holding tight, stopping him.

"David." Rose Brayden spoke his name in a tone frosty with loathing for him. Leaning closer, she brushed his cheek with her lips. Her offensive breath, smelling of a mixture of toothpaste and gin, washed over him. "This must just be awful for you." Her eyes were red-rimmed and he wondered if it were from crying or drinking.

They stood back from the rest of the crowd, isolated in one corner of the room. David eyed the door less than ten feet away. He had been so close. Turning his gaze back to Rose, he searched his mind for something to say. He finally settled on, "I'm going to miss her."

"Yes, well, won't we all." Pulling a white lace hanky from her purse, she dabbed at her dry eyes. "I just hate to think of the pain you're going through." Her voice held no concern. "First, the breakup and now this."

There was no mistaking the accusation in her voice, the incrimination behind the words. "I have to go." He took a step away but Rose moved with him.

"Yes, maybe it would be better if you left."

His anger at her dismissal was immediate. "Back off, Rose."

"I only meant that Leah wouldn't want you here after what you did to her."

"What happened between us is none of your business."

"My daughter's dead," she snapped. "You don't think you had anything to do with it?"

David stared at her. "Leah was the one who left *me*."

"Because you confused her. You took her from me. And then, after you left her—"

"She left me!"

"—she was so confused, she couldn't even come to me anymore. You left her with no one!"

David could not speak, could not defend himself. The words were too close to his own thoughts, his own feelings of guilt. He turned away, through listening to her. Rose grabbed his arm, digging her nails into the sleeve of his coat. "You killed her."

He yanked his arm away, guilt and frustration warring inside him. "Go to hell." Moving fast, he pushed through the door, heading out into the hallway. The air felt fresher outside; he could breath again.

Walking to the end of the hall, he stood at the window that overlooked the parking lot. He could see a limousine parked there and suddenly, dreaded going to the cemetery.

You're doing it for Leah, he told himself.

Leah.

Closing his eyes, David leaned forward resting his forehead against the cool glass of the window.

Why did she suddenly break it off with him? What had changed? He'd thought about if for so long now and no matter how he looked at it, he came to the same conclusion.

Nothing had changed.

She just stopped caring about him.

"Why did you leave me?" he asked quietly. God, he wished he knew.

Behind him, he heard a door open. He glanced around, hoping it was not Rose following him out in the hall to berate him some more.

A woman stood near the entrance, checking the directory. She glanced down the hall toward David.

There was a softness to her that struck him almost immediately. Maybe it was her hair. She wore it down, loose curls framing her heart-shaped face. The color, a soft blond, seemed bleached that shade by the sun. But it was more than just her looks. It was the way she carried herself. Something about the way she looked at him or moved. . . . It was familiar to him somehow, as if they had met once, a long time ago and he just couldn't recall when.

As he continued to look at her, trying to remember who she was, saying nothing, she shifted uncomfortably and looked away, back to the directory.

He took a step toward her. "Do you need help?"

"No." She walked past him, not looking at him. "I'm here for the Brayden funeral."

"Did you know Leah?" he called after her.

Stopping, she turned. Her brows furrowed as she looked at him, her expression a mixture of disbelief and pain. "She was my sister."

CHAPTER TWO

1

Hartwick, Michigan

Greg and Teddy Collins raced through the woods following the disappearing form of their hound dog, Rebel.

"Come on, Teddy," Greg called over his shoulder as his little brother fell farther and farther behind.

"I'm trying," Teddy shouted, his short legs pumping hard to keep up.

Greg jumped a log, his gaze locked on the dog's tail. He was gonna catch Rebel first, like he always did, then he'd get to pick the game. And it was always more fun when he picked.

Up ahead, Rebel stopped and sniffed a tree. Greg moved in on him, creeping slowly, careful to make no sound. He reached down, biting his lip, smiling wildly—

"Greg!"

Teddy's sharp voice startled the dog. Rebel looked up, barked twice at Greg and ran off. Greg stomped his foot as the dog quickly disappeared from view.

"Teddy!" He spun around. But his little brother was not behind him. He scanned the area but Teddy was nowhere to be seen.

Cupping his hands around his mouth, he yelled for his brother.

"Over here." Teddy's voice drifted back, giving Greg a direction. Sighing, he headed back along the path. He wasn't worried. He knew what had happened. It was what always happened.

Teddy had fallen.

No matter how often they played in the woods, no matter how many times Greg told him to watch where he was going, Teddy always fell.

Coming around the corner, he saw his brother. Teddy sat on the ground, his knee pulled up to his face, blowing on his skinned leg.

"What happened?" Greg moved slowly to him. "Are you hurt?" He knelt down, looked at the skinned knee and frowned.

Teddy looked at his brother, wide-eyed. "It was an accident. Is Mom gonna be mad?"

"Nah." He shrugged nonchalantly. "Don't worry. She won't get mad at you." *It's me she'll be mad at,* he thought wearily. Whenever he and Teddy were out playing and Teddy got hurt or dirty and went in the house crying, *he* was the one who always got in trouble. But he didn't hold it against Teddy. It wasn't his fault. At seven he was nearly three years younger than Greg. He tried hard to keep up but he was clumsy.

"We better get home." Glancing around, he could see no sign of their dog. "Rebel! Come on, boy!"

He stood and hooked an arm through his brother's, pulling Teddy to his feet. A moment later, they heard their dog, barking loudly and continuously some distance away.

"Rebel!" Greg shouted. The dog continued to bark, the sound not changing.

He wasn't coming.

"We're gonna have to go get him." Teddy started following the sound of the bark. After only a moment's hesitation, Greg followed.

The sound grew louder and louder as they walked. And as Greg listened, he realized that the bark sounded wrong. Rebel didn't bark much—maybe when he chased a rabbit or begged for food. But this bark was different. Rebel sounded . . .

Afraid.

Greg hesitated. He glanced around. They had never played in this part of the woods before. Rebel had wandered farther than they were allowed. The palms of his hands were sweating. He rubbed them over his shorts.

And in that moment, he wanted to go home. The woods felt bad. He wanted his mother. Wanted to be in his house, watching Popeye and eating ice cream. He wanted to be anywhere but here.

But what about Rebel? They had to get him, had to take him with them. He bit his lip, thinking. His gaze fell on his little brother. Teddy walked ahead, his pace never slowing. And Greg suddenly felt stupid. He wasn't a baby. Teddy was the one who was afraid to sleep alone, who jumped on his bed at night so the monster underneath wouldn't get him. Not Greg. He was brave. He was the protector.

"Teddy, wait up!" He jogged toward his brother, not wanting to lose sight of him.

Rounding a thick stand of trees, Greg saw Rebel. He stood only a few feet away, his tail straight out in back, his eyes locked forward, his teeth bared as he growled and barked.

Greg stopped cold. He felt his breath leave him as he looked at the forest before him.

It was all dead. That was the only way he could describe it. The trees, the grass, the weeds. Dead.

A breeze blew up. It caught the broken, peeling limbs of the trees, tossing them back and forth. They slapped against each other, pieces raining down, the branches creaking and groaning.

Teddy walked toward it. "What happened?"

Greg reached out and stopped his brother. He wasn't sure why, but he didn't want Teddy going there. "Let's get home," he whispered.

"But I wanna see—"

"Teddy." Greg pulled on his arm, his voice low, sharp. "I said we're going home." Moving to the dog, he grabbed Rebel by the collar and began pulling him away from the dead part of the woods.

2

Kelsey stood beside the grave, only half listening to the priest as he read the Lord's Prayer over her sister's casket. She stole glances at the people around her, murmuring the expected responses in unison. Leah's friends. Co-workers. Acquaintances.

Strangers.

At least to Kelsey.

She tried not to make eye contact with anyone. She didn't want to talk to any more strangers after the service, didn't want to have to explain who she was. She was tired of the shocked expression she got from each and every face when she said she was Leah's sister. They always managed to recover quickly but it was apparent the news stunned them. Her existence was a complete mystery to all of them. Kelsey had never been particularly close to her younger sister but it seemed that Leah had managed to completely erase her from her life.

But it wasn't just Leah, Kelsey thought, a feeling of guilt tugging at her. In the last twelve years, she had only been home three times. Her whole life, she had been waiting for the day she could leave. She hadn't achieved good grades and done extra credit work because she wanted to do well and get ahead. She went after them because she wanted to guarantee a full scholarship to a university—*any* university that would take her away from home, away from her mother.

Away from the guilt.

Rose had once told Kelsey that she had better do everything in life that she wanted to do before she had children, because once a woman had children, her life was over.

When Kelsey graduated fourth in her class of five hundred, she jumped at a teaching position offered to her in Minneapolis. Minnesota was far enough away so she wouldn't be expected to visit.

At first, she had tried to keep in contact with Leah, but for some reason, Leah defended their mother whenever Kelsey brought up the subject of Rose's manipulating ways. Soon every conversation escalated into an argument, their relationship growing more and more strained as each took a side and battle lines were drawn. Their last phone call had been nearly three years ago.

A breeze blew up, cutting through the stifling heat of the afternoon, ruffling the hair of the man on the other side of the grave. The man Kelsey had met at the funeral home.

David Ebersol.

Leah's ex-lover.

At least that's what so many people had been whispering.

She watched him, the way he kept is gaze locked on the casket, his hands fisted at his sides. A man stood beside him. Not quite as tall or as well-toned but they were related somehow. The resemblance was unmistakable. For a moment, David seemed to waver where he stood. The older man placed a hand on his arm, steadying him.

She could not picture this man with Leah. She hated to think it, but there it was in her mind nonetheless. What was this handsome millionaire's son doing with her shy, rather plain sister? Had Leah changed so much?

She remembered how he had looked at her when she told him who she was. His dark eyes seemed to try and penetrate her, to see inside.

He looked up and their eyes locked. For a moment, it

was as if they shared the same thought. *Why?* She wondered how much he knew about Leah's last days. Could he
help her find out the truth about her sister's death? Did he
know? She needed to find out.

As the casket began its descent into the ground, he turned
and walked away.

Kelsey started after him but stopped as her mother
stepped in front of her, blocking her way.

"You should have gotten a trim, dear. No one can see
your lovely eyes." Reaching out, Rose brushed Kelsey's
hair back from her face. "It was nice of you to drive all
the way here for Leah's funeral."

"What did you expect?"

"Expect? From you? Nothing really. I never do."

Kelsey had anticipated her mother's coldness toward her,
but this was different. Leah was dead. She didn't expect
hugs and kisses but she thought maybe . . . she hoped . . .
for more.

"The wake will be at my house. But I understand if you
need to get back on the road again."

Kelsey felt the anger inside flare. She was being dismissed from her sister's funeral as if she were a distant
acquaintance. "Mom, I'm staying in town for a while."

Rose's expression turned sour. "I don't have much room
at the house," she said, a trace of irritation in her voice.

"I'm not asking you to put me up." She could feel herself growing tense, defensive. The standard response to her
mother. "I thought I could stay at Leah's."

"I don't think so."

Kelsey stared at her. "Why not?"

"I don't think Leah would want you to."

Kelsey took her mother's arm, glancing around, and led
her away from the crowd.

"Mom," Kelsey began. "I'm not going home until I
come to terms with this whole thing." Rose opened her
mouth but Kelsey spoke first. "Let me finish," she
snapped, not allowing her mother to get even one negative

word in. "I didn't know Leah very well. That was both our faults but she was my sister. I want to know who she was. I want to see her house, her things. I want to know what compelled her to stand in the road in the middle of the night and be hit by a car." The words tumbled one over the other, out of control. "I need to know why she's dead!" For the first time, her voice cracked. She bit her lip, stopping herself, needing to get her emotions in check once again. She had promised herself before she arrived that she would not show any weakness to her mother. Would not give her the opportunity to exploit her emotions.

"You never wanted to know her when she was alive." Rose's eyes narrowed slightly as she looked at Kelsey, studying her. "Now suddenly you're interested in what her life was like?"

Kelsey took a deep, calming breath before speaking. "I don't have to explain anything to you. I'm off for the summer and I'm staying."

"You always were selfish," Rose muttered. "Have you given any thought to what I might want. I always told Leah—"

"Mother," Kelsey interrupted sharply. Her mother's mouth snapped shut. "Give me the keys to Leah's house."

3

David stared out the windshield of his car at the group still gathered around Leah's grave. It didn't seem real. Leah was dead and it didn't seem real. His eyes locked on the two women standing apart from the rest of the group. Rose Brayden and . . . Kelsey.

He thought he and Leah had been so close, thought they had shared so much. Yet Leah had never spoken about a sister. He began to doubt how well he knew her at all. Starting his car, he pulled out into the street and headed east.

As he drove down each street, not seeing any of the scenery around him, lost in his thoughts, he knew he was doing the right thing. Tomorrow morning, before he went to work, he would go to Leah's house and take a look at her diary. Then maybe he could begin to put this all behind him.

Making a left turn, he realized he was nearly to his father's house and he'd better start thinking about exactly what he wanted to say before arriving.

His father's house.

He shook his head. It was where he grew up, the only place he'd ever lived until he went to college. Yet whenever he thought of it, he always thought of it as his father's house.

He tried to think of the last time he'd been there. Two months? Three? He wasn't sure. Seeing his father at work was more than enough for him. He turned off the main road and onto the drive.

The house, surrounded on all sides by trees, sat nearly a half mile back from the road, hidden from any casual passersby. As he drove down the rough dirt lane, David caught glimpses through the trees. The large front porch. The second floor balcony. One of the three chimneys. Reaching the circular drive, he steered his car into one of several parking spots near the front entrance.

He took a deep breath, pushed his door open and stepped from his car.

He jiggled his keys in his hands as he stood in the driveway, staring at the house before him. Did he really want to do this?

The wind picked up, rustling the trees behind him, whipping the leaves at his feet into a whirlwind. He stared down into the spinning, swirling motion.

Strange.

The leaves . . . so much like . . . like . . . what? He strained to grasp the thought.

Sweat broke out across his forehead.

His keys slipped from his hand.

He watched as they dead-dropped to the pavement, hitting with a sharp metallic clatter.

The sound repeated in his mind. But it was different—louder . . . sharper.

Clang.

It reverberated in his mind.

Clang. Clang. Clang!

His knees buckled beneath him. The breath left his lungs. He fell back against his car as a dizziness swept through him.

"Damn," he muttered. Leaning over the hood of the car, still not sure if he were going to pass out or not, he squeezed his eyes shut and concentrated on his breathing.

What was wrong with him? But he knew, had only himself to blame. Since hearing of Leah's death, he hadn't slept through the night, hadn't had much of an appetite. That was it. He was simply paying the price for lack of sleep and nourishment.

"David?"

He turned with a start toward the voice behind him, swaying slightly from the sudden, unexpected movement.

Louis Stark stood a few feet away, the large oak doors of the house open wide behind him. "I'm sorry. I didn't mean to startle you." He smiled kindly. It was the only way Louis could smile. He was only five feet five, his back stooped slightly. But for the last thirty-five years, he'd run the entire household smoothly and efficiently without ever raising his voice. It was a quality David admired.

"I was watching you from inside." Louis took a few shuffling steps forward and reached down, groaning slightly from the effort, and scooped up David's keys. "Is everything all right?"

David took the keys from him, dismissing his concern with a wave of his hand. "It's nothing. I'm fine." Walking forward, he patted the man reassuringly on the back, smiling widely. "How's life treating you?"

"Just fine, sir."

Together, they walked to the house.

Once inside, Louis led the way to the library, neither man needing to tell the other where they were going. The library was the place Hal Ebersol met anyone and everyone who came to his house, including his son. Their shoes clicked loudly on the Italian tiles that criss-crossed the foyer, the sound echoing through the cavernous front hallway.

Reaching the library, Louis opened the two oak doors and stepped aside, allowing David to enter. "Is your father expecting you?" he asked as soon as David was over the threshold.

David turned to face him. "No but I need to see him."

"I'll check, but you know your father." Louis closed the doors behind him.

David remained where he was, listening to the man's retreating steps.

You know your father.

He shook his head. No, he didn't. He didn't think anyone really knew Hal Ebersol.

David strolled to one of the book-lined cases and began scanning the names printed on the spines of the books stored there.

Shakespeare. Twain. Dickens. All the classics. All beautifully bound. All never once opened and read. Their clean, unbroken spines a testimony to their disuse.

David sometimes felt he was like these books, existing only to improve his father's outward appearance. Reaching up, he ran his fingers down the line of books. His father was not a bad person, he often told himself. He's just indifferent. Hal Ebersol cared more for his company and the success it brought him than he did for his only child.

Envirospace.

David had hated the company when he was younger. It had kept his father away for weeks at a time when he was growing up. He always tried not to resent it. But after his mother died and he was left to celebrate his birthday and Christmas with his Uncle Edward, Louis and a few other servants, he couldn't help himself.

Turning, he stared at the portrait of his father that hung over the fireplace. He was a regal man, his thick silver-gray hair showing no signs of thinning, his face at the age of fifty-seven just beginning to show the signs of age. But it was his eyes that drew people in. They hinted at knowledge, a knowledge of things he knew that no one else would ever quite understand.

David walked toward the painting, staring up at the man on the canvas. His father had realized his dream of success, but at what price?

The doors to the library opened and Hal Ebersol stepped through. "David." He walked toward him. "Did I have an appointment with you?"

"No." David gripped the extended hand and shook firmly, just the way he had been taught to. "Leah's funeral was today. I thought you had planned on attending."

Hal walked to one of the leather chairs that flanked the fireplace. Sitting down, he gestured for his son to do the same. David complied.

"Leah?" Hal's eyebrows knit together as he tried to place the name.

"Brayden," David said, his tone flat. "Leah Brayden." His body tensed with the anger that now flowed through him. His father had never liked Leah, never accepted the fact that David was seeing her. "You know damn well who she was."

Hal picked up the cigar case that sat on the table beside him, opened it and took one out. Running it under his nose, he smiled at its richness. "The name's somewhat familiar but . . . ." He shook his head as if the memory still would not come.

"Familiar." David repeated the word, his jaw tightening with each passing second. "It should be familiar. She was here once for dinner."

Clutching the cigar between his teeth, Hal nodded absently at David's explanation. "Right. That girl you were seeing." Opening the top drawer of the desk beside him, he began fishing around inside. "I thought that was over. Why would you expect me at the girl's funeral?"

He watched as his father searched within the drawer, only half listening to what he was being told. In that instant, David wanted to reach out and slam the drawer shut, catching his father's hand inside. Maybe then he'd stop and listen. Maybe then he'd hear. "She worked at Envirospace for more than six years. The last two in the main office."

David waited for his father to say something. That he remembered her now. How could he be so stupid. But his father did not respond. Instead, he slammed the top drawer shut and yanked open the one beneath it.

"Where's the damn lighter?" he muttered, the cigar bobbing with each word.

"Would you listen to me!" David jumped up from his chair and snatched the cigar from his father's mouth and tossed it into the fireplace. "Her desk sat twenty feet outside your office. I can't believe you didn't know that." He towered over his father, glaring down at him.

Anger creased Hal's forehead and pulled down the corners of his mouth. "It's a big company. I don't know everyone."

"You knew her," David shot back. "I introduced you."

Reaching sideways, his movements slow, deliberate, Hal opened the case on the table and retrieved another cigar. He found the lighter inside the case. "Whether you were seeing her or not, she was an employee, nothing more." He slammed the case shut. "Did you really think I would attend her funeral?" His gaze locked with David's. His eyes, cold, angry, bore into him, daring him to answer.

David returned the stare, his gaze as unwavering as his father's. "Yes," he whispered. "Like an idiot, I thought you'd be there because Leah meant something to me. But I guess that doesn't matter." He waited for his father to tell him he was wrong. Waited for . . . he didn't know what. Some kind of acknowledgment that he did matter in some small way.

And as David continued to stare into his father's eyes, something changed. Instead of the strong, unyielding gaze he was so accustomed to, he thought he saw—for just an instant—doubt. It flickered across his face, a pinched, loss-of-control look so fleeting that if David had not been watching so closely, he might have missed it completely.

Hal dropped his gaze as if aware he had been caught.

The hair on the back of David's neck prickled. His stomach tightened. Never could he remember a time when his father was anything but in control.

Was something else going on here? Something his father could not talk to him about?

"Dad—"

"Were you still sleeping with this girl?" Hal's sharp voice cut David off. Flipping open the lighter, he held the flame to the end of the cigar and inhaled deeply. His gaze returned to David's. The doubt, if it had ever been there, was gone.

And David felt like a fool.

"You sit there—" David stopped abruptly, clamping his mouth shut. What was the point? In the end, what difference would it make whether Hal Ebersol remembered Leah or not? It was just a piece of his life. It had no real consequence to his father. So why should he remember it?

He turned away, running a hand through his hair, making an effort to calm down. "I came here today," he began when he felt he could speak again without sounding accusatory. "Because I thought Envirospace could do something in her memory." He turned back to his father. "We have a launch coming up. I thought we could dedicate it in her name, have a short ceremony."

Hal Ebersol sat in his chair. Stared at his son. Made his decision. "I don't want to set a precedent for this type of thing." His voice was dispassionate. "Where does it stop?"

"I'm asking you to do this." David ground the words out, his jaw stiff.

Hal tilted his head to one side, studying him. "Really, son. All this over a frumpy little secretary?"

David turned away from him. Pacing to the fireplace, he stared into the empty black pit, the cigar its only contents. As a boy, he'd spent most of his winters in this room, sprawled out in front of this fireplace reading comics and adventure novels. It had always been comforting to him. Not today.

David could hear the creak of the leather as his father rose from his chair and moved toward him.

"Son, I can see that you feel very strongly about this," he began, now standing directly behind him. "But I just can't do it." There was a long pause. "What can I say?"

David closed his eyes. The pat answer: What can I say?

When he was eight, his mother died one cold December night. Her death had not been unexpected. It had been slow in coming. During that time, his father had kept her locked behind the doors of the master bedroom as the cancer ate away at her body. In all that time, David was not allowed to see his mother, to comfort her. It would frighten him, he was told. But that night, after she was gone, David was taken inside to say good-bye. As he stood staring at her still form, her face almost unrecognizable to him after so many months of illness, his father had uttered those words for the first time.

What can I say?

"I shouldn't have come here." He moved away. Throwing the double doors wide, he exited the library.

Louis approached him immediately. "David, is everything all right?" His face was lined with concern.

David shook his head as he walked toward the front door. "It's never been all right."

4

Kelsey steered her car into the driveway of her sister's home and cut the engine. She sat inside, staring through the windshield at the house Leah had lived in the last three years of her life. It was a one-story brick with bright flowers just beginning to wilt against the front. It sat in a circular court, the woods surrounding the back of the house giving it a certain amount of seclusion.

Pushing her door open, she headed toward the house. The scent of lilacs drifted through the air, the smell strong.

Leah's favorite flower.

And walking around the side of the house, she saw several lilac bushes growing wild against the back of the house. A breeze blew up, catching the delicate purple flowers, making them sway gently back and forth. Walking to them, she reached toward the small flowers. Her hand shook as she touched the soft petals. She pulled it back, warm tears building behind her eyes.

To her left, at the edge of the woods, two boys and a dog emerged, running at a fast clip. Kelsey wiped at her tears, watching the trio, listening to their voices.

And without warning, a long forgotten memory flashed through her mind. Leah at the park, picking lilacs, begging Kelsey to help her smuggle them home under her shirt, only managing to crush them instead.

A cloud passed over the sun, blanketing the yard in dull gray.

She closed her eyes as the tears began falling. How had they grown so far apart? Why had they wasted so many years?

But it was too late for questions like that. Too late to go back.

Kelsey bit her trembling lip, swallowing the bitterness that welled up inside her. Opening her eyes, she wiped at her cheeks, her gaze locked on the delicate flowers her sister had loved so much. They were so beautiful, so—

Was someone there? She turned sharply. Left. Right. But the yard was empty, even the two boys and their dog were gone. Slowly, she turned and stared into the woods. Was someone there just beyond the trees? Hidden in the shadows? A chill stole over her body, shaking her where she stood.

She took a step forward, toward the trees. She needed to know, needed to see. . . .

The sun came out from behind the clouds, shining down on the yard, its warmth touching her bare arms.

Instantly, the feeling vanished.

And Kelsey felt alone once again.

Hugging herself, the sun's rays doing little to warm her, she stared toward the trees. But she no longer felt . . . watched. Still, she could not dispel the uneasiness that clung to her. Digging in her pocket, she found the key her mother had reluctantly given her. After taking one last look around, she headed back toward the house.

As she inserted it into the door, she stopped. Without thinking, she was entering the house through the side door. A habit their mother had ground into them as children.

The front door is for company. The side door is for little girls with dirty hands and smudged faces.

As her mother's words flashed through her mind, Kelsey debated going around to the front of the house and entering there. But she dismissed the thought. It would be a childish thing to do and she was no longer that child who was intimidated by her mother.

Pushing the door open, she could smell disinfectant and very faintly beneath that, moth balls. The smell of their mother's house, she thought, and her body tensed involuntarily as more old memories threatened to surface. She pushed them aside, not ready to deal with them yet, and entered the house through the kitchen.

The walls were white, the tile on the floor a light pattern with small flecks of color. The counter was clear of any small appliances or dishes. No dirty glasses sat in the sink. There were no cookbooks in sight. A tea kettle, white with a wooden handle, sat atop the stove. Kelsey stood in the center of the room, staring at the silent kettle. It was the only indication that a human being had actually lived here, that someone, at some time had used this kitchen. A sadness swept through Kelsey as she took in the emptiness of the room. Once again she was reminded of her mother's home, sterilized clean of any and all signs of life.

She walked through to the living room, expecting to see the same bland colors and unimaginative decor. Instead, she found a warm, cozy living room done in mostly earth tones, the cathedral ceiling crisscrossed with wooden beams.

Bright, colorful pillows covered the couch, waiting for someone to be swallowed whole by their plushness. The contrast to the kitchen took her completely off guard. It was as if two different people had decorated the house. Her gaze was drawn to the far wall. It was all brick with a large fireplace in the middle. An arrangement of pictures sat atop a small table in the corner, the frames a variety of sizes and designs. Kelsey walked over, leaned close and scanned each one. Childhood pictures of Leah with their mother, adult pictures of Leah again with their mother and a few of Leah with . . . David Ebersol. They stood together, David looking directly into the camera, Leah looking at him. They looked happy, carefree.

There were no shots of Kelsey.

Lifting a photograph of Leah, she stared at her sister's face, trying to imagine what her life had been like, why she would suddenly decide to end it. That was what plagued Kelsey. More than just the loss of her sister. The idea that she took her own life.

When they were children, their favorite uncle killed himself. Carl got up early one morning, retrieved his shot gun from the hall closet, went into the basement and splattered his brains all over the walls.

His family had been away at the time and it was nearly

three days before he was found. The funeral had been
closed casket. Kelsey still remembered the nights after that.
She and Leah suffered from nightmares for nearly a week.
They spent those restless nights talking about suicide and
death. As a result, the girls developed strong opinions about
both. During one of those long nights they had made a vow
to each other, whispering the words, memorizing the promise.

"I promise," Kelsey now whispered, the words choked
off as her grief resurfaced.

But her sister had not called her as she had vowed to do
so long ago. If they had been speaking would everything
be different? Would Leah still be alive?

She set the picture back on the table where it belonged,
no longer able to look in her sister's eyes.

For a long moment, Kelsey thought about what she was
doing. Did she really want to stay here with so many reminders, so many memories?

She knew the answer was yes even before acknowledg-
ing it in her mind. She could not go home until she felt
satisfied with Leah's death.

Going back to her car, she almost laughed at the thought.
Was anyone ever satisfied with someone's death? She
opened the trunk and began unloading her bags. As she
carried the third one inside, she noticed a woman walking
up the driveway toward the house. She looked to be in her
mid-sixties, her hair a mixture of gray and white. She
moved slowly, needing a cane to walk. Clutched in her free
hand was a small wicker basket

Kelsey-stopped, setting the heavy bag down on the garage floor and waited. "Hi," she said when the woman
finally reached her.

"That is some walk," the woman said, leaning heavily
against the cane, breathing hard.

"Are you okay? Do you need something to drink?" Kelsey wasn't sure if there *was* anything in the house to drink.

"No, dear but I could use a sit down." She indicated the house with a tilt of her head.

Kelsey turned, looking behind her. Two chairs sat on the front porch. This woman had obviously been here before. She led the way.

"I'm Eve Forrester. Leah's neighbor. We used to visit right here in these chairs." She sat down heavily, patting the arm of the chair she now occupied. "Lately though, it's been more at my place. I'm having a hard time getting around any more." She indicated the cane. "Couldn't find a soul to take me to Leah's funeral today. Sorry I missed it." She handed the basket she had been carrying to Kelsey. "Brought over a little bit of a care package. Didn't know if anyone'd be here but I wanted to show my respect. Not much. Just some vegetables from my garden."

Kelsey took the small basket, staring down at the fresh tomatoes, cucumbers, and radishes. "Thank you. I appreciate the thought."

Settling back in her seat, resting the cane across her lap, Eve smiled. "You must be Kelsey."

She stared, stunned. No one else had known her. No one at all. "How—"

"Leah talked about you a great deal."

CHAPTER THREE

1

David tossed his keys on the table beside the door and reached toward the light. His fingers touched the switch. He hesitated, his gaze traveling over the room before him. He'd bought the condo because he liked the open air feel. Large living room with tract lighting. Cathedral ceilings. Lots of windows.

But now it felt big, imposing.

He dropped his hand to his side, leaving the light off. He sighed, walking through the dark living room. It had been a long day.

Skirting the coffee table, he tossed his jacket on the chair across from him before collapsing onto the couch. He stared up at the silent ceiling fan, sweat slowly forming on his brow, his shirt sticking to his back. He had forgotten to turn on the air conditioner before he left and the house was hot. The air was thick, stale.

Uncle Edward had been right. He shouldn't have gone to his father's. The visit had left him feeling angry, depressed, and even a little embarrassed. When would he stop deluding himself into thinking that Hal Ebersol would ever care about anything but his damn company?

He closed his eyes. He should just get out. Leave the company. And his father.

"Hell, why not?" he muttered.

He could get a job anywhere. Eight years ago, when he graduated with a degree in environmental engineering, he'd done it. Everyone had expected him to go to work for his father. But he had wanted to prove to himself and everyone else that he didn't need Envirospace to find work, didn't need to rely on Hal Ebersol for his future.

Instead, he applied to Chem Tech Inc. in Boston. They had hired him immediately. He spent his years there writing clean up procedures, designing containers that would be safe for storing toxic waste and combining recycling procedures with waste management. The work had been satisfying. He had been offered a management position. He had been on his way to the future he wanted for himself.

And then his uncle had called.

Even now, over five years later, he could still remember the argument his uncle had used. They were on the verge of expanding. A new science building was nearly complete. They needed someone to come in, hire the staff, direct research and development.

At the time, it sounded good to David and it was exactly the kind of opportunity anyone would jump at. But he hadn't gone back because of that. He hated to admit it to himself even now but he knew it was true. He had come back for one reason and one reason only. He wanted to prove to his father that he could make Envirospace better than it already was. He could implement changes that would make the existing procedures seem archaic.

He wanted to show him up.

He laughed bitterly at the thought. In the years since his return to Envirospace, he'd implemented one project successfully. Soil cleanup. Instead of hauling away contaminated soil, his team had perfected a method of treating the soil on the job site. That was it. They were contracted out to clean up sites. Any other programs he tried to implement were turned down.

And he was sure his father had something to do with it.

His uncle offered the world. Expansion of his division after five years. Partnership after ten. But his father said nothing. In fact, David had no proof but he felt sure his father was deliberately blocking his efforts. That he would be more than happy to see his son leave. Forever.

Twice he had decided to do just that, and twice his uncle had talked him out of it. It was his mother. Edward was always telling David how much she wanted him working in the company. She had big plans for a better future. Plans she wanted David to help make a reality.

Sitting up, he glanced toward the bookshelf in the corner. He kept a photo of his mother there. He couldn't see it in the dark and as he tried to picture her face in his mind, he found he could not. His memories of her were too vague. His fourth birthday. Their sixth Christmas. Not much before she fell ill.

And in that moment, he made a decision. He couldn't keep his life on hold any longer. He needed to move forward. He needed to leave the company.

Leah always said . . .

Leah.

He leaned forward on the couch feeling as if he had just been punched in the gut, all the breath leaving him. My God, he had forgotten. For a moment, he had forgotten.

And even though he had just come from her funeral, had watched as they lowered her coffin into the ground, he still could not believe she was gone.

He closed his eyes as a memory swept over him. A picnic together. Only a few months ago. Laughing. Sipping orange juice from a wine glass. Toasting each other with silly sayings and goofy glances.

He ran a hand over his face, trying to wipe away his memories with the sweat.

It was wrong.

Leah's death. His life.

All wrong.

The thought repeated itself over and over in his mind, making him feel confused and angry. Reaching up, he attempted to loosen his tie. But as he pulled, the knot would not give.

"God dammit." He used both hands. Finally managing to pull the knot free, he ripped the tie from around his neck and flung it across the room.

At the same moment, someone knocked on his front door. He jerked toward the sound, irritated at the sudden intrusion.

He sat for a moment trying to decide if he wanted to answer. There was no one he wanted to talk to, no one he wanted to see.

The knock sounded again. Louder this time.

Pushing up from the couch, David walked over and glanced out the peephole. An eye stared back in at him. Sam's eye. It was one of his favorite jokes. A joke only he thought was funny.

Unlocking the door, David pulled it wide.

"Thought for a minute you weren't home." Sam stood on the porch, holding a basketball, wearing purple running shorts and a T-shirt with a picture of Yosemite Sam on it. His wild hair was once again free on his head making him look like a cross between Albert Einstein and Bozo the Clown.

"What is it, Sam?" He stood in front of the doorway, his arm blocking the way, making it clear he did not want company. Sam ignored him and ducked low, slipping under his arm.

"Whaddaya got to drink?" He moved through the living room and into the kitchen. David glanced over his shoulder as Sam disappeared into the next room. Sighing, he closed the door and going back to the couch, dropped down.

Sam reentered a few minutes later, flipping on a light, drinking directly from an orange juice container. "Jesus, Dave. Is it hot enough in here?" Moving to the thermostat, he flipped on the air conditioner. A moment later, the familiar hum of the unit sounded and cold air blasted out of the vents, instantly cutting through the cloying heat.

A chill passed through David's body as the cold air touched the sweat on his back.

Sam walked over and stood in front of the couch, staring down at him. "Come on. Let's hit the concrete."

"What?" He did not look up.

"Basketball." Sam's voice was light, as if today were any other day. "I know our regular game's not until tomorrow but I just got the urge." He bounced the ball once. It made a soft thud against the carpeted floor. "I plan to run you off the court."

Slowly, David turned his gaze upward. "Sam. I don't want—"

"Catch." Sam shot the ball toward David, cutting him off mid-sentence.

He dodged sideways. The ball hit the back of the couch and fell to the floor, rolling slowly away.

"See." Sam retrieved the ball. "You need this practice." He stood in front of David, once more staring down at him, his gaze intense. "Come on, buddy," he quietly urged. "Let's just go."

David ran a hand over his face, wiping away what was left of the perspiration there and said nothing.

Sam took the seat across from him and set the ball on the floor by his feet. "What were you going to do? Sit in this dark sweat box all night and think about Leah."

He did not answer.

"She wouldn't want you to, you know."

And in the back of his mind, David could hear Leah, her words so clear: *Go out with Sam. Have fun. I'll be fine.*

Slowly, he turned his gaze toward his friend, staring at his lopsided grin. "You really think we should play?"

"Like I said, I'm going to run you off that court." Reaching down, he grabbed the ball and began trying to spin it on the tip of his left index finger, a self-satisfied grin on his face.

"In your dreams, pal."

David left Sam in the living room and went to his bedroom to change his clothes. He crossed the room in the dark, moving to the lamp beside his bed. As he reached down to turn on the light, he stopped.

Lilacs.

The scent filled the air. And with it came a memory of Leah. The scent of her hair, her skin.

A shiver raced up his spine. Suddenly he no longer felt alone.

Straightening, leaving the light off, he stood in the darkness and listened. Except for the occasional sound of Sam thudding the basketball against the floor in the next room, the house was silent. The air conditioner still ran but the room felt colder than it should. David shivered. His breath plumed out before him.

He stood in darkness, waiting, watching.

"Leah?" he whispered. And immediately felt foolish. What was he doing? What did he expect? He certainly didn't believe in ghosts. Still, he felt . . .

Something brushed past him, soft and breezy, rubbing against his arm. With a startled gasp, he flinched back, trying to see, his breath coming in short, harsh gulps. A tingling sensation shuddered through his body.

Reaching down, groping for the light, he switched it on. The room was empty.

And a moment later, David realized the smell was gone. *Had it ever been there?*

He stood for a moment, thoughts of Leah still tumbling through his mind. *It's just the funeral,* he told himself. *I'm reacting to the stress of the funeral.*

But as he changed his clothes, taking off his suit and hanging it in the closet, pulling on his shorts and shirt, the feeling remained. No matter how hard he tried, he couldn't shake the feeling that he was no longer alone.

2

Hal Ebersol stood at the rain-splattered window of his private study staring down the gently sloping hill at the Envirospace complex in the distance. It sat less than five miles away, covering a forty-acre area. Administrative wing, three stories high, stood taller than both the science and the prelaunch building. But the processing plant was by far the largest building on the property. And the heart of the complex. All the garbage was brought to that building and packaged into viable units before being sent to the prelaunch facility. The launch area itself sat farther back on the property, separated from the other buildings by a man-made lake and a concrete wall.

His gaze traveled over the structures, as he admired their architectural perfection. The soft rain hitting the window distorted the buildings tonight, elongating them, twisting them into odd shapes. But Hal barely noticed. He saw only his perfect creation. In a short thirty years, he had achieved his dream of owning one of the most successful corporations in America.

But it could all end tomorrow.

All because of David.

He frowned, his stomach instantly turning to acid. Everything he had built, everything he had achieved now teetered on the edge, ready to crumble. All because of that self-righteous little bastard.

Hal turned away from the window, disgusted by thoughts of his offspring. His eyes locked on the miniature duplicate of Envirospace that sat against the far wall. Walking to it, he stared down at the scale model of his creation.

For a long time, he had thought his dream would never become a reality. As the son of a middle class working family, he did not have the capital required to start a million-dollar business. But then he met Claire and Edward Ross. The only children of multi-millionaire Howard Ross, they were eager to show their father they had what it took to succeed on their own.

With Hal's ideas and their money, they started the Envirospace project, dividing the shares equally among all three, each having the same power as the other. Hal was named president, Edward vice president, and Claire both secretary and treasurer.

At first, they worked out of a rented office space doing the required research, building capital. During that time, Hal began to realize that Claire could be more than a business partner. She was exactly what he was looking for in a wife. Smart. Beautiful. Driven. Wealthy. He decided then that she would marry him.

He could still remember the day he brought Claire to this spot, showing her where their future home would be. It was eight months into the Envirospace project, three months into their affair. They stood in the empty field, Hal designing the home around her. The kitchen here, the study there, the bedroom upstairs. She'd laughed as he pulled her from room to imaginary room. Before long, she was helping him, picking out the furnishings in her head, decorating the walls. When they were done, their fantasy house complete, he wrapped his arm around her shoulder and turned her west. "And down there," he'd said, pointing to a wooded lot. "We will build the company of the future. And you and I—" He turned her toward him, his eyes bright. "—will sit up here together and watch it become an empire."

They were married less than a year later.

For a wedding gift, Claire's father built them their dream house. It was exactly to their specifications, no expense spared.

Three months later, they broke ground for the first building in the Envirospace complex exactly where Hal had pointed it out on that clear spring day.

His life's plan was working out perfectly until the third year of his marriage to Claire, the year she began asking about children. They'd talked about it before they were married. It was the only subject about which they strongly disagreed. Hal did not want children. Claire was adamant in her insistence. Finally, he talked her into a compromise. They would wait until the company was well on its way before starting a family, maybe ten years. He was sure in all that time, he could convince her that they were perfectly happy the way they were.

But over the next two years, the company advanced more quickly than anyone could have anticipated. And Claire began planning. She bought baby books, looked at maternity clothes, selected names.

Hal ignored it all, refusing to acknowledge her growing interest and insistence.

One night as they lay in bed together, Claire babbling on about the newest birthing techniques, he could no longer stand it. He told her the truth. They would never have children. He was perfectly happy without them. He wasn't going to ruin their life together just to fulfill her foolish desire.

Things were never the same after that day. Claire substantially cut back her hours at the company. She joined clubs, chaired functions, attended meetings. And stopped talking about children. She had her friends, her charities. He was confident that in time she would see that he had been right.

He held onto that belief until she waltzed into his office at Envirospace and announced she was pregnant.

She had betrayed him, deceived him, made him believe she had given up on the idea while all along she had plotted behind his back.

And he never forgave her.

David's arrival ended her involvement with Envirospace. She stayed home full-time and raised their son. She finally had what she wanted. She was no longer interested in the business. No longer interested in Hal.

He began to put in more and more hours. The distance between them grew larger until they were simply two strangers sharing the same house. If Claire had not become ill, he was sure they would have divorced eventually. During the months that Claire lay in the upstairs bedroom, wasting away, he began coming to this room on a regular basis. Until then he had never been home long enough to enjoy the view. He would come to this room, stand at the window and stare out at his creation, his crowning glory.

And wait for Claire to die.

His anger toward her deepened with each passing day. She would leave him with the burden of raising the child he never wanted. She had never appreciated what he had built for them, what he had accomplished. She talked about only one thing, worried about only one person.

David.

Reaching out, he gripped the sides of the table. Fury welled up inside him. His hands shook, jostling the miniature copy of his dream.

Ungrateful. Undeserving.

A light knock sounded on the door.

Selfish. Parasite.

The knock sounded again.

"What," he barked, releasing the table, a few buildings and people falling over.

Louis opened the door, stepping hesitantly inside. "Mr. Brewer to see you, sir." He kept his gaze downcast as he spoke. "Shall I show him in?"

Hal paced back to the window. "Yes, Louis." He locked his gaze once more on the buildings in the distance. Behind him he heard Ken Brewer enter and the door close quietly. Hal said nothing. Ken did not make a sound.

Minutes ticked by. The night security lights came on around the buildings below, illuminating the parking lots. Fog crept over the buildings, hiding them in its white thickness. The rain increased until the pellets hitting the window almost obscured the view below.

Both men remained silent.

Hal could picture Ken standing beside the door, his back straight, his arms at his sides, his eyes locked forward. He could stand that way for hours, never moving a muscle, never flinching. Hal had seen him do it, had tested him on more than one occasion. It was his training. For twenty years, Ken had served in the marines. Now he served Hal Ebersol. And Hal enjoyed testing the man's endurance.

"My son came to see me today," he said, feeling satisfied with the length of time he had kept Ken waiting. Slowly, he turned to face him. "David was angry."

Ken raised one eyebrow. It was the only indication that he was listening.

"More angry than the moment called for. And it worries me. If he's already showing signs of strain . . ." he trailed off, not finishing the sentence. "I will not allow this to escalate out of control again." His voice was quietly threatening. "Do you understand me?"

For the first time, Ken moved. His body shifted ever so slightly to the left, his gaze landing squarely on Hal. "Yes sir," he said, his voice clipped, professional.

Moving to his chair, Hal sat down. Ken remained at the door, his eyes once again locked forward. He wore a double-breasted, dark blue suit, the lines in his trousers crisp and straight. No matter what time of the day or night Hal called Ken, he always showed up in one of his pristine double-breasted suits. His head, shaved clean, gleamed dully in the glow of the room's lights. Ken shaved it every morning at six A.M. with a straight edged razor. It took him less than three minutes. To Hal's knowledge, he had never cut himself.

"I wouldn't want what happened to the Brayden woman to happen to David." Hal shook his head. "At least not when we're on the verge of such a huge expansion. How would it look?"

"It will be contained, sir," Ken said.

"You said that the last time." Hal rubbed his eyes. He was tired of the whole damn thing. "I should have ended it that night," he said quietly. "Well, it's done now." He waved a hand, dismissing the thoughts. "We can't go back." Turning his chair around, he stared out the window once again. His gaze locked on the almost full moon that hung in the distance. "I trust that you're handling the rest of the problem effectively and will continue to do so."

"Yes sir."

Hal thought he could hear a hint of amusement in Ken's voice. Or was it satisfaction?

"And my son?" Hal stood, watching the rain slide slowly down the window. The drops hung on at the bottom of the window, swaying on the edge of the pane before dropping off into the distance below. "He is being monitored?"

"Even as we speak."

3

David grabbed the ball from Sam's hands and shot wildly. He watched as it bounced once off the backboard before falling through the hoop.

"Yes!" He threw his arms up in victory and began jogging around the court. "That's game."

Sam grabbed the ball. "You call that fair?" He bounced it several times, the hard rubber splashing against the wet ground.

Halfway through their second game, a drizzling summer rain had started. They told each other it was just passing over and kept on playing. Now at the end of their third game, they were both thoroughly drenched. The light shower showed no sign of letting up.

David stopped his victory dance and stared at Sam. "You think I cheated?"

Sam nodded, still bouncing the ball. "You always do."

"I spotted you ten points."

"Spot me fifteen this time." Sam glanced at the sky. "I still say it's going to stop."

Fog had already begun to move in, swirling around them,

wrapping their legs in its thickness.

"It doesn't matter how much I spot you." David dodged forward, stealing the ball. "I'll still win." He threw the ball and it shot through the hoop without touching the rim.

"I hate it when you do that."

The rain increased slightly, the drops heavier. David looked up, closing his eyes, letting the water fall over him.

He felt better. With each game, a bit of his tension dissolved. Poured off his body, along with the sweat and rainwater. Cleansed away. And he found himself wondering if Sam and Uncle Edward were right. Maybe he should just try and put this whole thing behind him. What did he really expect to learn?

"You want to quit?" Sam asked as the summer storm increased.

David eyed him sideways. "You chicken?"

Sam smiled and raised his arms to indicate he wanted the ball. David tossed it to him.

"I start with fifteen."

David nodded.

Sam immediately dodged left, skirting him. As David turned, he saw the ball hit the rim and bounce off the side. No points.

The ball splashed down into one of the many puddles that were now threatening to flood the whole court. David grabbed it. "You've still got fifteen." Turning, he took a shot. It fell smoothly through.

Sam wiped a hand over his face as water dripped in his eyes. "Lucky shot," he yelled.

David laughed. "Yeah, I've had my share of those tonight."

The rain increased, the fog now a thick swirling mass. David could no longer see the basket. Sam tossed him the ball. "I feel lucky tonight," he shouted above the sound of the rain. "I have a feeling I'm finally going to win a game."

"How do you figure that?"

Sam indicated the missing basket, lost in the fog. "We call this game, I'm high score."

"I spotted you those points."

Sam shrugged. "I'm not proud."

David laughed. "You think I'd give up that easy?" He bounced the ball. It splashed in the water. He eyed the area where he thought the basket was. Sam stood before him, trying to block, his arms raised overhead. David smiled and faked left. Sam followed suit to block him and David dodged right. Moving down the court, he could hear nothing but the sound of the rain pounding on the pavement and the ball splashing down and up.

Ahead, a dark shape emerged from the fog.

The pole. It's got to be the basketball pole.

He blinked, the water almost blinding. He grabbed the ball in both hands ready to shoot.

Leah stood beneath the net. Her wide eyes stared into his. Her hands reached for him.

David cried out. The ball slipped from his hands as he lost his footing on the wet pavement. He fell hard, skidding against the ground with the momentum of the run. A burning sensation streaked along his shoulder. Skin tore away. He skidded to a halt beneath the basket. Pushing up, groaning in pain, he sought the figure, straining to see through the rain, needing to be sure.

But Leah was gone.

Sam jogged across the court. "Jesus, Dave," he said, standing over him. "You okay, man?" He leaned over, water dripping from him onto David, his face concerned as he saw David's bloody shoulder. He knelt down. "You ripped the hell out of your shoulder."

David flinched back in pain as Sam touched the skinned area. "I thought . . ." he began, still looking around. Was he losing his mind? "I thought . . ." He looked at Sam, trying to form the words. But as he stared at his friend, he knew he could not say it, wasn't sure he believed it himself.

Sam's eyebrows furrowed. "What? You thought what?"

He shook his head. "Nothing. I . . . I just tripped over my feet." The rain continued to pour down on them. Suddenly, it no longer felt good to him, no longer cleansing. The rain was cold, the fog threatening.

"Let's call it a night." Sam stood and extended a hand. David took it, grunting in pain as he lurched to his feet.

His shoulder throbbed, his left ankle ached. As he limped off the court, heading back to his condo, he resisted the urge to look back over his shoulder.

4

Kelsey poured hot water over the tea bag before carrying the cup to the bedroom and setting it on the table beside the bed. Earlier, she had decided she would sleep in the guest bedroom, leaving her sister's room off limits. But after talking to Eve Forrester, she changed her mind. She wanted to be in Leah's bed tonight. Maybe only for tonight. But she needed to feel that closeness right now.

Slipping under the sheet, she reached for her teacup. She could hear the soft patter of rain against the house and glanced toward the window. The curtains billowed softly with a gentle breeze but so far the rain wasn't coming inside. She wanted to leave the window open as long as she could. She liked the fresh air, the smell of rain on the cool evening wind.

Kelsey took a sip of her tea. The heat felt good as it moved through her body. Leaning back against the headboard, she glanced around her sister's room, taking in the details. A bookcase, two dressers . . . her gaze stopped on a small cross-stitch plaque that hung beside the tallest dresser. Kelsey immediately recognized it. As a child, Leah had always enjoyed cross-stitching, working hours at a time, taking days, sometimes weeks for just one pattern. The hobby relaxed her, she always said. Once at Leah's urging, Kelsey tried it but the effect was just the opposite on her. Sorting the different colored threads, counting the stitches—all of it drove her crazy.

The plaque beside the dresser was one Leah had done when she was eleven or twelve. It had always been one of Kelsey's favorites. It showed a small girl hugging a bouquet of flowers to her chest, smiling brightly. *The world is beautiful* was stitched below in bright red. It seemed to Kelsey that if she stared at the picture long enough, she would see Leah in that small stitched face. The saying reflected Leah's attitude about life.

Or at least it had when Leah was twelve years old.

Suddenly, Kelsey felt strange sitting in her sister's bed, sipping tea out of her cup, staring at her things. Maybe it wasn't such a good idea to stay in her room. She pushed back the light blanket covering her legs. Out of the corner of her eye, she caught sight of a small beige book. It sat on the bottom shelf of the bedside table, a bright blue satin marker sticking out the top. Kelsey stared at it, her heart picking up its beat ever so slightly. It was a diary. Leah's diary. She was sure of it. Leah had always kept one as a child.

She reached toward the book.

If it is her diary, should I read it?

Her hand stopped midway, hovering.

She stared at the book. Damn, she wished she hadn't noticed it. Reaching down, she snatched it up before she could stop herself.

Kelsey turned it over in her hands for several minutes trying to cement the decision in her mind, offering herself a dozen good reasons for reading it.

Hesitantly, she opened the cover. There on the first page were the words *This Book Belongs to:* and in her sister's familiar handwriting, *Leah Brayden.* Kelsey stared at the name. The *L* a large, looping letter. The *B* the same way. She ran her fingers over the writing, tracing the loops and lines. Her hands were shaking slightly as she turned to the first page. The book began on January first. Each page after that was dated for this year. Leah's familiar handwriting glared up at her from page after page. The words blurred as unwanted tears flooded her eyes.

Kelsey closed the book. She ran a hand over the cover, trying to get her emotions under control again. Her sister's life was within her hands. She hugged the book close to her chest, feeling as if she were holding a part of Leah.

Should she read it? Was she ready to?

Kelsey set the diary on the night table beside the bed. No more tonight. She needed to think about it, needed to sort through her feelings a little more first. Reaching over, she grabbed her tea cup and took another sip. It was already beginning to cool.

The rain increased outside. Kelsey glanced at the window. Water was just beginning to hit the screen. Getting out of bed, she made her way to the window to close it against the storm. She stood for a moment staring out at the yard beyond the glass. Fog rolled in from the woods, covering the lawn in white. Wind blew, the trees bending to its demand. Kelsey barely saw any of it. Her mind was stuck on Leah. What did she expect to find staying at her sister's? In the end, would it really matter? Maybe her mother was right and she should just go home. After all . . .

Movement caught her eye. Kelsey glanced toward the woods that flanked the back of the house. A figure stood at the edge of the trees, shrouded in darkness. Kelsey took a step back from the window, feeling suddenly vulnerable. Afraid. The figure lifted an arm and pointed toward the woods. Kelsey's heart fluttered in her chest, her hair prickled on her scalp. Something about this person . . . something familiar . . .

But then the figure was gone as if it had never been there. Kelsey let out the breath she had been holding. Reaching up, she quickly closed the window, locking it. But she did not go back to bed. Instead, she remained at the window a few moments longer. She hadn't been able to see the person who stood in the yard, the dark and the storm hiding the identity. But as Kelsey turned away from the window, staring at her sister's bed, knowing she could no longer sleep in it, only one name whirled through her mind.

Leah.

CHAPTER FOUR

1

Haupt, Texas

Joe Novak sat inside his car staring at the modest ranch house across the street. He had been watching the house since dawn, nearly three hours. No one had noticed him. His gray midsized Oldsmobile blended in perfectly with the neighborhood. Slumped against the back of his seat, he ran his thumb absently down the side of his face, tracing the scar that ran from his eye back to his mouth.

He hated this part of his work. The endless waiting. Sometimes he spent entire days just waiting for something, anything to happen. His gaze fell on the pack of Marlboros lying on the dash board before him. He longed for one.

But he would wait until the job was done.

Right now he felt antsy, anxious to finish and push on. The cigarette would relax him, take his edge away. And he needed that edge. So he would wait.

The automated garage door across the street began to rise. Joe straightened. Taking a quick glance at the open file on the seat beside him, he studied the photo of Steven Ordmann. Looking up once more, he watched the car that slowly backed down the driveway. Ordmann was driving the Ford.

Flipping the file closed, Joe started his car and began to follow the man he had been hired to kill. He drove at an even, steady pace. He was not worried that he would lose his target. Joe knew where he was going. It had been in the file. It was always in the file.

Most of the information supplied to him by his clients was worthless. Personal information. That was what the majority of each file contained. Wife's name. Children's names. Favorite restaurant. Church they attended. To Joe, it was worthless.

He needed to know only their name, address, and occupation to do the job at hand. The rest did not matter. Joe was a businessman. He wanted it kept on a business level.

Once he knew something personal about his subjects, it changed things. So he did not read the files supplied, did not meet the friends or family. He simply watched them, waiting for opportunity to present itself. Sometimes it took days, sometimes only hours. And on rare occasions, he was forced to create opportunity himself.

This would not be one of those occasions. This one would be quick, simple. An easy kill without complications—just the way he liked it. He was not some sick pervert who enjoyed watching as his victims die, staring intently into their eyes, waiting for life to ebb away. To him, it was simply an occupation, like ditch digging or bartending. He provided a service and was paid for it.

That was why he still regretted his handling of Harvey Staller. He'd allowed himself to get frustrated and lose control, displaying a rare anger toward his target. Very unprofessional behavior.

But it was his own fault.

He'd spent too much time waiting for the right opportunity to present itself. He should have moved in sooner, taking Harvey out while he slept or using a high powered scope to take him out at work from long range. But those options were risky and Joe did not like to take risks. Looking back, however, he realized that was exactly what he should have done. Perhaps then he wouldn't have lost control.

It was the pressure of the time limit. His clients had given him one month to complete the job. He had wasted two weeks on Harvey Staller. Two weeks. He shook his head as he thought about it. Why had he let it go on so long? Now he could feel the pressure of completing the job within the allotted time. It was not the way he liked to work.

Joe slowed his car down as the Ford turned into the gravel driveway of an ongoing construction site. It was early. The site was deserted.

He did not follow the car into the site. He did not want to leave his tire tracks in the gravel roadway. Instead, he parked across the street in a church lot.

Slipping out of his car, he fingered the butt of the familiar 9-mm semi-automatic that was strapped under his arm.

He moved at a leisurely pace; there was no reason to rush. He glanced around as he walked onto the construction site but there was no one in sight. Reaching into his pocket, he withdrew a pair of formfitting plastic surgical gloves and slipped them over his hands.

The construction trailer came into sight. Steven Ordmann owned the company and he was doing what every boss did—putting in too many extra hours. He stood outside the trailer holding a blueprint, glancing at the paper and then at the building in progress. Joe took one last look around as he drew near him. The crane cab empty. The bulldozer abandoned. Nothing moved. No cars, no voices, nothing.

Ordmann looked up as he approached. Joe knew he did not look menacing. Except for the scar on his face, he could be every mother's ideal son.

"Are you here about the job?" Ordmann asked.

Joe smiled, an easy, no problem smile.

In one fluid motion, he withdrew the 9-mm and popped

off two shots, the silencer muffling the sound. Both bullets hit their marks—one to the chest, one to the head—and Ordmann fell to the ground in a heap. The blueprint he had been holding fluttered downward in a graceful descent. It landed beside his head, one side partially covering his face, hiding the shocked expression frozen there.

"No thanks. I've already got a job." Joe replaced the weapon in its shoulder holster and leaned down, placing two gloved fingers to the side of Ordmann's neck. He waited. Nothing. Satisfied, he scooped up the spent cartridges, slipped them into his pocket and walked back to his car.

Climbing behind the wheel, pulling off his gloves, he reached for the Marlboros. As he slipped the cigarette between his lips, he pulled a single sheet of paper from his breast pocket. Lighting up, inhaling deeply, he crossed Steven Ordmann's name off the list.

2

Hartwick, Michigan

Eve Forrester sat on her back porch tossing peanuts to the squirrels that foraged around on the ground for food. She liked to watch them, the way their tails twitched as they moved, how quickly their small paws worked to shell the peanuts. They were her pets. At least that was how she liked to think of them. Each morning and again each evening, they showed up in her yard for food. She enjoyed their company.

Even the rabbits that often invaded her garden to steal her vegetables were welcome. Since her husband's death seven years earlier, any company was welcome.

Tossing another peanut toward a particularly brave squirrel that sat less than five feet from her, she smiled. Her husband, Ed, had been the one who started the tradition of feeding the squirrels. He'd come out every morning, sit in the chair she now sat in and toss out the roasted nuts. She never understood why he did it until after he was gone.

Three days after his funeral, she had looked into the yard and noticed four squirrels nosing around, glancing every few minutes toward the house. They were waiting for Ed, she realized. And in that moment, she'd felt needed. As soon as she opened the back door and stepped into the yard with her small handful of peanuts, they came to her, heads up, tails swishing from side to side, and she felt the connection. She knew they would only come around as long as she fed them but it didn't matter. They needed her and acknowledged her and it was enough.

Eve's hand was poised, ready to throw out another handful of peanuts when suddenly the squirrels all stopped in mid-chew. Their tails began to twitch. All at once, as if an alarm had gone off, they dashed to the woods, to the safety of the trees.

Her brow creased as she squinted toward the forest. She was just beginning to wonder what had frightened the small animals when Rebel came crashing through the underbrush and into her yard. She should have known.

"Rebel!" she yelled, her voice curt.

The dog was always scaring the squirrels and tearing up her garden. Today, he was in for double duty. He headed straight into her vegetables and began digging furiously.

"Rebel!" Using her cane, she pushed up from her seat and hobbled toward the hound. "You get out of there!" The dog simply ignored her, his paws moving furiously, dirt flying.

Just as she reached the garden, Teddy and Greg emerged from the woods.

"Rebel," Greg yelled, slightly out of breath. He jogged toward the garden, Teddy right behind him. "Geez, I'm sorry, Mrs. F. I'll get him." And before she could stop him, Greg stepped into the garden, his sneakers causing more damage to the delicate vegetables than the dog.

Eve groaned inwardly as she watched her tomatoes and beans being trampled.

"I'll help," Teddy offered when Greg proved unsuccessful in his attempts.

"No!" Eve said but the boy was already weaving his way through her plants.

Together, Greg and Teddy managed to pull Rebel out of the garden, dragging him through the carrots and cucumbers. They stopped in front of Eve, holding the dog's collar tightly as he bucked in their grasp. She stared down at the two young boys, scowling slightly, then realized they were waiting for her inevitable anger.

But as she watched them struggling to hold the hound, their large eyes staring up at her, she was not able to sustain her outrage. Slowly, a smile broke across her face. If the rabbits could ravage her garden, so could two young boys and their dog. "Don't worry about it boys. The garden's mostly for fun. It's not a great loss."

Greg and Teddy glanced at each other as if they did not understand what she was saying.

"You're not in trouble," she explained, picking up on their confused expressions.

Immediately, both boys smiled with relief.

"He won't do it again, Mrs. F. I promise," Greg said quickly.

"Don't make promises you can't keep," she replied. "Now go on before I change my mind."

Greg and Teddy looked at each other again. Then turned and quickly disappeared into the woods. They released Rebel and the dog ran ahead of them, free once more to wreak havoc.

Eve watched them go before turning back to her mangled garden.

It was true. The garden was not very important to her. Now that she was alone, she needed very little. Most of what she grew either went bad or was given away. Still, she took pride in her plants and hated to see them ruined.

As she looked at the hole the dog had made, her brow furrowed. Using her cane, she stepped slowly forward. Rebel hadn't just been digging, she realized, staring at the small clump of earth. He had been trying to bury something.

Bending down, she tried to see the half-buried object but could not make it out. She moved the dirt around it with the tip of her cane. Within moments, she could see the small paws and long tail. A squirrel, its soft fur matted down with a combination of dirt and saliva. Poor thing. Rebel must have found the body in the woods.

Well, she couldn't very well just leave it in the middle of her garden. Going to the shed that sat on the edge of her yard, she retrieved her gardening gloves, a hand-held shovel and a plastic garbage bag.

She knelt down on the ground before the small hole and carefully lifted the animal out.

But just before she dumped it into the bag, she stopped. Leaning closer, she studied the animal's body. ''What the devil?''

3

''You said black, one sugar, right?'' Mary Glover set the cup in front of Kelsey.

Kelsey smiled, nodding. ''Yes, thank you.'' She'd spent several hours that morning at the police station reading the reports regarding Leah's death. She didn't know what they would tell her, if anything, but she needed answers to all the questions buzzing around her head and it seemed a better place to start than anywhere else.

Included with the standard police reports was a statement from Mary Glover, a woman who claimed to have seen Leah an hour before she died. Kelsey copied her phone number from the recount and immediately called her after leaving the police station. She was thrilled when Mary agreed to see her.

"According to your statement," she began as soon as Mary was seated again. "You saw my sister only an hour before she died."

Mary nodded. "Yes. I was coming home from shopping."

"Did she say anything to you? Ask you anything?" She wrapped her hands around her coffee cup, holding it tightly. The heat burned her fingers but she did not release the mug. "Did you see anyone else around? A car maybe?"

"I didn't see anything and she didn't say anything. I tried talking to her," Mary added quickly. "I asked her if she needed help but she didn't say anything. I'm sorry. I guess that doesn't help you much."

Kelsey was not satisfied. This couldn't be it. There had to be more. "Anything you can tell me." Her voice was hopeful. "Something out of the ordinary. Something that didn't seem to fit that night."

"I don't know exactly. This may not . . ." She paused, sighing deeply. "This is difficult to say." She stopped again. Her gaze darted downward and stayed there.

"Go ahead," Kelsey prompted, sensing her discomfort but not willing to stop. "I need to hear everything."

Mary looked at her. This time there was a trace of pity on her face. "I thought there was something wrong with her that night," she said, her voice quiet. "To be honest with you, I thought maybe she was drunk or on drugs."

"What?" Kelsey hadn't heard any of this before. And like everything else about Leah's death, it simply did not make sense. As a teenager, Leah had stayed away from drugs and alcohol. Kelsey found it hard to believe she'd picked up the habits late in life. "Why would you think that?"

"Her eyes." Mary averted her own. "They seemed unfocused. It was almost as if she had no idea what she was doing." She wrung her hands as she spoke, her eyes looking everywhere but at Kelsey. "Your sister scared me." She sounded embarrassed by the admission. "Something about that night, about her, was wrong. I could sense that much. But all I wanted to do . . ." And finally, her gaze found Kelsey again. "All I wanted to do was get away from her." Reaching across the table, she gripped Kelsey's hand and squeezed. "I'm so sorry I didn't do something more."

Kelsey stared at Mary Glover. She had come to this woman seeking answers. Instead she had found more questions.

4

The key slid smoothly into the lock. A moment later, the click of the deadbolt sounded and the door swung open.

David stood in the doorway of Leah's home, staring in at the shadowy living room. He remembered the first day he'd come here. The antiseptic feel of the whole house. The colorless rooms with their bland decor. It had changed so much.

Leah had changed.

Little by little, the house had become what Leah had always wanted it to be. And so had she. At least, that's what he had thought.

Maybe if I had been here that night. Maybe—

He shook his head. He couldn't think that way. It didn't help, didn't change things. He had come here hoping to find some clue as to why she had killed herself. Nothing more.

Last night he had been ready to forget the whole thing, just let her rest in peace. Until the basketball game. Until . . .

No. He had not seen Leah. It had been his imagination, too much coffee, not enough food. Something other than what? Her ghost? He did not believe that. Yet he had not slept last night, could think of nothing else.

He closed the door behind him, sealing his decision.

Walking to a window, he pulled the blinds open. Sunlight poured in, the slats creating a pattern across the floor and walls.

Like bars in a prison, he thought. And realized that that was exactly how he felt—trapped and unable to move forward in his life until he understood or at least accepted what happened. Without blame or guilt.

Because in the back of his mind, there was something—a nagging, don't-let-this-go feeling that he could not dismiss.

Out of the corner of his eye, he could see photographs on the small table on the far side of the room. Slowly, he moved toward them, not sure if he wanted to see them but unable to stop himself. Leah's familiar smile greeted him. His gaze drifted over the photos on display. A few of him were still scattered throughout the collection. Why hadn't she put them away?

Reaching out, he picked up the largest photo. It was taken on the day they met. The annual company picnic. He stared into her eyes, studying her face, remembering. She had worn a floral dress that day, shorter in length than most of the other things she owned. He had seen her wear it only that one time. She had been at the picnic with Rose. David could still see it all so clearly in his mind, the pained look on Leah's face as Rose commented on everything from Leah's hair to her shoes. The longer he watched her, the more he wanted to rescue her.

But did I ever love her? The thought ran through his head for the first time fully formed. It was a question that whispered through his mind and tore at his heart. But he'd never had the courage to do more than let it nag at him. Now, as he stood in her house, staring at her picture, looking at her things, he knew the truth and could no longer turn away from it.

All the time he was with her, he had tried to give Leah strength, determination, tried to help her become her own person. More than anything else, he had tried to help her break free from her mother's smothering grasp. But he had never really loved her.

And he wondered if she had known.

They had slept together twice. The second time had been so awkward, so forced. Even now as he thought about it he felt embarrassed. Had she sensed his discomfort? Had she stopped calling, stopped talking to him because of it?

"Should have left her alone," he whispered. Quickly, he set the photo back in place no longer wanting to look at her.

But as he turned away, he bumped the table and knocked several of the frames over. As he set them back into place, he noticed one picture in particular. It was Leah with Hillary West. He lifted it off the table. The two of them were so close. More like sisters than friends. His brow furrowed. Hillary. Hillary? He couldn't remember the last time he'd seen her. She . . .

. . . screamed and then was silent.

He dropped the photo as a flash of memories rocketed through his mind.

Faces swam in and out of focus . . . He struggled . . . Pain seared through his shoulder . . .

He fell back against the table, knocking several framed pictures from atop it. A blinding headache pounded against his temple, scattering his thoughts. He clutched at the table to keep from falling as the pain intensified.

Squeezing his eyes shut, he rubbed his forehead, trying to clear his mind. Finally, the headache began to subside.

Opening his eyes, trembling, he stared down at the pictures on the floor. He struggled to remember what he had been thinking. But as the thoughts began to regroup in his head, the pain surged, clouding his mind until it was the only thing he could think about.

Letting his thoughts tumble away, he felt the throbbing ease until it was just a dull ache. He wiped at the light sweat that had sprung up on his forehead and wondered briefly if he were coming down with something.

This is taking too damn long. Just get the diary and get the hell out.

He left the photos on the floor. With long strides, he made his way down the darkened hallway toward the bedroom. He knew where she kept the diary.

Stepping inside, he headed toward the bed. But the familiar beige journal was not on the table beside it.

David looked under the bed. On top of the dresser. Inside the dresser. In the closet.

Dammit. The diary was gone.

5

Ken Brewer ran a hand over his smooth head as he watched the house across the street. David had gone inside some time ago.

His eyes, hidden behind the dark sunglasses he wore, scanned the area, making sure he was not being observed. That was all he needed, a nosy neighbor calling the cops on him.

He turned back to Leah Brayden's house. It was clean. Ken was sure of that. He'd been inside twice. But why did David come back here? What did he know that Ken did not?

He turned the questions over in his mind but found no apparent answers. And he needed answers. His future and the future of Hal Ebersol depended on him and his assessment of this situation.

Just as it had before.

As Ken continued his survey of the grounds, his gaze lingered on the expensive car parked in the driveway. *Thirty and the kid's got a Jag.* Ken drummed his fingers against the steering wheel of his two-year-old Camero.

Everything David Ebersol had was a fluke of nature, a simple twist of fate. He hadn't worked for it, hadn't earned it, he'd simply been born to it. And he didn't appreciate any of it.

Especially his father. Hal Ebersol was a man of action who was not afraid to use his power and authority. He knew what he wanted out of life and had the ability to go after it. Ken did not understand how David could be so ungrateful, so shortsighted.

In the twelve years he'd worked for the man, Ken had watched Envirospace grow into one of the most influential companies in North America. And in all that time, he never once had a security breach. Until two months ago. Until David.

"Should have ended it that night," he mumbled, letting himself indulge in what could have been. But he still might get his chance. He sensed that Hal Ebersol had lost some confidence in Ken's ability to get the job done. Ken was determined to gain that trust back. No matter what it took.

He checked his watch. It'd been nearly forty minutes since the kid went inside.

"Whatcha doin', Junior?" he muttered under his breath. He needed to know.

Slipping out of his car, he moved toward the house, once more checking the area around him. He stopped in front of the door, cocked his head to one side, listened. No sound from inside. Leaning over, he glanced through the open blinds. He had watched from his car as David opened them wide, silently thanking the kid for making his job easier.

Fingering the key in his hand, he tried to figure out what lie he could tell if he walked in the front door and came face to face with Junior. What excuse could he possibly give for invading this home? His fingers caressed the key, feeling its smooth top, its harsh teeth.

It's just David, he told himself. If Ken couldn't handle him . . . He slipped the key into the door. Gripping the knob, he turned it. He heard the click as the spring shifted the catch, releasing the door. Ken stopped, holding the knob, holding his breath. Still no sound from inside. He pushed the door a quarter of an inch open and waited. Nothing. He moved the door again. Again nothing.

As the door swung wide, he paused waiting for David to call out, ask who was there. But that did not happen. Stepping inside, Ken closed the door quietly behind him. The living room and most of the dining room were visible from where he now stood. David was nowhere in sight. Sweeping the room with a single glance, he stared at the photos on the floor in the corner.

Moving to them, he crouched down. One stood out from the rest, the glass cracked. *Dammit.* Hillary West. He had thought he'd taken everything out of the house that pertained to her. Reaching down, he lifted the broken picture and slipped it into his coat pocket.

His attention was drawn down the hallway. He could hear movement. Junior was down there, searching for something from the sound of it.

Ken had been in the house before, looking for information, making sure the Brayden woman was not hiding anything. He was familiar with the layout and the contents. Moving slowly, not wanting to make any more noise than necessary, he headed toward the bedrooms.

He needed to know what the hell David was doing.

He moved slowly, keeping to the left hand side, avoiding any squeaks in the floor. He could hear David shuffling around. Inside the far bedroom on the left.

"Dammit."

The word drifted toward Ken, the frustration behind it clear. Something banged or was dropped. Then an exasperated sigh.

Ken could see David in his mind's eye, could hear the slow rise and fall of each breath he took. In that instant, he wished he could snuff out that breath.

That would fix everything. End all our problems, he thought. The muscles in his arms became tight as his hands clenched involuntarily at his sides. And for a moment, he could almost feel the younger man's neck in his hands, the pulse beneath his fingers beating fiercely as its precious oxygen was cut off. Ken began to shake, his body straining with anticipation. It would be easy, take only moments. Ken would stare into David's eyes and watch until the light within them faded. Until the problem was silenced forever. He took a step closer to the bedroom. It would be simple. Fast. He leaned closer. One quick snap and . . .

The front door opened behind him.

6

Kelsey pushed the door wide. She could hear movement at the end of the hallway, near the bedrooms. She glanced that way but did not move any further into the room. She noticed her sister's photographs scattered on the floor only a few feet away.

"Hello? Is someone here?"

The question was ridiculous. She knew someone was. The Jaguar in the driveway was a dead giveaway.

Her mother? No. Her mother could not afford that car. Eve Forrester? No. Same reason.

"I saw your car," she called when she received no reply.

There was only one person she could think of who might drive that expensive car and be in her sister's house.

A moment later, her suspicion was confirmed as David Ebersol walked into the room.

"Hi." He stopped a few feet from her, smiling casually, as if it were perfectly normal for him to be here right now.

Kelsey remained at the door, keeping it open behind her. She stared at him through slitted eyes. What gave him the right to invade her sister's home?

"What are you doing here?" she asked when he offered no explanation for his uninvited visit. She crossed her arms over her chest and waited. His answer would help her decide if she should call the police or offer to make coffee.

He shifted uncomfortably under her scrutiny. "I'm sorry.

I didn't think anyone would be here.'' He held up a book he had tucked under his arm. Kelsey had not noticed it. ''I realized I'd left this here and I wanted to stop by and pick it up.''

He sounded sincere but as Kelsey glanced at the book, she knew he was lying.

"How did you get in?"

Reaching in his pocket, he held a hand out toward her. ''I have a key.''

Stepping forward, her gaze shifted to the small object in the palm of his hand. She frowned. ''I'll be staying here for a while.'' She held a hand out toward him. ''I would appreciate your key.''

He hesitated. It was only for a moment but enough for Kelsey to realized that he did not want to give it up.

What were you looking for?

But before she could ask him anything more, he handed her the key, checked his watch and headed for the door. ''I'm late for work.''

Suddenly, Kelsey did not want him to leave. The police report had gotten her nowhere. She didn't know any of Leah's friends. This man had dated Leah. He *knew* her. If he left, so did her best opportunity to find out what happened to her sister.

''Why did you really come here?'' she blurted out just as he reached the front door.

Her words stopped him cold. Slowly, he turned to face her again. ''I already told you—''

''I know you didn't come here for that book.''

''Yes, I did. I remembered this morning—''

''*101 Needlepoint Patterns,*'' she said, cutting him off.

His eyebrows creased. He stared at her visibly confused. ''What?''

''It's the title.'' She pointed at the book tucked under his arm.

He glanced down and cringed. His gaze shifted from the book to Kelsey and then back to the book as he tried to

come up with something that sounded convincing, something that sounded like the truth. "It's for a friend. I . . .
she . . . loaned it to Leah." His eyes locked with hers, chal-
lenging her to call him a liar.

"How well did you know my sister?" she said, trying
to change the subject, trying to keep him here.

"We were close."

How close? She wanted to ask. Because no matter how
hard she tried, she could not picture this man with her sister. Maybe once she read—

The diary.

Her heartbeat quickened as the realization sank in. "You
came for her diary."

He stared into her eyes, searching . . . for what? She
didn't know. But she feared that if he did not find what he
was looking for, he would not tell her the truth. "I thought
it could answer a few questions for me," he said finally.

Kelsey smiled, relieved he had decided to be honest with
her. "I had the same thought."

His eyes widened. "Then you have the diary?"

"Yes."

"I think," he began slowly, his voice tentative. "That
Leah would want me to have it." He locked his gaze on
her, waiting for her response.

And as she stood before him, looking at him, she knew
what he was hoping. She would tell him he was probably
right. After all, he had known Leah better than she had. It
only made sense that he should have her diary. And for a
moment, she wanted to do just that. Because there was
something about the way he stared at her, an urgency she
could not completely ignore. Maybe . . . She looked away.
She had her own needs to think about. "Mr. Ebersol—"

"David," he interjected.

"David." She paused briefly. "I'm not giving Leah's
diary to you or anyone else."

"There's a lot of personal information in that book. I
don't—"

"I'm sorry but that's just too bad." She met his glance and held it this time. "That book is the only link I have to my sister and I'm keeping it."

His face fell with defeat. He nodded. "I understand." Once more, he turned and headed toward the door.

Kelsey let him go. She had the diary. She didn't really need him. But after taking only two steps, David stopped. Shifted where he stood. Ran a hand through his hair. But did not leave.

Slowly, he turned to face her again, his dark eyes intense. "I need to find out what happened to her."

Kelsey did not know this man. Did not know if he really wanted to help or . . . what? Did she think he was covering up for someone? Covering for himself?

She didn't know. But maybe Leah's diary could tell her. Either way, she wanted to keep in contact with him until she knew the truth.

"Maybe," she began slowly, "we can find out together."

7

Ken listened to the muffled voices from his hiding place inside the closet but he could not make out any words. He stood wedged behind Leah's winter coats, his back pressed against the wall. He could remain there for hours if necessary. But as he strained to hear, he thought he detected the front door opening and closing and then silence.

They were gone.

Slowly, he inched forward and pressed the door open. No sound. He slid around the frame and made his way quietly to the back of the house. He could hear their voices out front, on the porch. Something about dinner at seven. No matter. He had what he needed.

David had definitely become a problem. Again.

Now all he needed to do was convince Hal Ebersol that

his son was too much of a liability to keep around. That was what Ken had decided as he stood in Leah's closet listening to the voices only a few feet away. The only way he could end this problem was to end David Ebersol's life.

He slipped out the back door and made a straight line for the woods behind the house. He could use the cover of the trees to work his way down the street until it was safe to approach his car.

His boots crunched through the underbrush, crushing twigs and leaves beneath each heavy step. He listened to the sound, trying to weigh all his options. It could be dangerous to get rid of David. Especially after what happened to the two women. But as far as he was concerned, David was a ticking time bomb. He could go off at any moment. Was that risk any higher than just disposing of him? It was a gamble either way.

He stopped. The hair on the back of his neck prickled. Was someone watching him? He looked behind him. To his right. Left. Daylight filtered through the trees, mixing with the shadows, shifting every few seconds in the slight wind.

Darkness. Light. Darkness.

He saw nothing. Except . . .

A cloud of fog. It drifted toward him, seeming almost deliberate in its movement. He took an involuntary step backward as the mist of cold air washed over him. With it came a smell. Strong. Too strong. It wrapped itself around him, getting into his lungs, choking him. He coughed. Tried to inhale.

And couldn't.

He gasped for breath that would not come.

And then he saw her. A woman. Only a few feet away. Ethereal. Part of the mist. Her image blurring in the darkness and light, mixing with the shadows. Her hands stretched toward him. Twisting. Squeezing. His throat constricted with each movement.

Stop! Her voice screamed through his mind, knocking

him to his knees. He clawed at his throat. His straining pulse beat fiercely against his flesh. His air starved lungs burned. *Don't!*

A strangled cry escaped his lips. His vision blurred. Blackness closed in, trying to envelope him. He struggled to stay conscious, fighting against the encroaching darkness.

And suddenly he could breathe again.

He fell forward. Gasping. Sweating. Breathing. He scanned the area around him but there was no trace of the woman. Or the fog. Only the smell—strong, sickly sweet—remained behind.

Lilacs.

CHAPTER FIVE

1

David entered the main suite of the Envirospace corporate headquarters and headed directly toward Leah's desk. He hadn't gotten to the diary first, but he'd sure as hell check out her desk before anyone else could.

He skirted a receptionist who rushed past him, mumbling to herself about the unjustness of making coffee. As usual, the staff was in full swing. Secretaries typed memos, analysts worked on their computers, assistants faxed information, the machines beeping and humming as everyone worked.

David weaved between desks, sidestepped busy employees, responded to the occasional hello. But the hurried activity barely registered in his mind as Leah's desk came into view. He stopped cold.

The desk was clear. Only her computer and a few stray pens remained. Reaching out, he opened the drawers one by one. Each was empty.

Just like the diary, he was one step behind.

"They cleaned it out yesterday." Denise Witoski, the office manager, stood beside him, her presence jarring him slightly. He had not heard her approach.

"When?" It was the only thing he could think to say.

"Yesterday," she repeated. "Early. Before any of us arrived."

"What'd they do with everything?"

She shook her head, pushing her glasses up on her nose. "No one knows. Her files weren't given to anyone in the office."

"What about personal items?" David asked. "Her pictures? That frog paperweight she had?"

"I can check with personnel if you'd like," Denise offered. "They probably have it."

He nodded absently. "Thanks, Denise."

He watched her walk away before turning back to the desk before him.

Her files she was working on weren't given to anyone.

Denise's words repeated in his mind, sounding odd, wrong.

The desks of people who had left the company for other jobs didn't get cleaned out so fast. Files sat inside for weeks sometimes before they were reassigned. So why had someone been in such a hurry to empty Leah's?

2

Kelsey looked out Leah's front window, surprised to see Eve Forrester sitting on the porch.

She stepped outside. "This is a nice surprise."

Eve bowed her head toward Kelsey in acknowledgment of the compliment. "Thank you, dear."

Taking the seat across from her, Kelsey smiled as brightly as she could manage. It wasn't that she didn't want to talk with Eve; she was genuinely glad to see her again. It was just that she was tired. While driving back from Mary Glover's, she'd decided she needed a nap, time to catch up on the sleep she'd missed over the last few days. David Ebersol's unexpected visit had deterred her from that mission. Now with Eve . . .

"I didn't hear you knock. Have you been waiting long?" She smiled, sincerely she hoped.

"Not really waiting. At my age, I need a sit-down every time I come through those woods anymore." She patted the arms of the chair she was in. "I'm a fixture on this porch in the summertime so I hope you don't mind a visit every once in while from an old woman who needs a place to rest her bones."

"Not at all. I'm getting used to the traffic. You're my second visitor today."

"Who else was here?" Eve asked.

"A friend of Leah's. David Ebersol."

"David is a lovely man."

"You know him?"

Eve nodded. "Through Leah. He was over quite a bit for a while there."

She thought for a moment. "But not lately?"

"They had their problems," Eve said, sounding a little sad. "I don't believe it ever would have worked out between them."

"Did Leah talk to you about it?" Kelsey asked, trying to learn anything that might help her understand what her sister's life had been like. "Was she depressed over it?"

"Of course she was, dear, but no more than any other young woman whose relationship ends." Eve paused, her brow creasing slightly. "Why are you asking about this?"

She paused, not sure if she wanted to discuss this with Eve. She didn't really know the woman that well. Still, Eve had been close to Leah and Kelsey needed someone to talk to, someone to help her sort through the jumble of emotions that coursed through her. "I talked to a woman today who saw Leah that night . . . the night . . ." She stopped, unable to finish the sentence. She could feel tears building behind her eyes. Swallowing back her emotions, she continued, "She said Leah looked like she was on drugs or drunk. You knew her. Does that sound like Leah?"

"No," Eve said immediately. "Not at all."

"Then what happened?" She had never felt so frustrated in all her life. "That's what I've been trying to figure out. None of this makes sense to me."

"Kelsey," Eve began, her voice compassionate. "Your sister was a sad girl. She never knew what it would take to make her happy. Not even David, as lovely a man as he is, could do it for her."

"If I could have talked to her, maybe I could—"

"No maybes, dear." Reaching out, Eve took Kelsey's hands in her own. Her eyes locked with Kelsey's. "If a person cannot find happiness within themselves, then they never will."

Kelsey pulled her hands away. "So I'm just supposed to accept what happened to Leah?" Her voice was tinged with an anger she could not suppress. "Not try and find out what drove her to stand in that road?" Standing, she paced to the edge of the porch and stared out at the quiet street before her. Two boys rode by on their bikes. The same boys she had seen earlier with their dog. And once more memories of Leah as a child flashed through her mind. "I just don't understand . . . anything," she whispered.

"I don't think anyone will ever know what was going through her mind that night." Eve's voice, so soft, was quietly comforting.

"Then you accept it," Kelsey said, needing to hear someone else tell her that Leah's suicide was plausible, even possible. So that she could come to terms with it. When Eve did not answer immediately, she turned to face her once more.

"I don't know," Eve said finally. "The last few weeks of her life, she was different."

"In what way?"

"Well, I know she was having trouble sleeping. She told me she was having nightmares."

"Nightmares? What kind of nightmares?"

"I'm sorry, dear, but she wouldn't share the details. Only that they frightened her terribly."

"Anything else?" Kelsey asked, somehow sensing there was much more.

"There was one day in particular I remember," she began slowly. "She came to my house. Looked as if she'd been in the woods for some time. Leaves in her hair, mud on her clothes and face. I thought maybe she'd gotten herself turned around on the path. I asked her as much."

"What'd she say?"

"Nothing." Eve looked at Kelsey and there was an uncertainty in her eyes that had not been there only moments earlier. "I wasn't even sure she knew what I was talking about. She seemed distracted, unfocused."

"Was she sick?"

"I don't think so." Eve leaned back in the chair, her gaze turning inward as she contemplated Leah's final days. "I don't know how to describe it," she said after a time. "She just was not herself. Those last few weeks, she seemed troubled, even more so than usual."

Kelsey sighed. This really wasn't getting her anywhere. Eve's strange stories and vague descriptions were useless to her. "I'm sure you didn't come over here for this," she said, wanting to change the subject.

Eve focused on her again. "I don't mind talking about it."

"I think," Kelsey began, wiping at a stray tear that escaped her eye, "that for right now at least, I'm done." Taking a deep breath, she blew it out slowly. "So what *did* bring you over?"

Eve glanced at the paper bag sitting on the table beside her. "That."

Kelsey eyed the bag. She hadn't noticed it until now. "What is it?" she asked, making no move to touch it. Something about the way Eve was acting made her uneasy. The moment she'd mentioned the bag, her attitude had changed. Was it the unsure look in her eyes? Or the anxiety that seemed to be coming off her in waves?

"Please, look inside," Eve said when Kelsey continued just to stare.

Moving forward, still feeling a little wary, Kelsey reached out and picked up the bag. The paper crackled as she unrolled the top. A sour, rancid smell assaulted her senses. Kelsey turned away, coughing, her eyes watering. "What *is* this?" She held the bag at arm's length and glared at Eve.

"Please," the older woman whispered. "It's important."

Kelsey opened her mouth to protest but as she stared into Eve's eyes, she saw an intensity in them she could not ignore.

Breathing through her mouth, more than a little apprehensive, she leaned forward, peering into the opening. A small animal lay inside, glazed eyes staring up. Kelsey's stomach lurched. Her gaze shifted from the contents of the bag back to Eve.

"Why?" she began but then stopped. What could she possibly say? Why did you put a dead animal in a bag and bring it over for me to look at? Why am I now standing here holding it in my hands and wondering about your sanity?

Kelsey considered Eve. The older woman's face was calm, her eyes clear and bright. She waited patiently for the question Kelsey had started but could not finish. Unable to think of anything appropriate to say, Kelsey shifted her gaze back to the bag. Opening it wider, she tried to get a better look. Maybe this wasn't what it appeared to be. Maybe— The body shifted slightly at the bottom of the bag and Kelsey flinched backward, nearly dropping it. Was it alive? But she knew it was not. Her brow furrowed as she continued to stare inside. "What is it?" she muttered. But within the next instant, she knew. A squirrel, a dead squirrel. And as Kelsey continued to stare inside, she finally understood why Eve had brought it to her. Growing from its breast area were two small paws—two extra paws. "Where did you get this?"

Eve shook her head. "I didn't want to say anything. I wanted your honest reaction. I thought maybe I was over-reacting but now I see I wasn't."

Kelsey looked at her. "What are you talking about?"

"That thing." She used her cane to point at the bag. "Scares me to death." She looked back at Kelsey. "It's got you scared too."

And Kelsey realized she was right. It wasn't just a fear of the thing in the bag, but what that thing represented.

A mutation. That was the only word that came to mind, the only one that seemed to fit what she was now looking at. This animal . . . thing . . . whatever, was an aberration. The question to ask was how. Was it something natural or unnatural? And if it was natural, why had it happened? If it was unnatural, how had it happened?

"Where'd you get it?" she asked again.

"I found it—" Her gaze shifted to the street behind her. "Greg! Teddy!" she called to the two boys on their bikes. They turned in unison and she waved them over.

"What are you doing?" Kelsey asked as the boys dumped their bikes on the front lawn and jogged toward the house.

"Greg," Eve said to the older boy. "When Rebel was in my garden earlier, he was trying to bury something."

The boy shuffled his feet. "I'm sorry, Mrs. F. I've got him chained up right now."

"It doesn't matter." She gestured toward the bag. "Have either of you ever seen this before?"

They both leaned over and stared inside.

"Cool." Teddy reached toward the bag but Greg stopped him.

"What is that?" he asked.

"I thought maybe you would know," Eve said. "Did you boys maybe find this and were keeping it?"

"No." Greg's answer was immediate.

"I bet Rebel got it from the dead part of the woods," Teddy offered, his voice serious.

"The dead part of the woods?" Kelsey repeated.

The boys looked at her curiously.

"This is Kelsey," Eve said.

Kelsey smiled at them knowing they would need no more introduction than that. "What's the dead part of the woods?" she asked. For the briefest of moments, a vision of the ghostly figure she had seen the night before flashed through her mind.

"Rebel found it," Teddy said.

Greg nodded his agreement. "It's pretty far back."

"But what is it?" Kelsey persisted, hoping for a clearer description.

"It's just dead." Greg shrugged as if that were the best explanation he could think of.

"Yeah," Teddy agreed. "The trees and grass and stuff."

Kelsey tried to picture a place in the woods that had just died off. It didn't make sense to her. The boys must be mistaken or exaggerating. But still . . . "Can you show me this dead part?"

"If you wanna see it, sure," Greg said.

Kelsey glanced at Eve. "I do."

"Really?" Greg's voice was tinged with a mixture of disbelief and excitement. "You really do? When?"

Kelsey took a deep breath. "How about right now."

3

Edward Ross moved briskly down the hall of the Envirospace corporate headquarters, his long legs taking quick strides. The angry set of his mouth surprised everyone who passed him.

No one stopped to make casual conversation. No one asked him what was wrong. Instead, they let him rush past without a word.

They knew where he was headed. There was only one

person who could drive Edward Ross to this level of anger: Hal Ebersol.

Most people did not understand why the two men had gone into business together. Many knew nothing of Claire's involvement or that, in fact, it had been Claire who brought the two men together so long ago. When she was alive, she had been able to moderate between them, keep the lines of communication open. But in the years following her death, the two men had grown not only more distant but actively hostile. Now, the only emotion they nurtured between them was unabated animosity.

And as Edward made his way toward his brother-in-law's office, he was aware of nothing but his current anger.

How many times had his brother-in-law disappointed him? How many times had he ignored his phone calls?

Too many, Edward thought, answering his own questions. *I've let this go too many damn times.*

Walking past Hal's secretary, Edward slammed into the office.

Hal sat at his desk working on his computer. His eyes flicked from the screen to Edward and then back to the screen. He said nothing.

"Where were you?" Edward demanded.

Hal continued to type on the keyboard never breaking his pace. "Come in, Edward," he said dryly. "Don't be shy." And with practiced ease, he turned to face him full on.

Stepping forward, Edward leaned on the desk top, laying his palms flat. He looked Hal square in the eye and repeated his question. "Where were you?"

Hal sat back in his chair, rocking slightly. "Am I supposed to know what you're talking about?"

"We had a meeting with the lawyers scheduled this morning."

"Yes, I see you're wearing your meeting clothes." Hal's gaze traveled over Edward's suit. "I only wish I had a clue as to this monumental meeting you are referring to. You know how I hate to miss any one of your suit days.''

"I'm done playing games." Straightening, he continued to stare down at Hal. "This innocent act of yours won't work anymore. Ignoring me won't make me go away." The anger flowed through his entire body making his cheeks flush, the effort making him short of breath. "This is going to stop." He gasped. And laying a hand against his chest, he felt the heavy rhythm of his heartbeat.

"Are you all right?" Hal asked when Edward did not continue. But there was no sincerity in his voice, no real concern in his eyes.

A year earlier, Edward had suffered a minor heart attack although to him, it had not felt minor. Since then, he'd followed his doctor's instructions, carefully watching his diet and exercising daily. But neither of those things had caused his first attack. It was the man who sat before him, staring up at him with a self-satisfied grin on his face. The man who now gleaned a certain amount of pleasure watching his brother-in-law struggle for breath that would not come. He would not give him the satisfaction. Squaring back his shoulders, he closed his eyes and began taking deep, calming breaths.

"Do that in your own office," Hal grumbled as Edward began his relaxation technique.

He ignored him and instead, continued to concentrate on his breathing. It was a method he'd used on several occasions when dealing with Hal. He was quite aware of the fact that it drove his brother-in-law crazy. But to Edward, that was just another benefit. No matter how riled up Hal got him, Edward could always manage to get himself under control again by using the simple relaxation technique.

Slowly, taking his time, he felt himself relax, felt his heartbeat return, once more, to normal. When he opened his eyes again, Hal was busy working on his computer. But the intense scowl on his face told Edward that the deep breathing technique had gotten to him.

"You've forced me into this position," Edward said

more calmly this time. "I'm giving you an ultimatum. You show up at the next meeting or I'm going to go ahead with the lawsuit and get David's share of the company that way."

Hal stopped typing. His mouth grew tight, his lips thinning until they seemed nonexistent. "This company would be nothing without me." The words were bitten off one at a time and spit out.

"This company was built with Ross money," Edward countered.

"But without my idea," Hal shot back, "Envirospace would not exist. Besides." The smug smile returned. "You can't break Claire's will. You should realize that by now." His eyes never left Edward's.

"You damn well know Claire wanted David to have her third of the company."

Hal shrugged innocently. "Not according to her will."

"She told you she wanted her share to go to David. You agreed to it." Edward could feel himself wearing down. He had spoken these words so many times over the last few years. He was tired of the fighting, tired of the lying. "It is beyond me how you can continue to deny what you know is the truth."

"David is my son," Hal began, his voice low, controlled. But there was no masking the deep anger that now boiled within him—Edward could feel it. "I will worry about *my* son's share of the company. I will take care of *my* family."

There was the briefest of pauses before Edward said, "The way you took care of my sister."

Hal was on his feet in an instant. "What the hell are you talking about?"

"You deliberately kept her from me while she was ill," he spat out, not backing down an inch, determined to show Hal he was not intimidated by him. "She was not the same woman when I was finally allowed to see her. You broke her spirit," he whispered. "I will not allow you to do the same to her only child."

"Claire lost much of herself to her illness. You cannot accept that, but I can. I have." Hal's voice was cool, even patronizing. "David is perfectly fine and I don't like what you're implying."

"I'm not implying it, I'm saying it." He squared his shoulders. His eyes locked with Hal's and in those eyes, he saw a deep hatred that burned for him alone. "You will not do to David what you did to Claire."

4

Eve sat on the back porch tossing peanuts to the squirrels that had gathered for their evening feeding. As she watched them romp and play together, her mind turned to the animal Rebel had been trying to bury. What had it been? Once, years earlier, Eve remembered reading a story about a family that found an animal on their back porch. It looked as if it were half-rabbit, half-cat. They called it a cabbit theorizing that a cat and rabbit had somehow mated. Eve had read that story with doubt in her mind. Now she had to wonder.

Tossing the last of her peanuts, she leaned back in the chair, closing her eyes. Exhaustion tugged at her limbs, making them feel heavy, weak. Just getting out of bed in the morning was becoming a chore. Too much walking, she decided. No more trips to Leah's for a while.

"I'm getting too old to go tromping through the woods," she muttered, shifting. Her body was a little achy, and not since menopause had she experienced such hot flashes. Using her cane, she pushed up from the seat. If she stayed there much longer, she feared she'd never get up again. She was just so tired.

And the rash was back.

Two weeks earlier her arms had begun to itch, the skin raw and flaky. She'd covered the unpleasant rash with calamine lotion and within a week it was gone. But now it was back with a vengeance. This time the calamine wasn't helping, the itch was unbearable. But what was worse, the rash seemed to be spreading at an alarming rate.

Must have brushed against some poison ivy. That's what she had been telling herself since first discovering the rash. During one of her trips through the woods, she must have come into contact with some kind of poisonous plant.

She had not gone to the doctor yet. It was so difficult for her to get around. But now she was beginning to think she had no choice.

Reaching over, she scratched the back of her shoulder lightly, not wanting to irritate it any more than it already was but unable to resist any longer. After only a few light passes with her hand, she stopped. Moisture soaked her skin, stuck her top to her back, slowly trickled down her spine.

She gasped, pulling her hand away and stared at the blood on her fingers.

5

Edward sat at his desk, staring down at the attorney's latest report regarding the split of Envirospace.

He had been a fool to let this go on for so long. Had been a fool to trust Hal Ebersol.

Just as his sister had been.

But he really couldn't blame Claire. Hal had isolated her, kept her alone, dependent on only him. She'd been so weak in the end that getting the new will drawn up must have been easy.

Upon her death, Claire left everything to Hal, giving him two-thirds of the company and controlling shares.

But that was only half of it.

"David will receive my shares."

She'd whispered those words to Edward two nights before her death. He'd finally been allowed to see her after nearly six months. When he stood beside her bed and stared down at her, he barely recognized the woman before him. Her face so thin, her body shrunken as if her muscles had already begun to atrophy. As soon as her eyes locked on him, she'd grabbed at him with her thin limbs, weakly plucking at his clothes, unable to maintain any grip. Struggling to speak, Claire had fought for breath, her face pinched with pain.

He'd had to lean down, put his ear close to her lips. As her hot breath washed over him, each word laced with pain, every syllable an effort, he memorized her words, promised to make them come true.

She'd told him about her verbal will. A will Hal agreed to abide by. According to Claire, Hal was obligated to turn over her shares to David on the boy's twenty-fifth birthday.

Edward never told Hal of his knowledge. Until David's twenty-fifth birthday. Until Hal did not follow through on his promise.

When he confronted Hal with what he knew, Hal had a perfectly reasonable explanation. He had decided that David was simply too young and too inexperienced at twenty-five to take control of his third of the company. Besides, David didn't even work for Envirospace at the time.

Edward's solution was simple. Invite David to come back to the company. They had plans for an extensive research department, were already in the process of constructing a new science wing. David could simply come in to head up that project. He could gain the experience and knowledge he needed for the position he would be acquiring. A position Edward wanted him to attain within five years. Hal had only one stipulation. He did not want David told about his mother's shares. He wanted his son to come back because he wanted to work for the company. Not simply because he was due a portion of it. Reluctantly, Edward agreed.

But now, six months after David should have received his inheritance, Hal refused to acknowledge their agreement. He had missed three meeting with the lawyers to discuss the split and ignored any paperwork regarding the matter.

Instead, over the last six months, Edward was slowly being phased out of his own division. Because Hal owned two-thirds of the company, he began using his deciding vote to veto any and everything that Edward was involved in, keeping him at arm's length on all projects within the corporation at all times.

The same was being done to David. He'd worked on only one project of consequence since returning to the company. A project Hal had already given the go ahead for before David returned. Since then, the research and development department had done nothing. The building still sat half empty. Edward knew David was dissatisfied. He also knew it was time his nephew knew the truth about his mother's inheritance.

But how? That was what he had been asking himself for the last six months. How to tell him? Should he take him to dinner? Casually remark over a plate of clams that his father was trying to cheat him out of his inheritance? No. He'd tried. God knows, he'd tried. It wasn't that he was afraid he would shatter some illusion David had about his father. David knew his father was a bastard. But to Edward, this was different. More difficult to hear. It was so damn deliberate.

A knock sounded on his door. A moment later, David peered around the corner. "You busy?"

"No." Edward slipped the papers into his top drawer. "But I am a little surprised to see you here today. I thought you might be taking the day off."

David came toward him, a grin set on his face. "How could I miss today?" And reaching forward, he set a small box on the desk before him. "Happy birthday, Uncle Edward."

Edward's surprise was genuine. "With all that's going

on, I can't believe you remembered." He picked up the small gift.

"Of course I remember." David sat down in the chair across from him. "Open it."

Carefully, Edward tore at the brightly colored paper until he held only the small white box. Lifting the lid, he stared at the framed photograph. "Oh, David." It showed himself and Claire much younger, standing arm in arm at a lake both laughing at the camera. He still remembered the day it was taken. They were on vacation from school. Dad had taken the whole family up to the lake house for the summer. The two of them had spent nearly a week setting up a homemade diving board off the side of the lake. This was the proud moment of their unveiling. Holding the photo close, he could still see the board behind them. Crooked, half in the water. But it had been their project, together.

"How did you get this?" He touched the front of the photo, feeling as if somehow he were touching a part of Claire.

"I've had it for years. Mom showed it to me once. She used to love to go through the old photo albums." He gestured at the framed photo. "She told me about that day. And sometimes, after she was gone, I would take out those photos and try and remember the stories she told about each one. But that one." He paused. "That one always stood out so clearly in my mind." He smiled. "She told me that story a lot. It was one of her favorites."

Edward nodded. "Your mother insisted on going first that day," he said, adding his own memories to David's story. "We'd found some old boards behind the house. God only knows how long they'd been sitting out there rotting." He laughed aloud with the memory. "I can still see her climbing up on that board so sure she could do a double gainer." He looked up at David. "She jumped on it once. The damn thing broke in two and dumped her into the lake."

Both men laughed at the visual in their mind.

Edward set the photo on the corner of the desk, his gaze lingering on Claire's young face for a few moments longer.

"She would be very proud of you. You were everything to her."

David still smiled but there was a bitterness there that Edward had never seen before. "Uncle Edward," he began a few moments later. "We need to talk."

"You probably don't realize it but your mom once told me—"

"Stop!" David barked and Edward's mouth snapped shut. "I'm sorry. I didn't mean to shout."

"It's all right." Edward sighed. "It's just . . . I know what you're going to say."

"Good. That makes it easier."

"You can't leave."

"Don't try and talk me out of this because you can't." David stood and began pacing before his desk. "I'm tired of the bullshit around here. I'm tired of doing nothing." Running a hand through his hair, he added, "I'm sorry but I just can't stay."

Edward leaned forward, his hands clenched before him on the desk, his knuckles white. "David, I know Leah's death—"

He shook his head. "That's not it."

An uncomfortable silence hung between the two men, harsh in its remoteness.

"I don't want to waste another year hoping things will change," David began, his voice resolved. "They won't. The science building is virtually empty. We use one lab out of five."

"That will change."

"It won't," he said, clearly exasperated. "There are over one hundred and twenty-five people working for this company. Do you know how many are devoted to research and development?"

"I don't see—"

"Fourteen including myself," David said as if Edward

had not spoken at all. "My father doesn't want to allocate any funds to research. He doesn't need to research recycling or new cleanup methods and he damn well knows it. He's making a mint cleaning up people's trash. Why develop a system that lessens that garbage? It's antiproductive, don't you think? I'm sure my father does."

"I can talk to him. I can get you more funds, more people."

"It's funny when you think about it." He laughed bitterly. "The big money's all in garbage." He shook his head. "I'm not needed here. It's time for me to move on."

"Give me ten minutes." Edward indicated the chair in front of his desk, his eyes locked on his nephew. "If you still want to leave after that then you can do so with my blessing."

David hesitated, but only for a moment. He sat down.

"I've wanted to tell you this for so long, but I haven't known how." He glanced at the photo of Claire, gaining some strength from her smiling face. "Your father's been lying to you. It's time you know the truth." He paused, searching for the words that he hadn't been able to find for the last two years. There were none. "Your mother left you her third of the company."

David blinked several times. "What?"

"You own—"

"I understood you." His voice flared. "I just don't believe you."

"It's true."

"My mother left everything to my father. I've seen her will."

"In writing, yes. But her verbal will left her third of the company to you, to be turned over to you on your twenty-fifth birthday."

David looked down in his lap, back at his uncle, toward the door. "What am I supposed to say?"

"I'm sorry. I know this is a shock."

"You're damn right it's a shock. Why the hell wasn't I told before?"

"I was hoping I could settle this with your father without bringing you in on it."

"Settle what?" David paused. His eyes narrowed as slow realization set in. "What is my father doing?"

"Your father," Edward began slowly, "is contesting your mother's verbal will. He claims she never told him what she wanted. He claims her written will is the only documentation of her disposition of assets that he knows of."

"Maybe that's the truth?"

Edward could hear the hope behind the statement. Could see the disappointment in his eyes. But Edward knew it was not the lack of a will or the potential loss of company shares that had David depressed. It was the realization that his father, will or not, did not want to give David a portion of the company.

"Your father is lying to keep the company to himself. He wants you gone. He wants me gone." He shook his head. "I can't let that happen. I won't."

David leaned back in his chair, folding his arms over his chest. "I get it now." His face took on a sour look, as if this news had left a foul taste in his mouth. "This is where I'm supposed to jump up and vow to join you in gallant battle."

"No. That's not it at all." Although, deep down, Edward had to admit that that was exactly what he had hoped.

"Then what? Why tell me if you don't expect me to help you in some way?"

"I just don't want you to leave. If you leave, it'll be that much easier for your father to keep your shares of the company."

"He can have them."

"David, you don't mean that. Your mother—"

"Would not want me to stay somewhere that makes me

so unhappy.'' He stood, pacing away from the desk.

''I understand your frustration but please just stop and think for a minute.''

''I don't need to think.'' He faced his uncle again. ''I don't want to get involved in some bitter battle for this company with my father. It's not worth it. He's not worth it. And for the life of me, I don't understand why you want to stay. You've already had one heart attack. Wasn't that enough to open your eyes?''

''I can't let him have it all,'' Edward whispered. And for the first time, he found himself admitting the whole truth. It wasn't just David he was fighting for. It was himself. ''I know you don't want to hear this,'' he began, his gaze meeting David's. ''But my sister and I worked damn hard to build up this company. I'm not about to let Hal Ebersol steal it out from under me just because you don't think I should fight for it.''

''You can do whatever you want,'' David snapped. ''Just don't try to drag me into it anymore. It won't work.''

''You deserve what is yours.'' Edward pressed. ''If you leave now, it's over. There's no going back.'' He paused but only for a moment. When he spoke again, his voice was low, barely audible. ''It's now or never.''

''I can't stay.''

''At least give me until Monday.''

''Uncle Edward—''

''I'm going out of town tonight,'' he continued quickly, cutting off David's argument. ''I won't get back until late Friday. If you do this while I'm gone, then you give your father days to undermine me. By the time I get back, I'll have nothing left to fight for.''

David said nothing. Just continued to stare at his hands.

''It's my birthday,'' Edward inserted, knowing it was low but desperate to get his way.

David rubbed his eyes. For the first time, Edward realized how tired his nephew looked.

"All right." David paused briefly as if his next words were hard to speak. I'll wait." He looked up at his uncle, his eyes intense. "But this won't work again. You can expect my resignation first thing Monday morning."

CHAPTER SIX

1

Tulsa, Oklahoma

"I'm at the halfway point." Joe glanced around the diner but no one was watching him. No one cared about the man in the phone booth. "Was the transfer made?"

"Yes." There was no hesitation in the voice on the other end of the line. There never was. "When will the job be complete?" The tone was always the same—deep, controlled. Joe knew from the speech pattern that the man was military.

"By Friday. I'll check back with you at the arranged time." Joe never met the people who hired him. Arrangements were always done through a series of phone calls. When he took a job, he contacted his clients, checking in at prearranged times just to be sure everything was still on as originally planned. But they had no way to contact him.

"Good." The line went dead.

Joe walked casually back to his seat. The waitress had refilled his coffee cup while he was on the phone. She winked at him as she walked past. He nodded his appreciation.

Lifting the cup to his lips, he surveyed the people behind

him in the mirror that hung over the counter before him. A young couple holding hands. An older man reading a newspaper. A woman with two children. In every case, booth after booth, table after table, they were aware of nothing but themselves. He could follow any one of them home, kill them and then disappear, having no problem at all getting away with it.

He glanced around the diner once again. It was always best to know who was around you, be aware of what you were up against. But as his gaze travelled over the small group, someone else caught his eye. A lone woman stood outside the diner looking in through the large glass front. Her loose, shoulder length blond hair blew around her head, concealing her face for a long moment before blowing the other way. She stood with her legs slightly apart, her arms crossed over her chest, her eyes locked forward.

Locked on him.

He set his cup down, returned the stare, let her know he knew she was looking. Usually that was enough to make someone turn away. Not this woman.

She continued her silent perusal, never moving, never blinking. And he began to feel nervous.

Something's wrong.

Reaching down, he placed his hand on the butt of the weapon strapped under his arm. How many people were in the diner? He began counting, figuring the odds. But as he began making a mental plan of action, he realized the woman was gone. He had not seen her leave, did not even realize he had taken his eyes off her. But he must have because she was gone. He turned on his stool and scanned the area behind him more closely.

Nothing.

Licking his lips, unease still resting between his shoulder blades, he turned back to his coffee. He sat for several moments, his eyes locked on the mirror before him, watching, waiting.

She did not return.

He lifted his cup. Sipped the hot coffee. And decided he would have to be more careful. The woman may have been no one, just a stranger who caught his eye. But Joe didn't think so. He had a feeling, an uncomfortable something-is-wrong feeling that he had learned years ago not to ignore. Taking out a map, anxious to finish this job, he traced a route to his next appointment anxious to finish the job.

2

Hartwick, Michigan

David drove toward Leah's house. He had accomplished nothing all day. Nothing at all. The only thing he'd been able to think about was the confrontation with his uncle. And the inheritance he had never received. But no matter how many times he turned it all over in his mind, he always came to the same conclusion—he didn't want to fight his father for a piece of Envirospace. He just wanted out.

He pulled up in front of Leah's and shut off the car. He'd considered cancelling dinner with Kelsey but decided at the last minute to go. He wanted to see her. If for no other reason than to take his mind off work for a while.

He glanced at the house. It looked the same, as if Leah were home right now, sitting inside, sewing another of her many cross stitch patterns. But it was Kelsey who opened the door, stepping outside even before he reached the house.

She walked purposefully toward him, as if she were in a hurry to leave. But looking at her, he realized she was not dressed to go out. She wore shorts, her knees and calves stained with mud. Her T-shirt and face were also smudged with dirt. "Dinner is tonight, isn't it?" he asked.

"Great. You're here," she said, as if he had not spoken at all. "I was just going to take some pictures." She held up a small camera. "Had to run out and get this thing. It's cheap but it'll do the job.'' She talked fast, her voice hurried as if she were late for something.

"It'll do what job?" David asked, feeling as if he had somehow come in the middle of something he should understand but did not.

She looked up at him, curiosity burning behind her eyes. "I can't explain it." She took two steps back. "You have to see it while it's still light." She took two more steps back.

He watched her slow retreat but made no move to join her. "See what?"

"It . . ." She hesitated, then shook her head. "I just can't do it justice. You have to see for yourself." She continued to walk backward. "Come with me." Without saying another word, she turned and headed at a fast pace toward the woods.

David watched her go. He glanced toward the street and then back to the Kelsey. "What the hell?"

Just before she disappeared from sight, David knew he would follow. Moving quickly, he jogged to the edge of the trees and followed her path inside.

They had planned a casual dinner and he was glad he had worn jeans and tennis shoes. But even so, her behavior was odd. Where were they going? What was she taking him to see?

He stumbled through the woods, trying to follow whatever path Kelsey was leading him on. But she was so far ahead that he kept losing sight of her. And her pace didn't help. She moved fast, her feet crashing through the underbrush of dead leaves and twigs. As he strained to follow her, David realized it was the sound that was guiding him more than the sight. He could hear her constantly. But see her? Sometimes he would catch sight of her between trees, off to his left or over on the right and he would adjust his direction. But it was the sound that kept him moving forward. If she was following some sort of path, only she could see it.

She turned toward him. "Why not? What's wrong?"

He pulled her back beside him and taking in her soiled appearance once again, said, "How long were you in there? What did you touch?"

Even as he spoke, he saw the curiosity leave her eyes, replaced almost immediately by fear. "I . . ." She looked down at herself, at the dirt on her clothes, her hands. "I don't know how long. A while. I wanted to check it out. I touched . . ." She looked at David then back to the clearing. "Everything," she whispered.

Taking her by the arm, David began leading her away. "You need to shower," he said, hoping he was going in the right direction. "Leave the clothes at the door. Don't take them inside the house."

"David, you're scaring me." Kelsey stumbled behind him as he pulled her along.

David stopped and turning to face her said, "I'm not trying to scare you, Kelsey. But I don't know what caused that." He nodded toward the dead part of the woods. "We could be looking at some kind of contamination." Anxiety gnawed at his belly as his gaze flickered over her exposed skin. "I just don't want to take any chances," he finished quietly.

3

Leaning back in his chair, Hal Ebersol removed the expensive cigar from his mouth and said, "Tell me about my son."

Ken Brewer stood before him, his hands clamped behind his back, his body erect. "I spent the day watching him." He did not look at Hal when he answered. He did not need to. He knew Hal was listening to every word he said. "He went to the Brayden woman's house today."

"Dammit," Hal grumbled. He held the cigar out, staring

at it, watching the smoke rise from the lit end. "Why would he go there?"

Ken did not refer to notes. He did not need them. He kept all the information in his head. It was safer that way. Nothing to trace, nothing to trip him up. "I'm not sure. But I believe he went there looking for something."

"The house is clean?" Hal asked but with little concern. Ken was neat. Hal knew he would not leave such an obvious loose thread.

"Nothing inside." And for the briefest of moments, his mind flashed back to what happened in the woods behind the Brayden woman's home. No matter how he turned it over in his mind, he could not come up with a logical explanation for what he had seen and felt. Instead, he had decided to put it out of his mind, forget the whole thing. A momentary lapse, that was all. "I've been in twice," he continued. "But . . ." He paused then letting the unfinished sentence worm its way under Hal's skin and squirm there.

"But what?" Hal said, his voice brusque.

"It's unfortunate, sir, but I think we may still have a problem."

"And it is?" Hal prompted, his patience growing thin.

With calculated slowness, Ken turned and looked directly at his employer. "A woman showed up while he was there. I couldn't hear what was being said but I believe she is related to the Brayden woman. They're having dinner together right now."

Standing, Hal stared out the window at Envirospace below. The lights were just coming on all over the complex for the night. "Find out who the woman is." When he spoke, there was resignation in his voice as if what Ken were telling him was unfortunate but not completely unexpected.

"Already working on it," Ken assured him. "Sir, I believe if he drops all of this within the next twenty-four hours, we're safe."

Hal was silent for a long time, his gaze locked on the

activity beyond his window. "If not," he began, his voice controlled, emotionless, "then I want you to end it by whatever means you see fit." He turned to face Ken, his eyes cold, lifeless. "Whatever means."

4

Kelsey and David sat in the yard at the picnic table eating the hamburgers he had cooked on the backyard grill.

Kelsey took a small bite out of her burger. She didn't want to insult David but she just didn't have much of an appetite.

How could she be so stupid? That's what she'd been asking herself since going to the dead part of the woods with David. She hadn't even thought. She'd just tromped around, touching, smearing, groping every part of the area she could. *What had possessed her?*

It wasn't until David told her to wash that she realized how foolish she had been. Even now, after taking one of the longest, hottest showers of her life, Kelsey still felt dirty, contaminated. Staring at the burger, she knew she would never finish it, didn't even think she could take one more bite.

She watched as David ran a hand through his still wet hair. After coming back to the house and getting gloves, bags and a small shovel, David spent nearly an hour at the dead part of the woods, taking pictures, digging up soil and depositing it into small baggies, peeling back bark and dumping it into its own separate container. By the time he got back to the house, Kelsey was out of the shower, her clothes in a garbage bag on the back patio.

She sparked up the grill while he showered. When they finally sat down to eat, David turned on the outside lights, washing the yard in gentle brightness. But the brightness could not chase away the sense of foreboding that seemed to hang in the air all around them.

"What about the animal?" she asked, shoving her plate away. "What do you think about it?"

She had kept the bag and small beast Eve had brought over. When she showed it to David, he had stared at it the same way she had, with a combination of shock, amazement and curiosity.

"I don't know. If it came from that same part of the woods..." He paused. "We could be looking at some kind of environmental damage. My crew at Envirospace does soil work. We can test for toxins." His eyes narrowed as he went over it in his mind. "We could come in and do the cleanup ourselves."

"What about *it*?" She nodded toward the bag containing the squirrel. It sat nearly ten feet away, the distance giving Kelsey a small sense of security.

"Same thing. We'll test it, dissect it, look for the same kind of poisons in it that may be in the soil."

"How long do you think the results will take?" The picnic table sat at the back of the property. Kelsey had to resist the urge to search the trees for movement. Because no matter how hard she tried, she could not dismiss the feeling that something was out there, watching . . . waiting.

David grabbed the salad bowl, dumping a large helping of lettuce, tomatoes, and radishes onto his plate. "Only a day or two."

"Good. The sooner this is looked into the better." Despite the warmth of the evening air, she shivered, her body feeling chilled all the way through.

"Kelsey," David began. "I'm sure you don't have anything to worry about. You were only in there a little while. I was just being cautious earlier."

Kelsey nodded not sure if he was really telling her the truth or just trying to make her feel better. "I'm just afraid somebody's been dumping something toxic out there." And this time she was not able to keep her gaze from the woods as a vision of the figure she had seen the night before flashed through her mind. "Maybe they're still doing it.'' Staring into the trees, she tried to decide if she should tell him. "I thought," she began, her voice still unsure, "that I saw . . . someone out at the edge of the woods last night."

David was about to take a bite out of his burger. He stopped, setting it back on the plate before him. "When?" He turned to look at the trees behind him.

"Late," she said. "I was getting ready to go to sleep. I thought it was odd because the weather was so bad last night. I wondered why anyone would be going into the woods that late in the rain and fog."

David nodded his agreement, turning to face her once again. "Could you see who it was?"

"No, it was too dark to make out any features. But I'm pretty sure it was a woman." Kelsey paused not sure she could tell him the rest. "For just a minute . . . I thought . . . I . . ."She faltered.

"What?" He shoved his plate forward, leaning toward her.

She bit her lip, trying to swallow her hesitation. Why had she brought this up? But deep down she knew why. She needed to say it because she believed it could be true. "Last night when I saw the person by the woods, it seemed, for just a second it seemed . . ." She shifted uncomfortably in her seat. "I thought it was Leah," she finished quickly.

David's eyes grew wide. "Are you serious?"

Hearing the shock in his voice, she said, "I'm sorry. I shouldn't have said that. It sounds so crazy."

He shook his head. "No," he said, a little too quickly. His gaze left Kelsey and came to rest, instead, on his plate and his half eaten meal.

He thinks I've lost it, Kelsey thought. *This is where he gets up, tells me dinner was pleasant, and runs for his car.*

But David did none of those things. Instead, he took a deep breath, looked up at her and said, "I've seen her too."

CHAPTER SEVEN

1

Kelsey's face paled slightly. "You've seen her too?"

David nodded. He had not planned on telling Kelsey about his sighting of Leah, hadn't planned on telling anyone. He had, in fact, worked very hard to convince himself that it never really happened, that he was just under a lot of strain and that was why his mind had produced her image.

But if Kelsey had seen her too? "It was brief," he said. "Only a second or two. But I thought, just for a second, that I saw her reaching out to me."

Kelsey chewed on her lower lip. She did not look at him. Instead, she seemed to stare at a point behind him, lost in whatever thoughts were now tumbling through her mind. "Is it possible," she began slowly, her eyes once more finding his, "that she's not dead?"

"No," David said bluntly. "I identified the body myself."

"I didn't see her. It was a closed casket."

"Because of the condition of the body."

"But—"

"She's gone!" He cut her off, his voice louder than he intended. "She's gone," he repeated more quietly. "It may be hard to accept but it's a fact.'' He spoke with a finality that he hoped would close the subject.

''But we've both seen her,'' Kelsey persisted.

David ran a hand through his hair in exasperation. ''What did you really see? A dark figure at the edge of the woods?''

She nodded.

''You're sure it was Leah?''

She paused before answering. ''I *felt* it was Leah.''

''But you didn't actually see her face?''

''It was too dark. She was too far away.''

''So you're not sure.''

''I know it was my sister.'' Her eyes locked with his, daring him to tell her she was wrong.

''Her ghost?'' he asked, before he could stop himself. Because hadn't he had the same thought himself? Hadn't he wondered if it were possible?

She looked away, toying with the food on her plate. ''I don't know,'' she whispered, then added, ''But I don't believe she killed herself.''

''I don't want to believe it either. But if we don't even allow for the possibility, we may be blinding ourselves to the truth. And when I think about how . . .'' He shook his head, unable to deny the facts confronting them both. ''She stood in the road waiting for a car to hit her, Kelsey.'' His voice was quiet. ''Makes it hard to call it anything but suicide.''

''But there's more to it. There has to be.'' She paused. ''I talked to a woman today who saw Leah that night, a few hours before she died.''

''What?'' David was astonished. This was the first he'd heard about this. ''She was with Leah?''

''No. She saw Leah in the road. Stopped before hitting her. She reported it to the police.''

''I was never told any of this.'' He leaned on the table. ''What else did she tell you?''

''This woman, Mary Glover, she said that Leah looked

like she was drunk or on drugs. She said she was afraid of her.''

''That's just ridiculous. Leah would never do drugs.''

''And I checked the police report. Her blood alcohol level was normal.'' Kelsey paused. ''So why would Mary Glover describe her that way?''

''I don't know.''

Behind them, the moon rose slowly over the trees. It hung low in the sky, nearly full, bathing the yard with its gentle glow.

''Eve said she was having nightmares,'' Kelsey said after a time. ''Now with *this* right in my sister's own backyard.'' She gestured toward the evidence they had taken from the woods. ''Something else is going on. I don't know what and I don't understand what we saw. But I plan on finding out.''

David turned it over in his mind. He had to admit that having the situation with the woods right behind Leah's house did change things.

But in what way?

They sat in silence, both lost in thought.

''Is it possible,'' Kelsey began after a time, ''that Leah went into those woods and found what we found but it affected her in some way?''

''Made her suicidal?''

''Not necessarily suicidal. Maybe just confused.'' She paused, her eyes searching the tabletop. ''Where's that map you had?'' Earlier, David had gone to his car and retrieved a map of the area from his glove box.

He handed it to Kelsey. She spread it wide across the table. ''Here you've marked the dead part of the woods.''

He nodded, staring at the red circle he had made.

''Show me where Leah died.''

He looked at her. She continued to stare down at the map, her eyes scanning the terrain. He hadn't known exactly what she was going to ask him when he handed her the map. Hadn't expected the question that still seemed to hang between them, pressing in on him.

"Is it on this map?" she asked when he continued to remain silent.

He nodded, slowly looking down. It took him only a moment to locate the road. South of them, several miles away. David pointed, marking the spot with his finger.

"Look at this." She traced her finger from the dead part of the woods to the spot where Leah died. "The woods are connected, David. She could have gotten there from here. And Eve said that a few days before Leah died, she showed up at her house looking as if she'd gotten lost in the woods. Maybe Leah had found the dead part and had been inside. Maybe it was making her ill, confused. Maybe she just wandered into the road that night."

She looked at him, her eyes expectant. Waiting. "What?" he said, before he realized he was going to speak.

"Maybe that's what happened."

"Maybe it is. I don't know."

"But you can guess."

"You want me to speculate on whether there's a connection between Leah being in the road and the dead woods?"

"I just want your opinion."

"My opinion." He ran a hand over his cheek, feeling the roughness of his late-day stubble. Could Leah have gotten ill? Could she have become confused? He hadn't really seen her in the last few weeks of her life. No. It didn't make sense.

"David," she said, interrupting his thought processes. "We were in those woods tonight. If something in there affected my sister . . ." She trailed off unable or unwilling to finish the sentence. He wasn't sure which but for the first time, he could see her own fear behind her eyes.

"If Leah touched something, it would take weeks maybe even months to manifest," he said, working out his thoughts aloud. "My opinion is that something else made her step in front of that car."

"But what?"

"I don't know." Then a new thought struck him. "Did you find anything in the diary?"

"I glanced through the last few pages but there's nothing that stands out. Just random thoughts. I'm going to start at the beginning tonight. Read it from cover to cover."

He nodded but even more so than before, the thought of Kelsey reading the diary made him uneasy. What had Leah written in that book?

An uncomfortable silence hung between them. Kelsey continued to stare down at the map, absently running her finger from the dead part of the woods to the place where Leah died. David watched the slow movement. Her hand traced back and forth, back and forth, hypnotic in its rhythmic motion.

He dragged his gaze away, looking at Kelsey instead. She squinted down at the map, her forehead wrinkled, her lip trembling. A stray tear escaped her eyes, trailing its way down her cheek. What was going through her mind?

She looked up, wiping at the cheek, her pain so clear in her eyes. In that moment, he wanted to reach out to her, take her in his arms, comfort her. But then she looked away, as if suddenly embarrassed.

"Take that thing," Kelsey said, nodding toward the bag that contained the squirrel, keeping her gaze off David. "Find out what happened to it. What caused that."

"I will," he said, not sure if he could but knowing she needed to hear it.

She nodded, gathering up the plates. "Maybe whatever it was caused Leah's confusion. Maybe that's what put her in that road that night." Her eyes flashed toward David one last time. There was a desperation within them he had not seen before. "Maybe it'll affect me too," she whispered and standing, she hurried toward the house, plates in hand.

"Kelsey," David called, wanting to reassure her, tell her she was fine, everything was going to be okay.

But she did not stop.

Somewhere deep in the woods, he could hear the distant croak of bull frogs. All around him, tree toads chirped. Turning, he stared at the trees, his gaze moving up until he was staring at the nearly full moon. It seemed huge tonight, filling the eastern sky.

Memories of a night not too long ago drifted through his mind. He and Leah had been out here together, taking an evening walk in the woods and they had gotten lost. He had been ready to give up and just start calling for help, but Leah had looked up at the moon and told him it would guide them home. Staring up at it now, the moon looking so much like it had that night, he felt his own emotions well up to the surface.

Leah was gone.

The thought struck with a finality he had not felt before. Leah was gone.

"We both saw her."

David turned toward the voice behind him with a start. Kelsey stood a few feet away, her face lost in the darkness of the shadows covering the backyard.

"Maybe we did," he said, finding his voice. "Or maybe we just wanted to."

"Or maybe," Kelsey said, "Just maybe, she's trying to tell us something."

2

Edward Ross sat in the darkness of his home, wearing his coat, an old photo album in his lap. He glanced at the glowing dials of the digital clock beside him. He had missed his flight. He hadn't meant to. He had, in fact, come home, packed his bags and set them beside the front door. But as he was pulling on his coat, he noticed the photo album in the closet.

He had pulled it out while there was still some light left in the day. Since then, he had been trying to decide if he wanted to look at it, dredge up the memories. Now it was dark and he still was not sure.

And he had missed his flight.

Reaching beside him, he turned on a light. The soft glow glared off the cheap white plastic cover of the album. Slowly, he opened it and stared at the first picture in the book. It was an old one, taken the day of ground breaking at Envirospace. He'd had it blown up into a full size page. In it, he, Hal and Claire all held shovels, each poised to turn the first pile of earth. He could still remember the feeling of exhilaration he had had at that moment. Back then, the three of them had been a team. And now, he could barely stand to be in the same room with Hal.

What had happened?

"Too much, too soon," he mumbled.

Turning the pages, he stared at picture after picture of his sister. As he looked, the years going by, the memories framed within each photo, Claire's face began to blur in his mind, become one with David's. When had he grown to look so much like her?

He closed the book. David was not Claire. He could not force his nephew into a life he did not want. If David needed to leave the company, then he would just have to let him go. Besides, maybe David was right. The fight with Hal had gone on so long. And for what?

Setting the book on the coffee table before him, he rose and headed for the door. He could still catch a late flight out. When he got back, he would accept David's resignation. And possibly turn in his own.

3

Stepping into his condo, David locked the door behind him and hung his keys on the hook beside the door. He stood for a moment staring at the paper bag in his hand, trying to decide what to do with it. Should it be refrigerated? But just the thought of sticking the small rodent in his fridge next to his leftover Chinese and cold chili turned his stomach. Instead, he left it on the floor next to the front door.

He stood for several minutes staring down at the bag. Should he call Kelsey? Just make sure she's okay? He shook his head. No. She had assured him before he left that she was fine, even admitting to feeling a little embarrassed at her reaction to what they had found. It wouldn't make sense for him to call her. Besides, what would he say? Are you sure you're okay? He ran a hand through his hair. No. He would not call her again until he got the test results.

Envirospace.

The name of his father's company seemed to echo through his mind. He needed to hold a meeting, call together a few of his people and form a plan of action. Tomorrow morning. Early. Before anyone else arrived. If he could outline a plan and present it to the board, he might finally be able to actually accomplish something.

Could this discovery finally launch some of his programs? If he planned it right, if he presented it well, it was possible his entire division could take off.

He rubbed his eyes, shaking his head. What the hell was he thinking? Earlier, he'd been ready to resign from the company. Now he was making plans to start up a new project.

He rolled his head on his shoulders, weariness pulling at his mind and body. His shoulder ached where he had hurt it the night before. A hot shower and then bed. That was what he needed. He was just too damn tired to think anymore tonight.

The red flashing light on his phone machine caught his eye. Moving slowly, he walked to the machine and pressed the button.

"David? You there?" Sam's voice filled the room. "Didn't see you today at work. Just wanted to see how you were doing. Don't forget we have another game tomorrow night."

David made a mental note to talk to Sam tomorrow as the machine rewound and reset itself. He turned toward his bedroom.

The phone rang.

He hesitated, debating his options, the comfort of his bed calling out to him from the next room. What if it was Kelsey?

It rang again. Sighing, he lifted the receiver. "Hello?"

"David, dear." Rose Brayden's voice grated against his ear. "I'm so glad I caught you."

He tensed, silently chiding himself for choosing to answer the phone. "What do you want, Rose?" He would no longer play civil to her. He didn't need to anymore.

"I wanted to apologize for how I acted at the funeral. I said some things . . ." She trailed off. "I was distraught."

It was late. Too late for this. And he was just so damn tired. He eyed the couch with genuine affection. But he knew if he sat down, he would have a hard time getting up again. And he didn't want to sleep on the couch. Closing his eyes, he dropped his head back, mustering as much patience as he could. "It's all right, Rose. We were both upset."

"Thank you, David. That's very sweet of you." She paused. David waited for her to say that's it, gotta go. But he knew she did not really call to apologize. She called because she wanted something. Something from him. "I have a favor to ask."

No kidding, he almost said. "What is it, Rose?"

"I'm wondering if you could clean out Leah's house for me?"

"Are you serious?" he asked, incredulously.

"Of course I'm serious."

David's hand tightened on the phone receiver. He wasn't falling for this act of hers. Not again. "Rose, what are you really fishing for?"

"I don't know what you're talking about." Her voice went up two octaves.

"Kelsey is staying at Leah's," he said, unable to hide his irritation any longer. "You had to have known that."

She let out a long, angry breath. "So she really went there. I asked her not to." A long pause. He knew she was waiting for him to say something else but he had nothing to say. "Well, what are we going to do, David?"

"We?" He nearly laughed. "Nothing." He offered her no other solution, no options. As far as he was concerned, he was no longer involved.

"I need your help. I was counting on—"

"Rose." The anger in his voice cut her off. He did not want to get between mother and daughter—not again. "Kelsey wants to go through Leah's things herself. Maybe if you call her—"

"She is being ridiculous," Rose interrupted. "I can't wait forever. There is a monthly payment on that house you know." Another pause. When she spoke again, her voice was softer. "Did you talk to Kelsey? What did she say?"

David's glance shifted to the bag beside his front door. There was a pause before he said, "We didn't talk."

4

January 1: I celebrated New Year's Eve with David. It was wonderful. Envirospace threw a huge party at the Hilton. I've never had such a good time. Everything was beautiful, the flowers, the gowns. David made me feel so special. At midnight, when he kissed me, I was giddy from champagne. I told him I felt guilty for not calling Mother but David said there'd be plenty of other New Year's with my Mother—this one was his.

Kelsey sat in the kitchen, the diary open on the table before her. She had read the paragraph about New Year's

Eve three times. It was the first paragraph in the book, the only one Kelsey had read so far.

But as she reread the section again, she realized David was right. She would not only be looking at her sister's life, she would also be delving into the lives of the people around Leah, the people who touched her life. And she wasn't sure if she really wanted to do that.

She ran her hand across the writing, tracing the words with her finger. *David.* Her hand hesitated on his name. She didn't know what she had been trying to prove earlier. Pointing to where her sister had died. Pushing him to agree with her. To give her an easy answer.

David.

He was right here on the first page. She knew he would be, that was a given. But now, confronted with it, she felt . . . uncomfortable. After reading personal thoughts regarding him, would she still be able to look him in the face? And who else, *what* else might be between the covers of the book?

She flipped through the pages, staring at her sister's neat writing, trying to make a decision. The journal was set up as a yearly record, some days requiring less than a page, while others ran several. But with each new day, Leah had carefully marked the date at the top, clearly distinguishing one from another.

As Kelsey continued to flip past each day, she realized there really was no decision to be made. She had come to Leah's for answers, answers that might very well be within the diary. One month. She would read one month and then if she felt that it was wrong, she would stop.

Taking a deep breath, she plunged in. At first, she read slowly, rereading several pages, skipping backward when she didn't recognize a name or place. But as she continued to read, her pace increased. She quickly digested day after day, turning the pages faster and faster. As she read, she began to get a clear picture of Leah's life, her feelings, her habits. And she could not stop. She read into February without pause.

February 12: We had Eve over for a birthday dinner. Her sixty-fifth. If you ask me, she doesn't look a day over fifty. David actually cooked! (Or tried to.) I think it was supposed to be a casserole but I'm still not sure. Luckily, Eve brought her wonderful home-made rolls or we wouldn't have had anything to eat. I'm letting the pan he used soak overnight but I think I might actually have to throw it out.

I gave Eve a teapot. Nothing fancy—white with small roses on the side. But she loved it. She began to cry even before she finished unwrapping it.

As I watched her, tears running down her cheeks, I realized how much she had come to mean to me. Our dinners, the talks we share, the time we spend just being together, keeping each other company. Before long I was crying too. I think David thought we were both crazy.

I only wish Mother could be like Eve. I know I shouldn't feel that way. Mother is who she is but I can't help but wonder what life would be like if she were more like Eve or just more affectionate.

I've always wondered how different Mother would be if Daddy had lived.

Daddy.

Kelsey stopped reading. She had not thought about her father in years. He died of a massive heart attack when Kelsey was three, Leah barely one. Neither one really had any memory of him, just the pictures and stories from his sister Eileen. As children, Kelsey used to make up stories to tell Leah. Each one featured their father. He was the hero, defending against wrong, saving the world. But as they grew older, the stories slowly died away. Before long,

they were left with only their mother and her constant crit-
icizing.

For so long, Kelsey had wondered if her feelings about
her mother had been exclusively hers. The burden of that
question weighed heavily on her, nagging at the back of
her mind, calling her selfish, ungrateful. But she was no
longer alone, had proof that her sister felt the same way.
As that realization sank in, she felt the weight she had carried for so long lift.

She looked down at the diary. It was all here within these
pages. The more she read, the more she felt she could almost see her sister's life being played out all around her in
this little house. The days. The nights. Every moment carefully recorded, every emotion thoroughly explored.

She ran her hands over the book, flipping through the
pages. She had so many questions, so many things she
needed to know.

March 15: We got a break in the winter weather today. It was actually warm—everyone had spring fe-
ver. David surprised me with a picnic lunch. My first
one. We walked to the park with a basket of food
and ate on a blanket spread on the ground. He even
brought champagne and we toasted over our bologna
sandwiches.

Later when I told mother about the picnic, she
seemed angry. Did I ruin my clothes? Did I really
think it was the right time of year to do something
like that? I tried to ignore it but I felt hurt that she
couldn't just be happy for me.

She keeps asking me when David and I are going
to get married. I don't have the heart (or is it guts?)
to tell her that I don't think that day will come. How
can I explain our relationship to her when I'm not
sure myself. David's wonderful and I know he cares
for me. But there's something missing, something I
don't think he feels for me. There's a gentleness in

his eyes when he looks at me. But I'm not sure it's love.

Kelsey continued to stare at the words but she no longer comprehended what she was reading. For a moment, she found herself thinking about David. Leah was right. There was a gentleness in his eyes. When he smiled, it touched his whole face. But there was also a strength there that reassured her, kept her fear at bay. He made her feel comfortable, like she'd known him forever. Was that how Leah had felt? Did they barbecue in the yard together on hot summer nights the way she and David had tonight? Did they?—no. She could not think about the two of them together. Not *that* way. It was too hard. Too uncomfortable.

Turning back to the book, she hesitated for a moment, not sure if she wanted to continue. Leah's life, her emotions, seemed to fill the room, pushing in, making Kelsey feel as if she were suffocating from their weight. But she needed to know, needed to find some kind of peace. She turned the page.

March 16: I miss Kelsey.

Kelsey's hands shook as she held the book. It was the first time she had been mentioned. It took her off guard, stealing her breath, shaking her knees. Quickly, she continued to read.

She gave me strength. I think back over the years as children and I know that's true. Maybe that's why mother doesn't want me to call her. She's afraid Kelsey will give me the strength to say no to her the way she did. I envy Kelsey for that. The other day, I was watching television and I saw these two little girls. They were putting on a show in their garage for their friends. I started to cry as I watched. It brought back the memories of Kelsey, the time we put on a show of our own. That night, I almost called her. I don't know what stopped me but the next day when I told Mother, she said it was good I didn't call. She says it'll just be the same old problems between us. Maybe we've both grown up a little since then. I don't know. She's my sister and I wish we could talk the way we did when we were kids.

Kelsey stopped reading. Tears filled her eyes. Her sister had not forgotten her, did not hate her. Even though they had been apart for so many years, neither really knowing the other, they were still sisters. And Leah had wanted to talk to her. That was something Kelsey had always done for Leah. Whenever her sister got in trouble, Kelsey was there to step in and take the heat or comfort her. Suddenly, all the things they had done together as children raced through her mind in crystal clarity. The days spent pretending they lived in a far-off land with a handsome prince, the late night stories they told each other about fairies and goblins. How had they grown so far apart?

Kelsey looked down at the book, touching the small section that dealt with her. Leah had missed her. For the first time in days . . . years, she felt at peace.

5

Tulsa, Oklahoma

"Something's wrong," Joe muttered. The unlit cigarette that hung between his lips bobbed up and down with each word. "I can feel it."

He was sure he was right. *Instinct.* It had saved his ass on more than one occasion. He wasn't about to ignore it now.

Lighting a match, he held it to the end of the cigarette, the light of the flame momentarily dancing off the scar on his cheek, making it seem grotesquely long and distorted.

He shook out the match. The room fell dark again except for the end of the cigarette. Joe lay on the bed, his hands behind his head, smoking the cigarette, trying to decide what he wanted to do.

In the room behind him, he could hear a television blaring out the evening news. Outside, the sound of the occasional police siren or honking horn split the otherwise quiet area.

Joe ignored it all.

Since leaving the diner, his mind had turned time and time again to the woman he had seen outside the window. He couldn't forget her, couldn't get the image of her face, her eyes out of his mind.

"Something's wrong," he said again and rising, crushed the cigarette out in the plastic ashtray on the bedside table. He walked to the window of his darkened motel room. He felt restless and he didn't like it. His gaze traveled over the parking lot before being drawn upward. The nearly full moon hung in the eastern sky, its brilliance reaching down to caress his bare chest with its soft whiteness, outlining the muscles of his chest and arms.

He closed his eyes, soaking up the moonlight. Behind him in the darkness of his room, he heard . . .

Breathing. Slow and even, only a few feet back.

But there was something else.

A smell. Sweet, cloying. Like flowers. It drifted through the room, permeating the air.

Perfume? He wasn't sure.

Keeping his eyes closed, giving no signal that he realized he was no longer alone, he mentally went over the layout of the room, deciding on his best strategy.

The breathing continued, unchanged.

Joe darted to the left, threw himself over the side of the bed, and swept his gun off the table in one swift move. Bringing it up before him, bracing himself against the wall, he waited.

No one slammed into him, fists flying. Nothing was thrown against him. No movement. His own breath, now rasping in and out, was the only sound in the room.

He waited.

And then he saw her.

The woman from the diner.

She stood on the other side of the room, the moon washing her in pale light. She did not move. Did not speak.

"Don't move!" He trained his gun on her heart. But even as he stared at the lone figure, he knew there was something wrong. "Who sent you?"

She remained silent.

"I'm going to turn on the light. Move and I'll kill you." Reaching sideways with his free hand, he turned on the light.

The woman was gone.

6

Hartwick, Michigan

Kelsey yawned, the words on the page blurring. Glancing at the clock, she was surprised to see how late it was. She had been reading the diary for nearly three hours straight. But she still felt no closer to understanding why Leah was now gone.

Turning back to the words on the page, she frowned. Another Hillary passage. Kelsey hated to admit it but the more she read the diary, the more she grew to hate Hillary West, Leah's closest friend. According to the diary, the two of them did everything together. Kelsey couldn't help but feel a little jealous of that relationship. After all, this was the woman who had taken Kelsey's place in her sister's life. The two friends talked on the phone regularly, had dinners together, spent weekends shopping. All the things Kelsey should have done with Leah.

She hesitated for a moment, stretching her neck, feeling exhaustion pull at her. This would be the last passage.

April 2: Hillary came over today to help me with the final decorating details for the living room. She loves the changes I've made so far and so do I but she keeps pushing me to start on the kitchen.

I told her she sounded like Mother when she nagged me. I thought she was going to hit me after that but at least it stopped her from asking. It's the last room in the house and I do want to change it, but every time I go in there, I see Mother. She hates the changes I've made and I know the kitchen is the only room left that Mother still feels comfortable in. I think it hurt her when I changed everything. I know she meant well when she decorated the house for me when I moved, and I'm grateful—I've told her that a thousand times. But I still think she doesn't understand. I want the house to feel more like mine now. When I showed Mother the living room and bedrooms the first time, she nodded and said they looked nice. But whenever she comes over, she just sits in the kitchen. Her last hold on my house. It hurts my feelings but I don't know what to do. How can I change it? Will she stop coming over if I do?

Hillary says I listen to Mother too much, that I should just go with what I want and feel. But I'm not always sure what that is. There are so many people pulling me in so many different directions. I don't know what's right anymore.

Kelsey stared at the last line on the page.

I don't know what's right anymore.

Was that it? Had Leah become confused? Anxious?

Kelsey shook her head. She was grasping at anything now. How often did she ask herself that question?

But as she continued to stare at the words, a new question formed in her mind. She reread the section about Hillary, going over it again word for word. For the first time, she realized that she could not recall seeing the woman. Not at the funeral or the wake. And she had not phoned or stopped by. Kelsey flipped back through the pages then forward through the next couple. Hillary's name was sprinkled heavily throughout each one.

"So where are you?" Kelsey whispered.

7

David struggled up from sleep, the sound of his own voice crying out in the darkness of the room startling him. He sat up, panting, his body covered in sweat.

He jerked left, then right, looking for the people he had felt all around him, smothering him.

There was a scream and a struggle. . . .

He scrambled across his bed, trying to escape. His feet caught in the tangle of blankets he had thrown free during his sleep. He fell hard, grunting as his sore shoulder smacked the hardwood floor.

But he did not stop.

"Get away!" He pulled on the covers, trying to free himself. He shoved the sheets away. Clambered over them into the corner of the room. Pushed his back against the wall. Scanned the room around him for intruders. Tried to get his bearings. Control his fear. Until he finally realized . . .

It was a nightmare.

No one was in his house. No one was going to hurt him. But even as he tried to remember the dream, he realized it was gone. Just the panic that still pulsed beneath his skin remained.

He stood in the darkness of his room, clutching his left arm against his chest, rubbing his shoulder, trying desperately to remember. Because deep down, somewhere in the vast recesses of his mind, he knew with a certainly he did not understand that what had just happened was much more than just a nightmare.

CHAPTER EIGHT

1

David arrived early at Envirospace. But instead of heading to his office in the administrative wing, he parked his car in the lot behind the science building. Pushing his door open, he tucked his laptop computer under his arm, before grabbing his briefcase and the paper bag containing the squirrel's carcass. The stillness of the morning struck him almost immediately. He stopped for a moment, eyes closed and listened to the early morning silence, so refreshing after the rush of the last few days. As he continued his walk across the lot, he found it hard to believe that in less than two hours, the quiet peace around him would be disrupted by more than a hundred employees.

Unlocking the main entrance, he walked to Lab One, the only lab in current operation, and dumped his load on the largest work table. After retrieving a large plastic container, he donned a mask and gloves, and working carefully, removed the squirrel's body from the bag. He placed it on the center of the container, lying the small animal on its back, exposing the tiny extra paws as best he could before covering it with the lid. Next, he set out each of his photographs and soil samples.

Then he waited.

One at a time, they filed in. Peter Kerin, head of toxicology, was the first to arrive.

"What's going on, David?" he asked, pulling his lab coat on over his Hawaiian shirt and clipping his I.D. badge to the pocket. "What couldn't wait until normal . . ." but the sentence trailed off as his eyes locked on the squirrel. "What is this?" He leaned close, his nose nearly touching the hood covering the small rodent. "What *is* this?"

Before David could answer, Margaret Skyler, his most experienced biochemist, walked in. "Morning, gentlemen."

Pete turned toward her, motioning her over. "Take a look at this, Maggie."

Even as she leaned over his shoulder, Phil Winters, resident soil specialist, arrived. "I brought doughnuts," he announced, dropping the bag on the table. "I got dibs on the powdered." His gaze focused on the squirrel. "What the hell?"

David stood on one side of the table, his three best people, what he considered the core of his small department, stood on the other side.

Pete flipped through the photographs, stopping every few moments to show one to Maggie who continued to stare at the squirrel. Phil held the bags of soil and bark close to his face, checking them one by one.

Finally, Pete refocused his attention on David. "I guess it was worth getting me up so early."

"I thought you'd see it that way." They were curious, he could see it on all their faces. That was all he needed. "Grab a seat and we can begin."

Phil, true to his word, grabbed the only powdered doughnut from the box before taking a seat around the work table. Maggie and Pete simply sat down, both too stunned by all the information on the table before them to bother with thoughts of food.

Opening his briefcase, David withdrew three manila folders. "I've already gathered together some information." He handed one folder to each person before opening his laptop computer and switching it on. "The map inside shows the area where the squirrel was located. The photographs are of the actual site where I also collected the soil and bark samples." Each person leafed through the material as he spoke. "I believe this is the opportunity we've all been waiting for."

Peter Kerin spoke first. "What do you mean exactly?"

"Our department is stagnant," David said. "We've been doing the same work for the last two years. I want to expand. I want to take us into new fields of research."

"Beginning with this?" Maggie asked.

"Yes."

"Has the E.P.A. been notified yet?" Phil interjected.

"You know how they operate." David fiddled with a paper clip, unfolding each side. "They receive about twenty-six thousand reports a year on sites exactly like this one. If we report the site, it'll be added to their list to do a preliminary assessment. They may come out in a week, a month who knows? All they'll do is a quick site inspection, a hazard ranking, and then the site will go on a national priority list depending on that ranking."

"It'll be a year or longer before anything is done," Pete added.

"Exactly." David pointed the now straight paper clip toward him. "We can begin today. This is exactly the kind of work I've been trying to get this company involved in. We can assist the E.P.A. and maybe take over some of their burden for investigation and clean up. If we can devise a plan for clean up and present it to the E.P.A., it may be possible for us to contract out for work of this nature in the near future."

Pete nodded his agreement. "We have the facilities for exactly that type of work."

"All we need to do is convince my father and the board that this is economically and scientifically worthwhile." He drummed his fingers along the top edge of his laptop computer.

"And how do you propose to do that?" Maggie crossed her arms over her chest, her face taking on a sour look. Their division did not have a stellar track record with the company regarding the passing of proposals.

"You three start down here. Work up a report on the squirrel and the soil samples I brought. Find out what's in them. I'll work up a proposal we can submit to the board. I've already got a few ideas." He glanced down at his computer screen but before he could bring up a file, the door behind him opened. He had thought calling this meeting so early would secure their privacy. Obviously, he had been wrong. He turned and found himself staring at the last person he wanted to see. Hal Ebersol.

Dammit!

He had not wanted him to know about any of this until he was ready to present it to the board. His father could stop the whole project before he got a chance to even try and get it passed.

But it wasn't just his father who stood blocking the doorway. James Froth from the legal department stood beside him. And behind him, just to his left, stood Ken Brewer.

David's brow furrowed. A strange trio to be taking a morning stroll through the Science Building, a building none of them frequented very often. "Is there something I can do for you?"

James Froth walked to the table, his gaze locked on the tiny rodent. "What's going on here?" He leaned closer, squinting at the squirrel under glass. His eyes widened suddenly. He pointed at the creature. "Are those . . . ?" But he never finished the question. Instead, he pulled a handkerchief from his pocket and placed it over his nose and mouth. "Is that thing properly contained?" He backed away two steps. "Is this completely safe?"

"Of course it is," David snapped. The man had the nerve to come into his lab and imply negligence. "What business is this of yours?'' he asked the lawyer.

But it was his father who answered. ''Last time I checked, this was still my company.'' He spoke with quiet authority. ''I believe I do have the right to find out what is going on within its walls.''

David shifted his attention to Hal Ebersol. Impatience burned behind his father's eyes. But despite the man's obvious animosity, David did not back down. ''I just find it unusual for the three of you to be wandering within the walls of *this* particular building.''

Hal's eyes narrowed. ''I decided to hold an early morning meeting. When we arrived and saw all the cars in the lot at such an early hour, our curiosity naturally got the better of us.''

David nodded. But he was not completely convinced. He glanced at the three people he had called less than two hours ago. His people from his department. He had asked each of them to keep the meeting to themselves. Had one of them called his father?

Hal stepped to the table. His gaze swept over the squirrel before coming to rest on the photographs. He lifted them one by one, staring for several moments at each. He asked no questions, said nothing. As David waited for the ax to fall, waited for his father to grind this project into the ground the way he had so many others, his gaze shifted to Ken Brewer. He stood, his back stiff, his eyes locked forward, utterly silent. The man was completely emotionless, a walking corpse he often told Sam.

And his gaze shifted back to his father.

Completely emotionless.

For the first time, David realized his father, unlike anyone else who had seen his evidence, showed no emotion. Why hadn't he been surprised, shocked, disturbed? David ran a hand through his hair. Was it possible his complete lack of feeling was due to the fact that what was being shown was not completely unexpected?

A pang of uncertainty spread through him.

If Envirospace had somehow caused this disaster . . .

No! It just wasn't possible. They were in the business of cleaning up messes. Not making them.

Besides, he shouldn't read so much into his father's reaction. He was not the type of man to show great emotion, especially in front of so many people.

But what about Leah?

The thought invaded, unwanted. And with the thought came yet more questions.

Why had her desk been emptied so quickly? Had someone been trying to hide something? Had she found out something she should not have? Something in the woods behind her house?

He let his gaze travel over each person in the room. Betrayal? Covert operations? Hidden agendas?

He ran a hand over his eyes. Absurd. Even a little paranoid. He took a deep breath, trying to clear his mind. He needed to slow down, look at things clearly and simply.

"David?" His father's voice cut off his thoughts. "What exactly is going on here?"

"Just a short meeting." The answer came without thought, without additional explanation. He was so used to being turned down that he said as little as possible without even thinking about it.

Hal dropped the photos back on the table. "I think it's more than that."

David's jaw tightened. He was not prepared to lay his cards on the table. Not yet. But as he weighed his options, he realized he had none. "I've discovered an environmentally damaged piece of land in the nearby area." He kept his eyes on his father, trying to gauge his reaction to what was being said. "I want to put together a program that will work in conjunction with the E.P.A. for cleanup and investigation."

Hal nodded, lifting one of the manila folders. "And who would fund this project?" he asked, scanning the notes inside.

"I was going to propose to the board that my department be allotted additional funds in order to head up this particular investigation." He nodded toward his evidence.

His father continued to scan the pages inside the file. His expression did not change.

"This is the perfect opportunity to expand the research and development department," David continued. "If this goes well, we can contract out for this kind of work. It'll pay for itself."

Froth chanced a step forward. He removed the hanky just long enough to speak. "Do you know who owns the land?"

"No." David did not look at Froth when he spoke. "We're just now discussing how we want to proceed."

"Have you bothered to contact anyone yet? The E.P.A. The local authorities? Maybe some Boy Scouts?"

David gripped the sides of the table. His gaze slid toward the lawyer. "Listen, Jim, I don't need your condescending attitude."

"We are obligated to notify the E.P.A." He held the handkerchief a few inches from his face as he spoke. "They will want to launch an investigation of their own."

"Not immediately they won't," David shot back. He had wanted to talk about this with his people. Get their feedback before talking to anyone else. Now he did not have that luxury. "I want to go in on a preliminary basis. We don't even know what this is yet." He looked back at his father. There was no change to his uninterested expression. "I just want to take a few more samples, do a few tests. Then we notify the E.P.A. No harm done."

Froth shook his head. "It's too much of a risk." He too spoke directly to Hal. "We do it and we open ourselves up to one hell of a lawsuit. If the E.P.A. wanted to, they could shut us down for something like that."

David nearly laughed. "Come on, you really think the E.P.A. would shut us down? The public loves us. The E.P.A. wouldn't dare touch us."

"I think David's right," Pete Kerin said, giving David

the support he so desperately needed. "We keep what we have here, run a few tests, no harm done."

"A mistake," Froth insisted.

"S.O.P." Kerin muttered under his breath.

Froth turned toward him, his eyes narrowing above the handkerchief. "And what's that supposed to mean?"

"Standard operating procedure for you, Froth. We get shut down every time—"

"Your department is nothing more than—"

"Gentlemen." Hal's voice, the tone sharper than it had been earlier, immediately quieted the room. "We have plenty of time to debate this issue. Let's remain civil while we do so." He kept his gaze on Froth and Kerin, driving his point home. Then slowly, he moved his gaze around the room, stopping for a moment on each person.

David had only been to a couple of other meetings with his father. But he knew the drill, had seen it in each instance.

Hal Ebersol now wanted the floor.

And David knew, without uttering a word, or asking a single person, that everyone in the room knew it too. No one spoke. No one moved. They waited, all attention focused on the man who owned the company, controlled the outcome of this and every meeting. They would wait until Hal Ebersol was ready to speak again.

Finally, Hal's gaze found David and stopped.

Immediately, he wanted to look away, as many of the others in the room had, suddenly remembering a note they needed to jot down or finding a new fact in the papers before them that they needed to study. Anything that would turn their gaze away from the cool eyes of his father.

But David was determined to show the man that he was not intimidated by him, would not flinch beneath his assessing gaze. Not anymore.

"David," Hal began, his voice steely calm. "I would like you to put together a report outlining exactly what we would need to do if we decide to go ahead with your idea."

Satisfaction flooded through him. "I've already started."
He glanced down at his lit screen and scrolled down several
lines. But instead of the notes he expected, the screen was
filled, top to bottom, every available space with 1's and
0's.

Faces. Voices. Harsh. Demanding.
A flash of jumbled memories ripped through his mind.
She screamed once and then was silent.
His mouth went dry. His hands shook.
He struggled but . . .
"David?" His father's sharp voice drew his attention.
He looked up, blinking rapidly as if waking from sleep.
A headache pounded against his forehead. "What? I'm
sorry." He rubbed his temples. Swallowed several times.
And struggled to remember what he had been thinking
about. But it was gone. Only a haze of confusion remained.
"What . . . what was I saying?" He looked around the
room. All eyes were on him.

"Are you all right?" His father was watching him, judg-
ing him.

"I'm fine." A headache tugged at his mind. He tried to
calm his fast beating heart. Erase the anxiety that crept over
his shoulder and whispered in his ear—*Something's wrong.*

"It's my notes." He glanced down at the computer. The
series of 1's and 0's glared up at him. He hit the page down
key. Slowly at first but then faster and faster. Screen after
screen was filled from top to bottom. "Something's wrong
with my computer." He snapped the screen closed. "I seem
to have lost the rest of my notes." He tapped the top of
the computer.

"I want a proposal by Friday. No later." Hal's voice
held a note of impatience.

"Yes. Of course." David wiped the sweat from his brow,
clutching his hands into fists to stop the shaking. "But until
we determine exactly what we will do, I think we should
send out a small crew. They can block off the area and
warn everyone to stay out of those woods."

2

As Kelsey steered her car out of her sister's subdivision, she tried to remember the directions David had given her the night before. Eve's driveway was less than a half mile from the entrance to Leah's subdivision, off the main road.

She had told him the night before that she wanted to visit Eve today, update her on what was going on. He'd given her the directions, making her promise to stay out of the woods for the day. As long as they stayed away from the dead part, he was sure it was safe. But he didn't want to take any chances. She hadn't told him last night, but nothing could have gotten her back into those woods. Until she got the test results, she would not worry unnecessarily but she would also not go back into the forest.

A mailbox came up on her right. She slowed, glancing out her side window. A moment later, she turned down a dirt road. The trees grew close to the road. There was barely enough room for her car down the narrow lane and as she bumped along, tree branches scraping and scratching across the outside of her car, she felt as if she were driving straight into the woods themselves.

Finally, the road widened out and Eve's house came into view. It sat on a small lot of land, surrounded on all sides by trees. As Kelsey parked, she noticed a small garden beside the house, the vegetables green and ripe.

Stepping from the car, she walked toward the house. Solitude. The word swept through her mind and she stopped, once more surveying the area around her. She closed her eyes, listening to the quiet, soaking up the serenity of this private little home.

Although her sister's subdivision was only a short walk through the woods, the thick trees provided Eve's home with a peacefulness few enjoyed anymore.

Taking a deep breath and releasing it slowly, she opened her eyes. A calmness filled her as she stepped up on the porch and knocked on the door. A minute passed. There was no sound from within. She glanced at the house. No open windows, no movement from inside. She knocked again, louder, wondering if she had made her trip for nothing.

"Should have called," she muttered, beginning to turn away. A moment later, the door opened. "Good morning," she said brightly, turning back.

But as she looked at Eve, she realized something was wrong. The woman looked tired, her eyes half closed, her right arm wrapped in gauze.

"Are you all right?"

"Just a bit under the weather, dear." Eve smiled but the attempt was weak.

Kelsey looked at the crude bandage. "What happened to your arm?"

Eve waved her hand absently. "It's nothing really. A rash of some sort. Probably brushed against something tromping through those woods."

Suddenly Kelsey's mind flashed back to her own walk through the woods yesterday. The tree limbs that had scraped against her bare arms, the leaves that had brushed against her legs and face. What had she touched? *What had touched her?*

"How long have you had your rash?" she asked, her eyes locked on the gauze covering.

"I noticed it last night but I'm afraid it's spreading rather quickly."

An image of Eve handing her the bag with the squirrel's body inside flickered through Kelsey's mind. Had the old woman touched it? Had she handled it with her bare hands before putting it into the brown paper bag?

Eve opened the door wider. "Would you like to come in, dear? Visit a while?"

Kelsey dragged her gaze away from the gauze covered arm, trying to remember all she had touched over the last two days. "No, I . . ."

A rash of some sort.

The words whispered through her mind, cutting off any other thoughts.

Probably brushed against something in the woods.

Her throat constricted. She cleared it. "I, ah, just need a minute of your time." Her feeling of solitude melted away, replaced by a growing sense of claustrophobia. She resisted the urge to turn and look at the thick stand of trees behind her.

"That's fine." Eve moved away from the door. "But I need to sit down." Her voice trailed back to Kelsey as she disappeared into the house.

Kelsey hesitated on the doorstep, trying to block out the nagging fear that chewed at her mind. She stared inside but could see nothing. It was like looking into a deep, murky hole filled with dark, unfamiliar shapes that seemed to loom toward her. As she stood, staring into that black opening, she longed to turn and run from this place, forget about her sister, go back to Minneapolis and continue her own life. But then the sun came out from behind the clouds and the light inside the house shifted and brightened. The half-closed shades cast strange patterns across the floor and walls and the dark shapes became tables and chairs.

She took a step over the threshold.

"Eve," she called, squinting into the darkened hallway, searching for the older woman.

"In here, dear."

Kelsey followed the sound of Eve's voice, moving down the hallway toward the living room, deeper into the house. Overstuffed furniture, ceiling-high bookcases and knick-knack-covered tables packed the house, leaving little walking space. The furniture, a hodgepodge of different styles and colors, none of it really matching, looked to be at least several decades old. Kelsey weaved her way past each piece, skirting them.

Eve sat in the far corner, her face lost in the shadows. A grandfather clock towered behind her, the pendulum swinging slowly back and forth.

Kelsey stopped halfway across the room, her gaze fixed on the bandage on Eve's arm. "How fast is it spreading?"

"Come in and sit down, dear." Eve indicated the chair across from her. "I don't want to shout."

Slowly, Kelsey walked forward. As she drew closer, she could make out Eve's features—she sat slumped back in her chair, eyes closed, her breathing thick, slightly labored.

Kelsey took the seat across from her, sitting on the edge of the chair. "Maybe you should see a doctor." Her voice sounded foreign to her, alien, detached.

Eve nodded, the effort of the simple gesture seeming to tire her even more. "I've made an appointment for late this afternoon. I'm sure he can give me a lotion of some sort to take care of it. But I have to ask you a favor, dear." She looked at Kelsey, her eyes dull, filmy. "Could you drive me?"

"I . . . ah . . ." Kelsey stumbled over the words, taken off guard by the request.

"Leah was always good about taking me places, picking things up for me." Her voice was quietly reflective as she spoke. Reaching beside her, she lifted one of the photographs from the table at her elbow and held it out toward Kelsey.

After only a moment's hesitation, she took the picture.

It was Leah. She wore shorts, a T-shirt and a ridiculous straw hat.

"I took that one day when she came over to help me garden," Eve said as Kelsey stared at the photo. "She took to it right away. I told her she had a genuine green thumb." She closed her eyes, leaning back in the chair. "She was a real comfort to me. I miss her company terribly," she whispered.

Kelsey stared at Eve, her throat constricting from the sudden emotional rush of grief and pain. Here she was trying to rush away from Eve, not even give her five minutes of her time. And why? Because the woman had a simple rash on her arm.

I'm beginning to let my imagination run away with me.

As Kelsey set the photo of her sister back in place, she glanced at the other pictures on display. Most of them looked as if they had been taken some time ago. A much younger version of Eve in a few. Leah's photo seemed to be the only recent one.

Kelsey was struck with a sense of loneliness for this woman. When she returned home, who would visit Eve? Who would drive her to the doctor's or help her garden? She seemed so alone here, so isolated.

And then Kelsey thought about her own life. Who was waiting to greet her when she came home? Who missed her when she was gone? She had friends but none of them were close, mostly work friends.

Her eyes grew moist. She blinked back the tears. This was doing no good. Her life was fine. She was fine.

She cleared her throat.

"I'd be happy to drive you."

"Thank you, dear."

"But for now, why don't I make you some tea or toast?" she offered. "Have you eaten?"

Eve shook her head. "I couldn't eat a thing but that's sweet of you." She looked at Kelsey, her eyes brightening slightly. "What did David have to say about our little find?"

"Actually, that's what I came over here to tell you. But I don't think now is the best time. I think you should be in bed."

"Nonsense." Straightening in her seat, Eve stared at Kelsey. "I've been waiting on pins and needles all night for this. Now, tell me, child."

Kelsey leaned forward, her elbows resting on her thighs. "He thought it was as strange as we did. He thinks it must be from some kind of environmental damage." Once again, her gaze was drawn to the bandage on Eve's arm. "He's supposed to be at work right now talking to them about it.''

Eve nodded. ''I'm sure whatever it is, Envirospace can clear it up. They've done so much good.'' She glanced at the photograph again. ''Leah was so proud of working there. She loved the company. Talked about it a lot.''

''Did she ever talk about a woman named Hillary West?'' She blurted out the question before she could stop herself. It had been nagging at her mind all night.

''Of course,'' Eve said, her gaze still on the photo of Leah. ''They were good friends. Spent a great deal of time together.''

''You've met her?''

Eve nodded, returning her gaze to Kelsey. ''On several occasions.''

''She didn't come to the funeral.''

Reaching over, Eve took her hand and squeezed gently. ''Many people have a hard time when someone dies. They can't immediately handle the emotional drain.''

Kelsey stared down at her hand as Eve leaned back in her chair. There was nothing on her hand—nothing she could see. Yet it felt different somehow, unclean.

''I . . .'' She struggled to recapture her thoughts. ''I found her number in Leah's book.'' She looked at Eve again, her hands shaking lightly. ''Do you think it would be wrong to call her?''

''She'd probably welcome the chance to meet Leah's sister. I know I have.''

Kelsey smiled at the compliment but her mind was on Hillary West. She didn't admit it to Eve but deep down, she felt Hillary might be the key to discovering why Leah had died.

3

Hal swiveled in his chair until he was facing the window behind his desk. He stared at the launch site on the far side of the man-made lake. He wanted to increase the launches to two a month. Had plans to add a new wing to the existing processing plant. Was in the middle of negotiating an expansion in both Texas and Montana.

Now it would all have to be put on hold.

Because of David.

The sun glistened off the windows of the east wing of the science building. He shifted his attention to the nearly empty building. He never should have agreed to allow the building to be constructed. If it weren't for Edward and his constant interference . . .

Edward. His grip increased on the sides of his chair. He had brought David back. Edward had insisted on expanding into new fields of research. And now David was actually expecting them to become involved in cleanup operations in conjunction with the E.P.A. Where was the profit in that? What possible benefit could that program offer *his company?*

As far as Hal was concerned, Envirospace was already headed down the most lucrative path. All they needed to concentrate on was the collection and disposal of America's refuse. Everything else was a waste of time and money.

And he would not put up with it any longer.

A heavy knock sounded on the door. Hal turned around as Ken Brewer stepped inside.

"Did you get it all?" Hal asked, his gaze falling on the case in his assistant's hand.

"Yes." Ken spoke with his usual certainty.

"Let's have it."

Taking two steps forward, Ken set the case on the desk and carefully opened the lid. David's photographs, the soil samples and bark pieces lay inside. "The rodent?" Hal asked, reaching out to pick up the pictures.

"Confiscated and contained."

Hal nodded, studying the photos of the damage done to the wooded lot behind the Brayden house. "This changes everything," he grumbled. He kept several of the photographs but slammed the lid shut on the remaining physical evidence. "I want this to be your first priority."

Ken nodded, snapping the locks in place.

"Froth and Winters will keep their mouths shut but the others . . ." Hal mentally reviewed the events of the early morning meeting. "They'll talk. Maybe just in casual conversation to other employees, but they'll talk. And people will become curious."

"How do you want me to proceed?"

"I want them off grounds within the hour. Take them on site, set up some kind of temporary command post and keep them there. Tell them they are to answer only to you."

"Done."

"I want this handled quietly." He crossed the room, stopping before the glass-framed schematic hanging on the wall. His expansion plans on paper. His plans for the future. "Do whatever it takes, but make this problem go away."

"And your son?" Ken asked.

Hal shook his head, irritated by the constant aggravation David seemed to cause. "He won't drop this. And he certainly won't cooperate. We already know that." Moving back to his desk, he stood once more before the window, staring at the science building. "You worry about the wooded lot behind the Brayden house. I will handle the problem with David myself."

4

David stared at the computer screen in front of him. The 1's and 0's glared back. Earlier, when he'd noticed the numbers on his laptop computer, he'd thought it was simply a malfunction within the machine. But now . . . now he knew the truth. Knew he had typed the numbers himself.

Twice in the last hour, he'd erased them from his screen only to find himself, sometime later, sitting in front of the computer retyping them. Each time, he could not remember when he decided to retype them or why.

He looked down at the proposal laid out on his desk. It had been sitting on the same spot, the pages unmoved, for the last hour.

"What's wrong with me?" he whispered.

5

Hal stood at the window of his office. He watched as a truck drove toward the processing plant. Less than a week, he thought, mentally calculating how many days they had until the next launch. How many days before time ran out and the option he was considering was lost to them.

Behind him, he heard the door to his office open and close. He did not turn, did not acknowledge the man who had entered. Instead, he kept his back to him, making him wait . . . worry . . . sweat.

Minutes ticked by. The man cleared his throat, shuffled his feet, tried to do anything that would indicate to Hal that he was there. Anything but speak. Because Hal knew the man did not really want that.

"You were supposed to keep my son occupied." Slowly, he turned and locked his gaze on the man who stood beside his door.

Sam Wyatt ran a hand through his wild red hair, shifting where he stood. "I tried. But I kept missing him. He came in late. Left early. I called—"

Hal held up a hand, stopping him. "I didn't call you here to listen to your excuses." He crossed his arms over his chest. "I called you because we have yet another problem caused by one of your perfect solutions."

"Another?" Sam shook his head. "That's not possible. I . . ." But the sentence died off as the younger man looked into Hal's eyes. In that instant, he seemed to almost shrink in size.

The look. Hal used it often. To control. Intimidate. Dominate. Over the years, he had carefully honed it to perfection. Funny how easy it was to make someone uncomfortable. Embarrassed. With one simple look.

Except David. Earlier, he'd used the look at the meeting. His way of letting each and every person there know who was in charge. It had worked on everyone except David. For the first time, his son did not turn away from his gaze. And it was cause for worry.

He continued to stare at the younger man but it was only a matter of seconds before Sam looked away.

Picking up the pile of photos that lay atop his desk, Hal tossed them toward Sam. They fluttered through the air, scattering at his feet.

"*That* is the latest problem." Hal sat at his desk, keeping his gaze on the man before him.

Slowly, Sam bent and began gathering up the photos. He stared at each one, muttering to himself, shaking his head. When he had them all, he held them out toward Hal. "Is this . . . ?"

Hal nodded. "Yes. It's the site. Deep within the wooded lot behind the Brayden girl's house." He paused only briefly before adding, "David discovered it."

"Dave?" Sam's eyes widened. "This can't be . . . " He leafed through the photos again. "This can't be traced to you," he finished, his words spilling out in a rush.

"You've told me that before." Usually, Hal let Ken deal with Sam. He simply did not have the patience for this man. But things had gotten out of control and he needed Sam to realize exactly where he stood in regard to this matter. "I don't want panicked reassurances. I want the problem resolved."

Sam shook his head, his eyes darting from side to side as he thought. "This should not have happened." He took two tentative steps forward. "Those wells were environmentally sound. If they're causing a problem—"

"Then you will be the one to suffer for it," Hal cut him off. "It was your suggestion to use the injection wells. You designed them. You assured me that they would work.''

"And they should have. Even if they leaked, they should not have caused this kind of damage. Unless . . ." He looked at Hal. "What did you pump into those wells?"

Hal's stare, even and cool, met Sam's. "Waste."

"But what type? We talked before those wells went in. Nothing toxic. Just garbage. Normal everyday garbage. Just to get rid of what was piling up."

Hal remained silent, his gaze unwavering.

"If those wells were filled with toxic waste and it's leaking . . ." Sam let the sentence hang unfinished as he flipped through the photos one more time. "The ground water will have to be tested. The soil." He looked up, his eyes wide. "The people."

"That's already being done. At my expense, I might add."

"Your expense? How can you talk about cost?" He held the photos out toward him. "We have a real problem here."

"We?" Hal nearly laughed. "The problem is yours. You created it, now you must find a solution to it."

"You're blaming me?"

Standing, Hal leaned on his desk, his knuckles white where they rested against the deep mahogany. "Of course I blame you, Mr. Wyatt. I blame you for all of it."

"I did what you hired me to do. I followed *your* directions."

Hal smiled. A long, slow smile. "You're the expert, Mr. Wyatt. Your company was brought in to advise me. I'm a simple businessman who was duped by a shark out to make money and a name for himself. At least, that's what the records will reflect." He sat back down. "In other words, if this all comes to light, it will be you, your reputation, your team, who will be ruined."

Sam looked back down at the photographs. "You can't—"

"It doesn't have to go that far," Hal interrupted not waiting for Sam to form complete sentences. "I'm really not worried about the legalities of the situation. That can always be worked out.''

Sam's brow wrinkled in confusion. "Then what?" he asked with some hesitation.

"Questions, Mr. Wyatt." He kept his gaze on the man before him, watching for any weakness, any sign of defection. Right now he was scared and that fear would keep him in line. But Hal would have to take action at the first sign of desertion. "If this gets out to the public, then questions will be asked. People will want to know when we used the injection wells and more importantly, they'll want to know why. And it all traces back to you. Are you prepared to answer those questions?"

Sam looked back at the photos, his mouth open as if to speak. Instead, he just shook his head back and forth.

"I thought as much." He paused briefly. "Mr. Wyatt, you are going to get some answers for me."

Hesitantly, Sam moved forward. "What kind of answers?"

"The answers I wanted yesterday." He paused. "Who is the woman staying at the Brayden house? How involved is she? How committed to this project is David? Will his involvement in this effectively end his probe into the Brayden girl's death?"

Sam hesitated but only for a moment. "I have a basketball game with Dave tonight. I'll talk to him then and I'll give you a report in the morning."

Hal's eyes narrowed as he glared at Sam. "No. You'll give me a report later tonight."

CHAPTER NINE

1

St. Louis, Missouri

Joe parked the Laclede gas company van in front of the house. Flipping open the file on the seat beside him, he checked the number, making sure he had the right place. *Two thirty seven.* This was it.

Before stepping from the van, he glanced back at the unconscious driver, adjusting the slightly too tight jumpsuit he now wore. The man had been the closest to his size he could find in the immediate area. He would be out for at least another hour, possibly longer. The drug he had used on the man was not harmful, just effective.

Pushing his door open, he glanced up the street. No other cars in the area, no one out walking their dog or taking an afternoon jog. Just Joe. Yet as he strolled toward the house, trying to seem as casual as was possible, he couldn't shake the feeling that he was being watched.

He walked through the open gate into the yard virtually unnoticed. Crouching down in back of the house, he fiddled with the outdoor meter, checking over his shoulder every few minutes, just to be sure.

As he worked, he caught glimpses of his next target,

Tom Hardigan, through the back window. The house had a casual, open design to it. Joe could see from one end to the other. Hardigan sat in the living room, in front of a computer, typing. He stopped every few moments to write on the pad of paper beside him or chew absently on the end of the pen he held.

The child genius all grown up, Joe thought, watching the thirty-something young man. This hit was going to be more difficult. His victim wasn't some anonymous face. Joe knew who Tom Hardigan was. Most people did. Child prodigy responsible for several of the world's leading computer systems including Computech Worldwide. And that knowledge broke Joe's first rule: Know nothing about the target.

He didn't like it.

It felt wrong.

Everything felt wrong after last night.

In an instant, the image of the woman who had been in his room the night before, flashed through his mind in crystal clarity. And with that image, came the memory of her smell—sweet, cloying, seemingly harmless—but very possibly lethal.

And that was the problem. He just wasn't sure. Logic told him that he was being set up. But in the back of his mind, he just wasn't sure.

The woman had not threatened him, had not made any move to stop him. She had just been there—watching. But why?

A bead of sweat rolled down the side of his head. He glanced up at the sun. It was a sweltering day and he'd never been crazy about the heat. He'd be glad to get back in his car and leave this place. Glancing into the house, he watched as Hardigan rose from his seat and headed toward the kitchen. As he drew nearer, Joe knew it was time to make his move.

He pulled his cap down lower over his eyes, checked the fake I.D. one last time and gripped the 9-mm in his hand.

2

Hartwick, Michigan

Ken Brewer stood over the still form of the dog where it lay in the high grass. The animal's open eyes stared blankly. Its paws, raw and red with some bone showing through, looked gnawed on. Pieces were missing, torn away as if it had chewed on its own feet.

"Looks fresh."

Ken shifted his gaze to the man who knelt beside the animal. Frank Paulinsky. One of six men Ken had hand picked for this job.

They'd been at the wooded lot behind the Brayden house for almost three hours. None of the men working in the neighborhood wore the telltale blue jumpsuits with the Envirospace logo on the pocket. Instead, each wore plain, brown coveralls.

Upon their arrival, he had sent two of the men into the subdivision. They were instructed to go door to door, ask everyone to stay out of the woods, explain that they were doing a survey and would appreciate cooperation for the next two days.

Answer as few questions as possible.

He had divided the wooded lot into three sections. The remaining men were canvasing the other areas, searching for contaminated sections. So far, none had sprung up.

He turned his attention back to the man crouched beside the dog. Paulinsky pulled a long rod from a bag beside him. He prodded the animal's body, pushing the rod deeply into the flesh. Then slowly, he lifted the hound up and looked beneath.

"No sign of decomposition." He glanced over his shoulder at Ken. "Could have died earlier today. Once I get it to a lab, I can run some tests, tell you more."

"I want a full report by tomorrow morning." Ken walked back toward the subdivision. He had the situation under control. His men were working quickly and efficiently. The people in the neighborhood seemed cooperative. No one had come nosing around. But it would all be for nothing if they couldn't handle the problem with David.

Reaching the edge of the woods, he ducked beneath the yellow caution tape they had strung from tree to tree blocking off all paths into and out of the forest. His gaze immediately came to rest on the back of the Brayden house. And the woman who stood in the yard, arms crossed over her chest, staring at the trees. The same woman who had watched them when they first arrived from behind the blinds of her kitchen. Who was she? How was she connected to Leah Brayden? The questions ricocheted through his mind as her gaze locked with his. In that instant, he thought she might come over, ask what was going on.

Come on, he silently challenged. It'd be the perfect opportunity for him to get the information they needed, information Sam Wyatt had yet to uncover.

"Mr. Brewer?"

Ken turned to Paulinsky behind him.

"I just talked to Winters. He believes he's found a possible temporary site. He'd like to speak with you."

Ken nodded once before looking back toward the Brayden house. But the woman was no longer in sight. A moment later, a car backed down the driveway and into the street. He watched until the woman drove from view.

As far as he was concerned, the woman was as much a problem as David. He needed to come up with a solution for both of them.

3

Kelsey steered her car through the subdivision, heading toward Eve's private drive. Even here, this far from the house, she could see the yellow caution tape.

How large an area had they blocked off?

As she'd stood in her yard, watching the men at the edge of the trees, she'd been tempted to talk with them, ask them exactly what was going on.

Her eyes flicked to the rearview mirror. The road behind her was empty. She shook her head. What had she expected to see?

But she knew what. Or rather who.

The bald man. The one who seemed in charge. The one who had been watching her house so closely all afternoon. She had wanted to talk to someone but not him. The skin on the back of her neck prickled even now as she thought about him. The way he looked at her, the way he seemed to be scrutinizing her. Even when she peeked out from behind the blinds, she'd seen him watching the house.

But it wasn't just him.

The cars they'd arrived in had no logos painted on the sides, they wore no name tags, had nothing that would identify them.

Why didn't they want people to know they were from Envirospace? At least that's who she assumed they were. But if it was Envirospace, where was David? Why wasn't he out here running the show?

She turned into Eve's drive. She would phone David. As soon as she got back to Leah's, she would call him at work and ask him to fill her in.

Stopping her car, she stared at Eve's small house. At least this trip to the doctor would give her some peace of mind. She would take Eve to the doctor and he would tell her that Eve's rash was just that, a simple rash, nothing to be too concerned about. Then she could relax, at least as far as Eve's problem was concerned. Once she received reassurance, she could concentrate on something other than every small itch and scratch she felt along her body.

She pushed her door open and headed toward the house. As she drew near, she noticed a car pulled along the side of the house. Midsized sedan. Michigan plates. Nothing unusual. But it had not been there this morning.

Stepping up on the porch, she raised her hand to knock. But the door opened before she could rap on the hard wood.

The man who stood just beyond the threshold wore the same brown coveralls as the other men she had seen earlier in her subdivision.

"Can I help you?" he asked, his gaze traveling over Kelsey.

She took a step back, startled by the man's presence. "I've come to see Eve . . . Mrs. Forrester." And glancing back at her car added, "I'm driving her to an appointment."

The man nodded, his face taking on a serious look. "How well did you know Mrs. Forrester?"

"Know?" she repeated, her voice choking on the past tense of the sentence. She cleared her throat. "Not well."

Stepping outside the house, he pulled the door closed behind him. "I'm sorry to have to tell you this but Mrs. Forrester . . ." He paused, seeming to search for the right thing to say. "I found her collapsed on the floor."

"No," Kelsey said, finding it difficult to breathe. "She's okay?"

"I'm sorry, no. She died before help arrived."

"How?" Heat rushed through her body. She swayed where she stood.

The man took her arm, steadying her. "We don't know yet. But her family's been notified."

Kelsey stared down at his hand where it held her. "Notified?" she whispered.

He spoke again but Kelsey did not hear him. Her gaze was locked on his hand, feeling it there, touching her exposed skin. Just as Eve's hand had only a few hours earlier.

Just a bit of a rash.

Eve had touched her.

And now she was dead.

Kelsey jerked away from his touch, taking several steps back.

"Miss?" His brow creased. "Are you all right? Should I call someone?"

A breeze blew up, rustling up Kelsey's body, caressing her skin. She could feel the woods behind her, pressing in on her.

"Miss?" The man took a step toward her.

"Don't touch me!" she shouted. Turning, she fled to her car.

4

Sam stood in the production hub of Envirospace—first floor, administration building. His entire system ran from this end of the building. Computers monitored packaging, communication, satellite hookups, everything.

It was his greatest achievement and now possibly his biggest downfall.

How had he gotten himself involved in this mess?

He could still remember six years ago when he was approached by Ken Brewer. A simple job. Upgrade the system. But it had become so much more than that and now he saw no way out.

He could tell the truth. Tell David what they had done to him, to Hillary and Leah.

But it wasn't just him. He had to think about the others, the people he had brought in on this project. His team.

Hal Ebersol had made it clear that the records reflected Sam and his team were the sole culprits, duping Envirospace into this mess. How could he disrupt the lives of so many people? Friends. Colleagues. Business acquaintances. Each with a family, a life that he could not destroy. Not when he still had other options to explore. He shook his head. No. The truth was not a choice.

He'd talk to David, see what he knew. Then make his

decision. What happened to Hillary was an accident. And Leah . . . Leah had always been a little unstable, hadn't she? David was at no risk. As long as he didn't know the truth, he was safe, Sam was safe, life could go on smoothly.

Turning, he headed toward the stairs and the third floor. As he walked up the heavy, iron steps, his shoes echoing through the stairwell, he tried not to think about what he had to do tonight. Instead, he reminded himself that in the end, he was protecting David, just as he had before.

That thought was still running through his mind as he stopped outside David's office. He knocked on the door before opening it and stepping inside.

David sat at his desk typing on his computer terminal. He did not look up as Sam entered, did not acknowledge him as he sat down in the seat across from him. Instead, he continued to type at a fast pace.

"Should I come back?" he asked. David said nothing. "Hello?" Still no response and as Sam sat waiting to be acknowledged, he wondered if David even realized he was in the room.

"Dave?" he said louder, worry just beginning to gnaw at his belly. "Dave, do you hear me?"

Slowly, David turned to face him, his eyes finding Sam. *His eyes.*

Sam stared into them. Something about his eyes. The look. Where had he seen it before? And then it struck him. Leah. A few days before she—

"David!" He rose from his chair.

"Sam?" David blinked several times, his brow furrowing. "What's going on?" His gaze swept from the door, to Sam, to his computer screen and stayed there. The crease in his brow deepened.

"What's wrong?" Sam started around the desk.

Reaching out, David clicked off the screen. It went black. "Nothing," he said quickly. "Everything's fine."

Sam stared down at him. "Are you sure?"

David leaned back in his chair. "I'm fine."

Sam wanted to believe him, needed to. *It wasn't supposed to affect him. It wasn't supposed to affect any of them.* He sat back down, telling himself that he was just overreacting, reading things into David's behavior that simply were not there. He needed to concentrate on the task at hand—getting the information Hal Ebersol requested. And as he continued to watch David, he decided he did look fine, normal as ever. "You about ready to go?"

"Go?" David's brow wrinkled in confusion. "Go where?"

"Basketball. We have a game tonight."

"But that's . . ." His sentence dropped off as he glanced down at his watch. "Six o'clock," he whispered.

"You're not ready?"

"No." David's confusion seemed to deepen. "I didn't realize . . . I guess I lost track of the time." He sorted through the papers on his desk. "I can't go. I'm still trying to finish this damn proposal."

"Finish it tomorrow." Sam's stomach churned. In his mind, he could see Hal Ebersol glowering at him when he told him he had nothing to report. He could not afford to come up empty. Not again. "It'll still be here."

"I haven't made much headway." David glanced up at him, the look on his face telling Sam there was no changing his mind. "It can't wait."

Sam nodded. "Next week." The conversation was over. Sam knew it. More importantly, David knew it. Sam needed a way of opening up the conversation again. A way of finding out what he needed to find out without being too obvious. And as Sam continued to sit in his chair, staring at his friend, saying nothing more, the silence grew uncomfortable.

"So," he began, his mind racing. "Word through the grapevine is that you found a genuine environmentally damaged piece of property," he finished, happy with the results of his ad-lib.

"Seems that way." David ran a hand through his hair.

Sam tried not to notice how his fingers shook. "I wish I still had the pictures of that place. I'll tell you, they didn't do it justice. It was damn eerie."

"Maybe when you're done here, we could go there," he suggested, even more pleased as he continued to improvise. "You could give me the grand tour of the site. Show me where it all began."

David shook his head. "I'm going to be here late."

"I don't mind waiting."

"From the way this report is going, that could be to-morrow morning." David smiled for the first time since Sam entered the office. But there was a tiredness behind the smile that Sam didn't like.

He wanted to stop, let his friend finish his work, get home, get some sleep. But he still did not have what he needed. Maybe if he could report to Hal Ebersol that David would no longer be a threat, then this whole thing could be dropped. He would no longer have to play spy.

Taking a deep breath, he continued with his interrogation. "I heard this place is out behind Leah's house." He paused. He needed to be careful, phrase this question just the right way or David would simply close himself off. "How did you find it? You didn't go to Leah's did you? I thought you were going to try and put all stuff this behind you."

David shifted where he sat, his gaze not meeting Sam's. "That's what you thought I should do. But I can't."

An uneasiness stole over him. This was exactly what he did not want to hear. "Dave—"

"Sam, I can't just walk away," he snapped. His eyes locked on Sam. They burned with a determination he had never seen before. "Even you have to admit something's wrong with the situation in the woods behind Leah's house. There's something going on. And I'm going to find out what."

And Sam knew as he stared at his friend that that was exactly what David planned to do. He was going to continue down the path he had chosen, continue to look into Leah's death no matter what it cost him.

"How'd you find the damage?" he asked, when no other question came to mind.

David sighed. "It's a long story."

Sam could tell by the way he said it, that David did not want to tell it. He tensed. This was what he needed. And he knew it wouldn't take much prodding on his part to get David to talk. "Thanks to you, I have nowhere else to go."

David looked at him and in that moment, Sam was sure he was simply going to tell him he didn't have the time, maybe tomorrow or even over the weekend. But not now. His hesitation seemed like an eternity.

David took a deep breath. Glanced once at his watch. Leaned back in his chair. Finally spoke. "Kelsey's really the one who showed it to me."

Sam's guilt deepened. David wasn't going to try and rush him out the door. He was, instead, going to take the time he didn't have and fill his friend in on what was going on.

"Kelsey?" he repeated the name, shaking his head, knowing David would supply what he needed.

"Leah's sister."

Sister! The word struck Sam with an intensity he could not have anticipated. He tried his best to conceal his shock. He should have known . . . guessed. This changed everything. This woman was not some outside observer. She had a personal stake in this matter. She would not easily be stopped. And neither would David.

"I didn't know Leah had a sister," he managed, his voice somehow retaining its normalcy.

"Neither did I until the funeral. We had dinner last night."

"What's she like?"

"You'd like her." David's voice took on a reflective tone. "She's like Leah in a lot of ways but . . ." He trailed off not finishing the sentence.

"But what?" Sam pressed, needing to find out as much

about this woman as he could.

"She's stronger than Leah was. I see what Leah could have been. She . . ." He stopped. Sitting back in his chair, he stared up at the ceiling. "I can't believe I just said that," he whispered.

Sam remained silent. *Stronger than Leah.* Those were not exactly the words he had wanted to hear. "Are you going to see her again?"

David shook his head. "I don't know. With all this work . . ." He trailed off. "I don't know."

"I'd like to meet her. I always liked Leah."

"Sure." David shrugged noncommittally.

Sam nodded. He had nothing more to ask, nothing more to say. He knew he should leave. After all, he'd gotten what he needed, hadn't he? But he couldn't leave. Not yet. David looked tired, almost ill. Was it a result of the stress of the last few days? Or was it because of what they had done to him?

"Dave, are you sure everything's okay?" he asked before he could stop himself. He knew he was treading on dangerous ground. But he had to know.

"I . . ." David's gaze darted to the blank computer screen, then back to Sam. "I . . ." He stopped again, his voice filled with uncertainty.

"What?" he pressed.

Slowly, David looked up. His gaze locked with Sam's. Turmoil swirled behind his eyes. Sam leaned forward, silently urging David to tell him exactly what was twisting around in his mind. But David's mouth clamped shut, his eyes darted away.

In an instant, he closed himself off.

His gaze fell back on the papers on his desk and stayed there. "I've got a lot of work here," he said when Sam continued to sit and stare at him.

"Dump this stuff." Sam indicated the mess on David's desk. "Let's just go play some basketball." And in that moment, that was all he really wanted to do. Just play the game. Maybe if David said yes, Sam could forget about everything that had happened over the last few days. Maybe he could even bring himself to tell David the truth. Explain what his father had done to him. Help him.

"I can't." David's words cut off Sam's thoughts. Cut off any hope he had of changing future events.

He stood, nodding wearily. "Guess I'll let you get back to work then." Deep down, he had known David would say no, had known he could never really change things. Because at some point tonight, he had to go to Hal Ebersol. Report his findings. Continue to lie to his closest friend.

5

David sat staring at the door through which Sam had just exited. He'd come so close to telling him, so close to saying . . . what? I'm seeing Leah, having nightmares, writing things I don't understand? No. He couldn't tell Sam.

I'm drowning.

The thought struck him out of the blue, shaking him to his core. Something gnawed at his mind, creating a growing sense of desperation within him. But he could not grab hold of whatever it was. He bit his lip, concentrating. It was like a dream, vivid when you first awaken but growing more and more dim as the day wore on.

His gaze moved to the computer. He didn't want to look, didn't want to know. But he had no choice. Reaching out, afraid to touch it, he turned the machine back on. In a flash, the writing on the screen reappeared. Top to bottom, every available space was filled with the random 1's and 0's.

He did not remember doing any of it.

He had no idea what it meant.

Slowly, he began to page through the numbers. One after the other flew by his screen. Twenty-seven pages in all. He leaned back in his chair. How long had he been sitting in front of the computer doing this?

He shook his head. Between the stress of the funeral, his lack of sleep and the pressure of this new project, he just had too much on his mind. He was letting his thoughts wander out of control. He had to concentrate, refocus, regroup and everything would be fine. His father expected him to turn in a proposal tomorrow and he was determined to do just that. He erased the numbers from his screen.

Standing, he crossed the room and withdrew a file from the cabinet beside the door. He slammed the drawer shut, catching his hand in the process. ''Dammit!'' he yelled, as pain laced up his arm.

He struggled. They twisted his arm behind his back.

He stared at his throbbing hand. Saw two of them.

They dragged him upstairs. Strapped him in.

His vision blurred. He swayed where he stood.

''What?'' His knees buckled. He fell into one of the chairs that flanked his desk.

''I'm all right,'' he told himself, repeating the words over and over, the loud ringing in his ears drowning out the sound of his own voice. He leaned forward in the chair, willing the dizziness to pass.

Maybe she touched something and it affected her.

Kelsey's words from the night before skidded through his mind. ''It doesn't happen that fast,'' he muttered, trying to reassure himself. But why had he spent the day typing number combinations he did not understand? Why was he even now having a hard time concentrating?

He ran a hand over his face, unable to come up with any reasonable answer. Was he losing his mind? Could whatever have affected Leah now be affecting him? Would he wind up standing in a road—

No! It simply was not possible. Yet he needed to talk to someone, tell someone.

Kelsey.

His gaze shifted to his desk top. The report could wait— he could not. He needed to talk to someone before he lost control completely.

CHAPTER TEN

1

Hal stood in the control room of the prelaunch building watching the automation system beyond the glass. Each day, garbage was trucked in, compacted down, and packaged into barrels made on site out of recycled materials. Using an automation system, the barrels were then stacked into Envirolift One. When the ship was filled, the building split in two, the western wall slowly moving out, allowing the ship to be towed to the launch area. Once in position, the system, automatically again, launched the ship toward its destination. Everything was completely preprogrammed, requiring only small modifications over the last six years.

As he watched the barrels being stacked inside the ship, Hal shook his head. It still amazed him. His dream, a reality. And as he continued to stand and stare at his creation, he couldn't help but think about Otto Braisen. He could still remember afternoons as a child, sitting at his father's knee, listening to Otto as he talked about his theories on propulsion.

But it had been Hal, not his father, who contacted the man nearly twenty years later and asked him to put his theories into practice.

Otto had been sixty-seven when Hal hired him. Seventy-six when the first ship was ready to be tested. Dead by the time Envirospace opened for business.

It had been Otto Braisen's propulsion system alone that had made Envirospace a reality. Without his revolutionary system, the company would not have been economically feasible.

Even now, all these years later, Hal still enjoyed watching the whole process. Each month, a few days before launch, Hal came down to the observation center and watched his creation in action. He liked listening to the clicks and beeps of the computer as it put the system through its programs. It was a beautiful sight, clean and efficient.

He'd been standing, watching it for nearly two hours now, thinking about David, Edward and all the other problems that seemed to be piling up. He wished he could dispose of them as easily as he disposed of the garbage.

His back stiffened. None of them understood. None of them appreciated his genius. He had devised a way of cleaning up the planet but instead of thanking him, they wanted to condemn him.

Sam Wyatt approached from behind, his reflection clearly displayed in the glass before Hal. He was no better. Because of his incompetence, Hal could be exposed to a potentially damaging lawsuit. Or worse.

"What did you find out?" he asked as Sam stopped beside him.

He glanced all around before speaking. "The woman at the house is Kelsey Brayden, Leah Brayden's sister."

Hal nodded. He had expected as much. "When is he planning on seeing her again?"

"Not until he has that proposal done for you. He gave me the impression that he'd be here most of the night working."

"Good." David was distracted. At least for the moment. "The sister. How deeply is she involved?"

"She's the one who found the damage to the woods,"

Sam offered, his voice uncertain.

"That tells me nothing," Hal snapped. "Is she questioning her sister's death or just here to clean out the house?"

"I don't . . . I'm not sure."

"But you're going to find out."

Sam nodded weakly.

"Why doesn't that reassure me?" Hal continued to watch the younger man in the glass before him. Their talk was over. He expected him to leave. But he did not. "Is there something else?" he asked, his voice brusque.

Sam shifted where he stood. Ran a hand through his hair. Hesitated. "I'm worried."

"You should be worried."

For the first time, Sam turned and faced him directly. "Not about myself. It's Dave. He seemed . . . unfocused."

Hal inhaled deeply. He did not want to waste his time on this. "It's been a busy week for him."

"Leah Brayden killed herself," Sam continued quickly. "Tonight when I was in Dave's office, he had that same look she had just before . . ." He glanced around again, making sure they were alone. He lowered his voice. "What if he does the same thing?"

Hal stood for several moments, thinking. If David were on the edge, that was not good. He didn't need that kind of attention on top of everything else. "Contact Dr. Pearson."

"But . . ." Sam hesitated, shifting again. "We had little success with the first treatment. With what happened to the two women . . ." He let the sentence fall away. "You know what Pearson said about the odds of a second treatment working. Dave—"

"I didn't ask for your opinion," Hal interrupted, still watching him in the glass reflection.

"After what happened to Hillary West, I—"

"Mr. Wyatt." Hal turned to face him full on. "We are in this mess because of your incompetence. Do you really believe I will now take your opinion over my own?"

"But it didn't work!"

"Something has to be done," Hal said, speaking over Sam. "Explain the situation. Tell the doctor I want him here by the weekend." He turned back to the processing area. "We have a launch in three days," he said as the system continued to beep and click. "I want this problem solved before then."

2

David pulled into Leah's driveway and cut the engine. Glancing out his window, he could see the tape blocking off the woods strung from tree to tree.

At least no one else would be exposed.

Stepping from his car, he headed toward the house. A light wind blew up, tugging at his clothes. David stopped. He cocked his head to one side and listened. For a moment, off in the distance, carried on the soft wind, he had thought he heard . . . chainsaws. He waited, straining to hear the far off buzz again. Silence. Just the sound of leaves blowing in the wind, the birds singing in the trees.

"Now I'm hearing things," he muttered, shaking his head.

He stepped up on the porch. Kelsey answered on the third knock.

"Are you okay?" he asked as soon as he saw her. Her eyes looked red, swollen. Had she been crying?

She headed back inside, never speaking a word.

"Kelsey," he said, following her. "What's wrong?"

She stood with her back to him, hugging herself. "Eve's dead."

David stared at her shoulders, trying to comprehend what she had just said, trying to think of something to say in response. "How?" It was the only thing that came to mind, the only question he could think to ask.

She remained with her back to him. "I don't know."

David took a step closer. "What happened?"

And slowly, she turned to face him. The fear he saw in her eyes made him wish for a moment that she had not turned around.

"Kelsey" He reached toward her.

"I don't think you should touch me." She backed away, wiping at her eyes as a few stray tears found their way out.

He stepped closer. "I just wanted to—"

"Don't touch me!" she shouted.

David backed up several steps. "What the hell is going on?"

"I'm sorry." She touched her lips with a shaky hand. "I didn't mean to shout."

"Just tell me what's wrong?"

"I saw Eve this morning." She paused as if trying to gather her thoughts. "She had a rash." She pointed to her forearm. "Here, running up the side. It was covered when I arrived but I could see some redness showing through."

She stopped then, staring down at her own arm, rubbing the exposed skin.

"And?" he prompted when she did not continue.

She looked at him, her eyes intense. "She said she got it in the woods." She bit her lip as it quivered. "Leah was in the woods. Leah is dead. Eve was in the woods. She's dead." She paused again. "I've been in the woods," she whispered.

And finally, he understood. "Kelsey." He stepped closer. "There's nothing wrong with you," he said, trying to mask his own uncertainty.

She shook her head. "You don't know that."

And as she took several more steps back from him, her hands running the length of her arms, her eyes wide with fear, he knew he could not tell her about his day.

"I was in the woods too." He extended his arms forward, showing them to her. "Do you see any rash?"

"Not yet," she mumbled.

"Leah's death was not caused by some rash," he insisted. "Your sister was hit by a car. She took her own life."

"But why?" Kelsey asked. "I can't stop thinking about that. Even after last night. I keep asking myself—did Leah kill herself because she knew she'd contracted something horrible in those woods?" She began crying again, the tears running down her face. She turned away from David, her hands covering her eyes.

Going to her, he grabbed her shoulders, steadying her, trying to give her strength. After only a moment, he turned her to face him. "I saw Leah," he said, his voice filled with resolve. "She had no rash. And Eve . . . Eve was old. She had a mild stroke a year and a half ago. Don't drive yourself crazy thinking you're going to die because of something in those woods."

"But what—"

"How do you feel?" he asked, cutting off her question before she even got it out.

"How . . . ?" she floundered, swallowing hard. "I feel fine but that—"

"No headaches? No dizzy spells?" She shook her head. "Trouble concentrating?" And as he spoke, he began to wonder who he was asking for—Kelsey or himself?

"No. Nothing like that."

"Then what are you worried about?" He kept his voice light. But inside, his gut twisted. *Kelsey's fine. What's wrong with me?*

"If it'll make you feel better," he began, barely able to keep the tremor out of his voice. "I'll make an appointment with my doctor tomorrow for both of us. We can go in and have blood tests, saliva, the whole disgusting works."

She nodded, even managing to smile a little. "I think that's a good idea."

"Okay. That's what we'll do." He smiled back at her, mentally calculating how many hours he would have to wait, how many more hours he would have to wonder. "Until then, there's no sense worrying."

''Okay.'' She sniffed, wiping at her nose. ''I need a tissue,'' she whispered.

He waited until she was gone before turning toward the back of the house. Slowly, he walked to the window. With trembling fingers, he drew the blinds open. His gaze locked on the trees that sat on the edge of the property.

What the hell is in the woods?

3

Sam steered his car down familiar streets heading toward home. He tried not to think about the events of the day. Tried, instead, to concentrate on the road before him, seeing only as far as his headlights would allow. But as each mile dropped off behind him, he found himself unable to push aside the inevitable.

Tomorrow he would have to call Dr. Pearson. Sam had been the one to bring the man in originally. It had been his solution, his way of protecting David and the others. But now he had his doubts about the man's procedures. Had his doubts about the effects.

Would David be more damaged if he received a second treatment?

You're his friend, a small voice whispered in his ear not for the first time. *Help him.* But he didn't know how. Maybe Dr. Pearson could make this all go away. Maybe this time it would work. *It won't. It'll only make things worse.* He pushed the words aside as he had done before. But each time, his guilt became more difficult to ignore.

4

David sat on the couch staring down at Kelsey's face. She lay, her head in his lap, sleeping. Exhaustion tugged at his mind but he would not rest. It had taken him nearly an hour to calm her. Now that she was finally out, he wanted to make sure she remained peaceful, serene.

He stared down at her. The curve of her lips, the way her chest rose and fell almost imperceptibly. He reached toward her hair wanting to feel it in his hands, feel the soft—

He drew back. What was he doing? What was he thinking? He shouldn't . . . couldn't have these feelings.

Not about Leah's sister.

But no matter how hard he tried to fight it, he had to admit that he found her attractive, very attractive. But it was more than that. He felt drawn to her somehow. Had felt it the first time he saw her outside Leah's funeral. He just hated to admit that he was so cold he could be attracted to the sister of the woman whose funeral he was attending.

He stared down at her. Saw her slender, tanned hand tucked under her cheek. Her face—

No! He could not think about her, not that way. He was, after all, mourning her sister's death. So was she for that matter. But somewhere in the back of his mind, a voice whispered very quietly, *"Are you sure you are?"* He wanted to scream out yes. I miss Leah. I wish she were still alive. And he did.

But he did not think he felt the depth of pain he would have expected after losing someone. And his feelings for Kelsey were strong, so much stronger than anything he'd ever felt for Leah. .

5

The dream began in the darkness of the woods. Kelsey stood beneath the trees. They slammed into one another, whipping in the wind. Pieces of bark and branches fell all around her, the trees showering her with their dead limbs.

Covering her head, she raced through the woods, trying to find her way home. But each path, every twist and turn, always ended at Eve's. She stood unwilling, yet fascinated, in front of the house. It loomed toward her. Dark. Deserted. But beckoning.

Upstairs, a light snapped on. A beacon in the dark night. Kelsey stared at it, felt it drawing her toward it. She moved forward. But her steps dragged, each more difficult than the last. She looked down. The ground had turned to mud, sucking her feet deeper with every step. She struggled forward, her breath rasping in and out from effort.

Eve's door opened as she approached and Kelsey fell inside, landing hard. Grunting, pulling herself to her feet, she looked around. Shadows reached toward her. A sour, rancid smell permeated the air.

"Kel-sey." Her name drifted from above.

Kelsey's heart slammed against her ribs, stealing her breath. "Leah," she whispered, somehow feeling her sister near.

"She's upstairs."

Kelsey jerked toward the voice behind her. A figure stood in the darkness.

"Eve?" But before she could take a step toward the darkened figure, a hand shot out. Webbed fingers, covered in red blisters that oozed with a green liquid, pointed at the stairs behind her.

Kelsey took a step back, wanting desperately to block out the images before her. Shaking her head, she turned and fled up the stairs. The hall above stood empty, each side lined with doors. She tried the handles. But they were all locked. At the far end of the hall, one door stood open. Kelsey moved toward it, unable to stop her forward progression.

Inside, a figure lay on a bed, covered with a sheet. Kelsey stood over the body, staring down, knowing her sister lay beneath.

Fingers trembling, she reached out and pulled the sheet back. Her breath locked in her throat, her screams unable to break free as she stared in horror at what had once been her sister.

Leah lay on her back, unseeing eyes wide open. Her body, covered with scales, writhed, small hands growing from her shoulders, stomach, chest, from every inch of exposed flesh. They grew at an accelerated rate. Sprouting from her skin, reaching upward and then shriveling and dropping off. Kelsey's gaze shifted to her feet. Hundreds of the discarded hands lay around her, some still wriggling with life. She backed away, crunching through the shriveled hands that littered the floor.

''No.'' She shook her head, wanting to deny what her eyes were witnessing. ''This can't be!'' she screamed.

Something squirmed beneath her shirt, wriggling against her skin. Horrified, she looked down. A hand emerged from between the buttons of her shirt, twisting, growing larger and longer. Another sprung from her shoulder, extending down her back.

She felt them all over now. Sprouting. Growing. Dying. She slapped at them, wrenching left, right, trying to free herself. They tangled in her hair. Ripped at her clothes. ''Help—''

''—me!'' Kelsey jerked awake, her hands slapping at the growths she still felt all over her body. ''Help me!'' The hands held on, preventing her from leaving. She struck out, hitting flesh and heard a grunt.

''Kelsey, stop. Stop!''

She turned toward the voice, hands still striking, and found herself staring at . . . ''David?''

''It's okay. You're okay.'' His quiet voice soothed her.

She stared at him, at the room around her, as the reality of the situation slowly sank in. ''A nightmare,'' she murmured, hugging herself, telling herself to calm down, it was only a dream.

''Damn good one, I'd say.'' He sat beside her, his arm around her shoulder, holding her, calming her, keeping her safe.

She looked at him. His left cheek red, his hair disheveled. "I'm so sorry." She reached toward him but her hand stopped before touching him. "Did I do that?"

David nodded, running a hand through his hair in an attempt to put it back in place. "No harm done."

She wiped at her eyes, realizing she must have been crying.

"Do you want to talk about it?" He rested his hand on her back and began to gently rub.

"I was dreaming . . . about Leah." Suddenly, she felt uncomfortable, so close to this man. Her sister's ex-lover. She stood, pacing away from him. "But I don't want to talk about it."

"I understand," he said. "I've had a few of my own since this whole thing started."

His words stopped her. She turned to face him. "You've had nightmares?"

"Several," he admitted. "Especially the last few nights."

"It they were anything like mine, then you have my sympathy."

For a moment, they just stared at each other. His eyes locked with hers. She wanted to tell him how much he had helped her tonight. How she couldn't have gotten through the evening without him. But just as before, she didn't feel comfortable, couldn't find the words.

In the end, it was David who finally broke the silence. "I should be going."

She glanced at the clock. "Is that right?" she asked, stunned by the lateness of the hour.

He nodded, checking his own watch to be sure.

"I'm sorry. I didn't mean to keep you here this late. I shouldn't have fallen asleep."

"You needed the rest."

She looked at him, into his eyes. They looked tired, unfocused. "You look like you could use some rest too."

"I'm fine." But as he leaned back against the couch, his eyes drifted closed.

"David." She spoke quietly, not wanting to startle him.

"Hmm," he muttered, his eyes still shut.

"What are we doing?"

"What do you mean?" he asked, the words slightly distorted as he tried to stifle a yawn.

"I mean, what are we doing? What do we hope to accomplish?"

Opening his eyes, he leaned forward, his hands resting on his thighs. He blinked, his eyelids moving slowly, as if even that made him more tired. "I thought we were looking for the truth."

She nodded. "But it's become more than that. We're on the verge of something big. Something neither of us counted on. Something . . . dangerous." She paused but only for a moment. "I'm scared. I don't know what I expected to find when I came here but this is not it."

"This what? We haven't found anything."

"What about the woods?"

"We've been over this already. We don't know if it has any connection at all to Leah."

"But what if it does?" As she waited for him to answer, she silently wished she could just go home. Drive back to Minneapolis. Go back to the way things were before she came here. Forget about her sister. Forget about the squirrel and the dead part of the woods.

"Kelsey, everything will be all right." He spoke the words with quiet assurance. And with that one simple sentence, a sentence he spoke with such certainty, he managed to alleviate some of her fear. "I'll make you a deal. I'll worry about the dead part of the woods. I'll handle the squirrel, the cleanup, everything connected with it. You just finish reading Leah's diary. Who knows? Maybe all our answers are in that book."

She nodded, the suggestion sounding good to her. Maybe once she finished her sister's journal, it would reveal that

Leah was having emotional problems. Problems that caused irrational behavior that resulted in her suicide. Then Kelsey could leave. The problem in the woods would be David's to deal with. He would ask Envirospace to clean it up and she wouldn't even have to be here. "Okay. You've got a deal."

"Good. I'm glad that's settled." He leaned back again, his eyes closing before his head touched the back of the couch.

She stared down at him. His chest rose and fell slowly, rhythmically. He was close to falling asleep. She needed to send him home before he did. But she really didn't want to be alone tonight.

Would he stay over?

She was sure he would if she asked. But did she really want that?

Crossing the room, she stood at the window and stared out at the back of the yard. The trees were shrouded in darkness. What secrets were hidden out there? What would they find?

She turned back toward David. He lay half-asleep on the couch, looking so peaceful, so vulnerable. And in that moment, she knew that no matter what she found in the diary, she could not leave him here to handle all of this alone.

CHAPTER ELEVEN

1

Louis opened the door for Hal Ebersol, allowing him entry into the house. "Dinner will be ready in less than an hour," he said, accepting the man's coat.

"Thank you, Louis." Hal headed toward the library but stopped before reaching it. "Louis," he said, turning to face him. "I'd like to talk to you for a moment."

Louis nodded appropriately as he hung up the coat. "Of course, sir." He followed Hal into the library, closing the door behind him.

Something must be wrong in the household. The only time Mr. Ebersol talked to Louis was when he was unhappy with one of the staff or the way the meals were being prepared. Louis had a feeling it was the new groundskeeper. The man was just not doing the job.

Hal sat down heavily in one of the leather chairs, automatically grabbing the cigar box. Louis stood before him, waiting.

"Louis," Hal began, running the cigar under his nose. "How long have you worked for me?"

Louis tensed. Was he going to be fired? "Almost thirty-five years, sir."

Hal nodded. "David is thirty."

"Yes, sir," he said, not understanding why that was important.

"What do you think of my son?" he asked.

Louis was taken off guard. In all the years he'd worked for Hal Ebersol, the man had never asked his opinion about anything, much less David. He simply expected Louis to do his job like any other worker and not interfere in his life. Until today. "I think David is a fine man." And it was true. He'd watched David grow up, spending countless hours with him, helping him with school work, listening to him talk about the girls he was dating, often making Louis wish he had had children of his own.

"He's having some problems," Hal said lighting the cigar. "I'm worried about him." But he did not sound worried at all. His manner was casual, calculated. He turned to Louis, his gaze penetrating. "Don't you agree?"

Images flashed through Louis's mind. It was raining that night, pouring. The sound of the yelling almost drowned out by the pounding rain. Almost but not quite. "I'm not sure I know what you mean, sir," Louis said, trying not to think about that night.

"If something were to happen to him," Hal continued, blowing a smoke ring. It drifted above him for a moment before dissolving. "You wouldn't be too surprised, would you?"

Louis went cold. "What are you saying, sir?"

Hal looked directly at him. "I just want to establish with you that you're aware of David's erratic behavior and would not be shocked if something were to happen to him."

He'd been told not to come out of his room that night and he hadn't. But the screams could be heard through the whole house. And David's voice . . .

"We're in agreement, aren't we?" Hal said, waiting for an answer.

"Yes, sir," Louis whispered.

2

Going to the kitchen, carrying the diary with her, Kelsey made a cup of tea. She had come very close to asking David to stay over, stretch out on the couch for the night. But in the end, she had not. It just felt wrong. But he had made her promise before he left that she would go straight to bed. But she couldn't. Not yet. Not until she had finished reading the diary. She'd been putting it off. Afraid to read those last few days of her sister's life. But now, it was time.

Sitting at the kitchen table, she sipped her tea. She yawned loudly as she opened the diary, the words on the page blurring momentarily. As they came back into focus, she began to read. Only a few pages later, she came to an abrupt halt as she read the words on the page before her.

> I guess David is the only one I can go to at this point, the only one I can trust. Hillary is afraid. She thinks we should go right to the authorities but I want to give the company a chance before we turn over her readouts to the police.

Kelsey looked up from the words. Leah had been having trouble at work. Hillary had brought her a problem and she didn't know what to do about it.

Kelsey leafed forward looking for additional references to Envirospace, reading snatches here and there. But, abruptly, any mention of Envirospace and the problem were gone. She scanned the pages a second time. As she flipped from page to page, she realized that the dates did not match.

Leah had skipped several days in a row.

Kelsey's brow furrowed. She paged through the diary again. But as she checked each day, she only confirmed what she already knew. Leah had diligently filled out every day of the year. A few days she even wrote, nothing to say tonight—too tired.

Never once had she skipped a day.

"What happened on those three days?" she whispered.

With growing trepidation, she began reading again. This time, however, she read after the three skipped days, each page one at a time right up until the day her sister died. She had glanced through these pages earlier, had noticed the odd doodling of 1's and 0's at the end of the book. But it had all seemed harmless to her, even normal. Until now. Now she knew what her sister's life had been like. Knew what her habits had been. Knew that these pages were wrong. The penmanship was the same but everything else was different. The sentence structures, the topics, even the words she used. And there was no longer any mention of David or Hillary.

She sat at the table flipping the pages back and forth, trying to make sense of her sister's last few weeks. But as her fingers moved quickly through the pages, a piece of paper fell from the back of the book. Retrieving it, she opened the small, folded sheet. Five names were printed in Leah's hand writing across the page. Nothing more. Just the five names.

She stared at the short list: Steven Ordmann, Harvey Staller, Betty Cantor, Tom Hardigan, Ned Bringer.

She recognized none of them.

3

The ringing came from far off, tugging at his mind, dragging him up from sleep. David groaned, his eyes slowly blinking open.

He lay on his couch, still dressed, his shoes on the floor before him. The phone rang again. He glanced toward it, flinching as his neck protested the simple movement. He'd been so exhausted when he got back from Kelsey's that he'd dropped down on the couch and fallen asleep almost instantly.

Now he wished he had gone to his bed. His neck was killing him and his back felt stiff.

The phone rang again. Reaching over his head to the table beside the couch, he fumbled for the receiver, managing to pick it up just before his machine would have kicked on. "Hello?"

"David, it's me."

"Kelsey?" He squinted at his watch, trying to see the small hands, but it was too dark. "I thought you'd be asleep by now."

"I think I found something in the diary."

Her words brought him fully awake. "What? You found something?" He sat up, turning on the light beside the couch.

"Leah knew something about the company, something big." Kelsey spoke quickly, her words rushed. "Maybe what caused the damage to the woods behind her house. I don't know. But according to her diary, she was going to talk to you about it."

"Me?" He rolled his head on his shoulders, trying to release some of the tension there.

"She didn't?"

"No. Why? What exactly does she say?"

"Well, it has something to do with Hillary West."

"Hillary—"

She screamed once and was silent.

"—West?" His stomach churned. His head pounded. He wiped at the perspiration that sprang up on his forehead.

"Yes. From what I read, Hillary apparently brought a problem to my sister and dumped it in her lap."

Kelsey continued to speak but her voice sounded far off to David, as if coming from a great distance away. A fog of confusion settled over his mind, clouding his thoughts.

Hillary West. Something happened to Hillary West.

A memory bubbled to the surface of his mind. Hillary and Leah. They had a problem. They wanted his help. They—

"David!" Kelsey's voice penetrated his mind, sweeping away the memory that had been so close. "David, are you still there?"

"Yeah," he whispered, trying to remember what he had been thinking about only moments ago. But his mind was once again just a haze of jumbled thoughts.

"What's going on?" Her concerned voice rang in his ears. "Are you okay? You were so quiet. I thought the line went dead for a minute there."

"Sorry." He licked his lips, concentrating on her voice, her words. "I . . ." But he stopped himself before he said anything more. How could he explain what was happening to him when he wasn't sure himself? And after the way she reacted to Eve's death, he wasn't sure how much more she could handle. What could he say that wouldn't scare the hell out of her? "I just have a headache. What were you saying?"

"I was asking about Hillary West," she began hesitantly. "I've tried contacting her for the last few days. But so far I haven't had any luck. I was thinking—"

"Kelsey?" He squeezed his eyes shut, rubbing the area between them. The pain throbbed, intensified. "Can we do this tomorrow. I'm . . . tired."

"Sure." She paused. "Of course. I just thought—"

"I'll be over early." He gritted his teeth, working hard to get the words out. "We can talk then. Okay?"

Another brief pause. "Okay. Sorry. You get some sleep."

"I will."

"David?" she said, before he could hang up. "I wanted to thank you for being there for me earlier tonight. I was pretty upset." She was silent for a moment before adding, "You've helped me, David. You've helped me a lot."

"I'm glad," he whispered.

His hand trembled slightly as he replaced the receiver. He lay back against the couch, staring up at the ceiling. Already the pain in his head, the nausea that had twisted his gut, was subsiding. He breathed deeply, trying to relax.

"Sleep," he mumbled, trying hard to convince himself that that was all he really needed. A good night's sleep and then he'd be fine.

4

Louis walked through the darkened house. It was quiet tonight; Mr. Ebersol had already gone to bed. He liked the house at night. Often he walked through, making sure everything was in its place, ready for the next morning's activities.

He could remember when Mrs. Ebersol was still alive how much she liked to work with the staff. The house had a different feel then, a warmth it had lost since her death. The house no longer held fresh flowers, laughter no longer rang through the halls.

Louis stopped in the main room and stared up at the portrait of Claire Ebersol. It did not do her justice. The painting caught the depth of her beauty but not her heart. And he realized that that was what the house had lost—its heart.

As he stood there staring up at her face, he felt ashamed. What had he allowed to happen to her only child?

Turning away, Louis walked to the window and stared out. It was another windy night. *Just like that night.*

He had to do something. He could not turn a blind eye and pretend he did not know. If something were to happen to David, he would never forgive himself.

5

Kelsey lay in bed staring up at the ceiling. She'd been lying in bed for nearly two hours now trying to fall asleep. But each time she closed her eyes, all she could see was David, half-asleep on her couch. She should have asked him to stay. Then he would be here and she would be sure he was okay.

She glanced at the phone. He had sounded so odd when she talked to him, so distant. Almost as if he were having trouble comprehending what she was saying to him.

Outside, the wind howled around the house, whistled through the eaves. Kelsey shivered, drawing the sheet that covered her body up under her chin.

Leah had committed suicide. But had something driven her to do it? Something that confused her? Disoriented her? And was it possible that that something was now affecting David?

6

David struggled to wake from the violent nightmare. In his dream, he was being dragged into a dark room, his arm twisted painfully behind his back.

"Let go of me!" He fought against his captors. But there were too many.

"Keep him quiet," a voice called out.

"Strap him down," another yelled.

David tried to see their faces, to see his assailants as they forced him onto a bed and restrained his arms and legs. He struggled against the bindings, his watch slamming into the metal bars on the bed. The clanging echoed in the cavernous attic. "You can't do this!"

Somewhere, in another part of the room, he heard a

woman scream. He jerked toward the sound. "Stop!" he cried, seeing a struggling form on the other side of the room. They were holding her down, inserting a needle in her arm.

"Get this over with."

David turned toward the harsh voice.

A dark figure loomed over him. Fear stabbed through his body at the sight.

"Keep him quiet. We don't want to draw any attention."

David felt as if he were being smothered as something covered his face. He fought harder, his battle with his captors increasing.

He cried out, flinging his blankets from around him.

A scream.

Crawling from his bed, he pushed himself against the wall and slid down into a ball on the floor, pulling himself in tight.

His eyes rolled in their sockets, unfocused, unseeing.

"No. *No!*" He looked around, swinging his arms, trying to keep everyone away. Slowly, be began to realize where he was.

Home. Safe.

He stared into the darkness before him, trying to remember. What was he afraid of? What was he running from?

But no matter how hard he concentrated, he could not remember what had caused his panic, what it was in his dream he was so afraid of.

Pushing himself up, he wiped at the sweat on his face.

What's wrong with me? Am I losing my mind?

His eyes focused on papers scattered on the floor. Bending forward, he lifted the white sheets filled with the 1's and 0's. His hand shook rattling the papers he held.

He began gathering them up. Some from the bedroom, the kitchen, the living room. All over the house.

He dropped down on his couch, his arms full of the papers. He stared down at his handwriting. Sweat covered his body in a slick sheen. When had he written all of these? In his sleep? After work? After talking to Kelsey? He couldn't remember.

He should have told Kelsey, Sam, anyone about the numbers, the dreams, the blackouts.

Just in case . . . what? In case he killed himself?

No. He would never do that. But what about Leah? Hadn't he thought the same thing about her?

CHAPTER TWELVE

1

Kelsey was sitting on the porch when David pulled up in front of the house. As promised, he had come early. She watched him as he made his way toward her. He wore a wrinkled shirt, his hair disheveled. Dark circles stood out under his eyes.

"You look tired," she said as he stepped up onto the porch.

He ran a hand through his hair, messing it up even more. "Just having trouble sleeping."

"Same nightmares?" she asked, watching him carefully, the conversation from the night before still fresh in her mind.

"Yeah," he muttered, taking the seat beside her. "But I think we have bigger problems than that to deal with." He glanced at her out of the corner of his eye.

She met his gaze and held it. "What are you talking about?"

"I stopped by work this morning," he began. "I wanted to get an update from my team. Wanted to know what they've come up with but I can't get any information." He paused briefly before adding, "It's as if I never held a meeting yesterday."

"What about the squirrel? The pictures?"

"All gone. Just like my staff."

"Your staff?"

He nodded. "None of the people I met with yesterday were in the lab this morning. And no one there seemed to know exactly where they are. Apparently they've been gone since my meeting broke up yesterday morning. Wherever they went, they took everything with them." He stared ahead, his eyes unfocused. When he spoke again, his voice was low, almost as if he were speaking more to himself than to Kelsey. "And then there's Leah's desk."

"Leah's desk? What about her desk?"

He hesitated for a moment before answering. "I didn't tell you this yesterday, but when I went to check Leah's desk, it had already been emptied." Standing, he walked to the edge of the porch and stared at the woods with its yellow tape warning everyone to stay back. "I haven't been able to find out who cleaned it out and where her things went."

"Why would someone empty her desk?"

"There's more." He kept his back to her as he spoke. "When I was driving up, I went by Eve's road. Her drive's been blocked off. There's a chain strung across the front with a no trespassing sign on it."

"You think Envirospace put it there?"

"I don't know," he whispered. Turning, he sat on the porch railing, facing her again. "You said when you went to Eve's yesterday that you think the man who answered the door was from Envirospace."

"I think he was, yes."

"So why was he still there? If Eve collapsed earlier, why was he still at her house?"

Kelsey replayed the few moments when she had stood outside Eve's house. Now it felt . . . wrong. He had come out, shut the door behind him, as if not wanting her to see inside. "What do you want to do?"

"Do you still have that camera?"

She nodded once, slowly.

"First, I want to get more pictures of the dead part of the woods. My own pictures. And then I want to check out Eve's."

Kelsey's heart picked up a beat. "We're going back into the woods?"

"I need pictures of my own."

"But the woods?" She was just beginning to believe that she may not have contracted something horrible out there. But to go again? She wasn't sure she could. "Is that a good idea?"

"I can go alone," he offered.

She shook her head, not liking the idea of him going into those trees by himself. "I don't want that. But . . ." Her eyes darted from him to the tree line behind him. "I'm afraid." She turned away, embarrassed by her fear.

He crossed to her, sitting beside her. "You're allowed," he whispered, taking her hands in his.

She could not look at him. Instead, she studied the porch boards, staring at the knots in the wood.

"It's okay." His hands squeezed hers reassuringly. "I'll go alone. It'll only take a few minutes."

She shifted her gaze to him. "You'll be fast?"

"Very fast," he confirmed. "And I won't touch anything. I'll just take some pictures and then I'll come right back here."

Kelsey nodded. She still wasn't crazy about the idea but she saw no way of stopping him. Going inside, she quickly retrieved the camera. But as she stepped back outside, she stopped.

Once again, David stood at the far end of the porch, his back to her, watching the trees behind the house. A breeze blew up, rustling his hair, tugging at his clothes.

This could cost him everything.

The thought raced through Kelsey's mind, stopping her where she stood, rooting her to the spot. For a moment, she was struck with a great sense of danger. Danger for him.

It rippled through her, chilling her, rocking her where she stood. Did she really want to continue with this? Was it worth his life? Hers?

But could she let it go now even if she wanted to?

Kelsey took two hesitant steps forward. "David," she began but then stopped. What could she say? Go home. I've changed my mind about this whole thing.

"What?" He turned to face her when she did not continue.

Looking at him, she knew her words would mean nothing. At this point, he would go into those woods with or without her.

"Is something wrong?" he asked, when she continued to simply stand and stare at him.

"No. Nothing." She shook her head. "I . . . I have the camera." Walking to him, she handed it to him.

He checked to see how much film was left. "Be right back."

She gripped his arm stopping him. "I'm going with you."

"Kelsey—"

"I want to," she said before she could change her mind.

"Okay. If you're sure." Stepping off the porch, he headed toward the woods.

Kelsey stood for a moment, watching as he moved away. *My sister knew something and it got her killed,* she thought as she watched David draw closer and closer to the trees. She stepped off the porch, following just before he disappeared from sight.

What happens when we find out what she knew?

2

Sam moved swiftly across the parking lot, away from the science building, back to administration. It was the third stop on his search for David. After finding his office empty, his secretary told him to check research. Research told him to check science. Science told him to check with his secretary.

They had all seen him but not within the last hour or so. And Sam had the feeling that he was no longer on the grounds of Envirospace.

But he had a good idea where he might be.

He slammed through his office door and grabbed up the phone. But before he could finish dialing Leah's number, Hal Ebersol came into his office.

"Where is he?" Hal did not sit down. Instead, he stood before Sam's desk, glaring at him. Sam knew he was trying to intimidate him. And he hated to admit it was working.

"I'm trying to find out right now."

"You're supposed to know. You're supposed to be watching him."

"I have been." Sam set the phone back in its cradle. "But I can't be with him all the time."

Hal leaned on the desk. "Find out where he is and what he's doing. Now!"

3

"It's gone," David whispered as he stared at what had once been the dead part of the woods. Nothing remained. The barren trees, gray mud and dead bushes were gone. In their place was a neat clearing. The trees cut down. The ground covered with new soil. "They got rid of it." He turned in a slow circle, his fingers playing over the lens of the camera in his hands. "Yesterday . . . I heard power saws yesterday," he mumbled, trying to piece it all together in his mind.

"Have they already begun the cleanup?" Kelsey asked, keeping her distance from the clearing.

"I . . ." David fumbled for an answer. "I don't know. I guess that's possible." But if that were true, why hadn't he been informed? After all, this was supposed to be his project.

Kelsey chanced a step closer. "You still think we should go to Eve's?"

David stared at the bare clearing, still fumbling with the camera in his hand. "More than ever," he whispered.

They walked at a fast pace, moving quickly through the trees and brush. As they drew closer, David slowed his pace. Without saying a word, Kelsey matched him, staying a few steps back. Reaching the edge of the tree line surrounding Eve's house, David crouched down. Kelsey knelt beside him.

"What's wrong?" she whispered, her voice tense.

"I just want to check it out first."

They hid behind a thick stand of bushes at the edge of the trees. Slowly, carefully, David pulled back a few limbs. Eve's house became visible through the leaves. Two men stood in front of the house.

"What do you think they're doing here?" Kelsey asked, her voice a low whisper.

"I'm not sure but I have a pretty good idea." He nodded toward the men. "You see the way they're watching the woods?"

Kelsey nodded. "Like they're guarding it or something."

"That's exactly what they're doing." David raised himself up slightly as the guards scanned the area opposite his hiding place. He strained to see inside the house, looking for movement within. But the windows were dark.

"You think they're from Envirospace?" she asked.

"I'd put money on it." He crouched down beside her again.

"Look at Eve's garden," Kelsey said, directing David's gaze right. The vegetables that had been in full bloom the day before were gone. Instead, the earth had been recently turned. "It wasn't like that yesterday. Why would they ruin her garden?"

David stared at the small plot of land beside the house.

"Contamination," he whispered, the significance of the implication sending a chill down his back. "If Eve ate from that garden on a regular basis and the ground in this area is somehow contaminated then maybe that's what caused Eve's rash." He paused for a moment before continuing with the most logical assumption that came to mind. "And if Leah ate over Eve's enough, I don't know, maybe it affected her some way. I think . . ." But as he glanced at Kelsey, the words died off. She had gone white, her eyes wide. "What's wrong?"

"David." She swallowed several times as if her throat had suddenly gone dry. "We *ate* from that garden."

His heart thudded against his chest as her words sunk in. "No. I never—"

"The first day I arrived, Eve brought over a care package. Vegetables. I used those on our salad the night we barbecued."

The last few days rushed through his mind. The dreams about Leah. His visions of her. The memory lapses and blackouts. Could it all be a result of what they had eaten?

They would have to be tested, have to be checked for contaminates in their system. He'd—

Kelsey grabbed his arm, the gesture cutting off his thoughts. "Look there," she said pointing.

David changed his eye-line, following her pointing finger. "Dammit," he muttered under his breath.

Fifty yards to David's right, Greg and Teddy were moving along the brush, rustling it loudly.

"What should we do?" Kelsey's voice was tense with worry, her eyes never leaving the two young boys.

David glanced back at the guards. One of the men began walking in the direction of the two boys, his head bobbing around as he tried to see past the bushes. Teddy and Greg froze.

"I don't care how you do it," David said, his gaze locked on the guard, "but get those kids out of here." He began to stand.

Kelsey grabbed his arm and pulled him back down. "What do you think you're doing?"

"I'm going out there."

"No you're not. They'll know who you are."

The guard drew closer.

"I have no choice," he hissed.

Their eyes locked. Fear, confusion, hope all flashed within Kelsey's eyes. Neither one knew exactly what it meant to have these men out here but they were both sure it couldn't be good.

Kelsey leaned forward, kissing him gently on the cheek. "Wish me luck," she whispered in his ear.

And before he could stop her, Kelsey stood and stepped out of the brush and into the open. The guard, now only a few feet from Teddy and Greg, immediately turned, changing direction and jogged toward Kelsey.

David crouched even lower, his chest flat against the ground. He had not expected her rash behavior. If he had, he would have stopped her. He watched as the two spoke. He could not hear the words, only the sound of their muffled voices. The guard shook his head, pointing toward the drive leading back to the main road. Kelsey's voice rose in volume but her words were still unintelligible. A moment later, the guard began leading the way back to the house, Kelsey in tow. She did not turn, did not glance at the brush that concealed him, too afraid that even the slightest hint of someone else in the area would give him away.

Kelsey was ushered inside, the door slammed shut behind her. The other guard remained, his gaze locked on the trees. David did not move. His gaze shifted from the guard to the boys. As the seconds ticked by, he prayed the boys could sit still long enough for him to feel it was safe again to move.

Finally, after what seemed as eternity, the guard looked away. Then, as quietly as possible, David pushed up from the ground and picked his way through the broken twigs and weeds to Greg and Teddy. They still sat crouched both afraid to move.

David held a finger to his lips as he drew near.

"We're sorry," Greg said quietly when he was close enough.

"Let's just go," he whispered and ushered the two boys away. He glanced back once, staring at the house Kelsey had disappeared into.

As soon as they were out of the woods and back on the sidewalks of their neighborhood, both boys began talking.

"We didn't know there would be men," Greg began.

"We were just lookin' for Rebel. He's been gone since yesterday," Teddy continued.

"We thought he might have gone into Mrs. F.'s garden," Greg finished.

David smiled at the boys who were obviously shaken up from the experience. "It's okay. You didn't know but I don't want you pulling any stunts like that again." He stared at them sternly. "You boys were told to stay out of those woods."

"But we had to find Rebel," Greg said. "We thought maybe those men hurt him."

David sighed. "I know you're worried." He took the boys by the hands and began leading them home. "But you have to promise me that you'll stay away from the woods from now on."

Both boys nodded.

"What about Kelsey? Those men seemed mad when they saw her." Teddy's eyes were wide as he spoke.

David stared ahead, worry gnawing at his gut. Should he go back and see if he could help or should he wait? "She'll be fine," he muttered, praying he was right.

4

Ken stood in front of the line of monitors, his gaze moving from one screen to the next. Kitchen. Guest room. His gaze stopped on the screen that showed the happenings of the far bedroom upstairs. Several doctors, all in masks and gloves, stood around the table, the dog's body laid out before them. The dissection was going well but so far nothing concrete had shown up in his system.

"Sir?"

Ken turned toward the sound of the voice and found himself staring at Kelsey Brayden. His gaze shifted from the woman to the man who had addressed him.

Burke. Usually a good man. Ken could not understand why he had disobeyed him and allowed this woman inside the house.

"Problem, Burke?"

He nodded, glaring at the woman beside him. "This lady says she came to check on the house. Was a friend of the woman who lived here. I tried to assure her that everything is on the up and up. But before I could get a word out, she started yelling about bringing the cops out to see if we had permission to be at this house."

Ken's gaze shifted back to Kelsey. She stood before him but her attention was drawn down to the monitors behind him. She looked from one to the other finally locking on the monitor he had been observing before this interruption.

"Miss?" he said, moving slightly, blocking the monitor from her view.

Her gaze shifted back up to him. "Mrs.," she corrected. "Mrs. Beth Carver."

She lied with ease but Ken could sense a nervousness behind her cocky exterior. She was afraid, yet she had come here. For what? Just to see what they were doing? Get a look inside?

"Mr. Burke tells me you're concerned with our presence in this house."

"That's right."

"Let me assure you that we have spoken with the family and have been given full permission to use this home as long as we need to."

"What's with all the monitors?" she asked, her gaze shifting around the room again. "What are you looking for out here?"

"I'm sorry but I cannot discuss it with you at this time." He paused briefly. "Mrs. Carver," he said, purposely using the name, hoping to rattle her. "Are you aware that we asked everyone to stay out of the woods?"

She shrugged. "It's a short walk. I didn't think it would hurt."

He stepped toward her. She backed away, pressing herself against the wall behind her.

"That's where you're wrong," he whispered, his face only inches from her's. She stared up at him, her gaze meeting his. But he could see the fear in her eyes, noticed the small tremble of her lips. "Please do not go into the woods again. I wouldn't want anything to happen to you."

CHAPTER THIRTEEN

1

Aurora, Illinois

Joe leaned against his car, smoking. He watched from behind dark sunglasses as the older couple led their horses back into the barn. His eyes locked on the woman. She was his next target. He glanced around. Should be easy. The area was pretty secluded; the ranch sat on two hundred acres of wooded land.

There was only one problem.

He hated doing women. He knew it was a sexist, chauvinistic attitude but he really didn't think most women would mind.

The couple was older in age than the others he had taken out so far on this job. Picking up the file regarding the woman, he glanced inside. Betty Cantor. Married forty years to Howard Cantor, he read before he could stop himself. Looking up, he watched as Betty came out of the barn. Her hair was brown streaked with gray, her face did not yet show her age. She paused at the door to the barn and a moment later, the man emerged. They walked back to the house arm in arm, kissing once.

Joe flicked the cigarette away. He had seen enough. Getting in his car, he started the engine and began to drive away from the Cantor ranch. But as he stared at the passing road signs, his mind turned to Victor Green.

Victor had been one of his first assignments. One of his first hits.

He received the information on Victor. His brother-in-law wanted him taken out. Seems the business they owned together was being run into the ground by Victor and his loving in-law wanted him out before the whole thing collapsed. So Joe got the file, read every piece of information and headed out to Victor's home.

When he arrived, the man was on the front lawn with his twelve-year-old son. The two of them were playing baseball. For hours he watched them throw the ball, taking turns batting, running the bases. And he knew he could not kill this man. Bad business man or not, he was a good father.

So Joe drove away. But it didn't end there. Not only couldn't he kill this man, he couldn't let someone else do it. He called the police alerting them to the brother-in-law's plan. The next time the man tried to set up a hit, he found himself talking to an undercover police officer. He was indicted and charged for trying to solicit a murder. And for a while, Joe felt pretty good about the whole thing. He had done the right thing. But less than six months later, the man he had so valiantly saved was indicated for sexually molesting that twelve-year-old boy Joe had watched him play with so nicely that summer day.

That was the day he decided he could no longer know anything personal about his clients. Everyone had secrets. Everyone did bad things. Everyone deserved to die.

He sighed and pulling off the road, turned his car around, heading back.

2

Hartwick, Michigan

David stared out the window at the tree line at the back of the house.

Where the hell is she?

He'd been standing at the window watching for Kelsey for, he glanced at his watch, close to thirty minutes. Five more. She had five more minutes to get here or he was going to go back to that house—

The front door opened. He spun toward the sound. Kelsey walked past him and into the kitchen.

"Kelsey?" He followed, close on her heels. "What took so long?" He had to resist the urge to throw his arms around her.

"I had to walk all the way around the woods to get back." Turning on the faucet, she grabbed a glass from the rack beside the sink and took a long drink of water.

"What happened? What did you tell them?"

She filled the glass again. "I told them I wanted to know why they were in Eve's house. I told them I was going to call the cops." She half-laughed.

"And that worked?"

"I'm a harmless woman. Now, you . . ." She downed the second glass of water. "I shudder to think what would have happened if you had gone in."

"Who did you talk to? Did you get any names?"

She shook her head. "But I talked to the guy who I saw at the woods yesterday. I think he's in charge of the whole thing. Big guy. Completely bald." She shivered. "Gave me the creeps."

"Ken Brewer," David said, her description unmistakable.

"Who is he?"

"My father's personal assistant." Deep down, David had known that his father was involved. Had to be. But this was proof, concrete, indisputable. "What else?"

Her eyes narrowed slightly as she recalled the details. "They've shoved all of Eve's furniture and things out of the way, pushed it all up against the walls. In the living room, they've set up a long table with computers and monitors. I'm not sure because I couldn't really get a good look but I think they've got the whole place wired. And I could hear footsteps overhead so they must be using the entire house."

David could picture it clearly in his mind. He knew exactly what they were doing. "Sounds like they've set themselves up with a command post." He slammed a fist on the counter top. "Dammit! They're going to try and cover this up."

"You mean clean it up, don't you?"

"I'm not sure anymore." He leaned against the counter trying to sort through everything. That morning when he'd arrived at Leah's, he had been sure they could find a reasonable explanation for all that had been happening. Now he didn't know what to believe.

"You think they may actually be illegally disposing of waste in the woods?" Kelsey stood, hands on hips, waiting for an answer.

"I don't know. I sure as hell hope not."

"What about the ships they launch?" she asked, her voice incredulous. "If they're not filled with garbage, then why go to the expense of actually shooting them off?"

"That's the problem." David thought back over the years he'd been with the company. "I know those ships are being loaded with garbage. I've watched the process. Besides, there's too damn much to dump. Someone would have found out long before now. So the question is, why would they dump anything in the woods?"

"Maybe there was an accident? A spill? Something they couldn't prevent?"

"If that's true, why didn't they just clean it up when it happened? Why wait until someone stumbles across it?"

"I still don't see how you can be so sure they're not just cleaning it up."

David shook his head. "I'm not sure about anything anymore. But the more I think about it all, the more it just feels wrong." He replayed the conversation with his father yesterday. Hal Ebersol, listening to his suggestion, willing to look at a proposal, cooperative. Hell, that alone should have tipped David off that something was wrong.

A muscle in his jaw twitched. Was it possible that Envirospace had done something, something that had killed that section of the woods? And were they now trying to hide their mistake? David had no way of knowing, but now, more than ever, he was determined to find out the truth.

His gaze refocused on Kelsey. "What else did you see?"

She shrugged. "Nothing really. They rushed me out. But David." Her brow furrowed. "As I was walking back, I began to wonder if maybe this is the problem Leah talked about in her diary."

"No. Again, if they knew about all of this before Leah died, why would they leave it here for someone else to discover?" He shook his head. "They've moved too fast on this. They would have already cleaned it up. Leah must have known something else."

"But what?"

"I don't know." He ran a hand through his hair. "Why don't you get the diary. Read to me exactly what she says. Maybe I'll know what she's talking about."

Kelsey nodded. She left the room but returned within moments carrying Leah's diary. "I found a couple of strange things last night." Reaching in the back of the book, she pulled out a small, once folded piece of paper and handed it to him. "Do you know who any of these people are?"

"This is Leah's writing," he said, staring at the names. "I found it last night. I don't recognize any of them."

"This second name," he said. "Harvey Staller. He worked on the original design of the Envirospace Project."

"And the others?"

His brow furrowed. "It seems like I've heard of Tom Hardigan, heard that name somewhere but I don't know." He looked at her. "Why? What do you think this is?"

"I'm not sure. But Leah must have written them down for a reason. Maybe they're involved in whatever is going on."

"I agree." David read through the names again. "I think we need to find out who these people are."

"And look at this." Kelsey flipped through the pages of the diary. Then, finding what she needed, held the small journal up showing him the pages. "For some reason, she skipped three days in a row. She filled out every day up until these three. Then nothing."

David leaned forward, glancing at the dates. "That's right around the time the two of us stopped seeing each other."

Kelsey stared down at the book, fingering the pages, flipping them forward, backward, forward. "I didn't even think of that," she muttered.

He shifted where he stood, uncomfortable with the change in subject. The breakup had been sudden, painful, but it was behind him. He didn't want to dredge it up now. With Kelsey.

She held up the diary. "She never mentions it. She wrote every day since the beginning of the year. Good days. Bad days. Everything. Then suddenly, nothing for three days straight. And absolutely no mention of the two of you splitting up."

"It was sudden. Maybe she—"

"David," she said, cutting him off. "Think about it. Leah was having trouble at work. She wrote about it in her diary. She said she was going to talk to you about it but you say she never did. Then three skipped days. After those dates, there's no mention of the problem or you again. Like none of it ever existed." She leafed farther forward. "And look at this." She showed him a page filled with 1's and 0's.

He stared at the numbers, the blood rushing from his head. "How? She couldn't . . ."

"David?" Kelsey took a step closer. "Are you all right?"

He nodded, but was having trouble breathing, the air suddenly thick, stale. He looked up but it was no longer Kelsey standing before him.

It was Leah.

She held out armfuls of papers, shoving them toward him, speaking so fast he could not understand her. The walls and ceiling around him were filled with 1's and 0's, covering every inch of space.

A scream.

He spun around. And as he turned, the lights around him dimmed until he stood in almost complete darkness. Only one place remained lit. A cot. It sat on the other side of the room, tucked away in the farthest corner. A small group of people clustered around the small bed. A woman lay on the cot. She struggled against them, trying to get free.

He heard her scream once and then she was silent.

He covered his ears, trying to block out the sound. The 1's and 0's grew larger, invading his mind, crushing him.

"*No!*"

"David. David!"

A face swam into focus before him. Kelsey's face. Alarmed. Concerned. "David!"

He focused on her, the images fading away. He looked around but he was no longer in that dark place, surrounded by the strange happenings.

"Sit down." She helped him into a seat. Then, crossing to the sink, she filled a glass with water. "Drink." She handed him the glass, helping him hold it.

After only a moment's hesitation, he did as he was ordered.

Kelsey knelt down in front of him. "What just happened?"

"I don't know." And even as he tried to remember, he realized he could not.

"Has anything like this happened before?"

He hesitated. How much could he say? How much did he want to say? He set the glass on the table but his hand was shaking and he missed the coaster. The bottom of the glass teetered half on, half off the small round object for a moment before falling over. His gaze followed the trail of the clear liquid as it slid across the surface of the table and reaching the edge slowly dripped off. Just like—

"David." Kelsey took his hand in hers, pulling his attention away from the table, back to her. "What is it? I know you're holding something back." Her concerned eyes stared into his. "Come on," she coaxed. "Now is not the time for secrets."

He drew in a breath, held it for several moments then released it slowly. "This isn't the first time this has happened."

"What?"

"For the last two days, I've had other episodes like this one."

"You've been dizzy?"

He nodded. "Dizzy. Headaches. Nausea." Reaching out, he picked up the diary. Hesitantly, he opened the book to the 1's and 0's. "And all day yesterday, I found myself writing these numbers. And I don't know why."

"You what?" She stood, her voice sharp. "Why didn't you tell me? With everything that's happened . . . My God, you should have told me. You—"

"When?" he interrupted, cutting her lecture short. "Yesterday when you were so upset?"

She stared down at him, the expression on her face a mixture of confusion and fear. "Yesterday." She ran a hand over her face. "You're right. You couldn't have told me yesterday." Her voice softened. "Tell me now."

"I'm not sure I can." He glanced at Leah's journal. "I was looking at the diary," he began slowly, straining to recall the details. "And for a minute, it was as if Leah were here talking to me, telling me something." He rubbed his forehead.

"What?"

"I don't know. I just don't know."

"Okay," she began, her voice calm. "Let's go at this in a different way." She paused for a moment, thinking. "What are these episodes like?"

"It's hard." He searched backward through his mind. "It's like I'm remembering something that never happened."

"Like a dream? Are you remembering a dream?"

"No." He shook his head, concentrating. "I don't know."

Kelsey began pacing before him, trying to reason it out. "You mentioned Leah? Are they about Leah?"

"I think so."

"What about Hillary West?"

She screamed once and was silent.

"A scream," he muttered, his eyes squeezing shut as a headache pounded against his temple.

"A scream? You hear someone screaming?"

He licked his lips, shaking his head. "She only screamed once."

"David? What's wrong? Is it happening again?"

He nodded. "Headache."

"Let it go then." She spoke softly. A moment later, he felt her hands take his, holding tightly. "Let it go."

Within moments, the headache began to subside. He opened his eyes. Once more she knelt down in front of him, her face drawn in concern.

"Better?"

"Yeah. Thanks."

"Good." She smiled, running a hand down the side of his face. "Just relax for a minute, okay?"

He nodded, taking a deep breath.

Kelsey stood. She paced toward the window, back to the table, turned back toward the window but stopped. She stood silent for a long time, her back to him. When she finally spoke, the words came out slowly, as if she were working out her theory aloud. "You said it's like you're remembering something that never happened."

He nodded stiffly, his body taut with anticipation.

She turned toward him, her eyes fearful. "But what if you're remembering something that did happen?"

A chill stole over him. "What are you getting at?"

"It's possible that something happened to you, something so traumatic that you're now suppressing it."

David shook his head even as she spoke. "No. I don't see how that could be."

"But it makes sense." She sat across from him, her gaze intense. "Don't you see? Something happened, something so awful that you repressed it. But now it's beginning to break through to your conscious mind."

"You're forgetting about Leah and Hillary. If you're right, then all three of us repressed the memories. I find that hard to believe."

She leaned back in her chair, disappointment pulling her shoulders down. "You're right. Plus it doesn't explain the connection to Envirospace." She traced the edge of the table with a finger. "Unless . . ." she began, her gaze lighting up once again.

"Unless someone did something to us," he finished for her, knowing what she was going to say, coming to the same conclusion seconds earlier.

"Exactly." She slapped the table top. "What if Leah did tell you this problem and you went to Envirospace with it. Maybe somehow they did something to you—to both of you to suppress what you knew and now it's coming back to haunt you. Maybe that's what's causing the headaches, the dizziness. Your mind is trying to remember something that your body has been told to forget."

David rubbed his forehead, trying to release the tension that was slowly building behind his eyes. It couldn't be true. If it were, then his father would know. Their relationship was strained but would he do something like this? But in the deep recesses of his mind, he believed it and knew it was the truth. "What could I know?" he whispered.

"That's what we need to find out." She picked up the diary, flipping through the pages until she found the strange number combinations. "You have no idea what these numbers mean."

"None."

"But you've been writing them, so you must have seen them somewhere."

"I must have."

"Must have," Kelsey repeated, glancing through the pages, running her finger down each page as if looking for something specific. "Okay, right here," she said, opening the book wider. "Leah says that Hillary brought her readouts and that she was going to show them to you."

"But she didn't."

"If we're right, then we have no way of knowing whether she did or not," Kelsey corrected. "But that doesn't matter. What we have to figure out is what kind of readouts were they? Where would Hillary get something like that?"

He looked up sharply. "Communications," he said as realization sunk in. "She worked in communications at Envirospace."

Now it was Kelsey's turn to be confused. "I don't understand."

He searched backward in his mind to his computer classes in college. What had they called it? "Binary," he said, the memory still fuzzy but coming slowly into focus. "Computers communicate with a language of their own called binary. I'm not sure but I think the binary is made up of a series of 1's and 0's."

Kelsey looked down at the diary. "So this could actually mean something."

"It must."

"But you can't decipher it."

"No. I don't understand how binary works. Besides, I'm really only guessing."

"But if you're right, we should be able to get someone to decipher it for us." Kelsey looked at him. "So where do we go from here? Who do we talk to?"

"I don't know," David whispered. "I don't know who I can trust anymore." He stared at the diary, the list of names. It all led back to Envirospace. But who was involved? He had no doubt about his father and Ken Brewer. But what about his uncle? Sam? His staff?

"David?" Kelsey's voice drew his attention. "Are you all right?"

"I'm just trying to take this all in. I mean, I know these people. At least, I thought I did." He ran a hand over his face, through his hair. He was just so damn tired.

"What do we do now?" Kelsey said, voicing the question he was afraid to ask.

"I wish I knew." His gaze shifted to the list of names. He picked up the paper, reading through each one again. Tom Hardigan. Who was he? Why was that name familiar?

"I need to go back to work. I may not be able to decipher the binary." He held up the list. "But I think I can find out who these people are. If they're connected to Envirospace, then they'll be in the main computer system." He stood, stuffing the list in his pocket.

"You're going back to Envirospace?" Kelsey followed him as he headed toward the front door.

"I have to."

"David, I think whatever was done to Leah caused her to become confused. I think that's why she's dead." He reached for the door but Kelsey grabbed his arm, stopping him. "I don't want the same thing to happen to you."

He did not look at her. He couldn't afford to let her

change his mind. He needed to know. Needed this to end.
"It won't. I'm fine."

"What about the doctor? We were going to be examined.
Let's just go there first. Have a few tests run."

"I can't waste the time."

"Maybe he can help you remember."

"Kelsey, don't you see?" He turned to face her, holding
up the paper. "This list could be the key to everything. If
I can find out who these people are, I may be able to find
out what the hell is going on."

"Then let me go with you." She stared at him, her eyes
filled with dread. "I don't think you should be alone."

"And how do I explain that?" He pulled the door open.
"Don't worry. I'll be back soon."

"David," she began quietly, her hand once more grabbing his arm. "Let's just go to the police."

"And tell them what? We have no proof of any wrong-
doing."

"What about Eve's? The men in the woods?"

David laughed bitterly. "I was the one who argued for
them to do exactly what they're doing. I wanted this."

"David." The grip on his arm increased. "I don't want
you to follow Leah's pattern. I don't want things to end the
same way."

CHAPTER FOURTEEN

1

Kelsey waited until David's car was gone from sight before going back to the kitchen and putting a kettle on for tea.

She had just picked up the diary, ready to go through it again, trying to find anything she might have missed, when the sound of a key fitting into the kitchen door reached her ears.

"David," she breathed, going to the door and pulling it wide.

Her mother stood beyond the threshold. "You're still here."

"Good to see you again too, Mother." Kelsey took a step back allowing her mother entrance.

Rose brushed past her. "I would have thought that you'd be gone by now."

"Don't you mean you were hoping," Kelsey said, closing the door.

"Please, Kelsey." Rose took a seat at the table. "It's far too early in the day for this type of thing."

"I agree. So let's not do it."

Rose glanced at the stove. "No coffee?"

"I just boiled some water if you'd like tea."

Rose sighed. "If that's all you have."

Kelsey brought a cup over and placed it in front of her mother.

"I hope it's not too strong," Rose said quietly, just before taking her first sip.

"Mother." Kelsey sat down across from her, ignoring the face Rose made as she sipped the tea. "What are you doing here?"

"I can't come to my daughter's house?" Rose thumped the cup down, sloshing some of the hot brew on the table. "I can't visit my daughter?"

"You didn't want me to stay," Kelsey said, not falling for her mother's innocent act. Past history had taught her too well. Rose Brayden wanted something or she wouldn't be here. "You said when you got here that you were surprised to see me," Kelsey continued. "You haven't called me at all—"

"Do you have any cream?" Rose asked, cutting her off, sipping the tea again and repeating the expression of distaste. She held the cup forward.

Kelsey stood, obediently retrieving the cream from the refrigerator and setting it on the table. Her mother poured enough in to make the tea white in color. As she stirred her cup, her gaze shifted to the tabletop.

"What is this?" she asked, picking up the diary. "Is this Leah's?"

Kelsey stared at the small journal, trying to think of a good lie. Before she could speak, Rose began flipping through the pages.

"This is her diary." She looked back at Kelsey. "Have you been reading this?"

Kelsey took the diary from her. "This is none of your business."

"Is it David's business?" There was no mistaking the accusation in her voice. "Don't try and deny it. I saw him leave." She crossed her arms over her chest, waiting.

"I've seen him," she began haltingly, embarrassed by

her mother's innuendo. "We've been . . . He's helping me."
She stopped. Why was she trying to defend herself? She'd
done nothing wrong. Within seconds, without realizing it,
she had allowed herself to slip back into the same old patterns with her mother. Guilt, shame, each heaped on without remorse.

Squaring back her shoulders, she began again. "David
has been over a couple of times," she said, her voice
strong. "But like I said, this is really none of your business.
I won't—"

"None of my business." Rose's shrill voice cut her off
mid-sentence. "You're living in Leah's home, sleeping in
her bed, seeing her fiancé."

"They were not engaged," Kelsey shot back. "They
were never close to being engaged and you know it."

"They could have been. Don't you have any integrity?"
She stuck her chin forward, her eyes hooded slits. "I told
Leah." Her gaze traveled over Kelsey with obvious disdain.
"I told her if you came here you'd just have to have Da-
vid."

Kelsey slammed the diary onto the table. "I don't *have*
David," she said, working hard to keep from shouting the
words. "We're helping each other."

"I can imagine," Rose mumbled.

"Mother!" Kelsey's voice was sharp. "Let this go. You
don't know what you're talking about. You're making a
fool of yourself."

"Me? I'm the fool?" She laid a hand across her chest,
her eyes wide. "I'm not the one playing house—"

"We don't think Leah killed herself," Kelsey blurted out
ready to say anything to stop the accusations.

Rose stared at her, not blinking, not speaking, not
breathing.

"I know it's a shock," Kelsey began. "But we've been
looking into this and—"

"You've been looking into what?" Rose said, her voice

loud, unbelieving. "No one asked you to look into anything."

"Asked? No one had to ask. She was my sister," Kelsey whispered.

"Her sister?" Rose spit the words out bitterly. "What kind of sister were you? Never calling. Never coming to see her. Do you know how that made her feel? Do you know how much you hurt her?"

"It goes both ways," Kelsey said, before she realized she was going to speak. "She never called me either."

"So you blame Leah for your leaving and never calling?"

"No, I didn't leave because of Leah. I left because of you!" Her mouth clamped shut, her heart beating against her chest. All these years she'd held her feelings inside, never able to give words to them. Until now. "I left because of you," she said again, more quietly.

Rose glared at her, anger seeming to stream from every pore of her body. "How dare you."

"How dare I what?" Kelsey challenged outright. "How dare I finally speak the truth? It's about time I did." She stood, staring down at her mother. "You specialized in undermining us. Every opportunity you had to eat away at our confidence you took, making us feel guilty for who we were and the thoughts we had."

"I never—"

"You do!" Kelsey shouted. "You're doing it right now. I haven't done anything wrong. Neither has David for that matter. Yet you're acting as if we have."

Rose's eyes narrowed. Slowly, she stood. "Don't you dare try and blame me for the pain you gave Leah." She wagged a finger at her. "You hurt her by leaving. Not me."

"I regret it, mother. Is that what you want to hear?" She could feel the explosion of emotions that were now threatening. "I'm the older sister. I should have been here. I should have protected her." She bit her lip, turning away, not wanting her mother to see her pain, her guilt.

"Kelsey."

She flinched as if struck; her mother's voice still sharp, still angry.

"I want you to drop all this nonsense. I want—"

"Please leave," Kelsey said, keeping her back to her.

"Let's not—"

"Get out!" Kelsey shouted, her body shaking. "I want you to leave. Now!"

2

David fed the names into the computer and waited, letting it do the searching for him. He tried not to think about the theory he and Kelsey had come up with. He couldn't. It just seemed too impossible to him. Whatever might or might not have happened to him, they couldn't just erase it.

NO SUCH FILE FOUND.

The words blinked across the computer screen. His brow furrowed. No such file? He'd told the computer to search for any reference to the five names he had provided. He was sure at least Harvey Staller would show up and was hoping from there he could get the rest of his answers. But no such file found? That he had not expected.

"Okay," he whispered. "Let's try another approach."

He told the computer to search through the company history dating back nearly twenty years for any reference to Harvey Staller specifically. After typing in the information, he leaned back confidently, waiting for his readout.

A knock sounded on his door. He glanced at the screen. STILL SEARCHING. A moment later, Sam peeked around the corner into his office.

"Your secretary said you were back." He strolled in and plopped down in the chair opposite David. As David looked at him, he felt, for a moment, as if he were staring at a stranger. Did he know? Was he involved? Sam seemed dif-

ferent to him, the way he looked at him, almost seeming
to study him, watching for . . .

"Were you waiting for me?" he asked.

"Not really." Sam shrugged casually but seemed anything but relaxed. "Just wondering what you've been up
to."

"Why? Is something going on?"

"No," he said almost too quickly and David suddenly
got the feeling that Sam knew more then he was saying.

Or was he just being paranoid? Was he beginning to read
something into everything that was said to him, mistrust
everyone? Possibly. But if he laid his cards out on the table
and he couldn't trust Sam, then what?

He stared at his friend. How many games of basketball
had they played together over the years? How many times
had Sam come to David about his latest conquest or a problem at work?

He had to trust someone, needed to.

"Do you know who these people are?" he asked, holding out the list of names before he could change his mind.

Sam hesitated a moment before taking the slip of paper.
Quickly, he scanned the list. "What is this?" His gaze
darted from the paper to David and then back to the paper.

"Do you know who they are?" he repeated, not answering Sam's question.

"Why? What's going on?"

They sat staring at each other, neither answering the other's question. A standoff, David thought. But it was more
than that. *He's involved.* And as the words whispered
through his mind, his stomach convulsed with a combination of shock and anger. Sam, one of the few people he
truly trusted, had betrayed him. Had allowed or been involved in whatever had been done to him. His hands
clenched into fists, his pulse pounded an irregular beat.

"It's a simple question, Sam," he said, working hard to
keep his voice calm, natural, hoping to bait him into answering. "Do you recognize any of those names?"

"No," he said and his left cheek muscle twitched.

"You don't recognize any of them?" he pressed.

Sam rubbed his cheek as the muscle continued to jump and twitch. "Dave, I can't . . ." The sentence trailed off as he shifted once more in his seat.

"Sam," David began, not quite sure what he wanted to say but knowing this might be the only opportunity he would get to give his friend a chance to come clean before he found out the truth himself. "If you know something, if something is going on and you know about it, now is the time to tell me."

Sam stared down at the list in his hand, saying nothing.

"I'm having nightmares," David continued, hoping if he told Sam what was happening to him, he would tell him what he knew, he would help stop it. "I'm writing things I don't understand. Getting flashes of conversations I don't remember having."

Sam shook his head as David spoke. "This is nuts," he mumbled, his hands folding and unfolding the paper he still held.

"Someone did something to me," he continued, ignoring Sam's reaction. "I think someone is trying to hide something, something involving Leah and Hillary." Leaning forward, he lowered his voice. "If we were ever friends, if you know anything, tell me now."

David waited, willing Sam to talk to him, tell him what he knew. Silence descended, wrapping itself around the two men. As the seconds ticked by, one after another, David knew Sam was trying to decide, trying to make up his mind if he would talk or not.

Finally, when he could stand the waiting no longer, David broke the unending quiet himself. "Sam—"

"There's nothing to tell," he cut in before David could get any more out.

Disappointment rippled through him. "Okay."

Sam stood. "I have to get back to work." His gaze

darted to David but quickly moved away as he turned and headed toward the exit.

But in the instant that their eyes met, David saw fear. *He's afraid.* And that realization brought new understanding. Sam was being threatened or forced into this situation. He was an unwilling participant.

"Sam," he called just as his friend reached the door. Sam stopped but did not turn. David stared at his back, trying desperately to think of something to say to break through to him. Something that would make him see that he should tell him, could trust him. But as his mind worked feverishly, coming up with and discarding each idea within a matter of seconds, he realized he was wasting his time. Sam wasn't keeping quiet because he didn't trust David. He was keeping quiet for one reason and one reason only.

Hal Ebersol.

David knew firsthand how intimidating his father could be. If he were the one behind all this and he were threatening Sam in some way, then he would say nothing.

His gaze shifted to his desktop. But as he stared at the papers in front of him, a new ripple of disappointment coursed through him. "The names," he whispered, looking back to Sam. "I'd like the names back."

Without uttering a word, Sam turned and deposited the paper on his desk.

David stared down at his list. Sam had folded it twice more, until it was small enough to conceal in the palm of his hand, small enough to smuggle out without notice.

He picked it up, his hand trembling as he fought to control his growing anger. "I'd appreciate it," he began, before Sam could take a step away, "if you would keep this between us."

"Yeah, sure," Sam mumbled as he turned and paced back to the door. He reached for the knob but paused, his hand stopping midway. For a moment, David thought he might have changed his mind, would come back and tell him everything. But then he opened the door and stepped through without speaking.

As the door clicked shut, a sense of urgency spread through David. Would Sam keep it to himself? If he did, David doubted it would be for long.

Reaching out, he turned his computer screen back on.

NO SUCH FILE FOUND glared at him.

"What the hell?" he muttered. "No Harvey Staller for the last twenty years?"

Going directly to the history file, he attempted to bring up the information himself, search manually. The files were not there. He tried again. Again, not there.

He'd used those files countless times when preparing for a presentation. They gave the company history, how it all began, the people behind it. And now it was gone.

Next he tried pulling up an old proposal he knew contained that information. It too was missing. His brow furrowed. What the hell? He typed in several proposal names, all of them came up empty.

"They dumped the files," he muttered.

He sat back, his frustration growing with each passing moment. What were they hiding?

And then a new thought struck him. Standing, he left his office and headed toward the hard copy file room. But like before, he came up empty. Nothing in the filing cabinets. Nothing in storage. Missing. Just like Hillary West.

But at least now he knew he was on the right track. There was something in the files, something about those names that someone did not want found. He just had to think of another way, another place to find the information he needed.

As he walked down the hall, he passed the main office. Inside, he could see Leah's empty desk with the silent computer terminal on top. He stopped. Her computer terminal. Could Leah have compiled information on her computer? He glanced at his watch. In less than two hours, the office would be empty for the night.

3

Sam sat at his desk staring at the far wall of his office. Why the hell didn't he just tell him the truth? David was going to find out. He fidgeted with his tie, pulling the knot down and up, down and up. He had to tell someone, had to . . .

Let's just keep this between us.

David's words repeated in his mind. What would happen if he told Hal Ebersol? How far would he go to keep his secret?

But he already knew the answer to that. No price was too high—Leah and Hillary were proof of that. He pulled hard on his tie, slipping the knot out of its loop, before yanking it from around his neck and tossing it on his desk. Fingers fumbling, he opened the top two buttons of his shirt and sat back. He had to calm down, reason out his options, decide what he needed to do.

Tom Hardigan. Betty Cantor. Harvey Staller. Ned Bringer. Steven Ordmann.

David had all the names. It was only a matter of time before he found the connection to Envirospace, the connection to Sam. He ran a hand over his face, knowing he had no real choice. He had to tell Hal Ebersol what he knew.

4

David checked his watch as he walked toward the main office. Should have been empty for at least a half hour now. He strolled casually past, glancing through the windows at the office beyond the glass. Lights off, computers shut down. Everyone had gone home for the night. He walked to the end of the hall and glanced at the elevator. No activity. Going back to the office, he pulled out his key, slid it into the lock and turned. But the lock did not disengage as expected. He checked the key and tried again. Again, the lock did not budge.

When had the master locks been changed? And why hadn't he received a new key? He glanced down the hall, checking his watch again. The night cleaning staff would begin its rounds within the next half hour. He had to get in and out before then.

He looked down at the lock. Could he pick it? But even as the thought ran through his mind, he knew it was ridiculous. Did he really believe a couple of straightened paperclips were going to pop open the lock?

He looked back at the door, the windows beside it. And then he looked up. A simple drop ceiling. He stared at it, studying it. When he was in high school, he and his best friend, Tony Carlin, had climbed through the drop ceiling into the Spanish room. They stole all the language tapes, recorded vintage Beatles over them and then returned them. They were never caught and to this day, David did not think anyone ever figured out how they got inside.

Grabbing the potted plant in the middle of the hall, he dragged it toward the door. Then stepping carefully on its side, he reached above him and pushed up the first of the stucco material. Just like in high school, he was able to push it aside and grip the door frame inside.

As he locked his hands over the ledge, preparing to heft himself up, he hesitated. What if he got caught? There was no way he could explain breaking into the office. In his mind, he went over the last few days. Once more his gaze fell on Leah's computer. This might be his only chance. He pulled himself up.

Balancing on the door frame, he lifted the ceiling material inside the main office and slid it to the side. Moving slowly, not wanting to break any of the ceiling tiles, he rotated his body until he was able to drop down inside the main office.

He left the lights off as he made his way over to Leah's desk. Turning on the computer terminal, he pointed the monitor away from the hall not wanting the light from the screen to attract any undue attention.

He waited as the machine warmed up. The computers at Envirospace were all the same. They worked off of a main network system that was automatically booted up when the machine came on. Whoever was using the machine simply had to input their password in order to open their allotted files.

But instead of entering his password, David exited the network and called up the directory to Leah's terminal. He wasn't sure what he was looking for but he had a feeling that if Leah had found something, she might have used her computer to compile the information. And if it was in regards to the company, he doubted she would want to leave it on the network for anyone and everyone to see.

He checked the directory in her word processing program, paging past file names, scanning each one quickly but carefully.

One file name stood out from the rest: Myer.

His brow furrowed. Why was that familiar? And then he remembered. It was Leah's middle name. The file was dated one month before her death. Typing in the name, he pulled up the file. The screen filled with 1's and 0's. His vision blurred, his heartbeat doubled. The numbers seemed to swim out at him, wrapping around him, smothering him.

We've got to go to the authorities.

Not yet. Let me handle this.

Reaching out, gripping the side of the desk, he managed to hold himself in his seat. He lowered his head, taking deep breaths, willing the dizziness to pass. Slowly, he turned his gaze back to the computer screen. With some hesitation, he reached out and began paging down, scanning the numbers.

What does it mean? He had to know, had to find the solution. But not here. He needed to get out of here.

Going to the supply cabinet, David retrieved a computer disk. He slipped it into the computer and quickly typed the command to copy the file onto the disk. As the computer worked, he glanced around, his gaze stopping on his father's office door.

There was definitely some kind of cover-up going on. Was it possible that his father's office held some of the answers he needed?

Standing, he crossed to the door. But as his fingers brushed against the brass knob, he stopped. What did he expect to find? Incriminating evidence in his top desk drawer? No, his father was not stupid. Yet he had to be sure.

He turned the knob and pushed. The door did not budge. Locked. Slowly, he turned his gaze upward. Drop ceiling, same as the one he had just climbed through to reach this office.

Before he could decide what he wanted to do, he heard, very faintly, whistling. Someone was coming.

He dashed back to the computer and flicked off the screen. He left the hard drive working, copying the file as he slipped down behind the desk. He held his breath as he heard the soft voices of the night cleaning crew draw closer. But as they unlocked the office across the hall, he let out a breath of relief. He waited another few minutes before slipping out from behind the desk and checking the disk. Finished.

He popped it out of the computer and slipped it into his pocket. Reaching for the on/off switch, he hesitated. Obviously, no one had checked Leah's computer and found this file before him. He didn't want them finding it now. After only a moment's hesitation, he erased the file he had just copied.

Going to the door, he climbed back over the door frame, carefully putting each piece back in place. He kept his hand in his pocket, his fingers wrapped around the computer disk as he made his way back to his office. He needed to get out of here, needed to go home and check . . .

"David?"

He stopped dead in his tracks.

Slowly, he turned to face the man behind him, his hand clutching the disk a little tighter. "You're working late."

Hal Ebersol stood back a few feet, his face lost in the shadows of the hallway. "I could say the same about you."

Had he seen him inside the main office? Did he know he copied something off the computer? David swallowed hard. He wondered if his father, in the darkness of the hallway, could see the perspiration spotting his forehead. He had to resist the urge to wipe it away.

"Just trying to finish that proposal," he began, his voice slightly rushed. *Calm down. There is no reason to panic.* "Want to make sure you have it by the deadline tomorrow."

"What would the company do without you?" But David could hear the insincerity in his voice.

You'd love to find out, he thought. "I was just getting ready to leave." He took a step back but kept his gaze on his father. "Trying to get home at a decent hour."

"Of course. Don't let me keep you."

He turned to leave.

"David?" His father's voice, oddly questioning, stopped him again.

Slowly, David turned to face him.

"Your clothes?" He leaned toward David, his face coming into the light for the first time. "What is that on your clothes?" He brushed at the white dust.

David's hand shot up, covering the dirty area. White dust from the Styrofoam ceiling spotted his shirt and pants. His mind raced. "I had to dig through some boxes in the file room. Must have gotten it there," he said, knowing it sounded lame but unable to think of a better lie.

Hal shifted back into the shadows, any change of expression lost in the darkness. "Don't dig too deeply, son. You might not like what you find."

5

Joe sat on the hood of his car staring up at the full moon.
Tomorrow. This would all be over tomorrow. He would
take out the last one on his list and then he was done.

Maybe it was time to think about retiring? He certainly
had enough money. And he was getting older. Besides, this
latest job was really giving him the creeps.

6

Hal bent down, running the white dust through his fingers.
Then looking up, he said quietly, "Came through the ceiling."

Sam nodded. "Probably. But why? Why would he do
that?" He had called Hal, asked him to meet him at his
office regarding information about David. Now he regretted
making that call. Everything he did seemed only to get
David into deeper trouble.

Scanning the room, Sam's gaze stopped on Leah's desk.
Her chair was pulled away from the desk, as if someone
had just been sitting there, looking . . . for what?

With quick strides, he crossed the room and sat in her
chair. He opened the drawers but found each one empty.
His gaze scanned the desk top but there was nothing but . . .

"Dammit!"

He flicked on Leah's computer. He had checked the computer system, first erasing anything that might be incriminating, then looking for any files that seemed out of place.
But it had never occurred to him that Leah may have kept
information on her personal terminal.

Hal stood behind him. "What are you doing?"

"A hunch," he mumbled, bypassing the network, un-
knowingly duplicating David's earlier actions. He went directly into the main directory and began searching.

"Nothing," he muttered, his fingers moving over the keyboard.

Hal turned away as Sam continued to search. He walked through the office, glancing down at the various desks, picking up a paper here and there, scanning the pages. "Why did you call me here tonight, Mr. Wyatt?"

Sam's typing slowed. Although the words were spoken with casual ease, Sam knew Hal Ebersol felt anything but relaxed. With each passing day, the situation was escalating out of control, just as it had before. And what Sam was about to tell him would only add fuel to the fire.

He glanced over his shoulder, trying to decide if he really wanted to crank up the heat that high.

Hal Ebersol stood a few feet back, his eyes fixed on Sam, waiting. And for a moment, Sam felt like a rabbit caught in headlights, frozen with fear, unable to do anything but stare in frightened horror.

"Mr. Wyatt?"

The sound of Hal Ebersol's impatient voice broke through the haze in Sam's mind.

"Dave knows something was done to him," he blurted out, unable to lie under the man's unflinching gaze. "He told me he's having nightmares. I think he may be on the verge of remembering."

Hal's gaze sliced sideways, his eyes narrowing slightly. "Obviously, his memory has not yet returned."

"No, but he does have the list of names. He's trying to find those people. If he contacts any one of them, if even one of those people talks, David will know. He'll remember. The trigger will be so strong—"

"They won't talk," Hal said with a finality that Sam did not like.

"How can you be so sure?"

But Hal did not answer his question. "I had a conversation with Mr. Brewer before arriving here," he said instead. "He informed me that Kelsey Brayden was out at the site today."

Sam's eyes widened. Everything was falling apart. "Was Dave with her?"

"It doesn't matter." Hal walked toward his office, pulling keys out as he went. "David broke into this office. That's enough."

"Enough?" Sam stood, trailing behind him. "Enough for what?"

"Clearly, this cannot go on." Hal unlocked his office door and, stepping inside, went directly to his desk. "I'm going to have them both picked up. We'll keep them at the site until Pearson arrives. I want to take advantage of the weekend." And without waiting for any further discussion, Hal Ebersol lifted the phone and began dialing.

Sam stood in the doorway, unable to think of anything he could say to stop what was happening. Instead, he turned back to the office behind him and, crossing to Leah's desk, dropped down in her chair. He stared at her computer trying to comprehend all he had done, all that was going to be done.

They would pick up David, give him another . . . treatment. Sam ran his hand along the top of the computer keyboard. *Treatment.* Experimental. Untested. Damaging. Could David withstand another one of these treatments?

He glanced over his shoulder. He could hear Hal Ebersol in the next room, his voice drifting out the open door. How long before he came back out? Five minutes? Less than that? His gaze shifted to the phone on the desk. There was still time to call David, warn him.

Sam reached for the receiver. But as he brought the phone to his ear, listening to the loud buzz of the dial tone, he hesitated. What would he tell him? How could he warn him without exposing himself and his team? And would warning him now really make any difference?

He hung the phone up. The instant his hand released the receiver, a chill stole over him. At the same moment, a smell filled the room. Sweet. Like flowers. Like ... lilacs.

The hairs on the back of his neck stood on end. He spun

in his chair, knowing, somehow feeling, someone was behind him.

A woman stood a few feet away, her face lost in the darkness that surrounded her. She did not speak, did not move. But somehow, he knew it was Leah Brayden.

He jerked to his feet but before he could move away, she glided across the floor, sweeping over him. Sam cried out, shuddering, as he felt the presence enter him. For a moment, it was as if they were one.

"Stop this." His voice spoke her words. His body felt her emotions. "Help David."

Then she was gone as if she had never been there. Sam collapsed to the floor. He lay for several moments, shivering from the cold that seemed to be part of his body.

Using the desk, he struggled to his feet and stood on trembling legs.

Help David.

The words reverberated in his mind. But as Hal Ebersol reentered the room, he knew it was already too late.

CHAPTER FIFTEEN

1

*W*here are you?

Kelsey could not relax. She stood at the window, staring out at the street, looking for his car. She checked her watch. Again.

David.

Her heartbeat picked up slightly as his name ran through her mind.

Where are you? Are you all right? she thought for the hundredth time.

It had been nearly thirty minutes since he called. Thirty minutes since he told her to pack a bag, open the garage door, and wait for him. She tapped the diary against her leg. Where was he?

She had tried to phone him at work but only got his voice mail. Home was no better—his machine.

She paced to the back of the house and glanced out. A breeze blew up outside, fluttering the yellow tape that surrounded the trees in her yard. She watched it flap and twist in the wind. As she stared, an image of David disappearing into the woods swept through her mind. She couldn't get it out of her head, couldn't let it go. She felt almost as if

it were an omen of things to come, bad things that she
would not be able to stop.

What if something happened to him? What if—

No, she could not think that, could not face another loss.
And for the first time since coming to Hartwick, she realized how much David Ebersol had come to mean to her.

He listened to her, helped her, was there for her through
this whole ordeal.

The same way he was there for Leah.

She closed her eyes, trying to dismiss the words from
her mind, the feelings from her heart.

But she knew it would not be that easy. She was falling
in love with David. She tried not to but it was there,
stronger than she cared to admit and growing stronger.

"I'm sorry, Leah," she whispered, feeling as if she were
somehow betraying her sister by caring for this man. All
night, she had tried to dismiss what she felt. It's only grat-
itude, she told herself, because he's been there for me so
much. But she knew it was more than that.

When she first saw him at the funeral home, looking so
distraught, so lost, she had felt something. That was why
she spoke to him that day. She knew he needed someone
to comfort him and she had wanted to be that someone.
Later, when she found out who he was, she'd felt disappointed and then ashamed for feeling that way.

After that, she had pushed her attraction away, shoving
it deep inside herself. But this morning when David arrived
at the house looking so tired. And later when he had problems with his memory, she'd felt a swell of emotion she
could no longer ignore.

She turned as the sound of a car approaching the house
filled her ears. She listened, holding her breath, hoping. The
car slowed . . .

Please be David.

She rushed toward the front door, relief flooding through
her as she saw him pull into the driveway. He drove into
the garage and turned off his car. She grabbed up her bag

and headed outside, locking the front door and leaving the lights on just as he told her to.

As she stepped closer, she saw him unload two boxes from his trunk. His briefcase sat beside him on the floor. He looked up as she approached. His gaze took in her bag, the street, the house.

"We'll take your car," he said, lifting the first box. "They know mine. Probably already looking for it." He checked the street again before stepping out of the garage.

"David—"

"The trunk," he said, nodding toward her vehicle, cutting her off before she could speak. She opened it for him.

"We have a lot to talk about," he said, loading the first box inside.

But as he moved to step past her to retrieve the second box, she reached out, wrapping her arms around him, stopping him dead in his tracks.

"What happened to you?" she whispered, working hard to hold back the tears that threatened. "I was worried." Her voice hitched.

"I'm sorry," he stammered, his body stiff for only a moment before returning the hug. "Things just took longer than I expected."

"I thought something might have happened to you."

"I'm sorry," he said again.

They stood for a moment in the driveway, their arms around each other. Kelsey did not want to release him, but she knew she was holding on too long. As she let him go, she felt a strange flutter in her heart.

Passion? Or just fear?

She didn't know but as she looked into David's eyes, she felt uneasy.

"I have a lot to tell you," he said, retrieving the second box. She could hear the rush behind his voice. He had found something, something he needed her to know. "But not here."

"Not here?" Her heart fluttered again.

Fear.

"I don't think it's safe to stay here any longer."

"What's happened?"

"I'll explain on the way." Lifting her bag into the trunk, placing it next to his two boxes, he slammed the lid shut. "I'll drive."

2

Kelsey sat beside David, staring ahead, not speaking, waiting, just waiting.

"I don't know where to begin," he said after what seemed an eternity.

She looked at him, his face pinched, his hands gripping and re-gripping the wheel. "First tell me where we're going."

"To my uncle's. He's out of town until tomorrow. They might not look for me there. But even if they do, he has a security system that will alert us if someone comes on the grounds. I think we'll be safe. At least for tonight."

"Why are we going there? What happened?"

"I ran into my father at work. He knows I'm on to him." He glanced at her, his eyes flashing with anger. "I could see it in his face."

And suddenly she realized why they were going off into the night. "My God. You think they're looking for us, don't you?"

"I know they are," he said quietly, his eyes fixed on the road ahead.

Her stomach churned. What would happen if they were found? What would they do to them? Her gaze darted to the sideview mirror. Nothing. No cars. No headlights. They were not being followed. But that knowledge did nothing to alleviate the tension that had wrapped around her, holding her firmly in its grip.

"Kelsey, we're going to be fine," he said, as if he had

read her thoughts. Reaching out, he took her hand in his and gently squeezed. "We're one step ahead of them right now."

But his words did not quiet the fear that still rushed through her, making her stomach flutter, her heart beat faster. "Did you find anything at work that will help us?"

"It's what I didn't find that worries me." He slowed as they approached a red light, his eyes checking the rearview mirror as they came to a stop. "All information regarding the people on Leah's list has been erased from the main frame. Missing from the hard copy files. Gone."

"They got rid of it?"

"Whatever connection those people have or had to Envirospace . . ." He stopped, searching for the right words. "Someone doesn't want anyone to know about it," he finished.

"So you came up empty."

"Not exactly." The light turned green. David accelerated slowly taking the car back up to the speed limit. "I found a file on Leah's computer."

"Leah's computer?" She was confused for only a moment and then it hit her. "At work? You went to Leah's computer at work?"

He nodded, opening his mouth to continue but Kelsey's words cut him off, stopping him short.

"David, that was stupid. You could have been caught. You shouldn't have risked it. We're on the verge of something big. I know we are." Her voice rose in volume as she continued. "What if they had been watching you? They would have picked you up for sure. They might—"

"Kelsey!" His sharp voice stopped her flow of words. "Do you want to hear this or not?"

Her mouth snapped shut. What was she doing? "I'm sorry. I just don't want anything to happen to you." *Like it did Leah.* But she didn't say that, couldn't. "So what was this file?"

"It was the same 1's and 0's that I've been writing for the last few days."

"The same," she breathed. She stared ahead, unable to face him, knowing if he looked at her he would see the fear behind her eyes. "David, what are we going to do?" she whispered.

"You and I are going to figure out what the hell is going on." He spoke the words with a confidence she did not feel.

"But . . . how?"

"After I left work, I went to my house and pulled out every file, every piece of paper I had relating to Envirospace. Memos, old proposals, payroll readouts."

"That's what's in my trunk? In the boxes?"

He nodded. "The two of us are going to find the connection in those boxes. I know I have a couple of reports with Harvey Staller's name on them. I'm betting we'll find a few more."

"Then what?"

"Then we call those people and find out who they are and what their connection is to Envirospace. Because if we're right, and I have no doubt that we are, then sooner or later my father will have me picked up. He'll try it again. He'll take me. He'll take you and this whole damn thing will start all over."

Minutes later, David turned into the driveway of a large, private home.

"Wait here," he said, pushing his door open and stepping from the car. She watched him, outlined in the headlights, as he made his way to the garage and disappeared around the corner.

Kelsey glanced around. Had they gotten away clean or was someone watching them even now? Dread pumped through her veins like blood, flowing through every fiber of her body. She jumped as the garage door began to slowly rise.

A moment later, David walked out. Climbing back into

the car, he drove inside, the door closing behind them.

"Let's go." They carried the boxes and her bag inside, setting everything on the large dining room table. The house was impressive. Large, expensive, yet homey beyond what Kelsey would have expected. The open layout allowed her to see the living room from the dining room. Dark, rich wood accented the walls, while thick carpeting covered the floors throughout. The back of the house, nearly all windows, overlooked an expansive backyard that backed up to a wooded lot. Kelsey hugged herself as she stared out at those trees. Normally she would have found the view breathtaking but with all that had happened, it only chilled her.

Pulling the blinds closed, she turned to David. "Where do we start?"

He held up a small computer disk. "First I want to make a hard copy of what I found on Leah's computer."

She followed him through the house into a small study. He sat at the desk and flipping on the computer, slipped the disk inside.

As he worked, Kelsey glanced around the room. Her gaze stopped on two photos that sat atop the desk. She lifted one. It showed an older man standing beside David. She recognized him as the man she had seen with David at her sister's funeral. When she first saw them together that day, she had assumed it was his father.

"Your uncle?" she asked, holding it toward him.

He glanced up, nodded, and went back to work.

She set it back in place before lifting the photo beside it. The picture contained a much younger version of the same man. He stood beside a woman who looked a great deal like David. "Your mother?"

He didn't look up this time. Just nodded.

Kelsey wandered from the room as he continued to work. Stepping back out into the living room, her gaze fell on a white plastic photo album that sat on the coffee table. Sitting on the couch, she picked up the album and began flip-

ping through. The same people scattered throughout. David.
His mother. Uncle.

Behind her, she could hear the printer start up, spewing
out the information Leah had gathered.

She flipped back to the first page and stared at a photo
showing his uncle, his mother and another man all holding
a shovel full of earth.

"That's all three of them."

She turned, startled. David stood behind her, leaning on
the back of the couch. She had not heard him enter the
room.

"They started the company together. As a team."

She looked at Hal Ebersol. She wasn't sure what she
expected him to look like. But this handsome young man
in the photo did not fit the villain she had in her mind. "So
that's your father."

"Yes," he whispered, a remoteness in his voice that
went beyond their current situation.

She looked up at him. "Are you all right?"

David sat on the back of the couch, his back to her. "I
don't know. I guess I'm just having a hard time admitting
to myself that my father is doing this. It's hard to get it
straight in my head." He glanced at her. She could see the
pain in his eyes. "We've never been close. There's always
been a wall between us. But this . . . it's difficult."

"David, I—"

"Printer's done," he said, cutting her off before she
could get the words out. A moment later, he rose and went
back into the study. She stared after him, wondering if she
should follow, unsure what she really wanted to say, how
much he wanted her to say. Before she could decide, he
walked back out carrying a stack of papers and, bypassing
her, went directly to the kitchen.

Setting the photo album back down, she followed.

He sat at the table flipping through the computer printouts, comparing it to other papers he had with him.

Kelsey stood behind him, watching as he compared the

1's and 0's. He shook his head, mumbling to himself.

"What is it?" she asked when he offered no explanation.

He glanced up at her. "I brought some of the papers I've been writing." Holding them out, he looked from the computer printer to his own handwriting. "They're identical."

"My God." She took both from him and made her own comparison. "So you were right."

"Yes. It's not just random rantings. This means something."

"But what?"

"That's what we're going to find out." Rising, he began to unload the boxes, stacking the papers into different piles. "We have to go through each one of these files. Somewhere inside these boxes are the answers we need."

Sighing, Kelsey sat down and began sorting through the pages before her.

3

Kelsey yawned, stretching. She blinked several times, her mind foggy. *Where am I?* She looked at the unfamiliar room around her, puzzled. Sunlight streaked across the floor in narrow strips, sneaking in between the still-closed blinds covering the far windows. She lay on a couch, a blanket across her legs. What?

And then she remembered.

David.

She glanced around. He was not in sight. How long had she been asleep? She checked her watch. 9:00 A.M. She rolled her eyes. The whole damn night!

Throwing the blanket aside, she slipped her legs over the side of the couch and stood. She turned toward the dining room and the stacks of files they had been examining the night before. But as she approached, she noticed that the papers had been sorted into smaller stacks. Each name from the list had been given a stack. Some of the names were assigned a phone number or address. Some just had notes.

David had made progress. And she had slept.

She plopped down at the table, glancing at the notes, feeling useless. Thirty seconds later, David stepped into the room carrying a glass of orange juice and a plate of toast.

"You're up," he said, setting the food before her. "Good. I just made breakfast."

She stared down at the food, her guilt deepening. "Why didn't you wake me?"

"You needed the sleep."

"And you don't?"

He sat across from her. "I don't sleep anymore," he muttered.

She looked at him, at the dark circles under his eyes, the pallor of his skin and wondered just how true that statement was.

"What did you find?" she asked, taking a bite out of a particularly dark piece of toast.

He put his hand on top of one of the stacks of papers. "I was able to trace three of the people on the list to Envirospace." His eyes locked with hers when he said, "Two of them are dead."

"What?" Kelsey should have expected it, should have known what he was going to say but she had not. "How?"

"Murdered within days of each other."

Kelsey felt as if all the air in the room had suddenly been sucked out. Breathing became difficult. She stared at the papers. "And the other two?" she asked, somehow finding enough air to speak but not sure if she really wanted to know the answer to her question.

"I don't know. I haven't been able to find the connection . . . yet."

"What about the people you found. Who are they?"

"That's the really strange part." Reaching over, he picked up a pad of paper. "The people I could connect haven't worked for the company for years."

He handed her his notes. He had listed out the three

people and beside each name, their connection to the company.

Pointing to the first name, he said, "Harvey Staller. I knew his connection immediately. He did all the automation work, did the original plan for the moon units. I've referred to him dozens of times in past briefs I've written. I've even recommended his company to a few clients."

"And he's dead?"

"Shot to death in his home day before yesterday."

"This next one," she said, pointing to the list. "This Ned Bringer." She glanced over the notes David had written about this man. "He did some engineering work," she mumbled, flipping through the pages. She glanced back to David. "Is he . . . ?"

"No," David said, providing the answer to the question she did not finish. "He's alive."

Kelsey felt a measure of relief but it quickly evaporated as she realized what that meant. "Then this last one, Tom Hardigan, he's . . . dead."

David nodded. "A few days after Staller. Same caliber of bullet, also found in his home."

"Who was he?" she asked, glancing through the notes. "What did he do?"

"Remember I told you that name sounded familiar? Well, it wasn't any connection to Envirospace that I was remembering. He's that computer whiz. About fifteen years ago, he emerged from Cal Tech with a zillion degrees and just as many offers."

Kelsey tapped the name, nodding. "Yes, I remember now, too. The child prodigy. I read about him in *People* magazine. How is he connected to all this?"

David lay his hand on a small pile of papers. "He set up the original computer language that is still used today with the corporation," he explained. "He's the one who figured out how the computers at the plant could talk to the computers on the moon."

"This was a few years ago," Kelsey said, more to herself

than to David. She sat for several moments trying to put it all together, trying to figure out why Tom Hardigan would now, after all these years, suddenly need to be eliminated. "It all seems so incredible."

"No. The incredible part is that I asked a friend of mine at work if he recognized anyone on the list." He picked up the paper that had fallen out of Leah's diary two nights earlier, his fingers trembling. "He said he didn't."

Kelsey's brow furrowed. David's attitude had changed. Abruptly. And she wasn't quite sure why. "So?"

"Tom Hardigan was brought in by him. They were friends." He spit the words out, anger lancing each syllable.

"He lied to you," Kelsey said when he seemed finished.

David nodded once, curtly. "Sam is involved."

And as he spoke the words, his voice barely audible, Kelsey realized how deeply he was hurt by the admission, realized that Sam must be closer to David than he was admitting.

Reaching out, she gripped his hand. "I'm sorry," she whispered, wishing there was some way she could ease his pain. "Maybe we're wrong about all this, David. Maybe somehow . . ." She stopped talking, knowing how ridiculous she must sound.

A sad smile pulled at the corners of his mouth. "I wish that were true, I really do. But you and I both know it's not."

Kelsey sat in silence for the next few moments, unsure what to say. "So what does his involvement mean to us?" she asked when she felt their silence had gone on too long.

Taking a deep breath, he released it slowly. "It probably means my father knows we have this list." He tossed the paper with the names on the table. "Like an idiot, I showed it to Sam."

"You're not an idiot because you trusted someone you believed was your friend. His betrayal is not your fault."

"You don't understand," he said, his voice low, controlled. "Sam is . . . was my best friend. I thought I knew

him. I would have trusted him with my life. To find out
that he's involved, that he may have participated in some
way . . .'' He stopped speaking, turning away. But not before Kelsey noticed the slight quiver to his lips. She waited,
knowing there was nothing she could say, knowing he
needed her to remain silent.

"It's incomprehensible to me," he finished quickly.
When he faced her again, his jaw was set firmly, his gaze
hardened.

"So where do we go from here?" she whispered.

He cleared his throat, his gaze traveling over the files on
the table top. "I need you to go through the rest of these
papers. Keep looking. We need to find out who those last
two people are."

"Right." Kelsey slid several stacks across the table toward herself. But before she could open the files, David
laid a hand on top of hers, stopping her.

"Not here," he said. "I don't think we'll be safe here
much longer."

"But . . . where?"

"I'm taking you to the library. A public place. You can
work there safe, without worry. It's also a good place to
see what else you can find. Maybe some magazine or newspaper articles. Anything regarding Envirospace that might
help us."

"Why does it sound like I'll be doing this alone?"

"Ned Bringer, the man still alive, I'm going to see him
today."

His words jolted her. "You're what?"

"I called him this morning." He glanced at his watch.
"He lives in Toledo. Short flight. I've already got the tick-
ets waiting for me at the airport."

"Are you sure it's safe?" Kelsey asked, dumbfounded
by this news.

David smiled, a strange, half-cocked smile. "I don't
think it matters anymore."

He stood and began repacking the stacks of papers into the boxes.

She watched him work, her anxiety climbing higher with each stack of paper that disappeared into its container.

"David," she began as he closed the lid on the second box. "I can't just sit back here and hope you come back."

Lifting his briefcase on the table, he pulled a portable phone from inside. "You won't have to. I'm going to check in with you every half hour." He handed her the phone. "It's fully charged. Just keep it with you. I'll call that number."

She stared down at the phone, her fingers playing over the small buttons. "Why don't we just stay together? I could go with you to Toledo."

"If I'm falling into a trap of some sort, then I want you here to pull me out." Reaching in his front pocket he withdrew two business cards and set them on the table in front of her. "If the calls stop. If I don't come back—"

"That won't happen," she cut in, her voice breathless. "Don't even say it."

"I have to." He spoke quietly, his gaze intense. "Neither one of us really knows what we're getting ourselves into, knows what the consequences might be. Anything could happen." He tapped his finger on one of the cards on the table. "My uncle's numbers, here and at work, are on this card. He'll be back today, probably soon. If I don't come back, call him. Tell him everything."

She lifted the second card, staring at the purple lettering. "This other one? Sam Wyatt?" Her eyes widened. "Sam?" She glanced up at him. "Isn't he—"

"Yes," he interrupted before she could finish.

"But I thought we couldn't trust him."

"I can't believe that Sam would continue to lie if my life is on the line."

"David, how can you say that after all that's happened. If he was involved in the original cover-up then—"

"We don't know that," he cut in, his voice rushed. "He

may have only found out afterward. He may only know part.'' And as he spoke, Kelsey realized that he needed to believe it, needed it to be true. ''I know it may sound naive of me but I can't believe he'd do anything to really hurt me. If I'm missing, he'll help you. I know he will.'' He stared down at her, his body rigid, his eyes optimistic. Waiting. Hoping.

''Okay,'' she breathed, praying David was right about his friend, knowing if he weren't, it would cost them both dearly.

''Great,'' he said, his voice relieved. He placed another stack of papers in front of her. ''I want you to take this too.'' It was the printed copy of the file he'd found on Leah's computer, the number combinations he'd been writing for the last few days. ''Try and find out what it means.''

Kelsey flipped through the pages. ''How do I do that?''

''See if the library has any books on binary or computer programming. Anything computer related. Maybe you'll get lucky and actually find a way of decoding it.''

''And if I come up empty?'' she asked, looking to him once more.

''I'll be back tonight,'' he smiled grimly. ''We'll think of something then.''

''You're not asking for much.''

''I think that Leah already found the connection.'' He tapped the pile in front of her. ''It's in here. All of it. We just have to figure it out.''

CHAPTER SIXTEEN

1

Hal Ebersol had not slept well. And he blamed his son.

When he'd phoned Ken Brewer the night before and told him to pick up David and the Brayden woman, Hal had been confident that this entire situation would be under control before morning. But David had not gone home last night. Had not shown up for work this morning. He and the Brayden woman had effectively disappeared.

Dammit! He slammed a fist down on his desk, scattering the papers that sat atop it. Why hadn't he stalled David last night? Kept him here until Ken could arrive? Until they could take him to the site? Until—

He shook his head. This was pointless. He would not waste his time thinking about what he should have done. Instead, he needed to concentrate on what they would do when they located him.

He checked his watch. It had been less than an hour since Sam Wyatt called to tell him that Pearson had arrived as scheduled. The doctor would be on site and set up by nightfall. But as Hal leaned back in his chair, staring unseeing at the far wall, he knew Pearson was not the answer. At least, not for David. The treatment had not kept the memories suppressed for very long and, as a result, David had become more than a small inconvenience. A second treatment didn't seem like the best idea anymore.

But there was an alternative.

They could plant an idea deep in his subconscious. A simple suggestion, like the one they had given the Brayden woman to leave David. Only this time, the suggestion could be more . . . damaging.

Suicide?

No. It simply wouldn't look right. Not after what had already occurred. It'd have to be an accident. Loss of control of his car. Missed step on the stairs. A forgotten pan on the stove. His mouth curled into a satisfied grin. The possibilities were endless.

A knock sounded on the door to his office. Hal blinked several times, brought out of his reverie.

"Come in," he called.

A moment later, Ken Brewer stepped through.

"What is it?" he asked, his voice brusque.

Ken stood beside the door, his eyes locked forward, his back stiff. "David purchased an airline ticket to Toledo."

Hal immediately understood the significance. "Bringer?"

"I believe so."

"And the Brayden woman?"

"Still looking."

Hal nodded but did not dismiss his assistant. Not yet. "You don't like my son very much do you?" he asked after a time.

Ken did not move. His eyes remained forward. "No, sir, I don't." And without missing a beat, added, "He doesn't appreciate all he has."

"No, I suppose he doesn't." And in that moment, the reality of the situation seemed to lock into place for Hal Ebersol. There was really only one solution to this problem. Only one way to handle David.

But he's your son . . . your only child.

It was Claire's voice, whispering in his ear, making him

hesitate. But he had never wanted David, had not asked to be a father. Finally, taking a deep breath, he said, ''Add David's name to the list.''

2

David leaned back, the normally uncomfortable airplane seat feeling cozy, restful. But he had been up all night—any seat would be comfortable at this point. He checked his watch. They had just taken off but should be landing in less than twenty minutes, the entire flight no more than a quick up and down.

Nevertheless, it was twenty minutes he could use to catch up on the rest he'd missed the night before. Settling back, he closed his eyes.

Just as he felt himself drifting off into a gentle sleep, he heard a voice softly calling. The flight attendant. Even on these short jaunts, they still insisted you take your peanuts and soft drink. He sighed, opening his eyes.

But he was no longer on the airplane.

Instead, he was back at Leah's, sitting in the yard at the picnic table, facing the house.

''David?''

He turned sharply toward the voice behind him.

Leah stood only a few feet away wearing the floral dress she had worn that first day he saw her. Behind her, beyond the trees, he could see the path leading into the woods.

''Leah,'' he breathed. It was all he was able to say, all he was able to do.

''You have to be careful, David,'' she said, not moving any closer to him. ''They know where you're going. It's not safe.''

''Who knows? What are you talking about?'' He tried to rise but found he could not.

''I didn't kill myself, David,'' she said. And the warm summer day, suddenly turned dark. Fog rolled in. David was no longer in Leah's yard. Instead, he found himself standing on the side of a road he did not recognize.

"Leah!" he yelled.

"I'm over here, David."

He turned toward her voice. She was a vague shape in the darkness, only a few feet away. The wind blew, stirring the leaves around him, blowing them across his path.

"Be careful, David," Leah said, her voice holding a sadness he had never heard before. She fixed him with her deep blue-green eyes.

And before he could move, cry out, help—headlights swept over Leah. As the car slammed into her, he cried out, feeling the pain himself. Her body was thrown several feet.

He felt the movement, felt as if he were flying himself.

"Leah!" He jolted awake, his heart slamming against his chest, the beating seeming to drown out the sound of the plane's engines.

"Sir?" The flight attendant leaned toward him. "Are you all right?"

He ran a hand over his face, wiping away the perspiration that had formed in his sleep. "Yes. Thank you." His heart drummed an irregular beat in his chest.

"We'll be landing soon," she said, her voice warm, friendly. "I need you to put your seat in its upright position."

He nodded, doing as she asked.

But as he looked down at his lap, his body trembled. Reaching down, he touched the small, wilting lilac pedals.

3

Louis steered his car toward David's condo. He had phoned work but was told David had reported in sick for the day. When he called his home and got no answer, he began to worry. Was David not answering the phone or was he unable to answer?

Pulling up in front of the condo, he pushed his door open and headed toward the front of the house. He knocked several times before using his key to enter.

"David?" he called. Moving through the living room, he glanced into the kitchen. Each room was immaculate as usual. But when he reached the bedroom, he was surprised by what he found. Scattered all over the floor, some on the bed, were computer printouts and loose leaf pieces of paper. Stepping over the threshold, Louis bent down and began picking up the papers. Each one, from top to bottom, some on both sides, was covered with a series of 0's and 1's.

Leaving the bedroom, closing the door behind him, he went to the phone and called Edward Ross.

4

Kelsey sat at a desk in the library, rubbing her eyes. She'd spent the last hour flipping past pages of payroll records, wading through stacks of reports. But so far she had found nothing regarding the last two names on Leah's list.

She turned back to the latest report, trying to refocus her gaze. But before she could read the first line, the small phone in her purse rang. She snatched it out and flipped it open.

David was right on time.

"Hello?"

"It's me."

Relief sped through her at the sound of his voice. "Where are you?"

"The airport. I'm going to catch a cab to his house."

Her grip tightened on the phone. "David, are you sure we're doing the right thing?"

"I think we're doing the only thing we can at this point." He paused. "Any luck on your end?"

"Nothing so far but I'm not giving up."

"That's good. Just . . . don't stay there much longer. I

don't think you should stay any one place too long."

She glanced around the library, taking in the strangers all around her. "They won't look for me here." But even as she spoke the words, she noticed a young man a few tables over, his gaze locked on her. He smiled as their eyes met. She looked away, her heart picking up its beat.

"Where should I go?" she asked, working hard to keep her voice calm. *Don't panic,* she told herself. *He's flirting with you, that's all.*

"You have your car. Once you're finished, just drive around until I call you to pick me up at the airport."

"Okay." She licked her lips, nodding. "Okay. That sounds good."

"I'll call you in a half hour."

"You better. And David . . . be careful."

"You too."

The line went dead. Kelsey folded the phone up and slipped it back into her purse before chancing another look at the young man two tables over. He sat, head down, lost in whatever book was laid out before him, Kelsey forgotten. She let out the breath she hadn't realized she was holding before turning her gaze on the rest of the room. No one watching as she picked up another book and began her search. At least, no one she could see.

CHAPTER SEVENTEEN

1

Toledo, Ohio

David stood in front of Ned Bringer's house. His cab had driven past twice before David was able to point out the driveway. The private access road and the house it led up to were well hidden behind tall bushes and a high stone fence, making it difficult to spot from the street.

The house itself, an expensive two story Tudor, looked unkept, the bushes shaggy against the front, the grass a little taller than it should be.

He'd been standing now for several minutes, trying to bring himself to go up and knock on the door, trying to think of what he was going to tell this man.

If the guy is involved in some kind of cover-up, then he already knows more than me, he reasoned. Deciding to wing it and see what happened, he started toward the house.

The front door opened before he reached it. A man who looked to be in his late forties stood in the doorway, waiting.

"Finally got the nerve to come up," he said. As David drew closer, he could smell the beer on the man. "I was watching you," he continued, each exhale spewing more brewery fumes. "Thought maybe you changed your mind there and were going to leave."

"Almost did," David said, stepping up on the porch, extending a hand. "David . . . Cameron," he said, surprising himself with the lie. But as he shook hands, he realized that it had been the right thing to do. Instinct. He needed to let instinct guide him, tell him what to say and do.

"Ned Bringer," the man said, shaking David's hand. Come on in, Dave. Let's get down to it."

David followed the burly man inside. The house was decorated in neo-modern design that didn't seem to fit the man before him.

Entering the kitchen, Ned indicated the table. David took a seat.

"Sent my wife out shopping. Just gave her the credit card and told her to go crazy." He sat down across from David, a pot of coffee in the center of the table. "We should have plenty of time alone."

"That sounds good." He knew he needed to begin, get things rolling, but he didn't know what to say. "I feel a little like I did outside," he said finally.

"How's that?" Ned leaned back, crossing his arms over his considerable belly.

David cleared his throat. It felt dry, constricted. "I don't know where to begin."

"When you called, you said it was urgent. Something about Envirospace. Is there a problem with those boys? Hal having a fit about something?"

David nodded slowly, trying to think of the best way to draw this man out. Obviously, he knew what was going on, knew the truth. David needed to convince Ned Bringer that he also knew everything.

"You know Hal," he said, casually, watching for a reaction. "He goes nuts over the smallest problem."

"You bet your ass he does." Rising, Ned went to the cupboard behind him and withdrew a bottle of scotch. Sitting back down, he dumped a hefty amount into his cup before offering it to David. He accepted the liquor, hoping to draw the man closer.

David watched as Ned downed his first cup of "coffee" and poured himself another—this one straight from the bottle. Reaching into this jacket pocket, David withdrew the paper showing the five names Leah had printed.

"Actually," he began. "It's not so much you that Hal's having the problem with."

He slid the list toward Ned who was already nodding.

"Don't tell me," he said. "It's that pansy Hardigan. He's having second thoughts about the whole thing."

David smiled easily. "You called it."

"I told Hal to dump that little bastard right from the get go." He took another drink. "What? He threatening to go public?"

"Yes." David leaned forward, the anticipation nearly unbearable. It was all he could do not to jump up and choke this man into spilling it all. "I'm here to make sure you won't join him."

Ned shrugged. "I got my money. Whadda I wanna talk for."

"But if you're asked . . ." David let his words trail off, hoping Ned would jump in.

He did.

"I'll tell 'em Hardigan's makin' it up. The system works perfectly. Hell, I verified it six years ago and they believed me. They'll believe me again."

"But if they send in a new inspector?"

"He won't find nothin'. Nobody has yet." Grabbing the scotch, Ned downed a large portion directly from the bottle. "As far as anyone is concerned, Envirospace is doing everything it says it is." Belching loudly, the sound echoing through the large house, Ned stood. "Gotta piss."

David could hear the man as he made his way down the hall, his heavy footsteps loud, almost like stomping.

I verified the system.

They believed me then. They will again.

Ned Bringer's words spun through his mind. What the hell was his father covering up? Just a few more minutes with Ned Bringer and David would know everything.

2

Hartwick, Michigan

Kelsey sat at a desk in the library staring down at the book spread out before her. It was the fourth she'd gotten from the shelf regarding computer programming. So far she had found nothing that would help her.

She glanced at her watch. David should be checking in again within the next ten minutes. He'd already called once from Bringer's house. He felt safe there. Things seemed to be going well.

Looking up, she watched the other people who milled about, looking at books, checking racks for reference material, running things through the computers.

She glanced down once more at the book open before her and decided it was a waste of time. She simply did not understand computer lingo. Instead, she stood and went to the magazine reference computer. She punched a couple of keys going directly to the search screen. She chose all types of reference and typed in Envirospace.

After a few moments of searching, the computer came up with the closest reference: Environmental.

It wasn't exactly what Kelsey wanted but maybe it would lead somewhere. She paged through the references to environmental damage, groups that work to clean up damage, companies with innovative ideas. Under a subheading, she found an article on Envirospace.

Kelsey went to the word and, highlighting it, brought up files specifically regarding the company.

There were three articles listed. She wrote down the information and then going to the magazine files, pulled the film for each.

Slipping the first film in, she fast forwarded to the article she needed. It was almost eight years old. An update on the company in general.

Not what she wanted. Quickly, she rewound the tape before inserting the second one. But it too was of little use. Information regarding NASA's interest in the short-term propulsion system Envirospace used.

She moved too quickly through the third film, passing the article once before backtracking to it. This one dated back six years. As she scanned the article, she realized it dealt with the upgrade. Sam Wyatt's name was mentioned several times.

As she moved the film to the next page, she stopped. A picture, grainy, unclear glared at her. But it was not the faces she was interested in. It was the caption below the photo.

"New team brought in to upgrade one of America's fastest growing environmental companies." The photo showed six people: Sam Wyatt, Ned Bringer, Betty Cantor, Harvey Staller, Steven Ordmann, Tom Hardigan.

Kelsey began feeding dimes into the machine, copying each page.

3

Toledo, Ohio

Ned Bringer had passed out. David stood on the front porch breathing deeply, trying to clear his nose of the smell of alcohol that seemed to cover him. For the last hour, he'd sat with Ned as the man continued to drink and talk and drink. In all that time, David hadn't really learned much more. The man was so drunk in the end that he was just babbling, his words slurring heavily.

David was just about to tell Ned that he needed to leave, in order to catch his plane back to Michigan, when the man got up for another of his endless trips to the bathroom. David had waited, listening to the heavy footfalls.

But as he mentally counted each step, it took about twelve to get to the bathroom, he decided he could no longer wait. Rising, he moved toward the hall.

Just as he turned the corner into the hallway, Ned stumbled, fell backward, and passed out. David had debated for several minutes, trying to decide if he could just leave or if he needed to do something more.

In the end, he had dragged the large man into the nearest bedroom and after trying to figure out a weight pulley system and realizing it was impossible, left him on he floor beside the bed.

Now, as he stood on the porch trying to clear his head, he knew it was time to leave. Going back inside, he headed for the phone. He'd check in with Kelsey then call the airport and make arrangements to fly back. But as he began to dial, he heard movement in the back of the house.

"Great," he muttered, hanging up the phone. "He's up." David no longer wanted to talk to Bringer but he knew the man would need help getting into bed. That was all David was going to do. Get the jerk into bed and leave.

But halfway down the hall, he heard a sound, a sound that stopped him cold. Thud. Thud. Twice, in quick succession.

A gun?

He wasn't sure but before he could do anything, he heard an unfamiliar voice, the tone cold, unemotional.

"Nothing personal." The words drifted from within the room, permeating the air with their stiff coldness.

And his gut twisted in fear.

The other two men were murdered, shot with the same caliber gun.

David's heart beat heavily against his chest, making breathing difficult. Sweat broke out across his forehead and back.

Why the hell had he come here?

He stood frozen to the spot, listening. But no other sound came from within the room.

Get out of the house!

The words tore through his mind, shaking him. Slowly, he began moving backward, one step at a time. Afraid to make a noise, breathe. After only two steps, a man appeared at the bedroom door. His gaze found David's and in one swift movement, he swung the gun he still carried around and leveled it at David's chest.

"I could hear you breathing," the man said, his voice calm.

David said nothing. He stared at this man with the scarred face and easy manner. An assassin? Had to be. But even as David's gaze moved from the gun that would, at any moment, end his life, to the man who held it, he couldn't help but think this man did not look like what David had always imagined a hired killer would.

The assassin took two steps closer. "I'm sorry. I thought he was alone." He shrugged, raising the weapon toward David's head. "Getting careless."

"You killed them all," David said, finding his voice just as the cold muzzle of the weapon touched his forehead.

The gun hesitated.

"What?" His voice softly questioned.

It had been the only thing David could think to say. And it had stopped him. "Hardigan. Staller. You killed them too."

"Who the hell are you?" But before David could answer, the man grabbed him by the front of his shirt and slammed him into the wall behind him. "Empty your pockets," he ordered.

David hesitated but as the man raised the gun once more, he did as he was told, holding the items in his hands before him.

The man grabbed the wallet first. "David J. Ebersol, out of Michigan." He looked at David, seeming to study his

face for a moment. "Never heard of you." He flipped
through the rest of the wallet, past his American Express,
his Amoco card, his Envirospace I.D. but stopped when he
reached the photos.

The man looked up briefly, eyes narrowing, before continuing to sift through the other items—car keys, change.

"The woman," he began but stopped abruptly, his eyes
locked on the list of names Leah had written.

His gaze shifted from David to the paper back to David,
his eyes growing wide.

"Who sent you?" he demanded. But as before, David
was not given time to answer. Instead, the man yanked him
forward and slammed him once more into the wall behind
him. "Are you following me? Checking my work?"

David's mind raced. What would sound logical? What
would save his life?

"They hire you to take me out when I'm finished?" he
shouted, his anger red-hot. "Is that how this works?" Once
more, the barrel of the gun touched David's forehead.

"No one hired me. I'm here on my own," he blurted
out. Closing his eyes, he waited for the bullet to enter his
skull, rip through his brain, and splatter it on the wall behind him.

But that did not happen.

Instead, the muzzle moved away.

"Why are you here? Where did you get these names?"
The man's voice was once more calm. "Did you take out
the woman?"

David opened his eyes, blinking several times, shocked
to find himself still breathing. "What woman?" he asked,
puzzled by the man's question.

The gunman held a photo up in front of David's face.

"I saw this woman in Oklahoma yesterday. Did you take
her out?"

David stared at Leah's smiling face. "She died . . . nearly
a week ago. Suicide."

The man smiled, a strange, I'm-not-sure-if-I-believe-you,

smile. "You know, I've felt funny about this job for days. I knew something was wrong."

"You killed them all, didn't you?"

The man did not answer. He glanced at Ned's door then back to David. "I'll tell you what, David J. Ebersol." He motioned toward the kitchen with the gun. "I'm going to give you a chance." The two men walked into the kitchen together, David in the lead. Upon entering, the man ripped the phone cord from the wall. A moment later, he shoved David, face first, against the wall. "Put your hands behind your back."

"What—" David started to protest, pushing away, trying to turn around to face this man. But as the gun came to rest at the back of his head, he stopped moving, the words leaving his throat.

"I could just shoot you," the man whispered. "I'm trying to give you a chance to live." The gun pressed hard, forcing his forehead against the wall before him. "Now give me your goddamn hands."

Closing his eyes, David crossed his hands behind his back. He flinched as the man wrapped the phone cord tightly around each wrist, cutting into his flesh, binding them together.

"I have to make a phone call tonight," he said as he knotted the cord. "Supposed to be my last night of work." He gripped David by the shoulder and turned him around. "You're going to stay alive until I make that call." He stuffed the gun back into the holster at his side.

Moments later, they were outside, walking toward the gray Oldsmobile in the driveway. David glanced around, looking for help, hoping someone might be watching. But there was no one. The high bushes and stone barrier concealed them from the street. Concealing him from help. He swallowed the lump in his throat. He could do nothing here. But once they were on the road . . .

His mind sped through one possible scenario. He could wait until they were in a crowded intersection. Kick the

gear shift into park and jump from the car. What could this
man do with so many witnesses? He'd have to let him go.
Just drive off in order to save himself.

That's what he would do. Just wait for the right moment
and then . . . but instead of taking him to the passenger side
of the car, the assassin led him to the back and opening the
trunk, said, "Get in."

4

Hartwick, Michigan

Kelsey sat in her car staring at the place her sister had died.
After copying the article in full, she'd decided it was time
to leave the library. She had planned to just drive around,
aimlessly, exactly as David had asked her. But as she drove,
she realized she was going to the place where Leah died.

She needed to see it. Maybe only this one time. But she
needed to see it. Now, as she sat in her car staring out her
window, she wondered why she had needed to see it so
badly.

But she knew why. The more she looked into Leah's
death, the more she began to realize who her sister was and
that she had died because of something she knew. Kelsey
needed to follow her pattern, needed to discover what she
had discovered. Maybe then she would find the truth.

Had Leah wandered through the woods, confused,
scared? Had she simply stumbled into the road, looking for
help?

She glanced at her watch. Fifteen minutes late.

David where are you?

5

Edward Ross stood on the porch of his nephew's condominium and knocked. The door opened almost immediately.

"Thank you for coming, Mr. Ross," Louis said, stepping aside, allowing him entrance.

"No problem, Louis." Edward crossed the threshold, more than a little curious about what was going on. "I'm sorry I couldn't get here any sooner. I was in a meeting when you called."

Louis helped Edward off with his coat before hanging it by the door, automatically taking on the role he was used to, the role of the butler.

"You said this concerned David. Is he here?" Edward asked, glancing around.

"No," Louis said.

"Do you know where he is? He left a note at my house saying that he stayed there last night. But I can't seem to find him today. No one seems to know where he is."

"I've made some coffee." Louis indicated the couch. "I'll get it and we can talk."

Edward sat down waiting for the man to return. He didn't understand any of this. Why was Louis in David's condo? Why had David stayed at his house last night? And where the hell was David? He was just beginning to grow impatient with the wait, when Louis returned carrying a tray.

"Black no sugar, correct sir?" He handed Edward the cup.

"Yes, thank you." He set it on the table before him without taking a drink. "What's going on Louis?"

"I don't know how to begin." Louis's eyes were cast downward. He held his cup in both hands. "I'm ashamed for the part I played," he said quietly and did not speak again.

"The part you played?" Edward sighed. "I'm not following you. Please, what does this have to do with David?''

Louis sat for several moments. Edward was beginning to think he might have to ask again, when the man finally began to speak.

''About a month ago, Mr. Ebersol came home from work. He was very angry. He said he and David had had a fight. He asked me to call David and see if he would come over.''

''And did you?'' Edward asked when Louis did not immediately continue.

''Yes,'' he whispered. ''But I thought he was going to apologize. I had no idea...'' He shook his head. ''No idea.''

''Louis,'' Edward said, mustering all the patience he had. ''What exactly are you getting at?''

''It was a Friday. Mr. Ebersol had me dismiss the staff for the weekend. Before David arrived, several other men came to the house. I didn't know any of them except Ken Brewer. They all went up to the third floor.''

''The attic?'' Edward's brow furrowed. He knew from visiting his brother-in-law's house that the third floor was used mainly for storage. ''What were they doing up there?''

''I don't know. But they brought in a great deal of equipment.''

''Equipment?'' Edward did not like the direction this seemed to be going. ''What happened when David got there?''

''I was told to show him in, have him wait in the library as usual and then go to my room and stay there.'' He stood and began pacing. ''David only came over because I asked him to. He was so angry. I'd never seen him like that before.''

''What happened?''

''I went to my room,'' Louis said quietly. ''It was storming that night. A horrible thunderstorm.'' He turned to face Edward. ''But I could still hear the shouting. David and Mr. Ebersol fighting.''

"Could you hear about what?"

"No." Louis shook his head, his face miserable. "But I don't think they realized I could hear David when he began calling out."

"Calling out . . . how?"

"They took him up to the third floor against his will," Louis whispered. "Dragged him up there. He was calling for me, asking for my help." Tears began to fall from the corners of the old man's eyes. "He's like my own son and I didn't do anything."

"What happened after that?" Edward asked, almost afraid of the answer.

"Nothing for a while." Louis wiped at his cheeks. "It was quiet for a few hours. Then some of the men left. I watched as they drove off. It was the middle of the night then, maybe two A.M."

"David was upstairs the whole time?"

Louis nodded. "In less than an hour, the men were back but they'd brought others with them."

"Others?"

"Two women," Louis said. "They were also taken to the third floor against their will." Taking a deep breath, he said, "They were there all weekend."

"On the third floor?" Edward asked.

"I don't know what they did up there. I heard . . ." He paused, wringing his hands before him. "I heard a woman's scream at one point, long, agony-filled." He looked at Edward. "It cut off abruptly. Like . . . like . . ."

"Like what?" Edward pressed.

"I think she may have died," Louis said, his voice barely audible. He paused briefly. "Sunday night around one A.M.," he began again, "they all left. The men, the equipment, everything."

"David?"

"He left then too. I called him the next day to see if he was all right. I brought it up. Asked him what happened that weekend. He said he spent the weekend home in bed with the flu.''

Edward blinked. ''He lied?''

''No. I don't think so.''

Edward could hear the concern in the butler's voice, see the fear in his eyes. ''What then?'' he asked, bracing himself.

Louis's answer sent a cold chill down his spine.

''I think they made him forget.''

CHAPTER EIGHTEEN

1

David lay on his side, his hands behind his back. His cheek rested against the covered spare tire, his knees were drawn up against his chest. Every muscle in his body ached from the tight confinement.

The car stopped, started. Turned, slowed down. And David felt every agonizing inch of every mile they traveled as if he were a part of the road they bumped along. Dim light filtered in from the brake lights, washing the trunk in red each time the car slowed. Otherwise, he lay in darkness.

He tried not to think about where they were going. What might happen to him when they arrived. Instead, he closed his eyes. Concentrated on his breathing. Pushed the pain in his limbs to the back of his mind. Did his best to remain calm.

He needed to think.

He was unwatched and alone. It was possible this would be the only time that happened. He had to devise some way of escaping.

He wriggled his wrists back and forth looking for any leeway. But the binding was tight, cutting into the flesh of his wrists.

He had to think, figure a way out.

The car struck a pothole in the road. David was thrown against the lid of the trunk. The left side of his head and shoulder struck hard, sending pain down his back, numbing his mind. He tried to focus his thoughts, but found himself filled with a dread he could not shake. The trunk, so much like . . .

She screamed and then was silent.

No! He squeezed his eyes shut, blocking out the thoughts that threatened to overwhelm him. He could not remember. Not now. Whatever information was lost in his head needed to stay that way. At least for the time being.

He bit his lip so hard he drew blood. The pain helped clear his mind, gave him something else to concentrate on. He could not give in to the images that would carry him to the dark place in his past. A place he could not afford to visit now.

After a few moments, he had control. Once again he was able to concentrate on the problem at hand: finding a way out.

He thought about kicking the backseat out but immediately dismissed the idea. He didn't know how difficult it would be and it would surely alert the man driving the car to his activity. No, he needed something more quiet. Before climbing into the trunk, he had briefly studied the contents. But there wasn't much to see. He guessed that the car was rented. The trunk looked unused, completely empty of anything that might help him.

Except one possibility.

Shifting his shoulders back and forth, pushing with his feet, he began maneuvering around the tight space. Twice he stopped, his body shaking from the effort of the maddeningly slow movement. His wrists throbbed from the constant pull of the bindings around them. Each movement seemed to twist the cord tighter, cutting off the circulation to his hands until they felt numb.

After what seemed an eternity, he lay in the correct position. Using his hands, he felt around as best he could behind him. Within moments, he found what he had been looking for. The car's jack box. He moved his hands over it, feeling for the latch that would open it. Silently, he prayed that the last person to use this thing had put the tools back properly, that they would not spill out all over him when he got the thing open.

Finding the latch, he moved his fingers over it and popped it open. Nothing happened. The tools were secure. He felt inside, searching for anything with a sharp edge to cut the binding around his hands.

"Damn," he whispered as his finger sliced open against the edge of a tire iron.

Carefully maneuvering the sharp area into place, he began to slowly rub it up and down against the telephone line that bound his wrists. He bit his lip as he sliced his own skin time and time again. But it did not take long before the wire split in two. David almost cried out in joy as the binding fell away.

It took a little more maneuvering and shifting before he was able to pull his hands in front of him.

He rubbed his wrists where the cord had been, feeling fresh blood. But it did not matter. His hands were free.

The car slowed and then came to a stop.

David tensed.

One phone call and you're free.

That's what the man had said. But as the car shifted, a sign of his captor stepping out, he didn't believe it would happen.

Who would he call? Whoever hired him? David was almost sure it was his father. If this man, this hired killer, told Hal Ebersol who he had stashed in his trunk . . .

David's stomach clenched with fear. He knew what his father would say. He knew if the choice were David or the company, the company would win every time.

He concentrated on his breathing, working hard to keep it under control. Above all else, he could not panic. He had to keep his wits about him.

He strained to hear any sound. A car horn, a dog barking, traffic, voices. Anything. But as he lay on his side, smelling oil and dirt, he realized he could hear nothing. The man had obviously picked an out of the way spot to make his call. He was a professional. Smart enough to know David would call out for help at the first opportunity.

Quietly, almost inaudibly, David could hear the man's muffled voice. It lasted only a few seconds. Then a soft jingling. Car keys?

One phone call and you're free.

Was it possible? Was he coming back to let him out as promised? Would David simply be allowed to leave?

But then the car shifted as his abductor got back in. Moments later, they began moving again.

He would not go free. He would remain a prisoner, held against his will.

Just like that night. Just like . . .

He struggled but there were too many.

They took him upstairs—to the third floor.

She screamed once and then was silent.

"No," David whispered, squeezing his eyes shut as his mind filled with images he did not understand, did not want to remember.

Pain.

It ripped through David's mind, rocking him. "God!" he screamed, his hands going to the side of his head, as his mind threatened to split in two.

Her hand was crushed beneath their boots.

They carried her body out.

He felt warm. Cold. Dizzy. "Stop!" he screamed. His eyes rolled wildly in their sockets.

I've got to get away. I've got to get away. I've got to get away.

The words tumbled through his mind, the only coherent thought he could grasp, the only words he wanted to listen to.

Hands grabbed at him.

They held him down, strapped him in.

"Let me go!" he yelled, punching around him, hitting the sides of the trunk, kicking out, hitting his head.

Help me!

"Help me!"

He heard his desperate cry as if from another place, another lifetime.

Images flashed through his mind at dizzying speeds. He spun with them, lost within them.

Then it all went black.

2

Hal stood at the window of the library. But his gaze was not cast down at Envirospace. Instead, he stared up at the moon.

Beautiful in its simplicity, it hung low in the sky, full and bright. Clouds drifted past, distorting the round ball in a hazy mist before moving on. He smiled at what had been the inspiration to his entire empire.

The phone on his desk rang once. He lifted the receiver to his ear before the second ring.

"Yes?"

"It's been set in motion." Ken Brewer spoke the words without emotion.

Hal hung up without replying. He glanced at the grandfather clock in the far corner of the library and wondered how long it would take.

The front doorbell rang drawing his attention. His brow furrowed. He wasn't expecting anyone. And he certainly didn't welcome people just dropping by. The bell rang again. Where the hell was Louis?

Stepping out of the library, he listened. But he did not hear the shuffling sound of the old man as he made his way to the door.

"Louis?" he called. The bell rang a third time, echoing

through the empty house. Then silence. Shaking his head, impatience tightening his shoulders, Hal crossed the foyer in quick strides and pulled the door wide.

Edward Ross stood on the porch, light fog just beginning to roll in behind him. He smiled, beamed, his eyes sparkling with a look of satisfaction Hal had never seen before.

"Louis told me everything," he said, his voice smug.

Hal's eyes narrowed slightly. "What the hell are you talking about?"

Edward leaned against the doorframe, crossing his arms over his chest. "You know what I'm talking about."

Hal stared at his brother-in-law. *Louis told me everything.* But what could Louis know? He had been here that weekend but he hadn't been involved. Guesses. He'd told Edward something. But he could not know the truth.

"What is this Edward? Some new tactic you've devised to try and intimidate me? Like everything else you've tried, this won't work." He tried to close the door but Edward reached out and forced it open.

"Aren't you even curious?" he whispered.

"Not in the least." Hal released the door, stepping back inside his house, leaving his brother-in-law on the porch.

"I now know why you've been fighting me so vehemently for David's shares of the company." Edward stepped inside, closing the door behind him. "You've been hiding something, something that we'd find out if you didn't hold the controlling shares."

Hal crossed into the library and, taking a seat before the fireplace, withdrew a cigar from the box beside him.

"I'm not only going to take the company from you," Edward said, following him inside. He stopped in front of Hal and glared down at him. "I'm going to send you to prison."

Hal held the lighter to the end of his cigar and inhaled deeply, chuckling as he puffed out smoke. "How do you propose to do that?"

Reaching into his pocket, Edward withdrew a single

sheet of paper. He tossed it at Hal. It drifted into his lap, landing gently across his legs. "So dramatic," Hal said, casually lifting the paper and turning it over. 1's and 0's glared up at him. In an instant, his heartbeat doubled.

"They're scattered all over David's condo," Edward said. He pulled out a second paper filled with the same 1's and 0's. Then another and another. He dropped each one at Hal's feet. "You held David here against his will. And now something is happening to him because of it." He dumped out the last of his papers. "I want to know what it means. I want to know what you did to him."

Hal stared down at the pile of papers on the floor. *Betrayal.* The word echoed through his mind. After more than thirty years of loyal employment, Louis had betrayed him. Had gone to Edward and told him what had happened behind closed doors.

Slowly, he shifted his gaze to the man who stood before him, hands on hips, looking at him with arrogant self-importance. How dare he come into *his* house and accuse him. Threaten him!

His gut twisted in barely contained rage.

Keeping his eyes on Edward, Hal crumbled the paper he held and tossed it into the fireplace.

Edward did not flinch. "Louis knows. I know. It's only a matter of time before everyone knows.

"Get out," he growled.

"Fine. You'll be hearing from my attorney in the morning." Crouching down, Edward began gathering up the papers. "I'll be filing for a restraining order to keep you off the grounds of Envirospace. As soon as I locate David—"

"You don't know where David is?" Hal interrupted.

Edward stood, the papers a haphazard pile in his hands. "He was out for the evening."

Hal smiled then. A long, slow, satisfied smile. He inhaled deeply on the cigar, relishing its rich flavor. "David won't be home tonight."

Edward's eyes narrowed. "What are you talking about?"

Hal laughed, a deep, hearty sound. "Oh, how do I put this." He locked his gaze on his brother-in-law. He wanted to savor every moment of his reaction, take in every little nuance of shock and fear. Speaking clearly, slowly, he said, "David will be dead before morning and you'll never trace it to me."

The blood drained from Edward's face. He dropped the papers he had been holding. "You're lying," he whispered.

Hal took another long inhalation, releasing the smoke as he spoke. "You know I'm not."

Reaching out, Edward gripped Hal's shirt and yanked him to his feet. "Where is he!" he shouted, his face, red, strained, only inches from Hal's.

"Get your goddamn hands off me!" Hal shoved him backward.

"Damn you," Edward wheezed, the breath leaving him all at once. He stumbled a few steps toward Hal but then stopped, his hand going to his heart, his face taking on a pained look.

And Hal saw his opportunity.

"I told them to make David suffer," he taunted.

Edward's grimace grew wider, his face a combination of agony and horror. He gulped in air, trying desperately to breathe. His gaze rolled from one end of the room to the other before stopping on the phone. He stumbled toward it.

"I told them to make it as painful as possible," Hal jeered, following behind him, dogging his steps.

Edward went down on one knee, gasping for air that would not come.

Hal stood directly behind him, watching, his arms crossed over his chest.

"Do you need to call someone?" Taking two slow, easy steps forward, he lifted the receiver and held it out toward his brother-in-law. Edward grabbed for it. But just as his fingers brushed the receiver, Hal yanked it away. For a moment, their eyes locked.

"You can join your sister and nephew in hell," Hal whispered.

Edward collapsed on his side and stopped moving.

Hal stood over his still form for several minutes, the phone in his hand.

"Edward," he said as the phone began to blare its anger at being off the hook so long. "Edward, can you hear me?"

No answer. No movement at all.

He hung up the phone, waited another minute and then dialed 911. After explaining the situation, careful to have the right mixture of fear and shock in his voice, he hung up.

Turning back to his prone brother-in-law, he smiled. Things could not be turning out better. With Edward out of the way—

Hal turned, the thought falling away as a splash of color moving across the foyer caught his eye.

"Who's here?" he called.

No answer.

"Louis?"

Still nothing.

He turned back to Edward. "Must be losing my mind," he muttered. Kneeling down, he touched the back of his brother-in-law's head. "But you've thought that all along haven't you." In the distance, he could hear the sirens as the ambulance approached. "I bet you wish—"

Was someone behind him? He spun suddenly. The foyer was empty. But for a moment, no longer than a blink of the eye, he thought he saw someone there. A young woman, her blond hair hanging loosely around her shoulders. "Ghosts," he muttered.

3

Kelsey pulled into a slot between two cars and shut off her engine. She glanced around. A woman pushed her grocery

cart toward a car, a man emptied bottles from the trunk of
his car into an empty basket, two children stood by the front
doors of the store collecting for their school band. Everything felt normal. But Kelsey could not relax.

She checked her watch. Again. Nearly two hours since
she'd last heard from David. She looked down at the seat
beside her. The majority of the files were in her trunk. But
she had kept the computer binary, the diary, and the newspaper clippings with her. They were the key. The key to
finding out what had happened to Leah. And possibly the
key to finding David now.

Using the portable phone, she dialed the numbers on the
card for Edward Ross. But just like the last two times she'd
tried, she received only an answering machine.

She stared down at the second card. Sam Wyatt. She'd
debated calling him for the last hour. Could she trust him?
But no matter how many ways she looked at it, the answer
was always the same. She had no choice. She had to trust
him.

Reluctantly, she dialed Sam's number. Twenty minutes
later, a late model sedan pulled into the lot.

A man with wild red hair and a purple shirt stepped from
the car. She had never met Sam Wyatt before but from
David's brief description, she knew it had to be him.

Kelsey did not get out of her car. Instead, she waited
until he approached then slowly rolled down her window.
"Sam?"

As he nodded, she leaned over and unlocked the passenger door. He slid inside.

"What's going on? Where's David?"

She glanced around the lot. But everything seemed the
same as before. People with carts, kids. Nothing out of the
ordinary.

"David went to see one of the men on that list he showed
you," she said, watching him carefully.

His brow furrowed. "What list?"

Kelsey nearly laughed. "The list of names you lied about."

"Lied? I don't know—"

"Don't bother," Kelsey cut in, stopping him short. She shoved the article she had copied from the library into his hands. "You know them all. You brought them all in on this project. And at least two of them are dead now."

"Dead?" He paled slightly.

"Murdered." She paused for a moment, giving him a chance to digest her words before continuing. "David went to see one of the men on that list and now he's late checking in with me. Right now, I don't know where he is. And I'm scared."

Sam stared down at the grainy picture in his hands, not moving, not speaking.

"Sam," she pleaded. "Tell me what you know."

He ran a hand over his hair, managing to flatten some of the wildness out of it. His eyes shifted from side to side. He chewed on his lip. But he said nothing.

"David told me to call you if he stopped checking in with me. He thought you were involved but said that he didn't think you'd let anything happen to him. Was he *that* wrong about you?"

He glanced at her, his eyes uncertain. But still he did not speak, did not admit to knowing anything.

"They brainwashed David and my sister, didn't they?" she pressed. Still, he remained silent. Grabbing the diary, she flipped past pages. "Somehow, they made them forget what they knew," she continued, her voice rushed. "Made them forget anything was done to them. Here, right here." She held the book up, showing the missing dates. "They took them on these three days. That's why my sister skipped them in her diary. They took them and made them forget. Right?" She shoved the book toward him, her voice growing louder and louder until she was shouting. "I'm right, aren't I? Aren't I!"

"Yes!" he yelled. "Yes, dammit."

She blinked several times, shocked he had actually admitted the truth. She pulled the book back into her lap, fingering the pages. "You're supposed to be his friend," she whispered.

"I am his friend," he mumbled.

"How could you let that happen to him? He trusted you and you helped cover up what they did to him."

He looked at her, his face miserable. "My solution kept them alive."

"Not my sister," she said, her voice barely audible.

"I know. I'm sorry." He turned away, a shaky hand running once more through his wild hair. "There were just too many reminders, too many triggers. I thought I could limit them. Control them. I thought as long as I supervised them, everything would be okay."

"That's what killed Leah, isn't it? The memories?"

"Most likely."

"And Hillary? Is she dead too?" The question hung between, unanswered for several minutes.

"It was an accident," he said after a time, his voice low. "It happened during the procedure. We didn't know she had a weak heart."

"My God," Kelsey breathed. "You killed her trying to brainwash her?"

Sam nodded once but did not speak.

"Do you have any idea what you've done to David?"

Still, Sam remained silent, his gaze cast downward.

"He's having flashes of conversation he doesn't remember. Nightmares, dizzy spells. He's writing things he doesn't understand. Here, look at this." She shoved the printout from Leah's computer into his hands.

"What's this?"

"You tell me."

Sam flipped through the pages. "It looks like computer binary. Where did you get it?"

"My sister was writing it before she died." Holding up

the diary, she showed him the pages with the 1's and 0's. "Now it's in David's head."

Sam's brow furrowed. "What do you mean, 'in David's head'?"

"It's part of what he's remembering. Part of what was taken from him. Do you know what it means?"

He looked back down at the numbers. "I'm not sure but from the looks of it, I'd say it has something to do with communications." He lifted each page. "Hillary worked in communications," he said, more to himself than to her.

"Sam," she said, drawing his attention back to her. "What are you covering up? Is Envirospace dumping in the woods behind my sister's house?"

His eyes narrowed. He tilted his head to one side as if studying her for a moment. "You still don't know," he said quietly, his face taking on a look of sudden and complete comprehension. "Then David doesn't remember."

A chill raced up Kelsey's spine. "Remember what? What else is there?"

He looked at his watch. Glanced around the parking lot. "Maybe we've caught it in time. Maybe it's not too late."

"Too late for what? What are you talking about?" she nearly shouted, her nerves stretched taut. But as she waited for an answer, her chest tightening with each passing moment of silence, she noticed a man only a few feet from her car. A very familiar man.

Her heartbeat doubled as Ken Brewer drew near.

She reached for the ignition, a light sheen of sweat covering her body. But before she could twist the key, Sam put a hand on hers, stopping her.

"It's for the best," he said softly.

She yanked her hand away from his. "You lying bastard."

4

David awoke with a start. His body ached, his head throbbed. He felt as if he'd been battered.

It was dark, pitch dark. Where was he? What was happening?

He searched backward through his memories, straining for information that did not want to come.

And remembered. Everything.

Rage welled up within him, swept through him, nearly smothered him in its weight.

His father, Ken Brewer, Sam—they all knew. They were all involved!

He squeezed his eyes shut, fighting against the fury that threatened to overwhelm him. Because he knew, somewhere in the deep recesses of his mind, that if he let the anger take over, he was dead. He had to get himself under control. Had to think with a clear mind. He listened to the steady thrumming of the tires, letting the anger fall away with each passing mile. After a time, he was able to concentrate on the situation at hand.

He lay inside a trunk. Being driven to his death.

He took several deep breaths, working hard to clear his mind, release the tension in his body.

He had to think. Had to plan.

The car made a sharp turn left. It bumped and banged over rough terrain, dipping down in deep ruts.

They had left the main road.

The thought struck him with the force of a blow. And with the thought came the only logical conclusion. The man driving the car was taking him to a remote area so he could put a bullet in his head and then dump his body and leave.

David's heart pounded an irregular beat in his chest. A minute ticked by.

Think, dammit! Think!

He felt around in the darkness. A weapon. He needed a

weapon! He maneuvered his way around the tight space until he once more came in contact with the jack box. He moved his hands over the tools inside, feeling each one, looking for the tire iron. He pulled it from its slot, liking the way the heavy metal felt in his hands.

But before he could decide exactly what he was going to do with his new weapon, the car came to a sudden stop. He lay inside the blackness of the trunk, clutching the heavy metal tool to his chest. His stiff muscles ached, his head pounded. What could he do? What . . .

The car shifted as the scarred man stepped out.

David tensed. His mind raced.

He has to take me out of this trunk, David reasoned. *He can't turn the car in with blood in the trunk.*

And in the next instant, he did the only thing he could think of and slipped his hands once more behind his back.

Outside, he heard his captor approach. Keys jingled as they were inserted into the lock.

David rolled backward slightly, concealing the tire iron behind his back, and braced himself.

He would have only one chance.

"Sorry, friend." The muffled voice came through the trunk, the tone slightly mocking. "But they added your name to my list." A moment later, the lid popped open.

Reaching inside, the assassin gripped David's arm. "I just want you to know," he said, pulling David into a sitting position. "That this is nothing per—" He stopped talking, the words trailing off. His brow creased as if he *sensed* something were wrong.

"What—" was all he said before David pulled the tire iron from behind his back and swinging it high, hit the man square on the side of the head. A large gash opened just above his right ear. The killer staggered backward, his eyes wide with surprise. David climbed from the trunk, his limbs stiff from their cramped position. He stumbled a couple of steps but managed to raise the tire iron again and hit the man once more, this time on the back, driving him to his knees.

David went with him, his legs giving out. He and the man knelt on the ground, facing each other, breathing hard. David pushed up, struggling to his feet as the assassin fumbled around inside his coat, searching for his gun.

Pulling back, nearly falling again, David kicked him hard in the stomach. Then again, this time in the head. The man went limp on the ground, his breathing irregular. The scarred man lay on his side, his head bleeding. David bent forward and yanked the gun from its holster.

"Tables have turned," he panted, tossing the tire iron away. He stumbled backward, sitting down hard on the edge of the trunk. His hands shook. A wave of nausea washed over him. Closing his eyes, he leaned forward, taking several deep breaths. After a few minutes, his head cleared. As he opened his eyes, his gaze was drawn downward to the unconscious man on the ground.

He had done it. God dammit, he had actually done it!

But as he continued to stare down at him, a new thought struck.

"Now what?" he muttered.

CHAPTER NINETEEN

1

"It'll be different for you."

Kelsey did not look at Sam as he spoke. She could not. Instead, she kept her gaze on the bald man that drove her car.

How could I be so stupid?

Not only had she allowed Sam to trick her but she'd kept all the evidence they had collected with her. The newspaper articles, the computer printouts, the diary.

And now Ken Brewer had it all.

"You'll be given the treatment but I promise, it'll be different for you," Sam continued. "We'll send you home right afterward. You won't have anything to remind you, anything to trigger your memories."

Kelsey fought hard to keep her face neutral, keep hidden the fear that welled up inside her. She would not give them the satisfaction of knowing that the idea of receiving the same "treatment" that had drive Leah to suicide, absolutely terrified her. Instead, she set her mouth in a firm line, kept her back rigid and stared ahead.

"Dr. Pearson has assured me that he's made some improvements to his treatment." Sam's voice held a regretful tone, as if he were not completely happy with the turn of events. "You may have vague memories here and there but they'll be too fleeting to make any difference."

"And David?" she asked stiffly.

Sam remained silent for a moment. "I promise, you'll be safe." The tone of his voice had not changed but Kelsey could sense a discomfort she had not before.

She turned to face him. "That's not what I asked you."

He stared ahead, not meeting her gaze. "When David is found, he'll receive a second treatment." Again, his voice held the same hesitation and doubt.

"What does that mean for him?"

But before Sam could answer, the car came to an abrupt stop. A moment later, Ken Brewer shut off the engine. Kelsey glanced out the window.

Eve's house.

Abandoned. Isolated. The perfect trap.

She turned back to Sam. "Is it safe for David?"

Sam did not look at her. Did not speak.

Ken Brewer stepped from the car and reaching back, opened Kelsey's door.

She gripped Sam's arm, squeezing hard. "Will he be okay?" she pleaded.

Sam covered her hand with his, meeting her gaze. And in his tortured eyes, she saw the answer before he spoke. "I'm not sure."

Seconds later, she was yanked from the car. Ken kept one bruising hand on Kelsey's arm as they walked toward the house. Sam trailed a few steps behind.

Kelsey stared at the woods. Only a few feet away. Her salvation. Her only hope. If she could break away, somehow get to the woods, she was sure she could make her way back to the neighborhood on the other side of the trees. All she needed was people. Witnesses. Then she could find David. Warn him.

Shifting her gaze, careful not to let the man beside her know she was looking, Kelsey studied him. Did he have a gun? She couldn't tell. But it could easily be hidden beneath the covering of his jacket.

He stared ahead seemingly unaware of her. Unaware of her plans. She could easily—

"Don't."

He spoke the word softly, almost inaudibly. In the same instant, the hand around her arm increased in pressure.

And her hopes sank.

Stopping in front of the door, Ken inserted a key. Once inside, he did not break stride as he walked toward the stairs and began up, pulling her along behind him. She stumbled on the top step.

So fast. It's happening so fast!

He yanked her upright and continued on, leading her to a room at the end of the hall. Stepping over the threshold, they came to an abrupt halt. A man in a white lab coat stood on the far side of the room. Kelsey's gaze locked on the hospital bed beside him, restraining straps hanging over the sides. Her eyes grew wide.

"No." She struggled against Ken, pulling at his hand, trying to free herself. "No!"

Gripping her upper arms tightly, Ken swung her around to face him. "I will hurt you."

Kelsey froze. In his eyes, she could see a deep malevolence, a hatred that went beyond understanding. Fear rippled through her, making her knees weak, her mouth dry. Not only would he hurt her, but she suspected, he might enjoy doing it.

He shoved her toward the bed. She shuffled forward, feeling clumsy, useless. She couldn't help David. She couldn't even help herself. She closed her eyes as Ken Brewer strapped first her wrists and then her ankles down.

"Begin tonight." His voice penetrated the haze in her mind. "Mr. Ebersol wants this done before Monday."

She opened her eyes, turning her head slightly until the two men came into focus. She stared at the man in the lab coat. Younger than she had first thought. Thirty-five, maybe thirty-eight, his long, straight features giving him a severe look.

"This has greatly furthered my research," he said, pulling on latex gloves. "Any others you could bring would only help."

Ken said nothing. Simply glanced one last time at Kelsey before leaving, closing the door softly behind him.

Kelsey's mind raced. She had to do something. She pulled at the straps around her wrists but they held tight. She couldn't let them erase everything from her mind, send her home with no memory of the last week. It couldn't end like this!

2

David drove toward Hartwick. The highway, empty at this hour of the night, allowed him the freedom of speed. He only hoped a cop didn't decide to pull him over. This was not his car and he didn't know how he would explain the gun on the seat beside him.

He glanced in his sideview mirror, switched lanes and passed a minivan going too slow. He'd left the man with the scar where he lay unconscious on the ground. It was the only solution he could come up with. He didn't want to bring the man with him. And if he took him to the authorities, they would ask questions, questions he could not answer.

No, the man with the scar was not important.

Kelsey.

As soon as he'd reached a phone, David had tried calling her. But there was no answer. Next he'd tried Sam and his uncle Edward. But in each instance, he came up empty.

They're all together, he assured himself not for the first time. When he didn't check in with Kelsey, she'd taken his advice and called both men. Now they were somewhere safe, putting all the pieces together.

But why isn't she answering the phone?

The question swirled through his mind, unwanted. He slammed his hand against the wheel. Because deep down, he knew the answer.

Something went wrong.

He tried to piece together in his mind all his father had done to keep the truth from the public, how many people he had hurt in order to keep his empire.

When David first got behind the wheel of the car, he'd wanted to just drive. Put as much distance between himself and home as was possible. But he couldn't. He couldn't leave Kelsey to deal with it all alone.

Kelsey.

He had failed Leah. He could not fail her too.

His speed increased as he passed the sign welcoming him back to Michigan.

3

Joe came around slowly. Instinctively, his hand sought out the weapon at his side. Gone. He rolled over, groaning and sat up. He checked for the other weapons he carried. The smaller 9-mm Smith and Wesson was still strapped to his ankle. Same with the second one he kept tucked in the back of his pants.

David Ebersol was definitely not a pro.

He glanced around looking for the young man who had managed to knock him out, who had caused so much damn trouble. But the area around him was empty. His car and his target were gone.

He wiped at the blood that trickled from the cut on his head. Gently probed the lump on the back of his head.

Could be worse, he thought. *Could be dead.*

"This is what I get for being a nice guy," he grumbled, getting to his feet with some difficulty.

Reaching inside his coat pocket, he pulled out the wallet

he had confiscated from David. As he began going through it, an I.D. card fell out, landing at his feet. He stared down at it for a moment, an idea forming in his mind. Bending down, his head still pounding, he picked up the card.

"Envirospace," he whispered, running it through his fingers.

CHAPTER TWENTY

1

Hal slammed the front door open. "Louis!" he yelled. The sound of his voice echoed through the empty halls. "Louis!"

No answer.

Dammit.

It had taken much longer at the hospital than he had anticipated. So many questions. So many forms to fill out. He only hoped that Louis was still at David's condo.

Going to the phone, he dialed Ken's mobile number.

2

Sam sat in front of the row of dark monitors, wishing he were anywhere but here. Earlier, when he'd heard Kelsey's cry of protest from above, he had wanted to go upstairs, had wanted to do something to try and stop what was happening. But he had not. Instead, he had stared down at his hands and tried like hell to convince himself that he was doing the right thing.

Now as he sat staring at the blank monitors, Kelsey's words haunted his mind.

How could you let that happen to him?
You're supposed to be his friend.

He ran his hands over his face, through his hair.

Reaching in his pocket, he pulled out the grainy copy of the magazine photo Kelsey had given him. Dead. At least two were dead. Maybe more.

He stared at each face. He had brought these people in. They were his business acquaintances. Colleagues. His gaze fell on Tom Hardigan. Friends.

Is it safe for David? Will he be okay?

The questions echoed through his mind, repeating over and over, demanding an answer.

Is it safe? Is it safe? Is it—
No!

The single word blasted through his mind. And with it came the truth he had tried so desperately to avoid. No, David could not safely receive a second treatment. Pearson had made that clear during the first session. But what could he do now to stop it?

He glanced at the man on the other side of the room. Ken Brewer sat at the far desk reading through Leah's diary, angrily flipping from page to page. Sam's gaze shifted to the pile of computer pages on the desk beside Ken. The binary readout.

What did they mean? What else were Hal Ebersol and Ken Brewer keeping from him?

And as he sat watching Ken, he made a decision. He needed to get a page of that binary. Needed to find out for himself exactly what it meant.

The muffled sound of a ringing phone split the silence, echoing through the room, making Sam jump slightly.

Reaching inside his jacket, Ken withdrew a small flip phone. "Yes?" He listened for several seconds. "I'll take care of it."

Tucking the phone back inside his jacket, he turned to Sam. "Mr. Ebersol has an emergency I must take care of. You stay here until I return."

Sam nodded, his gaze slipping to the printouts then back to Ken. He stood, leaving the items he had confiscated from Kelsey on the desk, and headed toward the door.

Sam listened until he heard the car outside drive away. Then crossing the room, he picked up the binary readouts and went to a table with a computer. Flipping on the machine, he laid the 1's and 0's out beside him and began feeding the information into the computer.

3

David parked his car across the street from Leah's. He glanced around. No one watching the house. No one watching him. At least, no one he could see. But as his gaze traveled once more over the small house, he knew instinctively that it was empty.

Just like his uncle's place.

Kelsey. Sam. Edward. All missing.

But as he sat, staring out his window, unsure of what to do, he noticed movement at the edge of the trees. He turned just as a dark figure ducked into the covering of the woods.

"Kelsey," he whispered, squinting toward the trees, his brow furrowing. Was it her? He couldn't be sure.

Turning, he glanced down at the gun in the seat beside him. After only a moment's hesitation, he grabbed up the weapon, pushed his door open and jogged across the yard. Dipping beneath a low-hanging limb, he entered the woods. Instantly, he caught sight of her again. Only a few feet away, moving fast.

"Kelsey! Wait!" He crashed through the forest, pushing back branches, jumping small piles of brush, dodging trees. His breath raged in and out as he worked hard to keep up.

"Wait!"

But as he continued the chase, he suddenly realized where he was being led. A moment later, Eve Forrester's house came into view.

He stopped at the edge of the trees, just inside the covering of the woods. He felt the presence beside him before he saw her.

Slowly, he turned to face her.

"Leah," he breathed, barely able to believe his eyes.

She stood a few feet away. Her body, rippling in and out of focus, shimmering in the darkness, floated several inches above the ground. Their eyes met and a jumble of emotions thundered through him.

Fear. Regret. Love. Hate.

He took an involuntary step back, his breath leaving him in a rush, as the power of the emotions threatened to overwhelm him.

David could not speak, think.

"What's happening?" he whispered, managing to find his voice.

Leah shifted her gaze to the house in the clearing. And lifting a hand, she pointed toward Eve's.

Kelsey.

The name rocketed through his mind. And in that instant, he understood what she was trying to tell him. Kelsey was in that house. Held against her will. In danger.

Before he could decide what to do, Leah vanished. She blinked out of existence in the time it took him to inhale a breath.

And he was left alone.

He turned back to the house, surveying the grounds. No guards. But that didn't mean there weren't a few inside. He glanced down at the pistol in his hand suddenly feeling very inadequate to the task before him. How was he going to get inside? And once in, how the hell was he going to get them both out?

He shook his head. None of that mattered. All that mattered was getting Kelsey out. He would not let her go through the hell he had been through.

Taking one last look around, making sure he saw no one, David crossed the grounds. He moved from the covering

of the trees to the shadows of the house within seconds.
He hunkered down behind a bush on the north side and
waited. But no one came around the corner looking for the
man who had just approached. Standing, half-hunched, he
skirted each side of the house, looking for an opening—
something that would get him inside undetected. On the
west side, he found what he needed. A window, left open
a crack. Standing, he scanned the room beyond the glass.
Dark. Empty. He slipped his hands under the frame and
pushed up.

Moments later, he stood inside a bathroom. Light poured
through the half-open door. David crept forward and peered
out.

Computer terminals sat on the kitchen table, printers beside them. But there was no sound. The computers were all
turned off. For a moment, he wondered if the house were
empty. But then he heard footsteps overhead. He looked
up. Someone was on the second floor.

He pulled the door open slowly, very slowly, and stepped
out into the hall. As he made his way toward the heart of
the house, he could hear a sound. An erratic tapping. Like
. . . typing.

Reaching the end of the hall, he leaned around the corner
and peered into the room beyond.

Sam.

He sat with his back to David, glancing at a pile of papers beside him before returning his gaze to the computer
in front of him.

Sam's presence here confirmed the worst in David's
mind. His best friend, one of the few people he truly believed he could trust, had betrayed him.

And had quite possibly been the one to bring Kelsey
here.

David's hand clenched around the gun in his hand.

CHAPTER TWENTY-ONE

1

Louis sat on the couch in David's condo and sipped his tea. He had waited too long. He should have told sooner. But he had been afraid. He had worked for Mr. Ebersol for thirty-five years. Without him, where would he go? How would he live?

His gaze fell once more on the clock on the far wall. Two hours. It had been nearly two hours since Mr. Ross had left. And he had heard nothing.

What had happened? Where was David? How long should he wait here before . . . before what? Before he could go home? No, he no longer had a home to go to.

Setting his tea on the coffee table before him, he crossed the room and checked outside. But the street was empty.

He had done the right thing, he told himself. Losing his job meant nothing if it helped David.

Behind him, he heard the floor creak. Before he could turn, he felt hands on his neck and a sharp twist.

Louis Stark was dead before his body hit the floor.

2

The phone rang once. Hal leaned forward and lifted the receiver.

"It's done."

"Good." He stared down at the Envirospace complex below. "I want the disposal handled tonight."

3

Ken Brewer stared down at the old man's body as he replaced the receiver in its cradle. He had betrayed Mr. Ebersol. Gone behind his back. Tried to bring him down. And he got exactly what he deserved.

It was what they all deserved.

Bending forward, he lifted the papers that were stacked on the coffee table—1's and 0's covered each page, every inch.

He would get the call tomorrow regarding Junior. The man would tell him the job was done. David was dead. He had told the man to make sure the body was not found. Bury it somewhere remote. Maybe a hunter would uncover it ten years from now. Just not soon. He checked his watch. Less than twelve hours. He would celebrate the young man's death. It would mark the end of all their problems.

He dropped the papers, scattering them at his feet.

CHAPTER TWENTY-TWO

1

"This can't be," Sam muttered typing in another set of binary numbers from the computer printout Kelsey had given him. He leaned back, waiting for the computer to complete the translation.

A quiet voice spoke from directly behind him, so quiet he almost didn't recognize it. "Who else is in the house?"

His brow furrowed. "Dave?" He turned and found himself staring down the muzzle of a gun.

"Don't bullshit me, Sam." David kept his voice low, kept the gun trained on Sam. "I want to know how many others are in the house."

With some effort, Sam shifted his gaze from the gun to David. He stood directly in front of him, his shoulders slightly hunched. His face and clothes were smudged with dirt and what looked like blood. The hand holding the gun trembled slightly.

"Dave, I—"

David pressed the end of the gun against the bridge of Sam's nose, resting it between his eyes. "How many?"

"Two," Sam supplied quickly. His heart pounded in his chest. Perspiration formed on his brow. Would David pull the trigger? But even as the question ran through his mind, he realized he did not want to know the answer. "Just Kelsey and Pearson."

The gun did not move. "Where?"

Sam swallowed hard, his throat dry. "Upstairs," he rasped.

David glared down at Sam, his eyes filled with a dark anger. "Get up."

"Let me explain." The words came out in a rush.

"I said, get up!" David grabbed the front of Sam's shirt and hauled him to his feet.

2

Kelsey stared up at the ceiling, twisting her left hand slowly, methodically back and forth, back and forth. A light sheen of sweat covered her body. She had been working her hand for nearly a half hour but there was little difference.

She craned her head around, trying to see the machine behind her with its three electrodes. She was not hooked up to it but the doctor had turned the switch on several minutes ago. Would it monitor her heart? Her brain activity? She wasn't sure. But as Pearson crossed toward her again, this time carrying a small tray, she tensed.

He glanced at her, his gaze traveling over her prone body with cool detachment. Placing the tray on the small table beside her bed, he rechecked the straps, tightening her left wrist ever so slightly.

For a moment, his eyes locked with hers.

"Please don't do this," she whispered.

He cocked his head to one side, a strange half-smile curling his lips upward. "Don't worry," he began, one hand reaching out and wiping the perspiration from her brow. "You won't recall any of this when I'm through." And slowly, his hand slipped down her cheek, over her neck, moving slowly, almost casually toward her breasts.

"Don't you touch me!" she screamed, struggling against the straps.

He drew back, laughing at her inane attempts at freedom. "Don't worry," he said, turning back to the tray beside the bed. "I have no real interest in you."

Lifting an IV bag from the tray, he hung it from the pole beside her bed. With stiff dizziness, she watched as he spiked the bag with tubing, filled the long, hollow strip of plastic with the fluid from the IV and left it dangling beside her.

"I think it's time to get started." He picked up a thin rubber cord from the tray.

"No!" she yelled, renewing her struggle, twisting and fighting against the straps. "I won't let you do this!"

His left hand clamped down viselike on her arm, holding it against the bed. Using his right hand, he slipped the tourniquet under her arm and tied it in place.

Kelsey stared at her arm, at the veins that bulged under the sudden pressure. She bit her lip, working hard to suppress the scream she felt building inside her.

Lifting a syringe from the tray, he leaned toward her. "Just need to get some blood—"

But his words were cut short as the door burst inward. Pearson swung around to face the sudden intrusion.

Sam stood in the threshold. And behind him . . .

"David!" Kelsey cried out, her heart doubling its beat.

He stood behind Sam and slightly to his left. But as he shoved Sam roughly forward, forcing him farther into the room, she realized there was something . . . different about him.

And in a flash of comprehension, she understood what it was. *Hatred.* It boiled behind his eyes, flowed from every pore of his body, filled the room with a sense of impending violence. David seemed on the verge of exploding.

If he lost control . . .

She pulled uselessly at the straps that bound her. David's gaze, fixed on Pearson, cut briefly to her. And as she stared into his eyes, she saw none of the compassion she had come to love. Only a growing fury. And her fear escalated.

"It's over, doctor." David shifted his focus once more to Pearson. Only then did she notice the gun in his hand. "Back away."

Pearson did not move. Instead, he tilted his head to one side seeming to study David. "I remember you," he said, his voice annoyed.

David took another step forward. "And I finally remember you," he said quietly.

Kelsey shuddered, a chill rippling through her body as the meaning behind his words sank in, the source of his anger now clear to her.

Pearson drew himself up, his back stiffening. "That's not possible," he said with complete assurance.

"Oh, it's quite possible, doctor," David continued. "I remember you and everything you did. And I'm here to make damn sure you never do it to anyone again." Once more, David's gaze flickered to Kelsey then back to Pearson. "Now, back away. Slowly."

Kelsey looked up at the doctor. She could see the muscles of his jaw flexing and jumping as he considered his current predicament. He took a step back and she released the breath she had not realized she was holding. But her relief was short lived. In the next instant, moving with surprising swiftness, he swung back toward her. The syringe swept over her in a low arc, stopping just above her left eye.

"Put down the gun," he ordered. "Put down the gun or I'll puncture her ocular cavity."

Kelsey could barely breath. Her eyes locked on the needle mere inches above her. Pearson's hand shook, the needle wavering slightly from side to side.

"You won't do that," David said, his voice trembling with rage. Kelsey dragged her gaze from the needle to the man that now held her fate in his hands.

"Because if you do," he continued. "I swear to God,

I'll kill you.'' He smiled then and the darkness behind the wicked grin scared Kelsey even more than the needle currently poised over her eye.

She waited, her breath caught in her throat, her heartbeat pounding in her ears. After what seemed an eternity, the needle moved away. Pearson backed up several steps, pressing himself against the wall.

Kelsey's body went limp. She blinked rapidly as a few stray tears escaped her eyes.

David shoved Sam farther into the room. ''Undo the straps.''

Sam shuffled forward, his head lowered. With quick motions, he released her arms.

''I never wanted this,'' he whispered, his anguish-filled eyes finding hers. ''I never wanted anyone to get hurt.''

Kelsey slid off the bed. But before she could take two steps away, David spoke again.

''Get in the bed, Sam.''

Kelsey stopped halfway between the two men, David's words taking her off guard. Sam's gaze cut from the bed to Kelsey to David, his expression mirroring Kelsey's own bewilderment.

''Why?'' he asked, clearly confused by the request.

''I'm not going to leave you free to call Ken Brewer the minute we leave.'' David kept the gun pointed at the doctor but his attention was on Sam. ''Now get in.''

''Dave, I won't—''

''Get in!'' he shouted.

Kelsey jumped, startled by the fierceness of his voice.

But before Sam could take a step, Dr. Pearson lunged toward David using the syringe like a dagger.

2

Joe drove silently through the night. He was near his destination. Near the end of this job. All he had to do was find

David Ebersol, blow his brains out, and collect the remaining balance due him.

Then maybe he would retire. He'd been considering it for the last several years. But tonight, as each mile dropped off behind him, the idea became more appealing. He could move to Hawaii, sit on the beach all day, and drink Mai Tais.

He glanced down at the map on the seat beside him, still pondering his future. Maybe he'd find himself a local girl, get married, turn into a real family man.

Finding his next turnoff, he looked back up. And slammed on his brakes.

"Shit!"

He swerved sideways, narrowly missing the woman who stood in the middle of the road. The car slid toward the shoulder, his tires skidding on gravel and dirt. He yanked the wheel into the spin, both feet on the brakes. A tree loomed up before him. He braced himself for impact. But the car came to an abrupt halt, stalling out, inches from the thick trunk.

Joe did not hesitate. As soon as the car was stopped, he was out, moving low, keeping his back to the frame.

Because in that split second before he lost control of his car, he had recognized the woman in the road, the woman whose picture David Ebersol carried in his wallet.

And he was done playing games with her.

Reaching the hood of the car, the 9-mm in his hand, he raised himself up. But the road was empty. His gaze travelled over the area. Nothing. No one.

He stood, half-crouched. "Where are you?" he shouted, turning a three hundred and sixty degree circle. "I know you're following me! I know—"

And then he saw her.

She stood at the edge of the woods, watching, waiting. He moved toward her, the sweet smell that always seemed to accompany her appearance, growing stronger with each step he took.

He stopped a few feet in front of her, his weapon trained on her heart. "Who are you?"

She stared at him, utterly silent, her sad eyes boring into his.

"Why are you—"

But as he stepped closer, the words died on his lips. He stared unblinking, realizing for the first time that he could see the trees behind her—through her! His mouth went dry. His gut twisted.

She floated toward him, arms extended. Before he could react, she swept over him, washing him in her light. He convulsed, hot and cold pulsing through his body. In that instant, they became one. He knew who she was and what she wanted him to do.

3

Kelsey screamed a warning. David dodged sideways as the doctor lunged at him, needle jabbing toward his exposed neck. He fired once but missed, taking a chunk out of the wall instead. He raised an arm to protect himself as the syringe plunged downward. The needle sunk into the flesh of his forearm. He cried out. And fired again. Point blank. The sound seemed to reverberate off the walls. Fill the room. An instant later, the doctor crumpled to the floor.

David dropped the gun, his face contorting in a combination of pain and astonishment.

Kelsey rushed toward him, her eyes fixed on the syringe sticking in his arm. "Are you all right?"

He nodded, wincing as he checked the needle. "It's just a puncture. No tearing." He yanked the syringe out and tossed it away.

Kelsey threw her arms around him, her face nuzzling against his chest. "Thank God," she whispered, not just relieved that the needle had done little damage, but that he was there and they were together again.

He ran a hand down her hair, over her back, his body warm against hers. And for the first time since separating that morning, Kelsey felt safe.

"I think he's dead."

Sam's dread-filled voice drew her attention. Kelsey released David and turned to face him. He knelt beside Pearson staring down at the doctor, at the blood pooling on the floor all around him. His fingers fumbled on the man's neck, searching. Then slowly, Sam's wide eyes turned upward. "I can't find a pulse."

"David had no choice," Kelsey said immediately, her voice defensive. "Pearson attacked him."

Sam nodded numbly. "I know. You're right. But it wasn't supposed to be like this. No one was supposed to be hurt. Now look what's happened. Look—" His voice hitched. He stopped speaking, his mouth clamping shut. His body trembled as he fought to get back control of himself. When he spoke again, his voice had regained some composure. "No one was supposed to die."

"But people did die," Kelsey said quietly. "My sister. Hillary West."

"Most, if not all, of your staff," David added. "Hell, I was next on their hit list."

Kelsey turned toward him. "You?" she breathed, all of her fear rushing back in with that one statement.

David nodded, rubbing the area of his arm where the needle had punctured him.

Slowly, Sam got to his feet. "No. They were bringing you back here. Back to Pearson."

"They wanted me dead," David said, his voice harsh.

"No." Sam shook his head, his face pinched with dismay. "No. They told me you were going to get a second treatment. They wouldn't hurt you. They—"

"Listen to what I'm saying!" David reached out and grabbed Sam by the front of the shirt. "They wanted me dead!" He slammed him into the wall behind him. "Do you understand what I'm saying?" He yanked him forward and slammed him into the wall again. "Dead!"

"David, stop!" Kelsey wrapped an arm around his, trying to pull him away. "Stop!"

And David did, all at once, shoving Sam away. Kelsey stepped between the two men, keeping them separate.

David backed up another step, his breath rasping in and out. "I was tied up and stuffed into the trunk of a car!" He held up his hands. Kelsey stared at his red, raw wrists, the cord marks still clearly outlined in his flesh.

"My God." She reached out and took his hands gently in hers, running her fingers over the damage there.

Sam slid to the floor, mumbling to himself, shaking his head. "I never wanted anyone to get hurt. I was in too deep. I didn't know what to do."

"You could have come to me." David glared down at him. "You could have told me the truth."

Sam looked up, his face a mirror of agony. "I'm sorry."

"It's too late for apologies." Bending down, David lifted the gun from the floor. "Stand up, Sam."

He did as he was told. "Please, David, I just want to help."

"You really think I want your help? You expect me to trust you?" He laughed, a deep, cynical sound.

"I didn't know the whole truth. I didn't know about the communications."

Kelsey's brow furrowed. "What communications?" she asked, looking from one man to the other.

"I'm supposed to believe you?" David said, ignoring Kelsey's question, his eyes hard, unforgiving.

"I'm telling you the truth. You know that!"

"Why? Because you've been so honest with me up until now?"

Sam raked his hands through his hair, pulling it away from his face. "Do you really believe I would have let this go on if I had known?"

"If you had known what?" Kelsey shouted, her patience growing thin. "What are you talking about?"

David focused on her, his eyes softening. "The binary," he said simply.

Kelsey sifted through the information in her mind, trying to put together what he meant. "The binary is some kind of communication?"

"Yes."

"I managed to decipher some of it downstairs," Sam added. His gaze shifted to David. "I swear to you it was the first time I'd ever seen it." He paused, for a moment before adding, "They're warnings, aren't they."

"Yes," David hissed.

"Warnings?" Kelsey looked at David. "What kind of warnings?"

David nodded toward Sam. "He didn't upgrade the system six years ago. He reprogrammed it."

Kelsey shook her head. "I still don't understand? What did he do?"

"My father wasn't making enough money. He started out putting the garbage on the moon but the profits weren't what he thought they would be."

"So he began dumping in the woods instead," Kelsey supplied.

"No," David said. "Only for a short period of time. Only to cover up the fact that they had stopped the shipments while Sam worked on the system and came up with a solution."

A chill passed through Kelsey. "What kind of solution?"

David kept his gaze on Sam as he spoke. "It was too costly to land on the moon and unload the garbage. The system kept breaking down. Sam was brought in to fix the cost and the system. But he couldn't. There was no solution to what they were doing. So he became creative. He gave them a new suggestion."

"I was under a lot of pressure," Sam said, his voice defensive.

"Is that your excuse? Is that what you tell yourself so you can sleep at night?"

"I had no choice."

"You always have a choice, Sam."

"What did he do?" Kelsey asked, her voice once again overriding theirs.

David stared at Sam. "Tell her," he prompted.

Sam's gaze cut to Kelsey. He stared at her for several long moments, his fingers fumbling with the sleeve of his shirt. He opened his mouth as if to speak but abruptly turned away, shame creasing his brow.

"What did he do?" Kelsey asked again, deeply puzzled by this sudden turn of events.

David paced away, the hand holding the gun dropping down by his side. He stopped in front of the only window in the room and drew open the blinds. Kelsey could see the moon outside, just above the tree line, full and round.

"They send those launches up full of all our waste," he began, his voice sad, almost wistful. "And they dump it into open space."

Kelsey's brow furrowed. "They what?"

He turned to face her, his eyes void of emotion. "They eject our garbage into space at random."

"For how long?" she asked.

"The last six years."

Kelsey stared at him, trying to comprehend just how much refuse had been disposed of in this manner.

"Really, I should give you credit," David said, his gaze once more on Sam. "It was a pretty good solution. Would have worked too. I mean, who cares, so some garbage gets shot into space. No harm done, right?" he finished, his words laced with sarcasm.

"I didn't know about the messages," Sam insisted.

"Warnings," David corrected.

Kelsey said, "What warnings?"

"Hillary discovered them," David explained. "She worked in the communications department. She'd been getting what was categorized as space static for several months. Everyone told her to disregard it. To keep her eyes on her monitors. But she began to collect it. Compare it."

"And she deciphered it?"

"Yes," David whispered. "Seems someone up there was not happy with the new dump system and wanted us to stop."

"Are you serious?" Kelsey said, her voice tentative.

"Ask him," David said, pointing at Sam.

"I didn't know," Sam said again. "Your father never told me. He said you found out about the new program and threatened to go to the E.P.A. He said we could all go to jail for fraud. I didn't think what we were doing was hurting anyone. I didn't see why we should be punished for it."

"So you punished us instead," David shot back.

"Wait a minute," Kelsey said. "Let's back up here." She stepped toward David, her mind reeling at the magnitude of his statement. "You're saying that someone up there," she hooked a thumb toward the ceiling, "is sending warnings down here?"

David nodded slowly.

"And your father chose to ignore them," she said in astonishment.

"He didn't believe us," David said dryly.

Her body flushed with sudden warmth. She swayed where she stood, overwhelmed by this new knowledge. "What did they say? Were they threats?"

"No. Nothing specific. At least, not while Hillary was monitoring it. Just a general warning to stop."

"But . . . who are they?"

Tucking the pistol in the back of his jeans, David sat on the edge of the window sill, crossing his arms over his chest. "I thought about that a lot when we first discovered the communications." His brow creased slightly as he relayed his theory. "I believe whoever they are, they've been watching us for a long time, close by, because our garbage wouldn't have had time to go any real distance. I think maybe they've been monitoring our progress, waiting for an opportunity to present themselves to us, or maybe waiting for us to advance to the point where they would want to make contact with us."

Sam nodded his agreement. "That has been a popular theory for many years."

"So instead of shared technology," David continued. "Our first contact is over garbage. Who knows how far this may have put us behind in their eyes," he finished with obvious remorse.

Kelsey shook her head, her mind reeling. "So what do we do now?" she asked, looking expectantly toward David.

Sam turned too, his face mirroring her question. And in that moment, she realized she wasn't just waiting for him to give an opinion. She wanted . . . guidance. Leadership. And she knew Sam wanted—needed the same thing.

David leaned against the window sill looking haggard and spent. His gaze shifted from Sam to Kelsey, uncertainty creasing his forehead.

She wanted to tell him it was okay, he didn't have to be strong for them. But she couldn't. She knew it wasn't true. They needed David. Needed his strength, his determination.

And as if sensing that need, David drew himself up, blinked the exhaustion from his eyes and said, "We can't stay here," his voice strong, confident. His gaze traveled over the doctor's still form. "Ken Brewer could be back at any moment."

"But where do we go?" Sam asked.

David turned back to the window, his gaze once more finding the moon. "We have to end all this before another launch can be sent up," he said, the words simple but true.

"How?" Sam mumbled.

"We can go to the authorities," Kelsey suggested. "We have the printouts."

David shook his head. "They're not enough. My father could easily say we concocted those."

"Not if I extract information from the launch computer," Sam interjected.

David turned to face him. "What information?"

"The programming," he said. "If we can get into the control room of the prelaunch building, I can copy the launch programming onto a disk."

"What good will that do?" Kelsey asked.

"It'll tell everything. It has an internal log. Since the day I reprogrammed it, it's been collecting data."

"And that data could prove what the company has been doing?" David finished.

"Exactly."

"And," Kelsey continued, "if we combine that information with what we already know about the woods, Sam's team and Dr. Pearson, we've got a strong case against Envirospace."

"A strong case against my father," David said quietly.

"I think," Kelsey said, her gaze shifting from David to Sam, "that we need to get to Envirospace tonight."

CHAPTER TWENTY-THREE

1

David held the door for Sam and Kelsey as the three of them moved through the prelaunch facility toward the control room.

"How do you know you can get the information we need?" David asked, his eyes searching the grounds for employees. But the lateness of the hour had guaranteed them privacy.

"I set up the system. I know where everything is."

Stepping into the control room, they heard the unrelenting beeps and clicks of the computer as it continued loading the barrels into Envirolift One.

Sam immediately moved toward the main computer and began punching the keys. "This shouldn't take long," he said.

David nodded, his stomach tight. He knew the security cameras had picked them up. If anyone were watching . . .

"Hurry," he said, unable to suppress his tension.

Sam nodded, continuing to work. David watched as his friend's fingers glided over the keys, screen after screen flashing across the monitor. Less than a minute later, Sam stopped typing, his finger's hovering over the keys. "I'm in," he said, the words eager.

David stared down at the computer terminal, the jargon displayed across the screen meaningless to him. "How long will it take to copy?"

"I'm not sure," Sam said, opening the box of computer disks he had brought with him. "Could take a couple of hours."

David clapped him on the back. "Work as fast as you can." He glanced sideways and realized for the first time since entering the room, that Kelsey was not beside him. She stood several feet away, staring through the glass at the barrels beyond.

Going to her, he placed a hand on her shoulder and gently squeezed. "You okay?"

She sighed, shrugging one shoulder. "I don't know." She placed a hand over his. "I look at this," she said, indicating the commotion on the other side of the glass. "My sister died because of this. It seems so . . . unfair."

"She was trying to do the right thing," he said softly. "We all were."

Kelsey glanced at him. "And your reward was abduction, brainwashing . . . death."

David said nothing. Only stared at the barrels as they were loaded one by one onto the ship. "It ends today," he whispered.

Behind them, the double doors opened. David turned to see Ken Brewer enter, a waste barrel strapped to the dolly he pushed. Their eyes met. An instant later, David reached for the gun still tucked in the back of his jeans. But Ken was faster. He drew his own weapon and had a bead on David before David could even draw his weapon.

"Don't move," Ken ordered, the muzzle of the gun aimed at David's chest.

David stood, one hand behind his back, his fingers touching the butt of the gun. A bead of sweat trickled down the side of his face. He licked his lips. His gaze flicked from Ken's face to the gun in his hand.

How fast are you? His own hand tightened on the

weapon he held behind him. Maybe—

"David, please," Kelsey whispered from beside him. "Don't do it. He'll kill you."

"It's true, son."

David's gaze darted to the doorway. Hal Ebersol stood just beyond the threshold, leaning casually against the doorjamb. "He will kill you if you try it."

Slowly, knowing he had no real choice, David dropped his hand to his side.

"You." Ken nodded toward Kelsey. "Take out the weapon, put it on the floor and slide it toward me."

Kelsey shot an unsure look in David's direction.

"Do it," he muttered.

A moment later, he watched as the gun skidded toward Ken Brewer.

"Good girl," he said bending down and picking it up.

Kelsey stepped beside David, her arm encircling his. He could feel her tremble against him.

Crossing to Ken, Hal took the weapon from him. "Where in the world did you get this?" he asked, hefting the pistol in his hand.

David ignored the question, his attention instead on the barrel they had left beside the door. Why the hell would they be bringing a waste drum into the building in the dead of night? He nodded toward the receptacle container. "What's inside?" he asked warily.

Hal was silent for a moment, seeming to study the weapon in his hand. "You know," he said, a hint of amusement in his voice. "I really think you don't want to know,"

David felt Kelsey stiffen beside him. He glanced down at her and seeing the gray pallor of her skin, knew she was feeling the same sense of dread about the unknown contents of the barrel as he was.

"I have to say," Hal continued in the same casual tone, "this is the last place I expected to find any of you tonight." He looked at each one of them, his gaze stopping on Sam. His eyes narrowed as he took in the computer console behind him. "Mr. Wyatt, what are you doing?" He walked over and lifted the box of computer disks. "Making some copies, are we?"

Sam swallowed hard. He looked from Hal to David and back again.

"He doesn't want anything to do with you anymore," David said, taking a step forward, lending Sam the support he needed. "You lied to him."

"And he lied to you," Hal shot back. "He's reported to me everything you've done for the last month."

"I didn't . . . I . . ." Sam faltered, his eyes clouded with regret.

"It doesn't matter any more, Sam," David said, finding the words Sam could not. "He's trying to undermine you but it won't work." He turned back to his father. "Sam knows what's going on now. He knows the whole truth. And he's going to help me stop you."

Hal shoved the pistol he held against Sam's chest, forcing him backward. "Maybe Mr. Wyatt would like a chance to reevaluate that decision."

Sam's gaze shifted from the gun pressing into his ribs to the man before him. To David's surprise and admiration, there was no fear in his face. "I don't need to reevaluate anything. I'm not going to help you anymore." And without speaking another word, he crossed the room and stood beside David.

Earlier, when Kelsey and Sam had looked to him for guidance, David had faked his way through it. Saying what he thought they needed to hear, feeling unsure and more than a little afraid. But now, standing with Kelsey to his left and Sam to his right, he felt a strength flow between the three of them. And his confidence returned.

"You lied to a lot of people," he said, his voice firm. "And it's got to stop."

"Because you say it does?" Hal's gaze fixed on David, his eyes cold. "You ungrateful little bastard," he growled. "You don't appreciate what you have."

"You mean I don't appreciate you," David said, his eyes never leaving his father's.

"No one does," Hal whispered. "The public should be on their knees to me. I gave them the solution they couldn't give themselves."

"Solution?" David repeated, incredulous. "All you've done is create a larger problem. One beyond anything we've ever encountered before."

Hal's brow furrowed. "What the hell are you talking about?"

"The binary," Sam supplied. "I deciphered some earlier tonight. I know what it means."

"We all do," David continued. "You must know, it's only a matter of time—"

"Before what?" Hal cut in. "Before little green men come down and issue me a citation?" he laughed mockingly.

"We have the communications," Kelsey said. "They're no joke."

Hal Ebersol's laughter cut off. For the first time since entering the control room, he focused on Kelsey. "You must be Leah Brayden's sister," he said mildly. And as his father's gaze traveled slowly over her, David tensed. "My son involved your sister in something that resulted in her death. Now you're headed down that same path."

"Is that some kind of threat?" David took a step forward but Kelsey, her arm still encircling his, pulled him to a stop.

He glanced at her and with a subtle tilt of her head, she indicated Ken Brewer. David realized that the man had not moved since entering the room. He still stood beside the barrel he had wheeled in, his weapon aimed at David's chest. It was apparent from the wicked grin on his face that he would like nothing better than to blow David's head off.

"Leah went to David with the information," Kelsey said, correcting Hal Ebersol's version of the truth. "She involved him. She and Hillary—"

"Hillary West was trying to blackmail me," Hal said,

his voice overriding hers. "Somehow, she found out about the change to the system. She faked those communications to try and extort money out of me."

"She never asked you for a dime," David countered. "You wouldn't have even known about her involvement if you hadn't pumped me full of drugs and extracted her name. But it's over now. It ends tonight."

Hal smiled then but the smile did not touch his eyes. "For you it does."

Kelsey's grip increased on David's arm. "What do you mean?" she asked, fear lacing each word.

But David did not need it spelled out for him. He knew exactly what his father meant. Had known since the man with the scar forced him into the trunk of his car. "He wants me dead," he said, his voice a flat monotone.

Hal stared down at the weapon he still held. "So insightful tonight."

"He's your son," Kelsey uttered, astonished by his open admission.

Hal shrugged. "I never wanted him." He turned his gaze toward David, his brow wrinkling in disappointment. "You're too much like your mother. Too much like Edward."

The name hit David like a slap in the face. His uncle. He had completely forgotten about his uncle. "Eventually, he'll find out the truth about all this. And he'll shut you down."

Hal grinned wickedly, his eyes ablaze with new delight. "That's right. You don't know."

David's mouth went dry. "Know what?"

"Earlier this evening, Edward suffered a massive coronary." He leaned close to David, speaking low, as if sharing a precious secret. "He died en route to the hospital."

David couldn't breathe. His body flushed with sudden warmth. The lights seemed to dim and flicker. The room swayed, shifted, his body swaying with it. He felt an arm on his, supporting him.

"David?" Kelsey's concerned voice wrapped around him, holding him tightly in its grip. "Are you okay?"

He turned and stared into her frightened eyes. But he could not speak. Could not find the words to explain the grief that flooded his body.

He died en route to the hospital.

The words tumbled through his mind. And as the depth of his loss settled over him, an anger began to blossom within him. His father would not, could not win.

"I blame myself," Hal continued, relishing the moment, savoring each word. "If only I had called the ambulance a little sooner."

With a cry of rage and pain, David lunged at his father.

Sam gripped his arm, keeping him back. "Dave, don't. Don't!" he yelled, struggling to hold on to him.

"It's what he wants!" Kelsey shouted, joining in the battle to keep David back.

He struggled against them another moment before the truth of their words sank in. He stopped, backing away several steps, his breath raging in and out.

"Edward Ross was twice the man you'll ever be!" he forced out between breaths.

"Good for him," Hal said with obvious sarcasm. He looked toward Ken. "Finish this."

The next few moments happened in a flash of time, a blur of movement and light.

Ken Brewer corrected his aim ever so slightly, leveling the barrel of his weapon at David's heart. David grabbed Kelsey and shoved her away. He heard two shots as he dodged in the opposite direction. An instant later, he was thrown backward with the force of the bullets striking him. A burning sensation spread through his left shoulder and his stomach as he struck the wall behind him. Kelsey screamed. A third shot was fired. A blur of purple and red flashed before his eyes. It was a moment before he realized it was Sam, standing in front of him, blocking him from the next bullet.

His last coherent thought before crumbling to the ground was, "Hey, thanks, buddy."

2

"No!" Kelsey scrambled across the floor, crawling toward the two men.

Sam lay on top of David, not moving, not breathing. And she knew he was dead.

Biting back the tears that threatened, she heaved Sam's corpse from atop David. As his body came fully into view, a sob escaped her. *Blood. There's too much blood.* His shirt stuck to his chest, the crimson stain growing larger with each passing moment.

But he was still breathing. He was alive.

Kelsey pulled open David's shirt. Two holes marred his body. One high on his shoulder. The other lower, near his stomach.

"He needs a doctor," she said, her hands moving ineffectively over his chest. She turned, glaring up at the men behind her. "He needs a doctor!"

Hal stared down at her, a look of total disdain on his face. "Ken," he said, keeping his gaze on Kelsey. "Please dispose of Mr. Wyatt and my son."

Kelsey shifted her gaze to Ken Brewer. Stuffing the weapon he had used to shoot David into the holster on his belt, he reached down and began dragging Sam's corpse toward the glass doors that separated the control room from the loading bay.

She watched in horror as Sam's lifeless body was stuffed into one of the waste barrels. Desperation blossomed in her stomach. Her heart fluttered in her chest. The barrel containing Sam was sealed and shoved into line with the rest of the garbage to be loaded onto the ship.

She looked down at David. Back to the launch bay. Ken

had a second barrel open and was coming back. She turned to Hal Ebersol.

"You can't!" Her hands touched David's hair, chest, face. *Wake up!* she silently urged. *Get up so we can get out of here!*

"You think you can just load his . . . his body into that ship and send him off with the rest of the garbage?" she shouted, fighting hard to contain the scream that threatened to break lose. Because she knew if she started to scream, she might not be able to stop.

Insanity.

The word bubbled to the surface of her mind. *That's what this is,* she decided. *Pure and utter insanity!*

"You think no one will ask any questions?"

Hal nodded, his face passive. "That's how it worked with Hillary West."

Kelsey's eyes widened with dawning horror.

Ken moved toward her.

"Please don't do this," she begged. "There's still time—"

David groaned, his eyes fluttering.

"David!" she yelled, gripping his hands, holding them against her chest. "Wake up. Please!"

Ken bent down, gripping David under the arms.

"No!" she screamed, trying to shove him away. "Leave him alone!"

Drawing back, Ken backhanded her across the face. Her head snapped sideways, the blow knocking her flat on her back. She pushed up, wiping the blood from her lip and scrambled to her feet.

Hal reached out and grabbed her, holding her in place.

She struggled against him. "He's not dead!" she shouted. "How can you do this?"

As Ken lifted David, his eyes opened, rolling madly in their sockets. He groaned, his hands working feebly to free himself.

"Kelsey," he moaned.

"Stop!" she screamed. "David!"

But Ken did not stop. He half carried, half dragged David into the packaging bay. Kelsey screamed as David's head disappeared below the rim of a barrel. She crumpled to the ground as Ken sealed the lid.

The door swooshed open. Ken reentered the room.

"I want this launch to go off without delay," Hal said.

"It will," Ken reassured him. "I'll make sure of that."

"Good. Once this launch is gone, so are all our problems."

They stood over her, speaking as if she did not exist.

Finally, Hal turned his attention to Kelsey. "Take her back to the house. Tell Pearson I want this handled by Monday. I'll stay and make sure every barrel is loaded."

Kelsey looked up into Hal Ebersol's smug, satisfied face. "Pearson's dead," she whispered, gleaning a certain amount of enjoyment from seeing his face fall.

He glared down at her. "You're lying."

She said nothing, just met his eyes coolly, evenly.

"Dammit!" he raged, seeing the truth behind those eyes.

"Looks like you're stuck now," Kelsey said calmly. "Can't kill me. Not with Leah's death so close. But without Pearson . . ." She trailed off, knowing he understood the bind he was now in.

"Get her out of my sight," Hal seethed through gritted teeth. "Take her back to the house and just hold her there until I think of something."

Ken leaned toward her. His hand clamped around her arm. "Let's go." He yanked her roughly to her feet and led her toward the exit.

Moments later, they stepped out into the warm night air. They were three feet from the building when a dark figure drifted out of the shadows, raised a weapon and fired.

Two shots rang out.

Kelsey screamed.

Ken jerked spasmodically, eyes wide and unbelieving. Two more shots hit him in quick succession. He fumbled for the gun strapped to his side, staggered backward four steps, and collapsed to the ground.

Kelsey stared at his body, her own shaking uncontrollably. Her stunned gaze shifted from the bloody corpse at her feet to the dark figure walking slowly toward her.

Her savior? Or something else entirely.

"Who . . ." she began but found her throat too constricted to continue.

The stranger stepped into the light.

Instantly, Kelsey knew she had never met this man with the scar on his left cheek. Yet there was something about him, something . . .

Her brow crinkled. A face. A second face floated around his, melding with him, becoming one, then shifting back, splitting apart.

"Leah?" she breathed.

"Kelsey." The voice, both male and female, came from the stranger.

"What . . ." She shook her head, seeing her sister's face. The man's face. "How . . . ?"

"David," he said, with the strange male/female voice.

The name jolted through Kelsey like a shot of lightning, bringing her back to her senses.

She whirled toward the prelaunch building.

3

Hal stood outside the automation room watching as each barrel moved closer to the launch ship. His eyes locked on the waste drum containing his son. Almost gone, he thought, a great feeling of completion filling him.

He glanced over his shoulder at the receptacle still strapped to the dolly. The receptacle containing Louis's body. In all the commotion, they had left it beside the door. He'd have to remember to have Ken move it into the launch room. He needed to get all the containers aboard the ship before morning. Before a nosy employee became quizzical and looked inside.

He turned back to the ship. Two days. In two days, the ship would launch and all his troubles would be behind him. Or at least above him, he thought wryly.

He was still chuckling at his own joke when the door behind him burst open.

4

Kelsey entered the room at a jog. The automation system clicked and beeped, continuing the loading process. Her gaze swept over the multitude of barrels.

Which one? Which *one?*

She turned to face Hal Ebersol.

His easy gaze shifted from the man holding the gun to her. He appeared to be completely composed. The abrupt turn of events not jarring him in the least.

"Which one is David in?" she asked, her voice tight.

"I don't remember." His eyes locked with hers. And in those eyes, she could see the knowledge she needed. He knew exactly which barrel. But he would never tell her.

"Shut it down," she said, taking a step closer to him, letting him know she was now in charge.

"That's not possible." He locked his hands behind his back, rocking slightly on his heels. "The system is automatic. It can't be shut down."

Kelsey took another step closer, her heart hammering in her chest. "You're lying."

He smirked, one corner of his mouth drawing upward. But said nothing more.

The man with the scar stepped forward. Without uttering a word, he raised his weapon and shot out the control panel. Sparks flew, lights blinked out and the loading process . . . stopped.

Kelsey did not wait. Running to the door that separated

the two rooms, she stepped into the loading bay. As the door closed slowly behind her, she stared at the assortment of barrels, her gaze shifting from one side of the room to the other.

Where do I start? How do I find him?

The barrels seemed to almost loom toward her daring her to find the right one. But before she could make a decision, before she could take another step forward, a loud thud echoed through the room.

She looked up, the sound coming from overhead.

"What's that?" But even as she spoke the question, the far western wall of the building began to move slowly away, splitting the room into two, opening it to the world outside.

"What's happening?" Kelsey yelled, turning toward the glass separating the two rooms.

Hal Ebersol stood at the damaged console, pushing buttons. He looked up. And for the first time, she could see worry creasing his brow. He punched a button on the wall, activating the speaker system within the packaging area. "The ship is cycling up," he said, his face a mask of frustration.

"What does that mean?" she asked, working hard to keep the hysteria out of her voice.

"It means that the ship's been tripped into launch mode," Hal quickly explained, his fingers flying over the keys. "It means that unless I can shut it down, that ship is going to try and launch from that room in less than ten minutes. And when it does, it'll take out this building and half the complex."

A low-grade hum began to grow from inside the ship.

The western wall continued its slow, easy crawl outward.

Kelsey looked up. The moon crested overhead, the star filled night sky visible through the opening.

David.

The name whispered through her mind. She had to get

him out. Had to get clear of this place before the ship launched.

She grabbed the barrel nearest to her and ripped the lid off. "David!"

5

"David!"

Through the haze of pain, David could hear the faint sound of his name. Someone was calling him. He struggled to remember where he was, what was happening.

Kelsey. My father. Sam.

Vague pieces of memory floated through his numb mind. But he was unable to decipher them. Unable to grasp the meaning behind each word.

He shuddered, cold shivers of pain rushing through every inch of his body. He let himself drift away from the pain, toward the warmth of the dark place. But other sounds penetrated his small cell drawing him back.

He struggled to remain conscious. Struggled to remain aware. And then he felt himself move and shift. Light. Warmth. Hands.

"Please, David. Open . . ."

6

". . . your eyes."

Kelsey knelt on the floor, David's head in her lap. She held his left hand pressed to her cheek. He had not moved since she pulled him from inside the barrel. But he was alive. The slow rise and fall of his chest proof.

"You're going to be all right," she murmured. "You're going to be fine."

Behind her, the hum intensified. The ship began shaking, barrels falling over, spilling out.

They were running out of time.

She looked toward the two men in the room beyond the glass.

"Help me!" she screamed. But as the two words echoed through the room, reverberating off the walls, everything in the building suddenly snapped off.

The lights, the ship, the computers all shut down.

In an instant, the room was devoid of all noise except David's uneven breathing. Yet she was sure, as she sat in the darkness, that she heard something . . . more.

The hairs on the back of her neck prickled. Her skin broke out in gooseflesh.

A sound. Unidentifiable. Coming from . . .

Slowly, she turned her gaze upward. The moon and the stars were gone. The entire night sky was obliterated from view by the solid black mass hovering overhead.

A pinpoint beam of light snapped on from above. It swept the room, crossing from corner to corner. Kelsey stared, breathless, as the beam grew in size, filling every inch of space.

Squeezing her eyes shut, she bent over David, shielding him from the blinding haze of white light as it spread across their bodies.

"Stop!" she screamed, the light penetrating her closed lids, seeming to sear directly into her brain. "Stop! Please, stop!"

The light snapped off. Silence returned.

Slowly, Kelsey sat up. She looked overhead, wiping the tears from her eyes. The moon and stars shone brightly in the night sky.

A moment later, the lights in the room blinked on.

"Kelsey?" She looked down at the man in her arms. David stared up at her, his eyes bright, his breathing normal.

"You're okay?" She pulled his red-stained shirt open. But the only indication of the wounds were two small crescent shaped scars on his shoulder and stomach.

"What happened?" He touched his shirt. Looked up. Back to her. "What . . . ?"

She shook her head. "I . . . I don't know." She looked toward the control room. The man with the scar stood beyond the glass separating the two rooms. The ghostly image of Leah, which shimmered and swayed around his body, shifted away, smoothly gliding across the floor. The man collapsed to his knees, convulsed several times, and then went limp.

Kelsey stared, breathless at the figure of her sister as it moved toward her, arms outstretched. Her eyes bore into Kelsey's. Her mouth moved as if she were trying to speak but no sound came out. Kelsey stood on shaky legs. She took a halting step forward. But in a flash of brilliant light, Leah was gone.

"Kelsey?" David's voice, quietly questioning, came from beside her. She turned toward him. He stood, his gaze also locked on the room beyond the glass. "Where's my father?"

For the first time, Kelsey realized that Hal Ebersol was no longer in the control room. He too had vanished.

EPILOGUE

Hartwick, Michigan

David stood in Leah's yard staring at the wooded lot behind her house. It had been nearly a week since his father disappeared from the control room of the prelaunch building. Nearly a week since the man with the scar slipped out into the night and vanished without a trace. Nearly a week since the death of both Sam and Edward.

David sighed. So much loss.

Behind him, he heard footsteps approach.

Kelsey stopped beside him. "How did it go?" she asked.

"As well as can be expected." He'd spent most of the morning at Envirospace, opening the files for the E.P.A. investigators, handing over his evidence regarding the cover-up, explaining what happened the last night he'd seen Hal Ebersol. "There's a warrant out for my father's arrest."

"Did you tell them anything?"

He glanced at her. She stared ahead, her face passive. "No. I didn't know how much to say."

They had decided not tell anyone of the events leading up to the disappearance of Hal Ebersol. Nor would they disclose the communications. As far as anyone was concerned, Envirospace had been ejecting garbage into open space and was responsible for the damage in the woods.

Anything else would prove nearly impossible to explain.

"Are you okay?" she asked, her voice quiet.

"I just . . ." He trailed off, unsure what he wanted to say, what he was feeling. "I keep thinking about his disappearance. Wondering what really happened that night."

She turned to face him, her brow furrowed in confusion. "What do you mean?"

"I don't know. I guess, the farther I get away from the whole damn thing, the more I wonder if it really happened. He knew what was coming down. He could have faked everything you saw that night."

"He couldn't have faked this," Kelsey said, placing her hand on his shoulder, touching the area where the crescent shaped scar still marred his flesh.

He grasped her hand, squeezing gently. "So what happens now?"

She shrugged one shoulder. "Summer's nearly over. I have to get back to school."

He stared at her, uncomprehending. "You're leaving?"

"I have to. I have a life to get back to."

"But I thought. . . ."

"David, I can't stay here . . . with you."

"Why not?"

"You know why not."

And as he stared into her eyes, he could see the pain, the uncertainty behind them. She didn't want to stay with him because he had been with Leah. But he couldn't let her leave. He couldn't lose her like he had lost everyone else in his life.

"Please, Kelsey," he began, his voice low, barely audible. "Don't leave me. I need you."

A tear escaped her eye, slowly rolling down her cheek. "I need you too," she whispered. "I just don't know if that's enough."

Reaching out, he ran his hand gently across her cheek, wiping away the moisture. "I think Leah would want us to try."

She half-smiled, half-frowned. "Maybe you're right. Maybe that's what she was trying to tell us that night."

"Then you'll stay?" he asked, his voice hopeful.

She nodded, her smile increasing. "I'll stay. But what am I going to do here? I don't have a job."

He wrapped his arms around her waist, pulling her close. "I have a friend on the school board. I think I can pull a few strings."

She moved closer. "What about the fringe benefits?"

"The benefits," he whispered, kissing her neck, her ear, her lips, "are out of this world."

Harry Bosch's life is on the edge. His earthquake-damaged home has been condemned. His girlfriend has left him. He's drinking too much. And after attacking his commanding officer, he's even had to turn in his L.A.P.D. detective's badge. Now, suspended indefinitely pending a psychiatric evaluation, he's spending his time investigating an unsolved crime from 1961: the brutal slaying of a prostitute who happened to be his own mother.

Edgar Award-winning author Michael Connelly has created a dark, fast-paced suspense thriller that cuts to the core of Harry Bosch's character. Once you start it, there's no turning back.

MICHAEL CONNELLY
THE LAST COYOTE

THE LAST COYOTE
Michael Connelly
_____ 95845-5 $6.99 U.S./$7.99 CAN.

After the unsolved murder of his wife five years ago, Nick Cross and his teenage son, Jeff, are finally creating a normal life together in a small Michigan town. Nick's finishing a new book and giving lectures, and Jeff's looking at colleges. But when Nick's self-proclaimed "biggest fan" is found dead in an apparent suicide, and Jeff vanishes without a trace, Nick begins to know the true meaning of the word horror.

With help from Diane Nolan, the detective assigned to the case, Nick soon finds himself up against a dark force he has never encountered—nor prepared for. Now, with time running out, he must confront an imagination even more lurid than his own—or lose his son.

SCARE TACTICS

The Startling Thriller by
ELIZABETH MANZ